CONTENTS

• • •

- MORE CONTENTS -

†††

- QUICK PROLOGUE -

Three young girls are wandering through dark woodland.
They've just heard something.
Was that a scream, rising from beyond that ridge?
They are not aware of it yet, but their life as they know it —and as
they've known it for the last four hundred and ninety eight years—
is about to be turned upside down...

THIS STORY BEGAN
LONG BEFORE CHAPTER ONE

THE MYSTERY GLOBE

The rain has cast a freezing spell on the crowd in
attendance. Only the raven seems duly dressed to fend
off the elements. A drop just managed to cling onto his coat,
adding a glassy eye to a face missing one, and a somber
peculiarity to a bird in need of none. Two feet away, the
one-legged owl is not faring as well. Her ruffled
feathers have rendered the spongy raptor gloomier
than usual, and all but harmless to the tail-less
rat sitting nearby, getting his share of soaking.
Even more ill suited is the nearly bold
moth struggling
to hang onto
the tree.

Slowly blending with the gray bark, he will probably never fly again, having lost most of his already scant powdery fur. But as they say, the sight was worth the journey…

A few branches below, a ceremony has just begun: the burial of Celestine Finch. Despite the weather, her son Stuart is not rushing his words, now partially smeared and streaming off the paper.

"My mother's life has ended. An incredible life if I may add. She was said to be ninety years old. Perhaps a bit more. Nobody really knows. Her birth certificate was lost a long time ago…"

Sitting in a circle, two dozen friends and relatives have joined hands, frozen in silence. Standing out among the dark clusters of umbrellas, a light brown casket is ready for its final journey —a grand, vertical, six-foot trip.

Perhaps to better navigate the waters of the afterlife, the pine vessel has been adorned with a strange fish-like symbol. Saying it looks different than the crosses, stars and crescents carved on tombstones around, would be a major understatement. Consisting of a simple loop, like a shoelace, such a naïve drawing would seem better suited for the coloring book of a two-year-old.

Right below, a no less unusual inscription confirms Stuart's story:

CELESTINE FINCH
???? - 2018

He goes on to talk about her career as a writer:

"Her unique prose brought Celestine more success than she ever dreamt of, or sought. In fact, despite the bestsellers and the prizes, she always remained humble. You will never see a picture of my mother on any of her books, or anywhere else for that matter, except right here."

On top of a chair next to Stuart, a picture of Celestine Finch, no closer to looking ninety than she does sixty —sweet almond eyes, long salt and pepper hair parted in the middle, and a thin mouth carrying an almost childish smirk.

"To fame and distinctions," continues Stuart, "she preferred the solitude of her home, often disappearing for years at a time. Most known for the lost words she nursed back to life, she did the same with children, victim of wars, famine and other tragedies. Her legacy speaks for itself, as she leaves behind nearly fifty orphanages around the world."

Three people are seated slightly closer to the casket and the gaping hole in the ground. Two have their head down, Stuart's wife Kate and their teenage daughter Hailee. One has his head up. This is Archibald. Gazing at the busy branches above, the young boy is gobbling up rain, his long hair channeling drops directly into his mouth. Could he be the one who drew that "fish" on the casket? It's very possible. Archibald was never fond of Celestine.

"Why did you let Grandma give me this stupid name?" he often asks at dinnertime. A name he blames for all the teasing he gets at school, although in all fairness, he owes most of that treatment to his reputation —as a teachers' pet. A status he's gained rather reluctantly. Please don't get him wrong. By all accounts, and by far, Archibald sure is smarter than any other student at Amesbury High. And it's nothing new. As far as he can remember, he has always known everything —about everything. But that's not really his fault you see. For one, Archibald never studies particularly hard. In fact, he hardly studies. For some reason, he just happens to know a lot, from Mathematics to History, and pretty much everything in between. Should he want to be a millionaire, he would make the rounds of a few game shows and never have to work in his life.

The only thing that still eludes him, is why he knows so much. Teachers don't care about the why, how come, or by what means. They just love him —too much apparently. Archibald has tried everything to reverse that curse: lie, cheat, play dumb —which he is really good at as well. Unfortunately, it made no difference, because at the end of the day, when a question is asked, and no one else has the answer, Archibald can't help it, he's got to raise his hand.

It doesn't help that his favorite curse is "Holy Bejabbles". Not quite the best way to fit in and make friends. Nobody knows where it comes from. Or what it even means. Some say those were the first two words Archibald ever uttered. The ones he hears most often though, are "dweeb", and "brown-noser", usually right before getting slapped behind the head —both by boys and girls. But again, they are just telling him the truth, sort of, except for William Tanner. *He* is a bully. Last week, that brute even tried to kiss Archibald's sister. On the mouth. Twice. What did Archibald do to stop him? Nothing. He was far too afraid. And that's the other thing about him: while he dreams of blending in like a chameleon, his default move is to play opossum. To put it plainly, our hero is a bit of a wimp.

A few days after the funeral, Archibald and his family arrive at 8 Culpeper Lane. Why the address doesn't just read 1 Culpeper Lane is a mystery, since there seems to be only one house on this obscure road. Not just a house though, a grand, majestic, three-story manor —a big fat mansion for short.

Rising at the end of a long driveway, the humble dwelling boasts 27 windows —on its façade alone. This is the place they inherited from Grandma Celestine, in the town of Cuffley, in

Hertfordshire County. Their small car is followed by a not so big either moving truck. Archibald's family obviously didn't own much —until now.

"How could she hide this from us all these years?" asks Kate, taking in the endless grounds of the property, formal gardens with short hedges planted in the most intricate patterns —in swirls, in commas, in zigzags, but rarely in a straight line.

Whoever did this drank way too much beer, thinks Archibald, making himself chuckle.

For his part, Stuart just wonders why his mother would have needed such a big place. His best guess: "Maybe this was also an orphanage at one point."

"You think so?" asks Kate.

"You know my mother," he says, "she was so secretive."

"And so mean," adds Archibald. "What kind of name is that anyway? Archibald?" he asks once more from the back seat.

"She was not that bad," says Dad. "You should read her books. You never know, you could learn something. You too Hailee."

Learn something? Archibald doubts it. That would imply there's something out there he doesn't already know. Hence the frown, while Hailee barely strays from her frenetic texting rhythm.

"Why couldn't we stay in London?" she questions.

"Oh please", sighs Kate, "thirty minutes by train from the City, this is still London, in a way. Can't you focus on the bright side of things? We're so close, you will both keep your school, and your friends."

"I have no friends," mumbles Archibald. "And I wouldn't mind a different school."

"Are you crazy?" Hailee thunders at him.

"Hailee please, don't start," demands Stuart. "We've not even moved in yet!"

"Holy Bejabbles! Look at those topiaries!" exclaims Archibald, seeing two trees shaped like animals, one like a horse, the other like an elephant.

"How you even know these are called topiaries, I have no idea," says Kate.

"I have no idea either, I thought everybody knew that," he says.

"Why would we want to know that?" asks Hailee.

Archibald shrugs her off, focused on those weird trees, which remind him of something:

"This yard's so big, I can finally get a dog, eh dad?"

"I'm not sure you're ready for that, Arch," cringes Stuart.

"I'll call him Paws," says Archibald.

"Now that's original!" mocks his sister.

"A small dog maybe, like *this* big?" says Archibald, suggesting a lap-size pup, but slowly shrinking the width of his demand, all the way down to a rather rare breed that would fit between his thumb and his index. Verdict: still too big. Dad shakes his head in the rearview mirror as he parks by the fountain. They have arrived.

It's stunning how not just the kids but Stuart and Kate also look so little standing by the huge double front door.

"Giants must have lived here once", Archibald says to himself, staring at the massive knockers even his dad has a hard time lifting.

"Clang, clang…" The metallic knock reverberates through every corridor, every cracked stone, every soot-filled chimney, every wobbly pipe and chandelier in the house.

While they wait, Archibald strokes the two lions —winged and stoned— flanking the entrance.

"Flying cats! These would make great pets," he mutters.

The door eventually creaks open. Or was it the old skinny man greeting them who was creaking? Presumably tall but mostly extremely bent, Bartholomeo was Celestine's butler. He came with the house, in charge of a grand staff of one: himself, as cook, handyman, housekeeper, beekeeper, keykeeper, and apparently gatekeeper as well —definitely a keeper.

"So nice to see you again Bartholomeo," says Kate, "you did such a marvelous job planning the funeral."

"Thank you for taking care of my mother all these years, you're one of her best kept secrets," says Stuart, his hand disappearing into Bartholomeo's mitt.

"Yes," simply replies the servant, with a strong Italian accent, and a surprisingly sweet voice that offsets his dreary appearance — to a degree. A man of few words, that Bartholomeo. He uses about 14, including "maybe", "okay", "huh", and "no I'm not hunchback", in response to Archibald's question starting with "if you don't mind me asking", which sounded like one of Grandpa Harvey's slip-ups. But Bartholomeo does not, mind, and he goes on with showing his new manormates around, room after room, after room, after room, 56 in total.

"No doubt," whispers Kate, "it does look like an orphanage." The creepy kind, if you ask Archibald. The maze of drafty hallways brings chills down his —bourgeoning— spine. His —already shaky— hand freezes on every knob, for every door, he fears, conceals a ghost or a monster. The squeaky floors paralyze his — baby— steps. The clanging sound of those huge keys Bartholomeo carries around shakes him to his —still to be determined— core. The hairless dolls in the library seem to never lose eye contact — no matter where he stands. Not to mention the countless spiders, which reveal their real size —ginormous— as they slide down from stalactites of cobwebs on the highest of ceilings.

And then there's his fear of the paintings. It's not so much the ones lining the walls that scare the bejabbles out of Archibald. The landscape masterpieces are as boring as peaceful can be. Same thing with the rugs hanging around the house. Yes, hanging, against the walls if you can believe it. Archibald knows the culprits: *Probably the same drunk guys who planted those hedges all crooked.* He is only joking. Of course he knows what these are. And just like the topiaries outside, they have a special name —tapestries, they are called. Did he read about that somewhere? No, he just knows. These wall carpets might actually harbor something spooky in the midst of their hand-woven threads, but they are so old, and the colors so faded, that each scene is essentially a blur —a welcomed non-threatening blur. Even the still lifes in the kitchen are surprisingly harmless, *sans* the usual dead rabbit or bleeding pheasant the genre often calls for. *Thank goodness!*

The way Archibald sees things though, it's the paintings that are missing he is worried about, the ones that once decorated the wall alongside the grand staircase. They were obviously there for a long while, as the much lighter shade of wallpaper in two spots can attest. They now seem ghostly inlaid on the wall. It's easy for Archibald to make out their shape, based on the yellowish outline they left behind —vertical and rectangular, both about three and a half feet tall by three wide.

When and why those paintings were removed, where they could possibly be now, and more importantly, what —or who— they depicted, are all matters that torment the newcomer each time he goes up or down the stairs.

Should his parents decide to sell this house, Archibald would certainly not mind. Better yet, he'd gladly volunteer to write the ad himself: "For sale (ASAP), dumpy mansion, ideal as horror movie set, creaky throughout, ~~probably haunted~~, haunted for sure, smells funny, will trade butler for puppy or kitten. Did I mention ASAP?"

In the meantime, he insists on sharing a room with his sister, an idea Hailee reluctantly agrees to on the first night, at dinner.

"I can't believe this," she seethes, "there's a million bedrooms in this house and we've gotta…"

"Twenty," corrects Bartholomeo as he brings pudding to the table —the very end of the table that is, since 21 chairs are empty.

"I beg your pardon?" asks Hailee.

"Twenty, not million," he says.

"It's just an expression," says Hailee, hitting a wall, making no dent in Bartholomeo's poker face —more of a bingo face actually. "Okay fine, *twenty* bedrooms," she concedes, "so why would we have to share one?"

"What's the big deal? You guys were already sharing a room," says Dad.

"He keeps his light on all night! I can't sleep!" snaps Hailee.

"Okay he's scared of the dark, most kids are," explains Kate.

"Yeah Mom, most kids are, but not after they turn three!" says Hailee.

"Maybe he can use a flashlight instead, right Arch? Under the blankets?" suggests Dad.

Archibald shrugs a why not.

"It will be fine. Bedrooms here are twice as big," adds Mom.

"That's the point!" fumes Hailee, "I wanted a bigger room, and I wanted privacy, we're not kids anymore! We already share everything. Do you know what it's like to be in the same class as your brother, even though I'm two years older than him?"

"I never asked to skip grades," says Archibald.

"I know right, it just happened, you're just too smart! And I'm the dumb one," she says with a fake grin.

"Hailee, no one called you dumb," says Kate.

"You don't need to Mom."

"Look, it's only for a couple of months," says Stuart, "until Arch gets used to this new house."

9

That's if he ever gets used to it of course —and that's a big if.

Archibald is most fascinated, meaning scared, by the living room fireplace. Some people have a walk-in closet. This is a walk-in fireplace, under which one can literally stand. More than one in fact. As Stuart said when they arrived, "you could easily fit ten people in there" —or wood logs big as entire tree trunks.

It takes Archibald a week to get close enough to the stone mantelpiece to make out the carvings: five women, in long dresses, screaming, their head shaved, hands tied to poles, being burnt on top of infernal fires, while crazy folks are shown dancing around, waving pitchforks. Archibald immediately regrets laying his eyes on this dark spectacle.

What did they do to deserve that? he asks himself. But more importantly, *who would put such a horrible thing in their house?* — Grandma, that's who! Archibald already knew she was a bad person, for giving him that stupid name. Now, he is also convinced that Grandma, behind her innocent little smirk, was a monster.

What if this fireplace was used for something other than melting marshmallow? Archibald wonders suddenly: *Didn't Dad say "you could easily fit ten people in there?'* That rather unfortunate comment just took on a whole new meaning. Archibald's mind is assailed by a tornado of maybes and what ifs: *Maybe Mom was right… Maybe this house was an orphanage… Maybe Grandma went mad… What if she got rid of all the kids in this fireplace… Maybe that's why it's so big!*

Archibald is staring at the pile of ashes in the hearth with sheer dread. That weird tingly sensation is back in his legs, the peach fuzz on his prune-size calves standing on end. It happens each time he gets really scared of something —usually in the morning, evening and sometimes around lunch time as well. Before his whole body turns to concrete, Archibald takes off and runs up to his room.

Now he can't get that nightmarish scene out of
result, he winds up spending the next three days hid
under the blankets —when he is not at school gettir
roughed up of course.

Only when Christmas time shows its snowy nose does Archibald get somewhat of a break. The afternoon of December 1st is
still a tough one. William Tanner ridicules him once more at the
bus stop after stealing drawings out of his backpack —caricatures
of macaques, baboons and orangutans.

"Archibaldo thinks he's Picasso!" shouts Tanner, exhibiting the
sketches.

The bully monkeys around until other students point out a
rather intriguing detail: one of those funny apes seems to have a lot
in common with Tanner himself. Is it the teeth, fanned out like a
garden rake, leaving daisy patterns on toasts and apples? Maybe it's
just the leafy ears, quite convenient to pick up free satellite TV but
rather hazardous on a windy day? Unless it's simply the eyes,
intense as pond goop and in such close proximity to one another
they seem about to overlap.

Whether it be one or all of the above, the probably not so
accidental resemblance earns the artist one more smack behind the
head —and three extra knots to a school tie turned rope.

Archibald will have to wait until 19 minutes past 5 for his life to
get better. That's when he comes back home. Hands deep in his
pockets, looking down, kicking rocks on the driveway, his face
lights up at the sight of Bartholomeo dragging a twelve-foot tree
into the house. It's also seven feet wide, which matters greatly, as it
is big enough to conceal most of that evil fireplace from
Archibald's traumatized eyes. He can finally breathe a sigh of relief.

The whole family spends a whole quarter of an hour decorating that beautiful tree, with just enough tinsel, baubles and lights to cover the bottom fifth of the massive Noble Fir.

"I guess we'll need more ornaments," notes Stuart. "This is slightly bigger than the Pine tree we had last year!"

"The one barely taller than Archibald you mean? The one we put on the kitchen table?" says Hailee, chuckling.

"It was not that small!" protests Archibald.

"It was very cute," says Kate, coming in with several gifts in her arms, placing them under the tree.

"Where's mine?" asks Archibald, not seeing his name on any of the tags.

"You'll have to be patient," says Kate. "We thought about a gift for you but…"

"Does it bark?" interrupts Archibald.

"No, you're not getting a dog," says Kate. "It's far too much responsibility, and you are not ready for that."

"What about a pony?" suggests Archibald.

"What's next? A flock of sheep perhaps?" asks Stuart.

"That's a great idea Dad! Think about it, no more mowing the lawn! And there sure is a lot of lawn around here!"

"Okay look," says Mom, "every year, for the last four years, you've turned Christmas into an Easter egg hunt. Each time, you turned the apartment upside down looking for your present. That cannot happen here. Therefore..." she says, pausing for a second, gearing up for the breaking news, "we have not bought it yet."

Archibald cannot believe his ears. This is the biggest letdown since that TV guy on the "Eaten alive" show was *not* eaten alive.

"What?" he shouts. "But if you wait, there'll be nothing left!"

"Don't worry, we'll get it before Christmas," says Mom. You're almost twelve, you're a big boy, you can wait a few weeks, right?"

Archibald's answer comes only after some deep thinking:

"If I'm a big boy, can I get a cat then?"

"Oh my!" sighs Stuart.

Feeling the entire world is against him, Archibald retreats into hiding, not in his room, just behind his curtain of long hair, gobbling up a fifth candy bar for the day. To him, this whole thing is not so much about the gift itself, as it is about the tradition. Dead set on keeping it alive, he will wait until after dinner to start his search, convinced that his mother lied to him.

"Of course they bought my gift already," he mumbles.

Kate and Stuart had to go out to visit Grandpa Harvey. The timing couldn't be more perfect. This year won't be easy though.

First of all, the search implies for risk-averse Archibald to stray away from the relatively safe path he has stuck to for the last couple of months. Since the day they moved in, not once has he stepped foot, alone, outside of a narrow corridor spanning from the kitchen to his bedroom —except for a few daunting trips to the gargling toilet.

Secondly, this is not the tiny two-bedroom-one-and-a-half-bath-412-square-foot apartment the family lived in the years prior. There must be hundreds of closets in this manor. Bartholomeo would say 63 and he would be right. Archibald starts with the ones lining the hallways. As he quickly finds out, they are all empty. Same thing for that cupboard under the stairs, where he finds nothing but an old pair of round glasses.

One door left, and Archibald will be done with the hallway on the top floor —a door much shorter than the others, that he always believed to be a broom closet, until he steps inside. Nothing much to step on in fact, as the floor turns out to be completely hollow! For Archibald, it's like missing a step, only, a very, very high step! Totally caught off guard, he topples over. His heart drops. But *he* doesn't. He has grabbed onto something —a rope, strapped onto a pulley above. After a few twists and shouts, he finally stabilizes, stuck in the most precarious position. Turned into a corkscrew, his entire body ends up suspended in the air —his entire body, minus the big toe of his left foot, still hooked onto the edge of the hallway floor. Glancing at the void beneath, Archibald has to preserve an uneasy balance, between on one hand, that big toe, and on the other hand, well, both his hands, moving up and down with the rope, as if he was milking a cow. Should he let go of either side of that rope, he would tumble to who knows where. The pressure on his limbs and lungs is such that he can't even call for help.

"I'm gonna die," he simply coughs out.

About to give up, Archibald swings his body back, and then forth, lunging forward with all his might. Miraculously, he lands back onto safe ground, amazed he managed to dig himself out of this hole.

"Holly Bejabbles!" he lets out. "Is that a dungeon?"

Getting on all four, Archibald leans over carefully to check the depth of that pit. He fishes a penny out of his pants pocket and drops the coin into the hole.

"One, two, three, four, five" seconds go by —and still no sound. Not a clatter. Not a splash. No echo. Archibald gasps.

"A tunnel to the center of Earth!" he mutters.

He hurries down to the floor below, trying to find a similar opening. There's none. Then he remembers seeing another dwarf door downstairs, between the living room and the library. That's no broom closet either. It's the bottom of the shaft, and, nestled inside, a wooden cart, attached to the rope through another wheel. Archibald's penny fell not in China, but straight into the cart, on a stack of bed sheets.

"Door knobs for giants and now this? An elevator for elves!" he exclaims.

"And I thought you were clever!" drops Hailee as she walks by.

"What is it then?" he asks.

"You don't know Genius?" she says, savoring this moment. "It's for the laundry! Bartholomeo said to leave it alone though. It's broken."

"Like everything in here," he comments. "Another reason to sell this house."

"By the way," says Hailee, "careful with that small door upstairs, it's dangerous."

"Thanks for the heads-up," he says ironically.

"Thinking of it, do me a favor, use that door," she says, laughing.

For a moment, Archibald sees himself climbing into the cart, boarding this launch pad and being propelled up from the Earth to the Moon. But after little consideration, he shall pass. That was enough of a scare for tonight.

After grabbing a flashlight, to avoid another whoops moment, Archibald turns his attention to the bedroom closets. He is in for another surprise. Each of them is packed with linen gowns and wool dresses not seen on the streets since the Queen of England was a King —at least.

"What's with the old costumes?" he wonders aloud, exploring every dark corner. He won't venture too deep inside though, for fear of getting lost, or trapped, among those layers of fabric that feel like cobwebs.

Was that a hand touching my shoulder? he freaks out, unwilling to stick around for an answer. He is done with the closets.

Conveniently skipping Bartholomeo's quarters and the ogre-like snoring echoing from that area, Archibald takes his quest to his parents' bedroom, a relatively safer terrain. He combs through it quickly, in case they come back early.

"Where aaaaaare you?" he whispers, calling for his gift to magically reveal itself. "I'll find you anyway," he says, zeroing in on his Mom's dresser. That's where she put that painter's kit last year. No luck this time though. Just in case, he also checks his own room, under his bed to be exact.

"Looking for monsters again? Aren't you too old for that?" asks Hailee, seeing him crawl on the floor.

"That's not what I'm doing," he says. "Besides, if there's a monster, he's living in the toilet, I swear, that thing sounds like it's alive," he adds in a mumble.

Under the bed is where Dad admitted to hiding a game console three Christmases ago. A horrible souvenir, the only time Archibald didn't find his gift, too afraid as he was to stick his head under there —of course because of monsters.

"If you don't get your own room soon, I swear, I'll tell everyone at school you're afraid of monsters, and the dark," warns Hailee.

"I'm not afraid of anything," Archibald hits back, "except food maybe," he jokes. "Wait… food!" he shouts, banging his head on the bed slats.

"You are so weird!" says Hailee, as Archibald zooms past her screaming: "Food, of course food!"

He runs back to the kitchen, where he briefly wreaked havoc earlier. From the cabinets to the oven, all the way to the dishwasher, nothing was spared by that tornado, except for the food itself —but not for long. For the first time ever, our explorer ventures into the Terra Incognita, an uncharted land from which some are said to have never returned —the pantry. One small step for Archibald, a giant leap for Mankind.

"They don't think I can do this!" he says daringly, taking a large breath and pinching his nose. "But I can!" he adds, now talking as if he had a cold.

If he knows his mother well, the only thing he has to do is focus on the foods she would never expect him to even touch. Suffice to say, the list is endless. In Archibald's book, anything outside of the strict regimen he swears by (candy bars and ice cream) rhymes with garbage —among other poetry:

"Gross... awful... disgusting," he notes, with a twang still, as he scans the shelves.

He looks behind every crate of potatoes, every bag of carrots and every basket of beets. But all these weird-shaped vegetables quickly make him sick to his stomach, with all that hair growing on them, some with warts, some with eyes even! When a "yuck" turns into "burp", and that belch turns into gagging, Archibald escapes in extremis, swallowing back those five still undigested candy bars that had moved back up to fill his mouth.

Driven by desperation, Archibald heads to the living room, where he feverishly tears open the three gifts sitting under the Christmas tree. Who cares if they're labeled "To Hailee"? You never know, "they could have mixed my gift in here," he mumbles.

Alas, unless they bought him a new hairdryer, a pair of earrings and a pink casing for the phone he doesn't have, he was wrong on this one also.

Two hours into his grand effort, Archibald is still empty-handed. His legs are starting to tingle again. A terrible doubt submerges him. *Maybe Mom told the truth. Maybe they didn't buy me anything! Maybe they're never going to buy me anything!*

He panics suddenly. *Was I so bad this year?* he wonders. *Not worse than last year, and I got a gift last year!* That means there's still hope. The tingling goes away —for now.

Archibald has gone through every nook and cranny of this manor, leaving no stone unturned. But what about books? Come to think of it, Archibald has not checked the library, even though he's walked through it several times this evening. After scanning the room and its roughly 5000 books —the exact count is known only to Bartholomeo—, he endeavors to pull and tilt every one of them, to get a quick glance in the back. Doing so while evading the all-seeing eyes on those hairless dolls is no mean feat.

"I won't look at you, don't even try," he tells them, in a bid to avoid a staring contest he knows to be unwinnable.

When done with the titles at ground level, he turns to the ladder. Mounted on wheels and attached to a shiny bronze rail near the top, it is studied to slide all around the room —a convenient tool to reach higher shelves, although for now, Archibald might have a different purpose in mind for it.

"Let's see what you've got," he says, testing the wheels back and forth in a sawing motion.

Apparently, it didn't elude Archibald that the room is shaped like a peanut, meaning an 8, meaning… a racetrack. After taking a few steps back to get a good run-up, he rushes forward. Pushing the ladder as hard as he can, he runs alongside, then climbs onto it. It's like catching a moving train —at least the closest he will ever get to that sort of thrill.

"Here I come!" he shouts, riding the ladder like he would a horse, waving the flashlight above his head.

It all goes well, until he reaches the main curve in the wall of books —a turn the sliding ladder was never quite designed to take that fast, especially with someone on it…

"Slow down!" begs Archibald, suddenly aware of the potential hiccup to come. But it's too late. No time to jump off this train. The wheels come to a squeaking halt. Archibald loses his grip on the ladder. He is thrown against the shelves, some of which tilt forward as a result, unloading an avalanche of books on his head right after he himself falls on the floor.

It takes Archibald a few seconds to stand back up, dazed but unharmed, mainly worried about the mess he just made.

"Mom's going to kill me," he says.

Scrambling to quickly put the books back together, he notices something on one of the upper shelves, something his accident has unveiled by knocking down eleven of the fifteen volumes of Jules Verne's *Voyages Extraordinaires*.

"What is that?" he mumbles, not quite sure what he's looking at, something square for sure, but beyond that, no certainty, just a hunch that his quest might finally yield some result.

He moves the ladder over and climbs up. Victory at last! Between *The Child of the Cavern* and *Twenty Thousand Leagues under the Sea*, he finds the Holy Grail, a box, cocooned in a shell-shaped alcove.

"I told you I'd find you," he says to the box.

Archibald drags it forward. It's heavy —a good sign. This is a substantial present we're talking about. In a cardboard box though?

"They've not even wrapped it yet!" fumes Archibald.

At the same time, it is rather convenient. He'll be able to enjoy whatever is inside now, and then put that whatever is inside back in the box right before Christmas without anyone noticing, just like he did four years ago.

Mom definitely lied. But of course she is forgiven already.

Archibald takes the box down to open it. And there it is, the so sought present, the gift that took his parents weeks, if not months, to find, that special something, that unique reward for a unique son, that... dull, used, yellowish object with that weird odor attached to it —a mix of sweaty sneakers and hot croissant smell to be exact.

Archibald's expression changes from full of excitement to cringy and wondering. Pulling it out of the box, he discovers the contours of a 12-inch globe, a terrestrial globe, as old as... well, everything else in the house.

"What is... this?" he lets out, pouting.

Not quite what he expected, that's for sure. Still. That's *his* stinky globe. He decides to bring it back to his room.

"What is that piece of junk?" inquires Hailee as soon as Archibald enters with the globe in his arms.

"What do you think? It's my Christmas gift! I found it," he declares, full of pride. "And this is no junk. Actually, I'm sure it's more valuable than a blow dryer. Or earrings even..."

"What's that supposed to mean?" she asks.

"Nothing," says Archibald, all smirk.

Hailee doesn't care much anyway, busy looking at herself in the mirror, pressing on her chest a pink tee shirt that clashes heavily with her school uniform —striped tie, white shirt, gray sweater, pleated skirt and winter tights.

Archibald places the globe on his desk, getting a first close look at his find —an all but ordinary find undoubtedly.

Mounted on a wooden base consisting of three carved lion paws, the frame is made entirely of bronze —with that unique fool's gold tint. Studded with rivets, two rings wrap around the globe itself, to meet again at the top, where a contraption resembling a crank handle seems a bit out of place.

"I hope it lights up," mutters Archibald.

Not seeing any cord or switch, he turns to that crank, and winds it up like an old clock, as far as he can, as hard as he can. But nothing happens.

"No light I guess," he pouts.

As his dad comes in, Archibald tries to act normal, while standing in front of the globe to hide it.

"Grandpa Harvey says hello, he can't wait to have you guys over in a couple of weeks."

"Can't wait!" says Archibald, sounding abnormally excited.

"Can't wait," echoes Hailee, with a sarcastic tone.

Only after a minute does Stuart notice something new on Archibald's desk.

"Where did you find that?" he asks.

"What?" answers Archibald, now leaning awkwardly on the desk to better conceal his find.

"That globe!" insists Stuart, now pointing at it.

Archibald gives up. But not without a fight.

"Nice try Dad. You know where! I must say, the library, behind the books, high shelf, you guys did pretty well this year. It took me forever to find it. But I did!" brags Archibald, his arms crossed high on his chest full of air.

"Oh I see, you think this is your Christmas gift?" says Dad.

"Of course it is. Why would you hide it so well if it wasn't?"

"I'm telling you, it's not, but you don't have to believe me."

Doubts start creeping into Archibald's mind, as he knows his dad would never lie —not to him at least.

"Maybe it was hidden for a reason, like a treasure you know," says Stuart.

"A treasure?" mutters Archibald, thinking *pirates, black sails, rum breath, wooden legs and eye patches*, even though that cardboard box was no Captain's chest.

Stuart starts examining the globe.

"One thing for sure, it's really old," he says.

"How old?" asks Archibald.

"So old that America is barely on here, that's how old! Look it's just a smudge of a continent!" exclaims Stuart. "This globe was made four, maybe even five centuries ago. I mean, everything is in Latin on here. I know you're smart but, you don't speak Latin Arch, do you?"

"Pig Latin!" says Archibald, quite seriously.

"I'm not sure that's going to help!" grins Stuart. "Anyway, I think it's broken."

"Broken?" groans Archibald.

"Well, it doesn't spin," says Dad, trying in vain to rotate the globe on its axle. "And it's dented," he notes, showing a hole right in the middle of Europe. "Did you stick your finger in here?"

Archibald shakes his head in denial.

"Wait, what is this island right here? This island doesn't even exist," Stuart points out, referring to an unknown piece of land off the coast of Ireland. "Same thing with this one by Spain over here. Another mysterious island! I guess they still had a lot of exploring to do… Fascinating though, isn't it?"

"Yes, amazing Dad," nods Hailee from her bed. "Nerds," she whispers, shaking her head and rolling her eyes.

"And look at all the strange beasts everywhere," adds Stuart, poring over the globe. "What's this? A winged snake with an eagle's head, what did they call that thing?"

"A basilisk?" says Archibald.

"Yes, that's it! Of course you know!"

"Of course he knows," repeats Hailee, irritated.

"What a fantastic creature, with the power to cause death with just one glance, if I remember correctly," adds Stuart. "I bet you that if you look closely, you'll find all the monsters that kept people up back then."

"Monsters?" asks Archibald.

"You know, werewolves, dragons, manticores, griffons…"

"But those don't exist!" grins Archibald.

"You're right, they're legendary creatures. But in any legend, there's a part of truth. Just a slightly distorted truth, that's all."

"What do you mean?" asks Archibald.

"These beasts were not born out of nowhere Arch. They reflected people's fears. And believe me, people had a lot to fear back then. Imagine, waiting for the night to come, the darkest of nights, with no lights but torches, being surrounded by the woods, humongous, deep, impenetrable woods. A world where every shadow gave birth to a new monster. And a new tale. And beyond that, the oceans, even more vast, unexplored, full of danger and mystery. Think about sailors, think about what it meant to go out to sea at that time. They must have been terrified. So what did they do? They exaggerated their stories. Squids became sea-serpents, or giant krakens threatening to sink boats. Remember, the unknown is always scarier than what you can see and understand."

Archibald is breathless and speechless, staring at the globe with a more and more curious and inquisitive look. His chest has deflated. His mouth has fallen, wide open. He is in awe.

"Dragons and griffons," he mumbles…

Glued to a handheld magnifier, Archibald's oversized right eye is traveling through the globe. Naturally, he is most interested in the strange creatures populating the map. He has just spotted a rather interesting specimen near the city of *Herculu*, by the Strait of

Gibraltar, that funnel commanding the entrance to the Mediterranean Sea.

"What are you?" Archibald wonders aloud, addressing what vaguely looks like a pig, a rather wild pig, endowed with two mouths, eight legs, fangs made out of branches, and the tail of a lizard, it seems…

"A cat!" he exclaims a minute later, when he stumbles upon a special breed of (one of) his favorite animal, on the island of *Sicilia*, south of Italia.

Part octopus, that feral feline fellow has tentacles all around its neck, and eyes all over its body, scattered in a cheetah pattern. Unusual for sure, but almost tame compared to that quite unique bear he locates nearby, on the coast of *Slavonia*…

"A bear with a porcupine coat!" whispers Archibald.

Bloated like a blowfish, the entire body of that behemoth is indeed studded with horns of different lengths.

"Are these feet?" questions Archibald. "And that face, it's so… human," he adds, noticing perhaps the strangest detail yet: adding mystery to those already weird creatures, each of them also includes some kind of human-like feature —from head, to toe…

Drawing with quick, self-assured strokes, Archibald sets out to reproduce each monster on paper.

A day, a night and another day go by, and his bedside slowly turns into a mini zoo. Soon, his full-length portraits, claw details and snout close-ups, cover an entire wall and a third of another, creeping towards Hailee, who's not thrilled a bit.

"Can you stop already with that freak show? I'm going to have nightmares!" she yells.

"What about *your* freak show? Don't you think it gives *me* nightmares?" he replies, referring to the posters pinned above her bed, featuring rappers with dollar sign grills on their teeth.

"Look, after Christmas, you're out of here," says Hailee. "In the meantime, stay away from me and don't invade my space okay."

Archibald just nods, acknowledging that they couldn't put any more distance between their beds, crammed on opposite corners of the room.

"And please stop wearing my sweater!" begs Hailee.

"It's not even yours, it's Mom's from College, and it's been washed so many times it fits me better now," corrects Archibald, readjusting the hoodie with three large greek letters printed across the front: Gamma, Delta, Phi —Kate's sorority at Harvard.

Archibald is now studying one monster in particular, at the foot of the Pyrenees, in southern *Gallia* (France): some sort of wild horse with the head of an owl, and a wide pair of bird wings. He is trying to get every detail right, when his magnifier wanders to the side by accident...

That's when he notices the crack his dad was talking about, located near a country called *Moldavia*, in Eastern Europe, by the *Pontus Euxinus* (the Black Sea). The edges are too sharp and too straight for that hole to be a crack though. In fact, it looks machine made. And his dad was wrong on another point: Archibald's finger wouldn't fit in there. He does try though, but even his pinky is too small. Instead, he sticks his pencil into it. A faint click occurs right away, followed by a louder intestinal tumult of gear wheels and springs. Slowly, the bottom of the dent rises back up, ending flush with the surface.

"Wow!" just says Archibald.

Moving his magnifier as close as he can, he discovers other hidden cutouts on the globe. He can feel them under his jittery, half gnawed fingernails. Again using his pencil, he presses down on one of them, right next to *Bohemia*, a land part of the larger country of *Germania*, near the border with *Polonia*. This time, the tiny square

25

insert sinks into the globe, again, in a ruckus of moving nuts and bolts. Archibald doesn't quite know what those indents do but it doesn't matter.

"This is the best toy ever!" he lets out, holding the globe above his head like a trophy.

Hailee makes a comment but he doesn't even pay attention. Now looking at the globe from underneath, he notices something he had not seen before: a hole, lined up with a pin inside one of the rings connecting the globe to its base. Archibald looks closer.

"It's not just a hole, it's a keyhole," he says. But "where's the key?" he wonders aloud.

"What key, what are you talking about?" asks Hailee.

"Nothing, go back to your phone," he tells her.

Archibald again goes through each drawer in the kitchen, living room and library. He looks into that little cup by the entrance where Dad always leaves the car keys. And of course he checks behind the Jules Verne books where he found the globe. No luck. Time for bed. He passes an exhausted Bartholomeo snailing up the staircase. The old man looks more hunched than ever. Just the other day, Archibald overheard his dad say that "Bartholomeo is the main pillar of this house." And according to his mom, "without Bartholomeo, this house would collapse." *No wonder his back is so bent*, thinks Archibald, *with all that weight on his shoulders!*

The victim of some unfair reversed evolution, Bartholomeo walks like a gorilla, his arms dragging so low that the keys he carries are banging against the stairs. The clanging sound stops Archibald in his tracks. He just connected the dots.

"He has it," he whispers, staring at the ring of keys.

No doubt, his parents gave Bartholomeo the key to the globe, entrusting him with a sacred mission. After all, in every tale and adventure Archibald has ever heard of, there's always a gatekeeper denying the hero his prize. If not a three-headed dog, it's a two-faced giant or a single burner dragon —so why not a quasi-hunch-backed butler?

Sure Archibald could ask him for the key, but who knows, that cranky old man might say no —like the other day when he refused to serve Archibald a ninth spoonful of ice cream. Besides, it's so much more fun and challenging to try and steal it from him. Let the showdown begin. Archibald shall defeat the creature standing in his way.

He starts following Bartholomeo around, stalking him, scrutinizing his every move, waiting for that bony hand to let go of those skeleton keys. But the watchful Bartholomeo never leaves them out of his blurry sight.

When he prepares breakfast, lunch or dinner, the keys are on the countertop, next to a set of long scary knives. When he retires to his room for any one of his five daily naps, he takes the keys with him. Those keys are to Bartholomeo what chips are to fish, yin is to yang, Mars is to Venus, candies are to stomach cramps and Hansel is to Gretel —inseparable. He would probably feel naked without them.

Archibald has a plan. He's going to trick Bartholomeo by diverting his attention. One morning, before school, he bursts into the kitchen, gesticulating wildly, pulling his hair.

"Mom fell into that laundry elevator!" assures Archibald. Bartholomeo rushes —slowly— to help. But grabs the keys on his way out.

The day after, Archibald tries something else, taking the drama up a notch. This time, it's Hailee who's in trouble, supposedly...

"She fell from the swing into the well, she's drowning!"

And again, Bartholomeo comes to the rescue, limping down the long driveway —with the keys.

"Presto, presto," ("Quick, quick"), he coughs out, perhaps to give the impression of speed.

Archibald speaks as much Italian as he does Latin —niente (none). He never learned any of it. Yet somehow, he understands all five of those funny words Bartholomeo utters from time to time. Not that it's of any help. But Archibald doesn't give up. Day after day, he keeps trying, coming up with fresh ploys to catch Bartholomeo off guard:

Friday: "Mom ate one of Grandpa's biscuits, she can't breathe!"

Some unique biscuits those are, stale yet moist at the same time —a mystery only the Loch Ness monster could surpass. Archibald still remembers the day his dad forced him to try one. It tasted as though Grandpa Harvey had chewed on it for a few seconds before putting it back into the package.

Saturday: "Hailee dropped her phone into the well and jumped in to get it!" —the most credible of his claims by far, better at least than the one he makes up the day after.

Sunday: "Dad got stung by a thousand bees. His face is swollen like Grandpa's bladder!"

Bees out and about in the middle of winter? Really? You would think that Bartholomeo would stop paying attention at one point. But the loyal butler does not take a chance and always responds to the call —never forgetting his keys though.

Somehow, Archibald's technique pays off in the end. All that "running" has drained all the juice out of the already quite dried up Bartholomeo. By Sunday evening, the old man can't make it to his bedroom and falls asleep on a chair in the library. Better yet, the ring of keys is hanging from Bartholomeo's long fingers, as if saying: "You won."

This is a once-in-a-lifetime opportunity. Archibald approaches the sleeping giant carefully, but flinches suddenly. One of

Bartholomeo's eyes is wide open. This is not a six-eyed Cerberus Archibald is facing. But a Cyclops.

Gently, he frees the ring of keys from his weak grip and rushes up to his bedroom.

Archibald quickly figures that most keys are too big for the globe's keyhole. Only four smaller ones may qualify as a perfect fit. The third one turns out to be a match.

Following a series of intricate noises reminiscent of a bank vault locking mechanism, the pin that kept the globe immobile is released. Archibald can finally rotate his toy, which to his surprise, glows a bluish light.

"So it does light up!" he says.

"Can you turn that off?" asks Hailee, annoyed.

Something else happens, something really strange. When Archibald spins it a bit faster, he can feel the globe pulling him, like a magnet. At one point, his hair starts floating in the air towards the globe. Some of it even gets snatched off and disappears! Archibald gasps and leans back on his chair. Terrified, he runs downstairs with the ring of keys and places it back into Bartholomeo's hand.

That same night, he hides deep into his bed, uncovering the blankets just enough to keep a wary eye on that mystery globe.

Archibald has learned his lesson. *That's what happens when you give in to temptation of an adventurous life,* he reminds himself.

Now he has a missing lock of hair on the side of his forehead. It looks burnt to the root. He is afraid it will never grow back. His mother wouldn't mind. At least now she can see one of his eyes at all times. But Archibald fears this is another reason to draw attention at school —which he surely didn't need.

It's decided, he will stick to the safety of his old wimpy self, and stay away from that globe, no matter how strong his desire to know more about that mysterious light. Compared to what he has just experienced, the fireplace is a piece of cake to deal with, so from now on, he does his homework in the living room.

He'd like to put the globe away but he is scared to even touch it. When he is ready for bed, he goes up and tries his best not to look at it —not even a glance, the same way he vanquished those bald dolls.

The stratagem works, until that fateful evening, when Archibald forgets to close his bedroom window. Not the kind of forget that could have any dire consequences, you may think. And yet... through the open window comes a hissing wind. The curtains shiver. And so does the globe, spinning slightly...

Back from the bathroom, Archibald realizes something terrible:

"I forgot to lock it," he cringes.

"Yes Genius, you forgot to lock the window. It's freezing in here now," complains Hailee, who just got into bed, ready to write her last fifty texts of the day.

"No, the globe," he mutters to himself, realizing something else, which surely won't help: he gave the key back to Bartholomeo.

The wind blows once more, opening the window a bit wider, making the globe spin a bit faster. Now it's glowing again.

"Will you please turn that off?" says Hailee, just about to lose it.

Archibald squints his eyes shut almost. The outer shell of the globe seems to have completely vanished, morphing into an abyss. There's something going on inside. Archibald gets closer. Only a few inches away, he can now peer through the glow, like a fortune-teller would in a crystal ball. The spectacle is mind-blowing: lightning strikes on a background of dark angry clouds —if his eyes are not playing tricks on him. A dormant storm has awoken.

As it dims down, Archibald gives the globe a gentle tap to keep it alive, followed by a stronger push. At the top, that crank handle he tightened so hard, and completely forgot about, has begun to unwind, slowly at first but quickly gaining momentum. The globe itself accelerates as a result. Suddenly, it lights up the entire room in a flash of thunder. Hailee lets out a loud strident scream. Before Archibald can react, he gets absorbed into the globe, in a brief suction sound.

Stuart and Kate barge in within seconds.

All seems normal, except that pretty much everything is gone from Archibald's side of the room. His desk. His chair. His stuff. They've all disappeared, all but —the top— half of his bed. And the globe, tilted on its side.

"What happened? Where's Archie?" asks Kate, panicked.

Hailee can't say a word. Seating on her bed, she is frozen with fear.

Bartholomeo reaches the room out of breath. His eyelids are so heavy with fatigue that he needs to tilt his head back to see anything. But when he actually sees, the globe on the floor and the coral-shaped burn marks veining the walls, his eyes open so wide they seem just about to pop out of his head.

"Oh no!" he simply utters, a man of few words until the end, that Bartholomeo.

Unfolding his body one vertebrae at a time, he soon freezes, standing straight for the first time in nearly 33 years. Seemingly exhaling his whole life in one deep sigh, he topples backwards onto the floor, dead —the ever-present ring of keys clenched in his hand.

The wind is getting stronger outside, with snow now coming in through the window. Stuart looks out. "Archibald!" he screams. Twice. But the night brings back no answer. Just the echo of his broken voice.

It's the calm after the storm. Or perhaps simply a lull before the next one. Stuart doesn't quite know. Sitting at the dining table, his head down, he is staring at the darkest, most opaque cup of coffee —his fifth of the day. And still no answers.

Kate brings extra cups for two inspectors who've just arrived from London. These are supposed to be the big guns, Scotland Yard's finest. It's as though they were trying really hard to fit the part —tough, rough, cold as ice, rude almost, borderline French. Quite a contrast compared to the warm and considerate local officers who stopped by in the morning. These two even refused to take off their coats. Water is dripping everywhere on the parquet floors, along with ashes from the cigarettes they brought in. No room for smiles in their tight, seemingly sewn mouths. No room for small talk or comforting words either. They didn't even bother asking Kate if she was okay. Nor did they say they were sorry for what happened to Archibald —whatever happened to Archibald.

"Do you know of any reason why your son would have left like this?" asks one of them.

"He did not leave," says Stuart.

"Well he's not here now is he?" says the inspector.

"He didn't leave on his own," corrects Stuart. "You know what I mean," he says —which they don't seem to want to know.

"I see here that you adopted Archibald," says the other officer, reading from his notes. "Any problems since you got him?"

"Like what? Overheating? We didn't *get* him! He's not a vacuum or a car! We welcomed him into our life," corrects Kate, obviously on edge. Stuart takes over.

"Archibald doesn't know he was adopted. We never told him," he explains.

"Even his sister thinks he came from my belly," says Kate quietly, looking around, worried that Hailee might hear.

"Maybe he escaped," says one of the officers.

"Escaped from what, he is happy here," replies Kate.

"Kids at school, they talk you know," says the other cop.

"What did they say? Do they know something?" asks Stuart.

The officer glances at his colleague. He seems embarrassed. He explains, looking at his notepad:

"It's still early, we could only talk to a handful of students but, they said your son had some kind of a bruise on his forehead…"

"You know how that happened?" inquires the other inspector.

"We thought he had gotten into a fight," says Kate. "He is constantly bothered at school. It's that bully, William Tanner."

"Are you sure?" insists the inspector.

"Wait, are you implying that *we* did that to him so he escaped?" comments Stuart. Adding: "And how do you explain the missing furniture? Did he take all that in his backpack?"

Kate puts her hand on her husband's.

"Do you know if your son was into chemical experiments, or anything of that sort?" asks the same inspector.

"What does that have to do with anything?" asks Kate.

"We did buy him a science kit for his birthday, but it was more of a toy really," noes Stuart. "My wife is right though, how is that relevant with the matter at hand?"

"Well," says the officer, "there are some substantial burn marks on the walls, consistent with a fire…"

"Brilliant!" quips Kate, cutting him off.

"What my colleague is trying to say, Mrs. Finch, is that perhaps your son set his room on fire to conceal his escape."

"What?" erupts Kate.

"Don't be silly," says Stuart. "We're talking about a boy here. He's not even twelve."

"Because thunder stealing your son is a more plausible option?" says the inspector. "Why not Aliens then?"

"Have you seen the scars on the floor, and the walls?" says Kate. "What could cause something like that?"

"You're right, those marks are consistent with lightning," says the other inspector. "But with all due respect Madam, we have to look at all *plausible* scenarios and the most *probable* causes, including child abuse. Your daughter is barely talking, she seems traumatized as well…" he notes, with suspicion in his voice.

"Of course she is traumatized, her brother is missing!" says Kate, barely containing her anger.

Upstairs, Hailee moves under the *Police Line Do Not Cross* yellow tape and past an imprint of Bartholomeo's body, drawn in white tape —with a side bulge marking the location of his keys. Hailee goes straight for the globe, still on the floor. She squats down to pick it up but hesitates for a second. Finally, she takes a large breath and grabs it with her two hands, as if she were to hold a person by the shoulders.

"Where did you go Arch?" she asks, staring right at the globe.

MAYBE HE FLEW, TO CHAPTER TWO

FROM LONDON TO GRISTLEMOTH

Archibald wakes up peacefully, with a yawn so long he can talk through it. "It was just a bad bad dream," he kind of says.

It's still dark. He pulls the cover up to his chin. His eyes full of sleep, he discovers the blurry twinkle of small red lights above him.

"Christmas!" he rejoices.

Using the energy of an even bigger yawn, he sits up, and rubs the back of his head, which feels awfully sore for some reason. To his astonishment, what he thought to be his blanket is actually a huge leaf. And he is lying on the ground, outside!

Archibald's first thought, aloud: "Hailee kicked me out!"

His second thought, even louder: "Hailee, I'm gonna kill you!"

But wait... his bed is here, around half of it at least —the bottom part—, bent down by his feet. His desk is also nearby, a few leaves away, covered with the usual desk mess of books and candy bars. Only the lamp got knocked over, along with a few books, now sharing the ground with Archibald's drawings, strewn around, some of them burnt around the edges.

His head is boiling up with a million questions. Well, to quote the late Bartholomeo, just twenty: *Where am I? Why am I here? How did I get here? Who did this to me? Where is the other half of my bed? Am I going to die? Is my hair okay? Am I dead already?* And about twelve more like these. More importantly, and that's a much more verifiable number, he has zero answer.

After scanning the surroundings, he is sure of one thing and one thing only: this is not *his* backyard. The trees here are much higher and the vegetation much more dense.

"Hailee..." he now murmurs. "Dad... Mom..."

Suddenly realizing he is on his own, in a totally unknown setting, Archibald panics and ducks under his desk. Dead set on hiding there forever if he has to, he tries to grab his flashlight from under the table, tapping around with his hand. It takes him a minute but he eventually gets a hold of it.

"Yes!" he shouts.

He uses the same technique to get his candy bars. It works. He can proudly count out his stash: 3 KitKat, 2 Galaxy Ripple, 1 Twix and 1 Yorkie.

"At least I have food," he huffs.

He counts again though and he is pretty sure there's another Yorkie up there. And indeed there is. It's already open but he only took one bite out of it yesterday so it's definitely worth finding it. He is back on the hunt for that missing bar. His hand snakes out on the desk again. It almost has a life of its own now, pushing aside crayons, eraser, magnifier, books and miniature dog sculptures molded up in playdough. His fingers are getting warmer, only a few inches away from the Yorkie, when a tremendous noise interrupts the search.

The desk is shaking and squeaking. Someone —or something— has jumped —or landed— right above Archibald, who has stopped breathing. Paralyzed by fear, he can't even command his stubborn hand to get back down with the rest of his shaking body. He can hear some loud sniffling, mixed with some growling and, perhaps even more unsettling, a side note of purring. Maybe it's one of those wild boars Bartholomeo showed him last week on the edge of the property. They looked really mean with those big fangs sticking out of their mouths!

Archibald's face is stuck in a painful cringe, his eyes closed, his body twitching in synch with any vibration in the desk. His eyes snap back open suddenly. Archibald can now feel whatever is up there breathing on his hand. He is trying not to scream. One more minute of this and without doubt he will faint. And then, as abruptly as it showed up, that something or someone takes off and disappears in a tremendous racket, causing the desk to crack and partially fall apart.

Archibald only gets a glimpse of a shadow vanishing behind the trees…

Only after a couple of hours does he manage to emerge from under the desk. He is still on his guard, moving in slow motion. First assessment: whatever that thing was, it/he/she ate his Yorkie bar, leaving behind one good pound of drool that looks very much like the mint jelly Bartholomeo liked to smear on everything.

"Gross!" he comments while touching the gob with the tip of his finger, then almost throwing up when smelling the tip of that finger. Why did he do that? He is just one of those —many— people who like to smell their fingers.

As he starts exploring the woods, he'll use that expert finger one more time, to wipe a strange powder off leaves.

"That's not snow, it's just dust," he mutters, realizing the vegetation is half dead, smothered under that grayish veil.

Too bad that flashlight is not big enough or Archibald would gladly hide behind it, which is exactly what he's trying to do, holding it with both hands right beneath his nose.

Not that he needs it really. The sky has enough of a glow to light his path, the regular glow from a moon full night, plus a reddish undertone.

Maybe Mars replaced the moon, he says to himself. Archibald can't actually see the moon so it doesn't seem like such a crazy thought. As it turns out though, the red glow seems to be coming from the lights he woke up to. Those are some really strange stars! Not only are they red, but they're moving. Archibald had heard of falling stars —and even seen a few during a trip to Paris on Bastille Day last year. But these are different. They are not quite falling per se. They are spinning and swirling. What a fascinating spectacle! Archibald stops in the middle of a clearing in the woods to enjoy the show blazing overhead.

"Wow, these are incredible!" he exclaims, squinting about.

One of them even seems to grow right before his eyes. Wait, it has now split into two separate stars, getting bigger and bigger, in fact, getting closer and closer. Archibald doesn't worry much about it, until he realizes that those stars seem to be carrying a dark mass with them. *Is that an asteroid?* He rubs his eyes, for he thinks he might be dreaming still. It just occurred to him: what he thought to be stars are not stars at all. They are actual eyes, with some sort of enormous bird attached to them!

Archibald starts running for cover, looking for his desk but unable to remember where it is. The tingling in his legs tells him to play opossum. Or should he try his chameleon thing? Leaving his dilemma behind, he bolts for his life. And won't stop screaming.

That bird has landed. *Is it even a bird? It can't be, it started running like a buffalo!* And it's now in pursuit, smashing every tree branch in its way.

Archibald has never run so fast —even faster perhaps than that day William Tanner hustled after him at school to feed him soap. And that was a memorable sprint! Thankfully he has his favorite sneakers on and not those unwieldy sleepers his mother usually makes him wear in the evening.

He glances back over his shoulder from time to time but can't really figure out what's chasing him. A bird? A hog? A camel? A mixed breed for sure! There was a circus in town just a couple days ago. Maybe one of their exotic animals escaped! Or, *maybe this is the same beast that ate my Yorkie earlier*, thinks Archibald. That gives him an idea. He fishes in his pocket for another candy bar and throws it behind him. And… it's a dud. The beast zooms past it without paying any attention.

"He can't smell it!" realizes Archibald. He has to think and act fast. He grabs another bar, only this time, tears it open before dropping it. It works! The beast stops to snatch it.

"Yes!" he exclaims once more. But this is the equivalent of Archibald gulping down one reasonable scoop of ice cream. The beast is far from stuffed. And back on the hunt within seconds.

Nearby, Archibald's screams have caught the attention of three young girls carrying logs and herb bouquets in their arms. They don't just seem to be from another country —like those relatives you've never heard of from Ireland who show up at your door one day. They seem to be from another time period altogether —like those relatives you've never heard of from Ireland who show up at your door one day.

The giveaway? Probably the long sleeved embroidered blouses, topped with grey wool tunics, stamped with a weird sort of wave pattern on the chest. Tied at the waist, those thick aprons end in a skirt, partially covering fluffy black pants. Though usually praised as a fashion must, layering in this case would be more of a faux-pas, possibly even worse than wearing socks and sandals together.

And that's not even mentioning the water flask, horn and sickle attached to their belt, in addition to several pouches hanging like grenades from a shoulder belt. One of them even has a bow and arrow strapped to her chest! Compared to the rest of these outfits, the Vietnamese-style pointy hats, extending all the way to the width of their shoulders, would almost look normal —except for the twigs and leaves scattered on top!

One more high-pitched scream from Archibald and the three girls drop their wood, herbs and whatever it is they were doing.

They start running in his direction right away.

Reaching a ridge, they witness the dramatic scene unfolding around twenty feet below. Despite Archibald's good pace, the beast is gaining on him and will soon catch up…

"What do we do?" asks one of the girls, with fear in her voice.

"They're heading to Wigzigor's mouth, we gotta hurry!" says the taller and apparently older one —who's obviously in charge.

Archibald is running out of breath. To make matters worse, he comes face to face with a barrier of stone, shaped like a crescent, and profiled like a wave —Wigzigor's mouth. That cliff must be thirty to forty feet in height at least, ending in a curling top, making it impossible to climb. Archibald is trapped. His back against the wall —literally—, he seems to have given up.

Seeing the beast running towards him at full speed, he is surprisingly calm. Or maybe his blood just froze along with every muscle, nerve and organ in his body.

It's funny, he says to himself, *I always thought that big fowl mouthed Tanner would be the one killing me.*

To his left, the three young girls have made their way down the hill, but they are still far. What could they do anyway? They've

43

apparently picked up a few stones, but their improvised weapons seem rather pathetic in the face of this goliath. Perhaps of less futile assistance, one of them takes aim at the beast with her bow and arrow. Against all odds, cutting through leaves, flying between tree trunks, her projectile hits the beast in the rear. An absolute feat given the great distance and countless obstacles in the way — but an exploit with no effect whatsoever on the monster's formidable velocity. It doesn't even so much as flinch.

As if to try and see what will soon devour or obliterate him, Archibald points his flashlight toward his nemesis. He turns it on moments away from his certain demise. Blinded by the light, the beast turns its neck at a quarter to noon angle, but without veering much off course. The collision seems inevitable. Archibald has closed his eyes. Seven eighths of a second later, a loud boom echoes throughout the forest...

The three young girls arrive at the scene expecting the worst but hoping for the best, following an old Confucius proverb, itself based on a fortune cookie —or vice-versa.

They push aside one more fern bush and discover Archibald on the ground, in one piece. He sits mute. The beast is lying just six and a half inches away, inert and twisted like a paper clip. It came crashing against the cliff.

The size of a —European— car, that "thing" has a coat made not of fur but of dead leaves, making it hard to see where its body ends, and the ground begins. It vaguely resembles in shape a rhinoceros, only, a rhinoceros that could fly. Protruding from its back are indeed two pairs of batwings. As for the tail hanging from the rear end, it belongs to a rat —a giant rat that is! If it's still alive, the beast will owe its survival to the carapace on its head, a massive horn that arcs all the way to its spine, similar to the front shield of a beetle, connected to two more horns curved around the mouth, like the whiskers of a catfish.

What Archibald finds the most intriguing though is the face under those horns, for it is 100% human, hairy and scary as hell, but human still —just like two of its six legs by the way, which seem shockingly dull within this overall display of oddities.

"Gadzooks!" swears the tallest of the girls. "How did you do that?"

"I just... used my flashlight," answers Archibald, stunned by his own prowess —and obvious luck as well.

"Your what?" she asks.

"My flashlight," he repeats, turning it on, shining it right in her face.

Little does he know that he has just done the unthinkable.

The girl starts screaming, covering her head as if to protect herself, while the two younger ones start screaming as well, not too sure why, perhaps simply out of sympathy and solidarity.

Archibald immediately turns it off and the screaming slowly subsides.

The victim rubs her face, checks her hands, arms and hair, asking the others whether she's okay —which of course she is.

As for Archibald, he'd like to feel sorry, but doesn't quite know why he should. Stunned, he inspects his flashlight to see whether it might have some special attributes he was not aware of.

"What is your magic?" inquires the girl with the bow.

"My magic? I don't have any magic," he says as he stands up to straighten up his pajama bottoms.

Big collective gasp among his audience, with the smallest one, baby-faced, slapping her hand on her mouth.

"Is she a boy?" she asks, sizing him up.

"She? What? Of course I'm a boy!" confirms Archibald, offended, uncovering his face fully by pulling his long hair behind his ears —and of course puffing up his chest.

All three girls are looking at him with equally startled faces. Already intrigued by Archibald's sneakers (quite different than their boots, made of cloth and crisscrossed with laces), they seem unsettled by his sweater —that sorority hoodie he borrowed from his sister, and that she herself borrowed from her mom.

"Are you a wizard?" asks the main girl, now cold and inquisitive, while the other two whisper things to one another.

"I wish!" says Archibald. "My sister would be a toad by now."

"Where are you from?" she asks.

"London," he responds. "I mean, technically outside of London, because see my Grandma died and we…"

"Oh keep your flummadiddle to yourself!" snaps the girl.

"My what?" he says.

"Your balderdash! You know what I mean!"

"Huh?" interjects Archibald, still not getting it.

"And he doesn't even speak English," she says, turning to her friends, who grin. Then back to Archibald:

"Your balductum, your hogwash!

Archibald shakes his head, still in the dark.

"Your horse manure, your nonsense!" she yells.

"Oh okay," says Archibald, finally getting it.

"What is your business here?" she now asks.

"My what?"

"What brings you here?" she rephrases, annoyed.

"Not sure, I was up in my room with my Christmas gift and…"

"Oh shush at once!" she spits. And he zips it, making his lips disappear into his mouth. The girl taps a finger on her temple. She is thinking, her eyes fixed on Archibald the entire time.

"Okay you'll accompany us to the village," she finally says. "But first, hand me your weapon."

"My weapon?" he asks.

She points at his flashlight.

"Oh this, sure, it's yours," he says, extending it towards her, making her jump.

She detaches one of the burlap pouches from her belt and motions for him to drop the flashlight into it. After he does, she shuts it tight and hooks it back on her belt.

"We'll get to the bottom of this in Gristlemoth," she tells him.

"Wait, Grease what?" asks Archibald. "I can't, I have to go back to…"

"To where, huh? London?" she asks. "Let's see, you're only five, maybe four weeks away, that's if you walk fast of course, and if you can swim for twenty hours straight!"

"Am I still dreaming?" Archibald wonders aloud. "Pinch me," he says, which she does, on his arm, really hard, making him scream —like a girl.

While Archibald tries to comprehend what that bossy girl just said, she gives instructions to her companions.

"You take care of this one," she says, motioning towards the beast. Then turning to Archibald: "You, follow me. Close."

"What's with the hat?" he asks.

"Where have you been all this time? Under a rock?" she jokes.

"Under a desk actually," he says, in the most genuine tone.

"You know, camouflage," she says. "It's made of the same things you can find on the ground. Wood, dirt, leaves. From up there, the Marodors can't see us, we blend in. So again, you stay close okay. We're lucky, we've got all sorts of night creepers around here, but not many land Marodors. We'll avoid clearings anyway, you never know."

47

Again, Archibald doesn't have the faintest idea as to what she is talking about. But man is that girl impressive! So he just nods, and goes shoulder to shoulder with her, craning his neck to try and match her height. Other than that time he fell asleep against Emily Dorsey in the bus, he can't recall ever being so close to a girl before. It feels strange.

As they walk away, Archibald looks back and sees the two other girls kneeing to the ground, placing around the beast the stones they were holding.

"Is that thing dead?" he asks.

"Of course not," says the girl.

When he checks again seconds later, the beast slowly rises in the air, frozen, as if carved out of stone or freshly stuffed, its tail and wings dragging on the ground. Archibald swallows his saliva loudly, now wary of the strange girl next to him as well.

"What's that monster?" he asks her.

"Surely you've heard of Marodors, right?" Don't tell me you haven't. Then I'd say you're talking knavery to me for certain. You don't want to talk knavery to me, do you?" she says, frowning.

"Knavery?" he wonders aloud.

"Knavery, you know, guilery, falsary!"

Archibald shakes his head again.

"Trumpery?"

This definitely speaks more to him but it's still not 100% clear.

"Impostry! A ruse! A lie! You don't want to lie to me, do you?" she says, frowning again.

"Of course not, I just meant what *kind* of... merdar is it? I know what a merdar is," he mumbles. "I know everything."

"That sounds so cockish. Nobody knows everything!"

"No I didn't mean it that way, it's not something I brag about, that's just the way it is, I don't know why but I know everything."

"It's funny, you don't strike me as someone who knows everything, but we'll see," just says the girl, in a challenging tone.

Archibald has to admit though, there's a lot he doesn't get about this place, starting with that creature he keeps glancing at.

"By the way, merdar, is that French?" he asks.

"What?"

"No nothing," he mutters.

"So," she says, "that weapon of yours, how many Marodors have you defeated with it?"

Archibald hesitates, and starts counting on his fingers.

"Not sure," he dares to say.

"That many huh!" she exclaims, truly impressed.

"You know, it's hard to stop yourself, you see one, you've gotta fight it you know, you can't just let it get away right?" he brags nervously, all the while staring down, unable to cross her gaze.

"It's weird, if I didn't know any better, I'd say you were trying to run away earlier," she says.

"I know, it looks like it, to people like you I mean, who are not familiar with my moves, and my tactics. I get that a lot. Common mistake."

"And the screaming, that's part of your... tactics?"

"Part of it? It's half of it! At least. You need lots of screaming."

"Good to know, because it sure sounded like you were calling for help at one point."

"See I'm so glad you thought that, it's *exactly* what I wanted that beast to think. That's key to my strategy, confusing the enemy."

"Well, you succeeded, it sure was very confusing!"

"If you don't mind, I'd rather not say more about it," he says. "I could teach you though, one day."

"I can't wait," nods Faerydae, not quite convinced but after all, he did vanquish that Marodor, or whatever she calls that thing.

"What is your name?" she asks.

"Archibald," he says in a sorry tone.

"Pleased to meet you. My name is Faerydae."

"Fear of what?"

"Fear of nothing! It's Fae-ry-dae," she spells out.

"And I thought *I* was the one with the funny name!" he chuckles. She stops, obviously offended.

"I didn't mean it that way," explains Archibald. "It's just that… people usually make fun of me because of my name."

"I don't know why, Archibald is so common," she says.

"I know you're saying that to be nice. But thanks. What's *their* names?" he asks, turning to the two girls a couple hundred feet behind, walking on each side of the levitating Marodor, holding out those stones —which are now glowing.

"That's Rhiannon and Maven," says Faerydae.

Archibald would almost think that she is pulling his leg.

"Any middle names I would have heard of?"

"Cinnamon and Hazel, it's short for Hazelnut."

"And what's yours, Nutmeg?" he asks, chuckling.

"I have two actually, Dawn and Orla," she says.

"You're not from around here, are you, Faerydae Dawn Orla?" jokes Archibald, looking at her from head to toe, hinting at the outdated outfit, on top of the weird names.

"Who is really?" she answers in a deep manner, almost sad. "By the way," she says, "nobody makes fun of someone because of their name. They make fun of someone because that someone did or said things others can make fun of. Usually something stupid."

Archibald doesn't know what to say to that —and it definitely bothers him.

"Anyway, it doesn't matter, when we arrive in Gristlemoth, your name will be Ivy."

"What? No! Why?" he objects.

"Yes, when we get to Gristlemoth, you'll be a girl, you'll understand, trust me."

"No," he repeats with force.

Faerydae stops abruptly.

"All right, we'll have to leave you here then. And I'll keep your weapon. Good luck to you, Friend!" she says.

"I have to think about this," says Archibald, taking ample time to answer —meaning two seconds. "Okay fine, I'll be a girl," he says reluctantly.

"That's what I thought!" says Faerydae, withdrawing a lace shawl from her bag and fitting it on Archibald to cover his sweater.

"So cute!" she comments.

At this point, Archibald doesn't offer any resistance. If he ever wondered what it's like to be a Chihuahua dressed up like a ballerina or a ladybug, now he knows.

"I can't do that to you," says Faerydae.

She reaches into her bag once more and pulls out a more opaque, dark red cloak.

"Let's try this," she says, placing it on Archibald's shoulders and tying it at the neck.

He definitely doesn't mind the makeover.

"Wow!" he exclaims, "I've always wanted one of these, a cape, like a superhero!"

"Hero maybe, superhero, I'm not sure about that," she says.

"Do you have a black one?" he asks.

"No, why?"

"It's fine, I'll just be that other guy. Superhero for sure though," mumbles Archibald as they get back on their way.

Between the trees, Archibald catches sight of a light in the sky, standing out in the night. But what it is exactly, he cannot discern.

"Is that the moon?" he asks.

"Did you fall on your head or something?" she comments.

"It's huge!" exclaims Archibald, who can't stop staring at that bright halo.

"There is no moon. That, is Gristlemoth," says Faerydae.

As they get closer, Archibald can make up the shape of an almost perfect circle with jittery edges, detaching from the surrounding darkness. Inside, it's blue sky and white fluffy clouds —and no Marodor to be seen.

A few more steps and he can see the timber rooftops of a small village located right under the glowing hole in the sky. Rays of sunshine pour a bright glare on dozens of homes —huts more than actual houses.

"How's that possible? How can it be nighttime here and day-light right over there?" he asks.

"I thought you knew everything?" mocks Faerydae.

"At home I do," he says with a questioning look. Could it be, that his burdening curse would have been lifted at last?

"It's wonder how you survived all these years," says Faerydae, pressing ahead.

They soon reach the edge of the village, surrounded by giant boulders marking the limit of the area soaked by the Sun. Strange waves of light are also rising from the large rocks, a green and white glow, the like of which Archibald has never seen before — except on a screensaver maybe. The closest comparison would be the Aurora Borealis. Those hypnotizing lights are usually found by the North Pole though, not in the London suburbs!

"Holy Bejabbles!" just says Archibald.

"Remember, your name is Ivy," whispers Faerydae.

"I really don't know why it's…"

"Shush!"

"Okay my name is Ivy," complies Archibald, trying to talk like a girl.

"Oh no need to change your voice."

"What does that mean?" says Archibald, one the verge of a fit.

"I'm just shenaniganning with you! Just keep your hair in your face, and your mouth shut, and it will be fine," she says.

Oddly, the dirt road comes to an end, the huge boulders blocking the way.

"How do we go in?" asks Archibald.

Faerydae blows her horn, producing an enchanting two-tone sound that carries over for a mile.

"What now?" asks Archibald.

"Are you always so impatient?" says Faerydae.

Archibald is about to answer when the boulder right in front of them starts shaking —making *him* shake.

"What was that?" he asks, looking scared.

The monolith wobbles a bit more, before slowly detaching from the ground, as if on hinges. And to the side it swivels, like a 50-ton door naturally would.

"Voilà!" says Faerydae with a smile. Archibald is stunned.

The small convoy, composed of the three girls, half a boy and the floating Marodor, passes the narrow opening manned by four girls with yet the same kind of stones gleaming in their hands. Archibald looks with apprehension as the revolving rock thuds shut behind them.

"We don't need these anymore," says Faerydae, removing her hat, unleashing a flurry of wavy curls topped with a braided crown. The golden hair brightens up her face, making it all the more soft and angelic. Archibald can't help but staring at her, his mouth wide open. Faerydae is the most beautiful creature he has ever seen. He would call her bedazzling and mesmerizing, if only he had the courage —and if he knew those words of course.

"Close your mouth, Ivy," Rhiannon whispers in his ear while escorting the Marodor down a side road, under the cheers and applause of an improvised crowd.

Archibald regains somewhat his composure and takes in the beautiful simplicity of Gristlemoth. This is a small town, as in no red light around small, not even a stop sign small. Spread out before him is a summer camp more than a village, dotted with small cabanas and lots of trees sharing a gently slopped landscape. Surrounded on three sides by the woods, and anchored to a high cliff on the other, Gristlemoth covers a fairly vast space, shaped like a ball of rugby. An eagle flying at an average eagle speed —say 30 miles per hour— would tell you it takes him about 4 minutes to cross Gristlemoth from North to South, and a minute less from East to West. That's if there was an eagle around. But there's none.

As a matter of fact, the sky and the trees alike are empty. No screeching eagle. No cawing crow. No quacking duck. No dooking ferret. No nest. No chirping of any kind. No cat, and no playing mice either. Not even a squirrel jumping from branch to branch or burying his nuts for a rainy day.

"Where are all the birds?" asks Archibald, looking up.

"The Marodors got them all. They left us with bugs, and a few worms," says Faerydae.

Archibald might be able to handle Marodors. But a world without animals, that, he can't imagine. Wait —there might be hope after all. He just spotted something brown, white and fluffy zooming through a field of flowers.

"A dog!" he exclaims, his joy quickly dashed as arrows start raining on that fur ball.

"What are they doing? They're going to kill him!" he screams, running to confront the archers who just reloaded their bows.

"What got into you? It's just a pillow!" shouts Faerydae.

"A what?" he asks, interrupting his heroic charge.

"A pillow," she repeats. "For target practice."

"A running pillow?" lets out Archibald, even though the furry prey doesn't have any legs. Somewhat of a face, and somewhat of a tail, but surely no legs. It is in fact... flying. Still, it certainly acts like a dog, whereas those arrows don't look anything like arrows, their tips not sharpened to a deadly point, but rather, capped with a rounded helmet. The way Archibald sees it:

"Those arrows are wearing gloves!"

And that's not the least strange of things about this place. Not only can he still not see any (real) animals, but there seems to be only girls around, all very young, none older than fifteen probably.

"Am I the only boy here?" he asks Faerydae.

"No Ivy, you're not," says Faerydae with a smile.

Everyone seems to be part of a small army —an army of girls, some sawing wood, some washing clothes, others carrying baskets and rocks. Whatever their outfit, trousers and tunics, or long dresses, they all have that same double wave pattern logo sewn on the chest.

Archibald wants to ask Faerydae about it. But he's already intrigued by something else, the curious hand gestures she's making towards those in her path.

"What's that you're doing?" he asks, trying to mimic her.

"You don't know sign language either?" sighs Faerydae.

Archibald admits he doesn't —a rather rare occurrence.

"Well you know how to shake your head, that's a start!" jokes Faerydae. "See, when we first moved here, there were people from all over the world, with so many different languages, making it hard to understand each other. So we developed this common language. It changed everything. We still use it from time to time, especially when we're not right next to each other, so we don't have to yell across the village. It keeps us more peaceful."

Following in his guide's footsteps, Archibald starts waving at everyone meeting his gaze, and gives some thumbs up, which Faerydae slaps down right away.

"What did you do that for?" he asks.

"Stop being a mope!"

"A what?" he says.

"A cang."

"A cang? Like a kangaroo? I don't get it."

"No I mean a nup, a liripoop, a saddle-goose, a fopdoodle!"

He doesn't know any of those names —who does really?

"A fool?" she sums up.

"Why am I a fool? I'm just doing what you're doing," he says.

"No, we don't use that kind of sign around here," she explains. "Don't you know where it's from?"

Of course he knows. But he'd rather play dumb. So he shrugs.

"The Roman Empire? Rings a bell?" she asks. "Giant arenas, gladiators, stupid games, thumb up, you live, thumb down, you die."

"I didn't think about it," says Archibald.

"You mustn't do that again," she says. "It's totally barbaric."

As they stride deeper into the sun-drenched village, another odd reality is starting to register with Archibald: there are no adults around either.

"Your parents are away or something?"

"You can say that I guess," she says. An answer Archibald interprets as a hint to something tragic.

"I'm sorry, I didn't know," he says.

"You didn't know what?"

"Last week, my dad met one of those orphans my Grandma rescued. That's what he kept saying, that his parents were away. It's terrible."

Faerydae just nods, more concerned about some kind of crackling sound in the background.

"Did you hear that?" she asks.

"It sounded like firecrackers," he says.

"Not again!" she thunders, picking up the pace, her eyes fixed on a cloud of white smoke billowing above the treeline.

"It's coming from the river," says Faerydae.

By the time they get there, most of the smoke has evaporated, but not the mischievous twinkle in the eyes of four girls squatted on the ground. If it added guilt to their faces, the sight of Faerydae didn't put an end to their misdeed —on the contrary...

"Hurry!" says one of them as she stands up in the middle of their circle, pressing two stones against her chest. Three more are tied up with strings around her ankles, and a few words recited. The next second, she is projected up in the air in a geyser of sputtering sparks. Her accomplices are blown off their feet, balls of light whirling over their heads.

Only after two erratic somersaults and a painful twist does Rocket girl finally come back down, crashing to the ground on her back.

"Lenora!" screams Faerydae, rushing to the scene, switching from mad to worried —for a moment.

"Are you tired of life?" she asks, kneeing by the girl still reeling from the fall.

"But..." utters Lenora, befogged and disoriented, her sleeves smoking.

"Do you wish to die?" clarifies Faerydae.

"I almost made it, did you see?" says Lenora, holding her elbow in pain.

"Will you be alright?" inquires Faerydae.

"I think so," answers the stuntgirl.

"Good, then you know where you're headed!" says Faerydae.

"I know," pouts Lenora, as the others help her back up.

"No such experiment shall ever happen again," hammers Faerydae. "Is that understood?"

All girls walk away giving a reluctant nod. Lenora cracks a smile as Archibald gives her a thumb up.

"What are you doing? Don't encourage her!" fumes Faerydae.

"Sorry, it just seemed fun!" he says.

"It was foolish, she could have gotten herself killed!" says Faerydae, collecting those mysterious stones strewn around, some blackened, some still glowing.

"What are these?" asks Archibald. "They look like those stones Raymond and Maverick used on that beast earlier."

"It's Rhiannon and Maven," spells out Faerydae. "And I'll tell you what these are *not* intended for... fun, whatever *fun* even means," she says, bashing two stones against one another, knocking the light out of them.

"Fine, don't tell me, they're just stones anyway," he says.

"Just stones?" repeats Faerydae angrily. "Follow me," she says —which is exactly the reaction Archibald was betting on.

Right around the block, just a stone's throw away, Faerydae and Archibald enter an immense vegetable garden. They weave between rows and rows of lettuce, cabbage, tomatoes, cucumbers, beans and more. To Archibald, this feels like one of those scary mazes with no end in sight. He was hoping they would get out of here soon, but Faerydae has just found someone she knows.

"Aye up Naida! This is my friend Arch... Ivy," she says, hesitating for a second, biting her tongue.

"Hello Ivy, where are you from?" says Naida, with a warm voice spiced up with exotic accent.

Not sure what to say, the Archibald asleep in Ivy responds with a weird cough mixed with a hiccup, followed by the oddest nod and shrug. Faerydae elbows him, urging him to act normal.

"By the way, what was that noise earlier?" asks Naida.

"You know, Lenora and her experiments," says Faerydae.

"You can't blame her for trying," comments Naida.

Faerydae rolls her eyes.

"So what are you doing?" she asks.

"I was just about to plant some carrots!" says Naida.

"Yuk!" blurts out Archibald, coughing to cover his comment. Faerydae elbows him again. Then turning back to Naida:

"Go ahead, show us."

They all kneel down on the ground.

"Too bad we don't have any bees, we wouldn't need to do all this. They would pollinate the plants for us," explains Naida.

"I'll bring you some. We have a million in our garden!" claims Archibald.

"Of course you do!" she says, with a doubting face.

Naida proceeds. Brushing aside the long black curls that blend with her skin, she pours a few seeds in the ground, to which she adds a bit of water. Other than that, there is nothing too out of the ordinary in her routine, until she opens a bag full of those strange looking stones. She surrounds the planted area with three of them, two black and shiny, one brown and translucent. Archibald is close enough to notice the markings on those stones, basic signs made of lines, rectangles and circles, similar to the hieroglyphs used in Ancient Egypt —nothing he has ever seen outside of a book though. He is also close enough to hear the strange words Naida is muttering. But can't understand any of them. One thing he can see clearly is the result of her spell: the stones start glowing, causing a tiny stem to emerge from the ground almost immediately, turning into a fuzzy green bouquet in the blink of an eye.

"You think they're done?" Faerydae asks Naida, excited.

"There's only one way to find out," says Naida, who wraps her hands around the crown and pulls up swiftly, unearthing the fastest grown carrots ever.

Even though Archibald hates carrots, he is amazed. Still, he does hate carrots so when Naida shakes them in front of his nose, he takes a step back, with that profound look of disgust on his face.

"What's wrong, you don't like carrots?" asks Faerydae.

"No!" he says, as if the answer were self-evident.

"What do you eat then?" asks Naida.

"Real food," he proudly says, pulling a KitKat out of his pocket.

"What is this?" asks Faerydae, pulling him aside by his cape. "It'd better not be another one of your magic tricks? What kind of potion is this?"

"Just food," he replies, "and you're kidding me right? You think my flashlight and my candy bars are magic? *You* have the magic!" he says, pointing at Naida's carrots.

"Don't be silly," says Faerydae. "We're not magicians, we're only witches."

Shocked and awed, Archibald gasps, in fact swallows the whole piece of KitKat he has just put in his mouth. And coughs heavily. Faerydae taps on his back.

"Are you okay?" she asks as he slowly gets back to normal — kind of.

"I'm sorry, what did you say you are?"

"Witches," she repeats, with that "no big deal" on her face. "I mean, unfortunately, that's the way people called us, you know, that and other bad names like sorceress, she-devil or eye-biter."

"Eye-biter," repeats Archibald, partially shielding his eyes with his hands and rapidly turning as green as those veggies he hates — not "ate" or he would then be turning purple.

"We actually call ourselves witches, we don't mind, we wear that name as a badge of honor," says Faerydae. "We are so much more than the caricature though. Personally, I see myself as an enchantress. It sounds better too, don't you think?"

"Enchantress," Archibald mutters slowly, his lips trembling.

He is staring at Faerydae, squinting.

Is there something I missed about that girl? he wonders. Some unmistakable clue as to who or what she truly is?

For one, she doesn't quite fit the stereotype of the witch. Her nose is rather small and cute, not swollen and crooked like a banana. Neither is her chin. And there's no giant, coarse, multilayered wart growing on that nose —or that chin for that matter. Sure she was wearing a peaked hat earlier but it looked definitely more weird than scary. Besides, she seems to have all of her teeth, not just two or three brown ones sticking out of her mouth. Faerydae can't be a witch! Unless this is the disguise of an old hag, as beautiful as it is deceitful…

"I have to go home," says Archibald.

Faerydae is surprised and deeply disappointed by his reaction.

"If you put it that way," she says, cold. "But let me show you one more thing before you go," she adds with a much nicer tone.

"I'm not sure I have time," says Archibald.

"I would feel insulted," she says. "We wouldn't want that to happen, right?"

Archibald shakes his head, fearful.

"That's what I thought," smiles Faerydae, motioning for him to follow her. Naida can tell something fishy is going on.

Using an arch bridge, they cross the narrow river running through Gristlemoth. There's nothing much on the other side, except for three tiny cabanas, in a rather remote area of the village. Faerydae leads Archibald to one of them, right next to a small graveyard —which is not to reassure him on that young witch's intentions.

"I really have to go," he repeats.

"It will just take a minute," she tells him. "After you," she says politely, inviting him to go in.

As soon as he does, she bangs the door shut and locks it with a wood plank swiveling from vertical to horizontal.

"What are you doing?" he yells.

"I don't trust you," she explains.

"But, I did everything you asked, I just want to go home," pleads Archibald.

"Sorry but you shall not. I have to figure out what's in you. Until then, I will see to it that you don't go anywhere," she says, walking off.

"What if I want to go to the bathroom?" he asks.

"That *is* the bathroom!" she laughs.

"Are you joking?" he chirps, sighing in the same breath, as he sees a bed in the corner of the room.

Archibald is trapped. He can't see much between the wooden slats of the door, just enough to realize Faerydae is indeed going away. He doesn't seem too mad though. He even breaks a smile. What could he possibly have in mind?

"She thinks she's so smart," he mumbles.

From the sweater under his cape, he pulls out three stones he obviously stole from Naida in the vegetable garden.

"I'm going home!" he says, in a very confident tone.

Imitating Naida, he lines up the stones at the foot of the door. Then he takes a step back and, extending his arms and waving his fingers toward the door, he orders:

"Shazam!"

He walks to the door, which, to his surprise, is still locked. He takes another step back. This time, no doubt, he's got it.

"Abracadabra!" he yells. "And now this," he says, pushing on the door, which apparently didn't quite get the message.

"What is it she said already?" he mutters.

Scratching his head, he tries something else:

"Balamoo Ragadoo Malabarus Tonotra!"

Close. But the door still doesn't budge. Shocker! Somehow, it just doesn't speak Archibald.

Realizing he won't hocus-pocus his way out of here, he sits on the bed, the only thing in this windowless room. The floor is dirt. The walls are dirt. If not a bathroom, this certainly looks like a jail.

"Are you done in there?" asks a voice coming from outside.

"Who's that?" responds Archibald.

"I'm in the hut next door," says the voice, which sounds kind of familiar.

"Lenora?" asks Archibald.

"That would be me," she confirms.

"They put you in jail too?"

"It's okay, it was well deserved. Besides, this is not really a jail," she says.

"That girl Faerydae, she's so tough!" he whines.

"I know right, I wish I could be just like her."

"What? Are you serious?"

"Of course, she's like a big sister, a role model for all of us."

"A role model? But she's barely older than you."

"It doesn't matter. Just in the last hundred years, she has been in more battles, and captured more Marodors, than all of us combined."

"You're funny," says Archibald.

"To be honest, I thought you were her secret boyfriend."

"What? No. I can't be... my name is Ivy..."

"I'm not stupid you know."

"I don't know what you're talking about," tries Archibald.

"Anyway, she seemed pretty mad at you. What did you do to get locked up?"

"Nothing. I just want to go home."

"Don't we all?" says Lenora.

"I thought you were from here."

"None of us is really."

"What?" mumbles Archibald, not too sure what to make of those foggy comments.

"Sorry my whole body hurts, I think I'll try to rest," says Lenora.

"Can I ask you something?"

"Sure," she says.

"What were you trying to do back there?"

"What we all want to do," she says.

"What's that?"

"Fly. To fight Marodors on equal ground."

"Or escape them?" says Archibald.

"That too," she agrees.

"But... you're a witch, aren't you?"

"So?"

"So... don't you have a broom for that?"

Lenora cracks up.

"That's a good one!" she says. "Okay good night... Ivy."

"G'night then," he says, lying down.

Through the top part of the teepee roof, where tree branches meet in a cone shape, Archibald experiences his first sunset in Gristlemoth. The night comes like an eclipse, slowly filling the hole in the sky, from an orangey blue to a creamy yellow, to finally blend in with the darkness around.

With no flashlight to keep him company, Archibald finds some comfort in those strange lights rising above the village, undulating and rippling against the night.

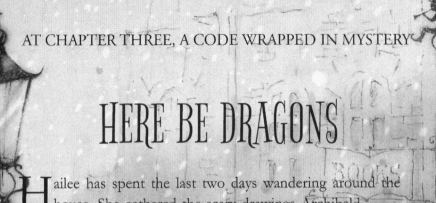

HERE BE DRAGONS

Hailee has spent the last two days wandering around the house. She gathered the scary drawings Archibald left behind, scribbled on napkins and toilet paper. She folded some of his sweaters, t-shirts and socks. The rest of the time, she just went through countless pictures of that dear, loved, and missed brother she wished gone just a few days ago…

Now she is on her way back to school, sharing the 8am train with gaggles of other teenagers. Most of them are texting and goofing around. She, is not. The tears streaking her cheeks mirror the raindrops slaloming against the window. Her lost gaze detaches from the horizon to turn to the seat next to her, where her coat partially covers a cardboard box.

An hour later, in History class, that box is sitting at her feet. Obviously unfazed by Archibald's disappearance, the notorious bully, William Tanner, is trying to get Hailee's attention by throwing air kisses her way, and paper balls on her desk. Her friend Emily picks up one of them and opens it up. It's Tanner's theorem, a blend of subtlety and finesse, reading: William Tanner + Hailee Finch = a childish drawing of two shapes vaguely resembling people, exchanging what vaguely resembles a kiss.

"Gross!" says Emily, showing it to Hailee, who has no apparent reaction. Inside though, she's boiling up.

Closing her eyes, she pictures herself jumping from one desk to another, going to that jerk and shoving that stupid paper ball in his mouth. *Why not?* she says to herself. *What a great way to channel all that stress and blow off steam!* Not that her teacher would care.

As usual, Mr. Absconce doesn't see any of Tanner's shenanigans. A 5000-pound Marodor could walk through the classroom in a Santa suit asking for directions, and Mr. Absconce would still be completely oblivious to what's going on. Once more, he is too busy discoursing on his favorite subject: what happened to the passengers and crew of the Mary Celeste, the Ghost ship found empty at sea in 1872; totally outside of this year's program —any year in fact.

For the first time, Hailee is listening to the story with a totally different outlook. But no one else is paying attention. Besides, Mr. Absconce is always hard to understand, as if he had wet vermicelli stubbornly stuck between his tongue and his palate. Bored students spend the hour challenging each other to count the hairs left in his comb over. Some say twenty-three. Some bet on twenty-five. Others, more audacious, speak of thirty —but that's probably far-fetched.

When the school bell rings out, Mr. Absconce dives into his notes, wagging his index in the air.

"Please read the first chapter of the 'Making of the Modern world', we'll discuss it on Thursday," he reminds all.

When he lifts his head back up, all have scurried off —except Hailee.

"Do you have a question Miss Finch?" he asks.

She approaches his desk with the box in her arms.

"I was hoping you could help me with something."

"Of course young lady. But first, let me say, if I may, that it is very courageous of you to come to class today, considering what happened to your brother. I commend you for that. What a shame, a great student, that Archibald."

"I know," sighs Hailee, still a bit tired of hearing that.

"Now, what can I do for you?" he asks.

Hailee pulls the globe out of the box.

"Well well well, what a fine piece of History you have here!" says Mr. Absconce, tilting his head back and adjusting some old-fashioned spectacles to see more clearly. "A family possession I presume?"

Hailee goes straight to the point.

"Have you ever seen a globe like this?"

"Not exactly no, this looks quite old and rare," he answers, noting: "It's too bad though, it seems broken."

Again, the globe doesn't spin. It must have locked itself automatically after Archibald used it, but of course, neither Hailee nor Mr. Absconce is aware of that.

"What can you tell me about it?" she asks.

"What do you want to know?" he asks.

"Anything really," she sighs.

"Well, the first thing you'd want to find out is how old it is and where it was made. That's usually a good start," he says. "Wait, does it say Made in China right here?"

"Where?" asks Hailee.

"I'm sorry, I'm just pulling your leg," giggles Mr. Absconce. "Now, let's see what we've got here," he says more seriously.

Hailee bends down to explore the globe with him, not too sure what to look for.

"Well you don't see this too often!" says Mr. Absconce.

"What's that?" asks the student.

"Right here, Hic Sunt Dracones," he says, reading from an inscription at the top of the globe.

"Is that some kind of code?" she asks.

"In a way yes," he confirms. "It's Latin. It means 'Here be dragons'. You'd find that on ancient maps. A code indeed, to identify territories still unexplored. Dangerous lands obviously, though it doesn't mean there would be actual dragons there. Besides, the creatures on this globe don't quite look like dragons, wouldn't you agree?"

Hailee nods in approval.

"Now, did you see any other markings that would be of any help in this matter?" he asks.

"I don't think so. Just a few letters, on this arm, right here," says Hailee, showing him the engraving on one of those ribs circling the sphere:

LDVMDXV

"See Miss Finch, this is not an arm. It's called a meridian. And these are not quite letters. They are Roman numerals," he corrects.

"What's that?"

"That," emphasizes Mr. Absconce, "is what we spent an hour discussing in class just last month, Miss Finch."

"I'm sorry," Hailee lets out.

"It's alright. Given the circumstances, I won't increase your burdens," he says, tapping her gently on the shoulder before heading to the chalkboard.

"It's fairly easy really," he says. "Do you know what this is?" he asks, writing a capital I.

"That stick?" says Hailee.

"Not quite a stick, but rather a one in Roman numerals, Miss Finch," says Mr. Absconce, rolling his eyes in dismay. "But don't worry, I have heard that before, unfortunately. In fact, I think I've heard it all."

"I knew that was a one," says Hailee, semi-honestly.

"But of course you did! So from here, to make a two, you'll need two *sticks*, and for a three, you'll need three of those *sticks*," he says, turning around with a teasing smile.

"That's pretty easy," comments Hailee.

"Well, it gets a bit more complicated," he says. "Five is this capital V you see. The reason why I skipped four is because you need to know five before you make a four. Since four is five minus one, we'll just place that capital I before our capital V, which you'll just reverse to get a six. Are you following?"

"Yes," says Hailee.

"Good. Same for ten, with Capital X as ten. Then based on the same logic, you'll have fifteen made of a ten followed by a five, and then twenty, thirty, etcetera, until you reach fifty."

"Is that 5 Xs?" asks Hailee.

"No, you see, to make things more convenient, they came up with specific signs for some numbers. Remember when I told you ten was X and five was V?"

Hailee nods.

"So fifty is capital L. Then C equals a hundred, D five hundred and M is a thousand. Are you still following?"

"Yes," says Hailee.

"Perfect. Now let's apply this to your globe. So what do we have?"

Hailee starts reading the numerals on the meridian, starting with "L."

"That's 50," notes Mr. Absconce, writing it down on the board.

"D," continues Hailee.

"That's 500."

"V."

"That's 5."

"M."

"That's a thousand," he says, pausing suddenly. "Wait, no, you must have read this wrong, can you please start over?"

"Okay," says Hailee, "L-D-V-M-D..."

He interrupts her.

"I'm sorry, this can't be right."

"Why?" she asks.

"Well, we have 50, 500, 5 and then a thousand. There is no logic to this. It's simply impossible to make a date out of it."

Mr. Absconce checks the globe for himself.

"I'm sorry to tell you this but I think this is a copy, which could explain why they made a mistake when engraving the numerals. That's the only thing I can think of."

"I see," sighs Hailee.

"I'm sorry I couldn't be of more assistance. Now if you'll excuse me, I have a teachers' meeting to attend and I'm quite late already."

"Of course, I understand," she says, putting the globe back in the box.

As Hailee is about to exit, Mr. Absconce has one more piece of advice for her:

"Miss Finch, I'm thinking, you might want to bring your globe to an antique store, perhaps they could help you further."

"I didn't think about it. Thanks Mister Absconce," she says before leaving.

ᚠ

Back home, sitting on her bed, Hailee is looking at those puzzling Roman numerals, flipping the globe upside down, when her dad knocks lightly at the door half open.

"Hailee?" he calls.

"Come in," she says.

Stuart sits on the bed next to her.

"You know, you mother and I were wondering... maybe you should move into another room, you know, just for now," he tells her.

They both take a quick look around. The room has been cleaned up. But the burn marks are still visible under a fresh coat of paint. And Archibald's side is still strangely empty.

"No, I'm fine Dad, I'll stay here until Arch comes back."

"Okay, we'll leave it up to you," he says.

An awkward silence ensues. Hailee can tell her dad obviously has something else to tell her.

"What's wrong Dad?"

"Nothing, why?"

She tilts her head and stares at him, meaning "I know better." Stuart hesitates a second. Then he begins:

"I don't want to upset you. I just wanted to know if... perhaps you could tell me more about what happened, that night."

"I told you already. There was a big bright light. The sound of thunder. And then nothing. Arch was gone. That's it," says Hailee, sighing heavily.

"I'm sorry," says Dad, putting a comforting hand on her leg. "Anything else though? Any other detail you could think of?"

Hailee looks down at the globe sitting on her lap.

"Arch certainly loved his globe," Stuart notes with a smile, before standing up and heading out.

"Dad!" says Hailee, calling him back in.

"Yes," he answers right away.

Hailee looks conflicted. She wants to tell him the bright light she mentioned emanated from the globe. But what would he think? That she is crazy. Or that she made it all up like so many other things she lied about these last few years.

"No, nothing," she finally says.

"I'm here for you okay, anytime," he tells her.

"Thank you," she utters.

Hailee is carrying her box under a mix of cats and dogs, unless it's just rain and snow. She's roaming the narrow streets of Covent Garden, in the center of London, scanning the storefronts. Enchanting as usual, the holiday decorations are totally invisible to her eyes, bloodshot after another restless night. Hailee passes by clothing stores she would normally be glued to, now without even a glance. Obviously, it's something else that brought her here…

"There's one!" she says suddenly.

Her pick: *Edmund's Antiques*, with a façade becoming an antique in its own right, thanks to custom cracks and a paint color nearly impossible to replicate —greenish moldy gray.

"Ching-a-ling…" Attached to the door in clusters, jingle bells have woken up an old man napping in the back. He looks very much like an Edmund, his pants and four-button waistcoat blending in perfectly with the striped fabric of a moth-eaten sofa. He is up in a jiffy —and a wince.

"Hello hello!" he says, greeting Hailee with the warmest tone.

"Hello," replies Hailee.

"How can I help you? Looking for a gift?"

"No , not real…"

"Don't tell me!" he shouts, cutting her off. I know. It's for your mother. You want to surprise her, and instead of buying one of those cheap knickknacks on Nebay, Oh I hate that Nebay, you said to yourself, I'll go to Edmund's and make my mom happy. Well you were right. As they say, come to Edmund and he'll give you the moond!"

Spinning around while a few cuckoo clocks go off, he's like one of those toys that just got wound up, and won't stop until the stored energy is all used up.

"I have just what you need," says the salesman, and before Hailee can utter a word, "I know what you're going to say," he tells her, "you've seen these somewhere else, but no, they don't make them like this anymore. And just between you and I, the Duchess of Cambridge herself wore these for her first ball. Who could say no to these huh?" asks Edmund, pulling out the most hideous pair of shoes ever made, yellow, with purple stripes, orange polka dots, and a missing heel —a flaw Edmund has apparently just become aware of.

"That's a quick fix. I'll glue a heel from another shoe. Free of charge. The color might not match exactly, but your mom deserves something unique, right? And five percent off! What do you say?"

"No sorry, I'm not here for shoes," says Hailee.

"A necklace then?" he suggests.

"No!"

"Pearl earrings?"

"No!"

"I know, a purse, I have one just for your mom."

"Please no, I'm not here for my mom," says Hailee.

"Don't tell me. It's for your best friend, isn't it?

"No."

"Your sister?"

"No!"

"Your brother?" he says, cringing at the shoes he's still holding. Hailee shakes her head.

"I'm not looking for anything! I just need some help with this globe," she says, opening the box.

Edmund barely looks inside.

"But of course young lady, why don't you take a seat and we'll look at it together"… is the reaction Hailee expected. Edmund's is… a tad different:

"Sorry Miss, I have enough globes to create my own solar system!" he tells her, pointing at shelves after shelves of globes covered with dust.

"You don't understand, I'm not trying to sell it, I just need some information about it."

"Information? What do you think this is? Booble? Or one of those yahoos? You're at Edmund's here, you're not on the Internets, I happen to work for a living Miss, I sell things, I'm a busy man can't you see?" he says, as he stands there, in the middle of mountains of unsold bibelots, a spider already starting to build a web from the corner of his hat to a chandelier above.

Back on the street, Hailee starts looking around again. No less than five times within an hour does she get a variation of the same —no— answer from different shop owners, whether they be old or young, male of female, awake or not. Hailee wants to call it a day. A bad day. She heads back to the subway. She has almost reached the Leicester Square station when she sees one more antique store across the street, "the Realm of antiques." She gives it a shot.

This time, Hailee makes a point to be crystal clear as soon as she enters:

"Hello, sorry to bother you, I'm not here to buy or sell anything, I just want to know more about this globe." That's when she realizes there might be no one in the store, until a voice responds, coming from behind a desk —a rather young voice.

"I'll be with you in a minute," says that voice. And about a minute later, a head pops up from behind that same desk —a rather charming head.

"Sorry I was cleaning up," says a boy, around Hailee's age but with a rough look to him, and no trendy clothes, very different from the boys at school. She is taken aback. And still a bit wary.

"As I said, I'd just like to know more about this globe," she explains, glancing at her box on the counter.

"A terrestrial globe?" says the young man.

"Yes," says Hailee.

"I love those. Let's put it over there by the light?" he suggests, motioning towards a table by the entrance.

"Great!" says Hailee, startled by such a rare display of basic kindness.

She pulls the globe out for him to look at.

"Nice!" he says right away before getting closer.

As he starts inspecting the globe, Hailee starts inspecting him.

"This is not your store, is it?" she asks, making him chuckle.

"No, I'm fifteen, it's my dad's," he says.

Hailee nods.

"This is very interesting," he says.

"Very," she concurs, not sure what she is referring to exactly, him or the globe.

"The monsters, the map, all of this was painted by hand, can you believe that?" he says.

"It's great," she nods. "Anything *different* about this globe though?"

"Compared to what?" he asks.

"Compared to other globes I guess."

"Ancient globes like this all have their own little quirks," he says. "Some maps showed California as an island for a while.

Others even had a totally fictitious mountain pop up in Africa, the Mountain of Kong, they called it. I'm not kidding. That mistake lasted for almost a hundred years. But in general, most globes and maps have a lot in common, just because they're based on science, you know, triangulation, that's just basic geometry."

"You talk like my brother," says Hailee. But she wants to remain focused on the questions that brought her here: "By different, I meant something out of the ordinary, something strange, you know what I mean?"

"You want something out of the ordinary? This is, right here," he says, pointing at the carvings on the meridian.

"Yes I know but it doesn't make any sense," she comments.

"LDV," he spells out.

"No, those aren't letters actually," she says.

"I'm sorry?"

"That's not LDV. Mr. Absconce, my History teacher, he told me those were Roman numerals. No offense by the way, I made the same mistake."

"Well, Mr. Absconce is only partially right," he says. "See the four letters that follow LDV, *those* are roman numerals, they read fifteen hundred and fifteen. I'm not certain but most likely, that's when this globe was built. But the three letters before that, these are actual letters. And they tell you something out of the ordinary for sure."

"What's that?"

"They tell you who built this globe."

"Who's LDV?" asks Hailee.

"Leonardo Da Vinci," he spells out. "Ever heard of him?"

Hailee is amazed, her thoughts instantly awash with images of well-known drawings and paintings from the Italian master. She has seen them in class, online or in museums with her parents.

"So I guess you *have* heard of him!" says the boy, just based on the awe on Hailee's face.

"But I didn't know he built globes, I thought he was just a painter?" she says.

"Believe it or not, but there's only about fifteen paintings from him out there. He's actually much more than just a painter! Wait a second," says the boy, heading to the "antique books" section of the store.

"Here," he says, pulling one jumbo book from the bottom shelf and opening it on the table next to the globe. Of course it's a book about Leonardo Da Vinci.

"Let me show you. That guy was a genius," he says, leafing through. "Look, not only he was a great artist but he also invented tons of things. The first tank, that's him. Same thing for the parachute, his idea. And look at his sketches for a flying machine… reminds you of something?"

"It looks like a weird helicopter," says Hailee.

"That's exactly what it is! He was such an incredible designer," explains Oliver.

"I didn't know that," says Hailee, amazed by the level of details in the sketches.

"Most people know Da Vinci for the Mona Lisa and that's it, it's kind of sad," adds Oliver, going back to the cover.

"That would be me, most people, kind of sad," says Hailee, joking but almost ashamed at the same time.

"I'm sorry, I didn't mean it that way. By the way, it's never too late to learn. Look, now you know!" he says, bringing a smile back on her face.

"Another Archibald!" she jokes.

"What do you mean?" he asks.

"My brother, he knows everything. It's annoying sometimes."

"Well, *I* don't know everything, nobody does."

The front door opens suddenly. Someone barges in, a frail little man, gangly frame, skinny arms and slumping knobby shoulders. He brings a whiff of cheap wine along with the outdoor breeze.

"Didn't I tell you to call me when we've got a client?" yells the man, sounding drunk. And to Hailee, with a slightly nicer voice and a fake smile: "Hello young lady, good day, what can I do for you?"

"Sorry Dad, I didn't want to bother you at the pub," says the boy, apologetic and submissive suddenly.

"Oliver, that's the point of me having a drin... a coffee right across the street, so I can be here in a twinkle," says the man, nearly losing his balance.

Pushing his kid away, he turns back to Hailee:

"What were we saying?"

Hailee doesn't know what to say. Oliver comes to her rescue:

"Dad, she brought a globe she'd like you to look at."

"I don't need no globe," says the father.

"Dad, I really think you should look at it, says Oliver, grabbing the globe from the table."

"I told you Boy, I don't need no goddam..."

One glimpse from afar is enough for him to stop talking at once. He approaches the globe with obvious interest. He takes it from his son and inspects it from top to bottom, passing his hand gently on the surface.

"Could this be?" he mumbles.

"I told you Dad," says Oliver.

"How much?" the shop owner asks Hailee.

"I'm sorry?" she says.

"How much do you want for it?"

"No, I'm not here to sell it, I just..."

"Everything has a price young lady, name yours," he says, staring at her, his eyes hesitating between creepy and drunk.

"I'm sorry Sir, as I said, I'm not interested."

"Miss!" he yells.

Oliver puts his hand on his dad's shoulder to stop him.

"Dad! She said she's not interested."

His father looks at the hand on his shoulder and manages to calm himself down.

"Okay, okay, no problem young lady," he says with a much more conciliatory —and clearly fake— tone.

"What is your name sweetheart?" he asks her.

"Hailee," she answers, fearful.

"And Hailee, where is it that you live?"

Now she is really freaked out.

"I'd like to go now, it's late," she says with a trembling voice. And indeed it's getting dark outside. "Can I have my globe back please?" she adds.

"Of course you can!" says Oliver, prying the globe from his father's hands and putting it back into the box for Hailee.

She leaves without turning back.

Oliver's dad looks at her through the window as she enters the nearest subway station. He then turns to his son, grabs him by the collar and pushes him against the wall.

"Do you know what you've done?"

"I didn't do anything," says Oliver.

"You've just ruined our lives. Mine. And yours," his father says.

"I was just trying to help her."

"Your job is to help *us*!" he yells. "Have I taught you nothing?"

"I'm sorry," says Oliver.

"What did you tell her? And what did she tell you? I want to know every detail," says the creep, pressing up on his son's throat.

"Nothing, I just told her that History teacher was wrong," says Oliver, now having problems breathing.

"A History teacher huh!" says his dad, loosening his hold.

R

A few minutes later, Hailee is sitting —semi— safely in her subway train, clutching her box to her chest the way she hugged her stuffed rabbit until just a few years ago.

Meanwhile, Mister Doyle is dialing a number on his old rotary phone, holding a business card.

A deep cavernous voice answers:

"Who is this?"

"Mister Heinrich?" asks Oliver's dad.

"Yes. Who is this?"

"Mister Heinrich, this is Mister Doyle, James Doyle, I'm the owner of the Realm of Antiques, in London. We met a few years ago, you came to my shop. You bought that old book from me, the Malleus… something, pardon me, I'm getting old."

"Go on," says Mr. Heinrich.

"Well maybe you don't remember but back then, you told me you were looking for something dear to you, a very particular globe, a terrestrial globe, you called it the missing link or some-thing like that?"

"Continue," says Mr. Heinrich with the same monotonic, almost robotic voice.

"I don't know if you're still interested but if you are, I think I can make you happy, Mister Heinrich. We would just have to find some agreement of some sort of course…" says Mr. Doyle.

An eerie silence has shrouded the other side of the line.

"Mr. Heinrich, are you still there?" asks Mr. Doyle.

"I'm in New York, I'll be at your shop in the morning," says Mr. Heinrich, before he hangs up.

"No more debt," mumbles Mr. Doyle. He is smiling. Oliver is not. Hiding behind an armoire, he listened to the entire conversation. He looks really worried.

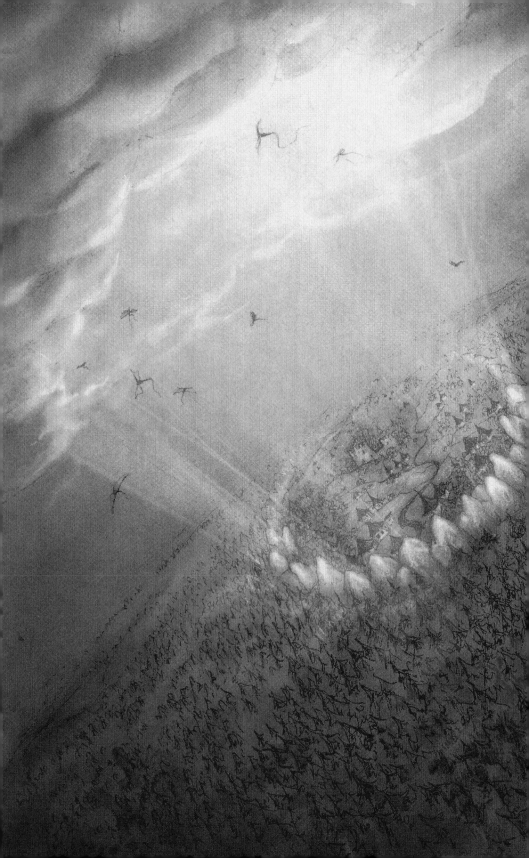

GOLEMS VERSUS MARODORS

The day has just dawned on Gristlemoth. Archibald wakes up in another long yawn, again talking through it, with essentially the same thought: "What a bad dream," he says sleepily.

Of course giant boulders don't just float in the air. Nor would carrots ever grow that fast —Thank Goodness! No way did he feed a Marodor his candy bar. Merdar or Marodor, there's no such thing anyway. Besides, even if he was running for his life, he would never waste a KitKat like that. And what did that girl call him? A fopdoodle? A liripoop? A fool? How could he imagine such a fallacy? No one talks to Archibald Finch that way. Especially not a girl...

"And you're a puggard!" yells a voice, startling him out of his fantasy.

It's Faerydae. She has just discovered Naida's stones scattered on the ground behind the door.

"Nothing but a petty puggard," she repeats, fuming.

From the look on his face, she quickly understands he doesn't understand.

"You're a goodfellow!" she now says.

"That doesn't sound too bad."

"Maybe you didn't hear me well! What about gonof, snatcher, thief?" she yells.

"No, I just... borrowed these," mutters Archibald.

"And again your flummadiddle!"

Same bewilderment on his face.

"Your non-sense hogwash!" she says.

Archibald pouts, finding nothing to say in his own defense.

"If you want me to trust you, we have to set some very clear rules," she yells.

"Like what?" he asks.

"Like you won't lie or steal anymore. Can you do that?"

"I think so," he says, not quite convincing.

"Can you do that?" repeats Faerydae, spelling out each word.

"On one condition," requests Archibald, sheepish.

"I'm not sure you're in a position to bargain!" she says. "But what would that be?"

"That you don't turn me into a rat or anything like that."

Faerydae cracks up.

"And why would I do that?" she asks.

"Because you're an… eye-biter, an enchantress."

Faerydae bursts out laughing again. But she also sees an opportunity to use his fear to her advantage.

"You're right. I *am* a witch and therefore, I *could* do that," she says. "But I tell you what, you have my word, if you stop lying and stealing, I won't turn you into anything."

Archibald looks relieved, as if a sword had been hanging over his head since he got here.

"Okay then I'll stop," he promises. "One more thing though," he adds.

"What now?" she says.

"The stones, will you show me how they work?"

"Well," she says, "if you really want to know, you'll have to go to school."

Archibald doesn't like the sound of that.

"Please no I'm on vacation. I hate school," he laments.

"How can you hate school? It's fun!" she says.

"School? Fun? I don't think we're talking about the same thing."

Faerydae has walked out, leaving the door open. But Archibald seems in no hurry to follow her.

"I don't want to go to school," he whines.

"You'll love it, trust me!" she shouts from outside.

"You wanna bet?" mumbles Archibald.

Borrowing Bartholomeo's unique style as a marathon runner, he drags his feet out of the cabana, just as that target pillow comes zooming by, panting, tongue out and with the most frightened look on his fluffy face. Five seconds later, a horde of archers follows, led by Rhiannon.

"What a freaky place!" lets out Archibald.

He slowly catches up with Faerydae, making no secret of his lack of enthusiasm for a last minute trip to school, however "fun" she thinks it might be. He pouts, he sighs, he huffs, he puffs, he looks down, he helps his shoulders sag, he kicks some rocks. He literally uses every trick in the book. And why not? It worked more than once before with his Mom. They ended up spending the day watching TV at home instead.

"Why don't we go fishing or something?" he suggests.

"Stop it, you're going to love it, I'm telling you," she repeats.

This is real torture for Archibald. The road has turned into his *via dolorosa*. In fact, looking at his face, you would believe he is being dragged to his death. Or at least that he has just caught an instant case of the Plague. Nothing could make him feel better. Not even the gigantest scoop of ice cream. Nothing, except perhaps what was hiding past that green curtain of tall elm trees...

"Welcome to Cleofa!" says Faerydae, as a large castle comes into view.

This is Gristlemoth's Rome. All roads lead to it. How could Archibald miss it? It's located at the very center of the village. But more importantly, how could Faerydae not show this to him earlier —instead of wasting time growing stinking carrots?

Unlike all the mud and wood dwellings around, the castle is made out of stone —massive, impressive stone blocks. From the crenelated fortifications to the arrow slits, deep moat all around, and turrets on each corner, it has all the attributes of a medieval fortress.

"Holy Bejabbles! This is just like the castles in my History book!" exclaims Archibald.

"You're awfully amusing," says Faerydae.

"Did you build this?" he asks, astounded and excited.

"No, it was here when we arrived," says Faerydae, "we used it to protect ourselves from Marodors."

Archibald cannot quite picture Faerydae and her friends fighting off armies of monsters from behind these ramparts.

"Not quite the fairytale castle I expected, that's for sure," he comments.

"Don't tell me you believe in fairytales!" says Faerydae, amused. "Cause this is no fairytale. It's the real thing!"

He would have imagined something a little different, more "girly" for sure —maybe some larger windows, a few towers of all sizes here and there, with funny pointy hats and probably some pink little flags fluttering in the wind. The only flag up there is more on the gloomy side, emblazoned with yet again that obscure double wave symbol —cream on a brownish red background.

Past the moat, through a wobbly drawbridge, they enter a wide courtyard effervescent with laughter, discussions and prayer-like recitations. While some people —meaning girls— are studying or reading on benches, many others are seated or lying directly on the ground. All faces, though, are turned towards three large chalkboards, around which most of the action seems to revolve, with yet more girls. The drawings include some trees, plants and flowers. But the focus is definitely on Marodors, featured in parts, or whole. Arrows point at the beasts' "weak points," "sides to avoid" and "danger" zones. Also specified are more basic yet potentially life saving details, such as "head" and "tail," which for some Marodors is rather hard to figure out —like that round millipede with about fifteen separate heads, puzzling to many observing it.

"Where's the teacher?" asks Archibald.

"We are all teachers," explains Faerydae. "We all have things to learn from one another. The key to learning lies in observing, listening and sharing. And that's not just true for Marodors."

Archibald is fascinated, though his main takeaway from her speech was rather predictable:

"No teacher? That's so cool!"

"I told you you'd love it!"

Past the chalkboards, Faerydae leads Archibald inside the castle itself, through a corridor carved under a huge double staircase. The first room they access spans both sides of the hallway. On the right, mounds of herbs in baskets, and rows of jars all around.

"Our apothecary," says Faerydae proudly, "with six different kinds of herbs: healers, damagers, protectors, numb-makers, paralyzers and brain-crackers."

"I think I'll pass on the tea," says Archibald.

Faerydae cracks up.

"Many of our plants are unique. To locate them, we've travelled weeks, crossed valleys and peaks, often to the far edges of the world," she explains. "Itch weed from Worgonia, Mugwort from the Sargung river, Voodoo lilies from Arachnagar, Dracula orchids from Lobulia, Octopus stinkhorns from Gurguria. Some you see here, you cannot find anymore," she laments.

"I hope so," he lets out under his breath, guessing the potency of these herbs solely based on the frowning faces of those cutting and bunching them together.

Across from this collection of stinky rarities, Archibald discovers a grand library, very much like his Grandma's, only, with a twist. Running from floor to ceiling, the shelves continue on the ceiling itself, where books are somehow hanging upside down without falling. It's all the more impressive that the books are enormous, some of them taller than Archibald, looking as heavy and overwhelming as the knowledge they surely carry. The students working here don't seem too inconvenienced or deterred by this sort of detail. With the help of a few glowing stones, they have made those oversized books lighter than feathers, passing them to each other across the room. An unusual ballet that has all but hypnotized Archibald.

Faerydae pulls him along. Maybe he will get some answers down the hallway, where unfolds the holy of holies, the main workshop for the manufacturing of those mysterious stones. The well-oiled production line is organized around a single, extremely long table. At one end are unloaded buckets of rough rock fragments. By the time they reach the opposite end, the rocks have become a more finished product, shaped like a bar of soap, thanks to the polishing work of dozens of hands working in concert. The stones are now ready for their markings. Armed with hammers and chisels, Maven is among those taking care of the engraving.

"Are these the magic rocks?" Archibald/Ivy asks them.

"Golems, these are golems," corrects Maven.

"Golems?" repeats Archibald. "What are those signs you're adding on the stones? I mean, on the golems?"

"It's what makes a golem a golem. The runes alphabet," says Maven.

Archibald examines the stones scattered on the table, fascinated and confused at the same time. Some kind of look like regular letters. But not really.

There's one that could almost pass for an N, if not for the arrow running through it —N⃗.

That ᛉ is rather unbalanced for an R, and just about to fall on its back.

As for that ᛒ, that's one angry B, seemingly giving the others the "don't mess with me" attitude.

Most runes, though, are as close to regular letters as margarine is to butter. From a tree of arrows, ↟, to a circular target, ⊕, to other cryptic symbols vaguely resembling a crocodile's eye, ⴲ, or a giraffe's head, ᚠ, this is a different language altogether. For Archibald, they might as well be Chinese logograms.

"That's one complicated alphabet!" he says.

"A bit trickier than a, b, c, d, etcetera, if that's what you mean," says Faerydae. "These might look childish. But don't be mistaken, they're based on ancient signs, handed down from our ancestors."

"How many letters?" he asks.

"It depends," says Maven.

"It depends? How can it depend? Try to remove the T from the alphabet, and let's see how we... alk!" chuckles Archibald.

"It's not set in stone, if I can say that," Maven chuckles back.

"We constantly have to adapt to new breeds of Marodors," explains Faerydae. "As a result, runes change over time. Some disappear, others are born. It's just the regular cycle of life. That's why their number varies. Right now, we're using around thirty."

"There's a crack in this one," notes Archibald, sticking his finger through a small hole in the stone.

"It's not a crack, it's a slit we drill into each golem, so they can be mounted on arrows, and reach their target more accurately," says Faerydae.

"Arrows with gloves," remembers Archibald, amazed at the basic ingenuity of this weapon.

"Each letter has a particular power," explains Maven. "Take this one here," she says, pointing at the stone he picked up, with two arrows pointing in opposite directions, ↕, "this is Incarnata, it can compress, squeeze or shrink pretty much anything."

"Marodors' heads mostly!" notes Faerydae.

"Hey, it's that sign you guys wear on your clothes!" says Archibald, grabbing a golem with a wave engraving: ≈.

"This is Prama, it's linked to water," says Maven.

"The source of life," adds Faerydae. "One of our most sacred runes. We chose it as the emblem of our colony," she says, placing her hand on the blazon embossed on her tunic, as if to pledge allegiance to a flag.

"It's also one of the base runes," says Maven.

"Base runes?" he wonders aloud.

"They are the foundations of our alphabet", she explains. "Can you use the others without these? Sure. But they won't work as well. They're the key runes if you will. This is my personal favorite, Moonesterum," she says, picking up another golem with some sort of pyramid marking on it: Δ.

"So what does... Moonesterum do?" he asks.

"It's so powerful," marvels Maven. "As a link between the Earth and the Sky, it has a unique ability, to defy the burden from the heavens, you know, that weight that keeps your feet on the ground."

"As in... gravity you mean?" notes Archibald.

"What's that?" she asks.

"What you're describing, I'm pretty sure it's gravity."

"Uh uh, the burden from the heavens," repeats Maven.

Archibald just nods, yielding to the poetry of that synonym, and eager to learn more.

"So this rune can make you fly?" he asks, looking excited.

The girls grin from ear to ear.

"Not quite, but it can move mountains," says Maven, giving an indication as to how she made that Marodor hover above ground, and how those books can remain glued to the ceiling next door.

"You know, your friend Lenora, I think she'd rather fly than move mountains," he says.

"Lenora doesn't need to fly, she already has her head in the clouds!" jokes Faerydae.

"She might have better luck with this one," says Maven, switching to another stone on the table, engraved with three stacked up horizontal lines: ☰.

"What's that one?" asks Archibald.

"Eolare, focused on wind power," says the teacher.

"What about fire?" he inquires.

"I kept that one for last. Since most Marodors spit fire, that's a crucial rune," says Maven.

"Spit fire? Like dragons?" he says.

"Not *like* dragons, many Marodors *are* dragons, but you know that right?" questions Faerydae.

Archibald nods nervously, a slight tremor of tingling itch going through his spine. "Dragons and griffons," he whispers, echoing the reaction he had to his dad's stories the night he found the globe.

"If we're talking fire, we're talking about Ignifera," says Maven, grabbing a stone with another pyramid, made of dots this one: ∴ "And here you have all four base runes, the most important."

"Which doesn't make the others negligible," notes Faerydae. "Base runes trigger or multiply the powers of other runes. But they all have a crucial role to play. That's the whole point, the golems are made in our image. Alone, they won't achieve much. But combine them together and you have real magic on your hands," she says, adding a stone to the ones Archibald was holding already.

"And the best part is, there's an infinite number of combinations," says Maven, motioning towards a second blackboard, against the back wall of the workshop. No Marodor on this one. Instead, a web of those arcane symbols, scrawled into different sets of equations, in which variables are runes.

In fact, the sum of each formula is not a number either. In Gristlemoth, $\text{B} + \infty + \Delta$ or $\text{X} + \approx + \text{P}$ does not equal anything but a headache, a real headache, among other medical conditions and ailments —some relatively mild, such as dizziness, loss of balance, blurred vision or nausea; others a tad more severe, like total paralysis, hallucinations, legs crumbling, instant weight loss, or ribs crushing.

"This has nothing to do with growing carrots, does it?" comments Archibald. "These are magic spells!"

"You can call them that," says Faerydae. "What you see here is more of a battle plan. This is the number one purpose of runes and golems, to fight Marodors."

"To hit the beast from within, you have to add Perfidrae," Maven advises a girl stuck on one of those equations.

"I get the legs crumbling or the ribs crushing, but what's a looping tail?" he asks, reading from the board.

"That's a good one!" says Maven. "It's when we make a Marodor tie up his legs with his own tail!"

"I have to say, this is much more fun than Math class!" notes Archibald.

"And I had to drag you here!" smiles Faerydae.

"Have you shown Ivy the fish yet?" asks Maven.

"Not yet," responds Faerydae.

"What fish?" asks Archibald, excited again.

"This workshop is only the tip of the iceberg," explains Maven.

"Let's dive a little deeper!" says Faerydae.

Making their way south, Archibald and Faerydae soon find themselves near the cliff Gristlemoth is leaning against. Riddled with holes of all sizes, from huge at the base to small towards the top, the steep rock façade has been terraced over time, to progressively turn into a gigantic staircase —surely a way for giants to reach for the skies, in Archibald's mind at least. Each step is connected to the next through ladders. Two dozen girls are digging and scraping at the mountainside with hammers and picks, while buckets are floating up and down, like the books in the library.

"This is where the golems come from," says Faerydae as she picks up rock fragments from the ground. "We also use amber from trees but this is much better."

"What is it?" asks Archibald.

"Magnetite, it's charged with natural energy," explains one of the girls guiding the buckets, holding out golems.

Archibald recognizes her despite the mask of black dust covering her face.

"Lenora?"

"Aye up... Ivy!" she says, confirming she is indeed the acrobat who shot up in the air and nearly killed herself yesterday.

"They let you out already?" he asks.

"The door was never locked, I went in there on my own."

"What? That stunt must have damaged your head! Who would choose to go to jail on their own?" he chuckles.

"It's not like that," she says.

"It's about acknowledging our mistakes," says Faerydae, "and take time to reflect on those mistakes, so we don't repeat them."

"Sounds real good," he says, skeptical. "So, Lenora, you've learned your lesson? In one night? You'll never do that rocket thing again?" he asks, drawing loops in the air with his finger.

Even under Faerydae's stare, Lenora struggles to offer a straight face.

"I shall not," she finally swears to Faerydae in an overly theatrical tone, punctuating her oath with a wink to Archibald. By a rather fitting twist of fate, she drops one of her golems in the process, causing all the buckets to tumble to the ground behind her.

"That's what I thought," laughs Archibald.

"Those buckets don't feel pain, but *you* sure will the next time you fall!" warns Faerydae.

"By the way, why is *my* door locked then?" asks Archibald.

"Let's just say that some people need more reflection than others," smiles Faerydae.

"I'm fine," he says. "Nothing to improve thanks."

"We all have it in us to be better, we just need a little push. Even this magnetite here, born with great powers, but its potential is even greater. So we add a little something to it," she says, motioning towards two canoes sitting by the river nearby.

Lenora runs ahead, picks up bread from a basket and throws some into one of the boats.

Archibald takes a look inside.

"Fish!" he cries out.

"We rarely use these boats so we converted them to raise our raad," explains Faerydae.

"Rad? What kind of fish are these?" he asks.

They are indeed unique, with their long thin tail, bug eyes and flat wide bodies that look like they've been squashed between a rock and a hard place — or inside a huge waffle-maker.

"I've heard there's a similar species in the ocean, bigger than you and I combined, but these raad live in rivers," says Faerydae. "They have so much energy they can multiply the power of each of these rocks by a hundred."

"How?" asks Archibald.

"Just like this," she says, dropping a piece of magnetite into one of the boats. As soon as the rock hits the water, several fish wrap and spin around it. Their dance makes the water seemingly boil instantly.

Lenora swaps her loaf of bread for a pair of large tongs. She carefully extracts the stone from the tight embrace of the raad fish.

"Hot hot hot," she says, puling it out.

"It will cool down and go back to its original state. But now it's fully charged," explains Faerydae. "Magnetite has unique qualities. It can attract and repel, energize and weaken. We use the runes to reactivate and harness those powers when needed. But none of this would work without the herbs and plants I showed you earlier."

"What are those for? Seasoning?" jokes Archibald.

"Well, we do boil them with the magnetite. They definitely spice things up!" smiles Faerydae. "Only then can the rocks be sent to the workshop."

Archibald is feeling dizzy.

"Energy stones, thunder fish, poison plants, tricky symbols, crazy names, freaky spells… those golems are one hell of a magic weapon!" he says.

"And don't forget the bread!" jokes Faerydae.

Archibald laughs.

"How do you call that bread by the way?" he asks.

"Just bread! What do you want to call it?" she says.

"I don't know, it's just that you have all those funky names for everything, so I thought…"

"What?" she says, obviously not seeing his point.

"Never mind," he says, biting onto one of his candy bars.

Smarter than he may sound, Archibald starts connecting the dots:

"Those big stones around the village, are those… golems too?"

"Good thinking," confirms Faerydae. "They took years to install. We used them as a shield at first. But then little by little, they liberated enough energy to carve a hole in the sky. *That* was magical. And key to creating more colonies. We even have one in Umbraea now."

"Where's Umbraya?" asks Archibald.

"Where's Umbraea?" she corrects, stunned he wouldn't know. "You know Naida? My friend with the carrots?"

Archibald nods, twitching his nose.

"That's where she's from," says Faerydae. "Where's Umbraea?" she mumbles, shaking her head, amused and upset all at once.

"What's wrong?" asks Archibald.

"Remember, you said you wouldn't lie anymore, so I'm going to ask you a question. And you you'd better not lie."

"Okay," he agrees.

"Who are you?" she asks, her expression darkening fast.

"I'm just… Archibald," he answers, a bit frightened.

"When we showed you the runes earlier, you acted like you didn't know anything about them."

"Because I didn't," he says.

"Really?" she insists.

"I swear!" he assures.

"So what is this then?" she asks, ripping off his cape and uncovering his hoodie underneath with the ΓΔΦ letters sewn across.

"That's just my sweater," says Archibald, on the defensive.

"Just a sweater?" she repeats. "You have three of our most powerful runes drawn on your clothes and you're going to tell me it's just a coincidence?"

Archibald is really scared now. Maybe Faerydae will turn it into a skunk or a turkey after all.

"It's my sister's, I just took it from her," he says, as honest as it gets.

"Stole it you mean?"

"Yes," he admits.

"Where is your sister?"

"In London," he answers.

"Will you stop saying London!" snaps Faerydae. "There's only colony in Gulli Terra —Whifflecliff."

"I'm sorry, I thought it was Cuffley, I'm not too familiar with the names, we just moved there a few months ago, but I trust you," says Archibald.

Faerydae calms down a little.

"Okay, it's your sister's, it makes sense, I guess. Sorry for your cape," she says, trying to put it back together around his neck.

Archibald might be off the hook.

"It's okay," he says.

Faerydae grabs him by the shoulders suddenly, scaring him again. But her face is softening:

"Look, I'm trying to put myself in your shoes, whatever shoes these are," she says, glancing down at his sneakers. "I know it must be hard for you, just to be here, as a boy. I mean, you're only a mislimp after all."

"I'm what now?" he asks.

"A mislimp, you know, an accident. I can only imagine how it feels," confides Faerydae, "I'm sorry if was a little rough with you."

Archibald smiles really big. He is amazed and relieved that she seems to know everything.

"Rough with me? No, not at all, I'm used to much worse, trust me," he says, images of William Tanner —and his sister— coming to his mind instantly. "I find you pretty chill actually!"

"Chill?" she asks. "Are you saying I'm cold?"

"Not at all, what I meant by chill is you're cool you know."

"Wait, so I'm not cold but I'm cool, isn't that essentially the same thing?" she says.

"Trust me, where I come from, it's a compliment, don't ask me why, I don't even know! I just really like you!" he lets out.

Faerydae is caught off guard. She blushes a little, looks away, runs her hands through her hair —looks awkward.

"Oh um okay..." she mumbles. "Well, I'm sorry but I'll still have to put you in that cabana, and lock the door, just for your own safety. You don't quite know your way around. Living here can be challenging you know. I'm not sure you're ready yet, that's all."

"I've heard that before," groans Archibald.

Another morning, another instance of talking through yawning for Archibald, who still dreams of getting out of this nightmare.

"This was just a bad, bad... Nope, still here," he mutters as he opens his eyes once more to the blue sky of Gristlemoth and the comfort of his charming cabana/prison.

He digs into the right pocket of his hoodie, surprised to find nothing. He tries the left pocket. Nothing there either. The wrapping papers scattered on the ground confirm his worst fear: he has run out of candy bars.

Faerydae is knocking at the door.

"Can I come in?" she says.

"Sure," he answers.

"Everything okay?" she asks, seeing slightly more disarray than usual in his pout.

"I'm fine," he says weakly.

"I have something to cheer you up," Faerydae tells him. "Something I've been working on for quite a while now," she adds, handing him a thick book.

"Wow, it's heavy!" says Archibald.

"That's centuries of research, what do you expect," she notes.

The title reads:

THE GRAND
(PURPOSELY INCOMPLETE)
BESTIARY OF MARODORS

CAUGHT & WITNESSED
(OR DEPICTED BASED ON
FAIRLY RELIABLE DESCRIPTIONS)

In order to read all the fine print (where the devil usually hides), Archibald has to brush aside clumps of feathers, leaves, fur and pine needles sown or glued to the wood cover.

"What's all this, a bunch of charms?" he asks.

"Nope, just some of the many things Marodors are made of," she says.

And indeed, Archibald discovers a menagerie of the most ragtag makeup. Winged or scaled, horned or clawed, furry or bald, all

Marodors look like the product of some botched experiment. The sum of their many parts, whether they be from animals, birds or insects, hints at something gone terribly wrong. And that's not even mentioning the human parts, chief among them that ghostly face located somewhere on their body.

Page after page, each Marodor, fully drawn or roughly sketched, is scarier than the last, with names alone capable of inspiring the worst fears. Humciferae Sulfuratus, Choleoptus Mortifare 1, 2 and 3 (depending on the head count), Megaptera Plaguare, Enominum Obscurus... Just whispering some of them makes Archibald tremble.

"So they were not scary enough, you had to give them crazy names too!" he comments.

"These are just their official names, their smart names if you will, all plants and animals have those you know," explains Fae-rydae. "But of course every Marodor also has a more common name, see right here," she says, pointing to the "also known as" section in the Marodor's description chart (on the opposite page).

"Socks... Clafoutis... Dingo... Stripes... these sound more like pet names!" says Archibald.

"It's just a way to show we're not afraid of them, even though we are of course!" she jokes. "The point is: we have nothing to fear but fear itself."

"Sounds good!" concurs Archibald, who might have heard that somewhere before...

Not all of those nicknames have a friendly tone though. Some, like Booger, Meathead, Doomdumb, or Big Bertha, are clearly intended to ridicule the monsters, while some seem more rooted in History —the darkest side of History...

"Genghis Khan!" exclaims Archibald. "That's one bad boy right here!"

"Considering he's responsible for the death of millions, yes, I think you can say that," nods Faerydae. "They really look similar though, I swear, sometimes I think the actual Ghenghis Khan got reincarnated into this thing."

Messy blend of cat and moth, plus bits and pieces of cockroach, the Ulanbatore Golgothae, indeed owes his nickname to an obvious resemblance with the bloody Mongol conqueror, from the long goatee to the thin scary eyes —and possibly the rough childhood.

"That's not even the worst, check out page 125," says Faerydae.

Archibald finds it quickly.

"Maculatus Ferocipare, also known as... Arthur," he reads. "That doesn't sound too bad!"

"He is, trust me, I named him after an ex-boyfriend of mine. They both had really bad breath."

Archibald cracks up, while also turning his head discreetly and blowing into the palm of his hand —just to make sure.

"As long as you didn't name him Archibald," he notes.

"No, Archibald is page 173," says Faerydae.

He has stopped laughing suddenly, not eager to reach that page. And when he does, he is definitely not too pleased with the DNA of that particular beast: naked mole rat, locust and snake, among other weird bits.

"Man he looks terrible! What's wrong with this one?" he asks, exploring the chart that details his average size, weight, speed, capture location, strengths and weaknesses.

"If I remember correctly," says Faerydae, "this Marodor has multiple tongues. Naida picked the name. Another ex-boyfriend I think. Terrible kisser I heard."

"Really?" asks Archibald, bummed out.

"I'm just bourding with you," she laughs, "this is a pretty average Marodor, nothing too special about him. He's sneaky though, you never quite know what his next move's going to be, so you've got to keep an eye on him…"

"It's weird, it says nothing about that in here," he comments.

"Trust me, I know *all* about him," says Faerydae, in a not too subtle nod to her experience with this Archibald from Cuffley —or wherever he claims to be from…

"And he's a crawler, that's just great," sighs Archibald, reading more details about the weird beast that bears his name.

"Yes, some of them crawl, some of them fly, some run, some swim. And some, well, they do all of the above," she explains.

"What a freak show!" says Archibald.

"Hey look, this is the Marodor who chased you," she says, showing him the Apiumare Mellifera, AKA Ram, on page 29.

"Who drew all these?" he asks.

"This is kind of my pet project but I'm not very good at it, so others contribute. One of my best friends, Parnel, she drew a few," says Faerydae, looking sad suddenly.

"Everything okay?" asks Archibald.

"Yes," she says, meaning no.

"I don't think I've met Parnel yet."

"Not yet," says Faerydae.

Flipping through more pages, Archibald pauses on one beast, the Tetraodonte Bacillus (page 111), which looks strangely familiar.

"Hey I've seen this one before!" he exclaims.

"I doubt it," says Faerydae, "but again, you fought so many!"

"I did?" asks Archibald, "oh yes, yes, I did, so many!" he corrects, reminding himself of his own lie.

"I'm impressed," says Faerydae, "this Marodor is rather rare. No one I know has ever seen one. In fact, I've never seen one!"

It's some kind of bear, not black, not white, not brown either, or maybe it is. But it's not the color one would remember. What makes that bear so different is the pair of huge horns in the front and a hundred smaller ones shielding his body. It suddenly comes back to him —that's one of the monsters he was drawing at home.

"I know where I saw it!" says Archibald. "On my glo…"

He is interrupted by a loud rumbling noise from down under.

"What was that?" asks Faerydae.

He knows. He just doesn't wish to tell her. But the roiling noise is back, even louder, and more of a gurgling sound this time.

"Was that your stomach?" she asks.

Archibald nods, reluctantly.

"What happened to your *real food?*" she inquires, quotation marking "real food" with her fingers.

"I finished it all," he admits.

"Well, let's go to the kitchen and see what we can find for you!" Faerydae tells Archibald, pulling him outside.

"Where's the kitchen?" he asks.

Archibald has only been in Gristlemoth for two days but he already noticed a curious pattern. Every evening around the same time —hard to tell when exactly since there's no clock around—, all the cabanas, and the village as a whole, seem to empty out at once.

Where's everyone going? he wondered each time, peeking through the door of his cabana. Now he knows —in Cleofa, across the courtyard, up that grand double staircase, all the way to the second floor, into this majestic hall he followed Faerydae off to.

Archibald can't believe his eyes. No, his astonishment has nothing to do with the size of the cauldron sitting in the middle of the kitchen —even though that giant pot could easily cook 200 pounds of rice in one batch. It's not the size of the dining hall either —even though it seems designed to feed an army, with dozens of tables organized in circles around the cooking area. It's not even the chandeliers, as whimsical and unique as they can be, made out of dead oak trees rising from all four corners of the room, with constellations of glowing jars in their arms extended left, right and center, sometimes overlapping one another.

No, Archibald is in awe because there's a man in that kitchen! A real man, with hair on his hands, on his knuckles, on his arms, on his cheeks and plenty more in his nose and ears, some even growing *on* his ears —but none where you'd expect it the most, on the top of his head, smooth as a polished golem.

"That's a man!" shouts Archibald, a big smile on his face.

"It sure is!" confirms Faerydae —if needed. "That's Wymer, the best cook in the world, and the best handyman in the world... Wymer, this is Ivy, and she's hungry!"

"Ivy huh?" says the round-bellied, barrel-chested man, with a fatherly voice. He doesn't seem too convinced, "Okay, Ivy, I am indeed Gristlemoth's cook, and Faery's right, the best one in town, probably 'cause I'm also the only one in town," he chuckles. "And yes, I'm the handyman around here as well, so I'll try not to put too many nails in your mint sauce!" he says, chuckling some more.

"Mint sauce is bad enough," jokes Archibald.

"What are you preparing?" asks Faerydae.

"Not carrots I hope," mumbles Archibald.

Wymer heard that. But he's not the one answering.

"No carrots today," says a metallic voice.

"What was that?" asks Archibald, trying to figure out where it came from.

"Oh that's just Karl," says Faerydae, giving the cauldron a friendly tap.

"Karl?" says Archibald, now distinguishing a face on that cauldron, also sitting on his own three hands. "You turned him into a crockpot!" he says, fascinated and afraid.

"The opposite. Wymer was a little lonely cooking in here by himself, so we gave life to his cauldron," she explains.

"Hello Ivy!" says the cauldron.

"Hey you," lets out Archibald, waving, full of amazement.

"And since Karl felt lonely as well, we then gave him some company. That would be Karla over there," explains Faerydae, motioning towards a smaller cauldron lost among pots and pans.

"Pardon her, she's sleeping, she cooked a heavy meal last night," says Karl.

"How is that possible? Is this what happened to Paws?"

"Who's Paws?" asks Wymer.

"The dog pillow," says Archibald.

"I can't believe you gave that thing a name," sighs Faerydae. "But to answer your question, no, to be honest, Karl was more of an accident," she says, covering her mouth. "We were boiling golems in the cauldron and we got this unexpected... side effect."

"A side effect?" says Karl, his feelings hurt.

"Yes, but a very welcomed side effect, with the most fantastic taste buds," says Wymer, petting his cast iron sous-chef.

"So what's for dinner?" asks Faerydae.

Archibald was glad to hear carrots were not on the menu. But a quick look at the ingredients lined up on the table is not to reassure the picky guest.

"Let me see," says Wymer, "what do we have here? Stale bread, fish, black treacle, cinnamon, what could I be making?"

"Flummadiddle!" shouts Karl as Faerydae high fives Wymer.

Archibald has heard that word before: "I thought Flummadiddle was some kind of non-sense?" he says.

"And what do you think this is, if not non-sense?" Wymer chuckles again.

"That's where Flummadiddle comes from! We just mix a lot of things that shouldn't really be mixed together, it's *total* non-sense!" sums up Faerydae. "The bug patties make it pretty tasty."

"Did you say… *bug* patties?"

"You know, caterpillars, termites, cockroaches. Worms and larvae are the best though, the most nutritious," she assures.

Archibald is looking pale again.

"The only bugs we don't eat are these," says Faerydae, pointing up at the glowing mason jars.

"What are they?" asks Archibald, squinting at the swarm of tiny bulbs.

"Fireflies!" she says. "All those years we were lost in darkness, they were our only hope. You can't imagine how much they mean to us."

"I can actually!" he sighs.

"Way too precious to end up in a crockpot," she adds.

"Lucky them," mumbles Archibald, as he watches insect heads, tails and wings getting smooshed under Wymer's rolling pin.

"You're supposed to use pork fat in Flummadiddle but the only pig we have is a Marodor with a pig body," explains the Chef. "And we're not gonna eat that!" he cracks up.

"What do you mean you have a Marodor with a pig body?" says Archibald. "You keep those things around here?" he asks.

"Where else are we supposed to put them?" responds Faerydae.

"I dunno," he says.

"Wanna see that book of monsters come alive?" she asks.

ß

Ten minutes later, Faerydae has led her curious guest to the very edge of Gristlemoth, opposite from the cliff. They are walking alongside the giant golems surrounding the village. Suddenly, Archibald jumps as he spots two Marodors flying on the other side. They swoop down low and come really close, but eventually swerve away, as though an invisible brick wall was standing in their way.

"Don't worry, we're fine here," says Faerydae. "You can enjoy your pudding!"

"Is that what this is, pudding?" he says, biting on that thick slice of dark brown cardboard he has a hard time chewing —not to mention swallowing.

"And I thought Grandpa's pudding was gross!" he grimaces.

Faerydae laughs.

"By the way," he says, "what was going on in the kitchen? I saw you guys doing those weird things with your hands. Were you making fun of me?"

Faerydae cracks up again.

"Not at all," she says, "it's just part of our sign language, remember, I told you about it."

"I guess," says Archibald, not convinced.

"We actually borrowed a lot of those signs from monks. You know, in monasteries, they don't really have the right to talk, so they came up with a whole system of signs. It's pretty ingenious."

"What does this mean then?" he asks, forming a circle with his hands by joining his thumbs and index fingers.

"Bread! I was just asking Wymer to make more for dinner!"

"That's pretty neat!" says Archibald.

"I know right," says Faerydae. "And look, for fish, you do it like this," she explains, waving her hand, mimicking the tail of a fish in water. "And for the raad fish, it's like this," she notes, making her hand shake frantically as if electrocuted.

Now it's Archibald's turn to laugh.

"So, when you fight Marodors, do you use that kind of signs?" he asks.

"Yes, just simple ones. They have to be. When you're in the middle of a fight, you don't have time for anything too complicated," says Faerydae. "For example, when we're ready to approach a Marodor, we do this," she says, turning her hand into a bird's head shape, her fingers all curled up together. "To retreat, it's the same sign, just the opposite direction," she explains, now pointing towards her chest. "And there's also this one, to create a diversion," she says, placing her left hand fingers into the palm of her right hand.

"You're like a commando, or a ninja!" says Archibald.

"I'm not sure what that is but thanks I guess," she says.

A dreadful scream soars from the area ahead. And another shortly after.

"What was that?" asks Archibald.

"That, would be the Marodors," says Faerydae.

"It sounds like they're crying," he notes.

"I wouldn't say crying, now are they happy we caught them? Probably not," she says.

They soon enter a woodsy area that gets darker and darker as the trees get bigger and taller. Some flaming torches light their way. The moaning is growing louder. They are close.

Some cages come into view, dark and dreary, covered with a thick canopy of branches blocking the few rays of sun that managed to pierce through the trees above. The Marodors are barely visible, pacing in the shadows, popping out for brief moments, one scary glimpse at a time —here a growling muzzle, there some salivating saber teeth, next door a semi-human hand with nails long as knives scratching the ground.

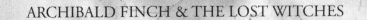

"Eeww!" lets out Archibald, breathing in a stench of near-death that makes his flummadiddle smell like cotton candy.

Patrolled by a few girls armed with golems, the sinuous path divides into secondary arteries, each lined with cages on both sides. There must be dozens of them, scattered across a rather large swath of land, making it a village within the village.

GOLEMS VERSUS MARODORS

"Wow! This would make a great ride at the fair," mutters Archibald, advancing between two walls of frightening mugs.

"Just make sure you stay in the middle of the road," says Faerydae, "don't go too near the cages."

There are naturally no markings on this dirt road but Archibald definitely sticks to the center, curled up into a turtle posture, chin tucked deep between his shoulders, and arms glued alongside his body.

"You said the book would come alive but… these creatures look dead almost," he comments, noticing that most Marodors, if not wounded, are in really bad shape.

"That's the thing, Marodors won't die, that's why we have to park them here," notes Faerydae. "Look, here's the one that attacked you," she says, pointing at one of the cages. Its neck still painfully bent into a question mark, the Marodor also seems to have lost one of his eyes, as only one glows red.

"We'll call this one Cyclops!" jokes Faerydae.

Archibald is amazed, scared and sad all at once. Even though these are obviously horrible monsters, they remind him of the animals from that shelter he visited last month with a friend.

"We keep them in the dark, their natural element. We don't want them to go too crack-brained with the Sun," she says.

Another word Archibald obviously doesn't get.

"Too crazy," she translates. "Anyway, just being here makes them extremely weak. Not only the golems around the village keep the Marodors out, they also sort of hypnotize the ones inside. Be careful though, they are still dangerous," she warns him.

"What happens if they catch you?"

"You don't know?" she says, surprised.

"I have an idea," he sighs. "I saw the graveyard by my cabana."

"That's different, those sisters died in battle," she says. "Marodors don't usually try to kill you. They don't mean to at least…"

"Well that's reassuring!" jokes Archibald.

"If they do kill you, it will be by accident, most likely, or because you made them really mad," explains Faerydae.

"I don't understand, what do they do to you then?" he asks.

"Something worse than death," she says.

"What can be worse than death?" argues Archibald, while not really eager to find out.

"Just a few weeks back, a friend of mine got too close to a cage. Within seconds, it was too late," says Faerydae.

"I'm really sorry, what was her name?"

"Parnel," says Faerydae, sighing.

"Wait, that's the one you told me about earlier right? She drew some of the Marodors in that book!"

"Yes, she was so talented, so beautiful. And so full of life…"

"So… what happened to her?" he asks.

"When one of us gets caught on the battlefield, we are never to be seen again. We are usually lost forever, probably for the better. This was definitely not easy to witness," she says.

About a hundred yards later, Faerydae stops in front of a cage isolated from the others.

"This is Parnel," she says.

At first, Archibald can only see an undefined shape curled up in a corner, until a pair of eyes light up, bright red. Coming out of the shadows, a pale face emerges, that of a young girl. Faerydae was right, she is beautiful. Parnel would almost look normal, if not for the huge roots creeping up her neck.

The rest of her body slowly unfolds. Her arms look intact but her legs have partially disappeared, replaced by claws, and a double hook, at the end of a curved tail. It's as if she was being devoured by a giant pincher bug.

"It's horrible," lets out Archibald.

"She is slowly turning into one of them," explains Faerydae, fighting off tears. "This is what Marodors do to you. It's one way for them to multiply."

"What causes that?" he asks.

"We call it the final embrace, or the hug of death," says Faerydae.

"How does it work? They suck your brains out or something?"

"No, they don't take anything from you. They inject something into you, some sort of virus. We still don't know exactly how it works but it happens quickly. You can get infected within seconds."

Parnel is crawling on the ground, moaning, trying to get closer to them, but she is having a hard time.

"She seems in pain," says Archibald.

"When she got caught, we tried to rescue her. The problem is, by using our golems on the beast, we hurt Parnel in the process. I think her arms are broken. We don't know though, she has not said a word since," explains Faerydae.

Parnel suddenly shrinks back to her corner, as two girls come running, screaming Faerydae's name.

"Willow, what's happening?" asks Faerydae.

"It's Naida," says the girl, out of breath.

"Is she okay?" worries Faerydae.

"She saw something," says Willow. "You've got to come with us."

Archibald and Faerydae find Naida on the way to Cleofa, surrounded by many. It looks as though half of the village has thronged to hear what she has to say. Slumped on the ground, she is obviously shaken.

"What happened?" asks Faerydae right away.

"I was out, looking for new herbs. That Marodor appeared right behind me. It's enormous. I've never seen anything like that before," explains Naida, fear imprinted in her eyes.

"Can you describe it?"

"It was so dark, I didn't see much, a shadow mostly. I just ran, sorry."

"Don't be sorry, you did the right thing," says Faerydae. "Any detail you'd remember? Anything at all?"

Naida leans over and starts drawing something on the ground with her finger. The beast takes shape little by little: the legs first, arched and wide, then the serpentine necks, twice as long, four in total.

"That's impossible," whispers Faerydae.

Maven has brought the Bestiary of Marodors. Faerydae knows it by heart. She jumps to page 155.

"Is this it?" she asks, almost scared of the answer.

"I think so," nods Naida. "Only…"

"Only what?" asks Faerydae.

"With more necks," she says.

Unfinished, the drawing itself doesn't offer much more details than Naida's sketch in the dirt.

Archibald peeks over Faerydae's shoulder, discovering the one they call Krakatorum Gargantus, a meaty and mighty beast, with two faceless necks mounted on an eight-legged furry body.

"Two nightmares in one," says Faerydae, "50% spider, 50% basilisk."

"And 100% spine-chilling," notes Maven.

"A basilisk? Is that the one with the death gaze that can petrify you?" asks Archibald, remembering his dad's story.

"Not quite," smiles Faerydae. "Don't get me wrong though. Could you be petrified by just looking at the basilisk? Certainly, but petrified with fear you will be. That's probably where the legend comes from. I'm sure the Krakatorum is a sight to behold, but only for those lucky enough to actually remember. The thing is, most who laid eyes on this beast probably never survived to tell of their encounter."

"Is that why the drawing is not more detailed," asks Archibald.

"When you witness something like this, you do the same as Naida, you run, you need not to stick around for details," says Maven.

"What's a Krakatorum doing here anyway?" wonders Faerydae out loud. "I thought they lived deep in the forests of Basquery." Then turning to Naida: "Where were you when you saw that thing? How far?"

"Near the Neander pass," says Naida, triggering a loud gasp through the crowd.

"That's less than ten miles from here!" realizes Faerydae, even more worried now.

"The Krakatorum is said to be a slow crawler," notes Maven.

"Still, it would take him only a day or two to reach us," fears Faerydae.

"We're fine here right?" asks Archibald.

"Maybe, maybe not," says Faerydae.

"But you said the golems around the village would protect us?"

"They should," she corrects.

"Now that's confident!" he lets out.

"Those golems can resist regular Marodors. The Krakatorum is much larger, and much more powerful. Most likely, our arrows will have no effect on him. Gristlemoth could fall," she predicts.

"It happened to another village a few years ago, in Myrmecia. I was there," recalls Naida. Her eyes say it all.

"Why don't we just stay here and wait, maybe it will just go away," suggests Archibald.

"No, we can't take that risk," says Faerydae. "We'll have to fight him outside."

She turns to the crowd to address everyone:

"There is danger at our walls," she says. "But I have some great news for us all," she adds, calming the clamor a bit. "We have a secret weapon that was sent to us at this very uncertain and perilous time."

Archibald looks relieved. He can't wait to hear more about that secret weapon.

"Here it is," she says, yanking Archibald's cape one more time, unveiling his hoodie with the three Greek letters —which to the girls in the assembly, read as runes of course.

"His name is Archibald," shouts Faerydae.

Archibald is stunned and overwhelmed, as weak applause turns into cheering, to greet the coming of the savor.

"I think it's time I give you back your magic weapon," says Faerydae, handing him the pouch containing his flashlight.

THE DARK PRIEST

James R. Doyle was definitely not born ready. This morning though, he sure is —as much as he can be. He arrived at his antique shop at 7am, two full hours earlier than usual, just in case his esteemed client showed up first thing. He has sobered up. His is wearing his nicest suit, two sizes too small, washed out and adorned with a mustard stain from a wedding night in 1982, but his nicest suit nonetheless —his only suit to be perfectly clear. And, a wrinkle-free shirt, of the yellowest white, matching his teeth, which he made sure to leave all night in mint water with five effervescent cleaning tabs. Now he keeps looking at his watch. He is getting impatient. After all, Mr. Heinrich said he'd be here "in the morning", but didn't give any specific time. Mr. Doyle once more peeks out the window, biting his fingers, nearly losing his denture in the process. This could be a life-changing day for James Doyle.

A long black Mercedes pulls to a stop curbside. The driver comes out first, then two more men from the back seats, each panning left, right and back, like owls. Only after that routine does a tall, shadowy figure finally emerge, his face obscured by a fedora hat. The man is escorted to the door hastily.

Mr. Heinrich comes in followed by one of his bodyguards, a muscle man with a chest so wide, and arms so short, that clapping is not even an option. Because henchmen usually come as a pair, like pliers, sneezes and bad news, his twin brother blocks the entrance, squeezing his square peg of a body into the oval frame of the doorway.

"Welcome!" shouts Mr. Doyle warmly.

He offers a handshake that only meets the hat his guest has just removed, revealing a monk's haircut that screams 1455. Archibald got the same two years ago —by accident. His mom was in a hurry. She placed a pasta bowl on his head and trimmed everything sticking out following the edge. He got teased at school for three weeks. Mr. Heinrich's mistake possesses one unique twist though. Cut short on his forehead, the scattered line of hair ends abruptly in a dent, right above his left ear. A dark, slanted dent that runs all the way to the back of his head, as if a chunk of his skull and brains had been chopped off by a sword.

Despite the high collar of his black leather coat covering part of his chin, Mr. Heinrich's face looks unusually long and emaciated. Due to a receding tide of skin never to rise again, the arched bones protrude around cavernous eyes besieged by deep shadows. All features have collapsed to form two deep parentheses framing a tight mouth, itself sagging at both ends. To sum it up, an ideal face for a radio career.

"Where is the globe?" he asks right away, quite nicely.

"Why don't we sit down?" suggests Mr. Doyle. "Please make yourself comfortable. I have tea in the back if you wish. I think there are just a few details we need to discuss first, to make sure we are on the same page."

Mr. Heinrich remains silent, simply slapping the palm of his left hand with one tight leather glove he has just taken off.

"Of course I'm prepared to be reasonable, by the way, just out of curiosity, what did you have in mind?" asks Mr. Doyle, rubbing his hands together, swallowing his saliva, as if getting ready for cake.

"I'm not happy," murmurs Mr. Heinrich.

"I beg your pardon?" asks Mr. Doyle.

"You said you would make me happy. I'm not happy," says Mr. Heinrich.

And before Mr. Doyle can even think of something to say:

"Where is the globe Mr. Doyle?" he repeats, letting out a cough mixed with a scary growling sound.

"Look, I don't need to tell you how this works, we are both business people here, am I right?" tries Mr. Doyle.

Mr. Heinrich slaps his hand with his glove again, only harder this time, yet showing no pain.

"Boris," he utters, motioning for his bodyguard to make a move. And a swift move it is. With one heavy blow to his chest, the colossus tackles Mr. Doyle to the floor, pressing his size 16 boot right against his neck.

Mr. Heinrich clears his throat and comes close, towering over that poor Mr. Doyle.

"Don't you dare insult me with your cheap bargaining tactics," he yells. "Money is not an issue. This is so much bigger than you and I. This is about History. This is about fulfilling a promise, made half a thousand years ago."

"Did you hear what Master Heinrich told you?" asks Boris, blessed with the singular talent of talking from the back of his throat, while barely moving his razor-thin lips.

Mr. Doyle can't talk. So he offers a whimpering nod.

"Good," says Mr. Heinrich. "So I'm going to ask you one last time Mr. Doyle… Where is the globe?"

Boris lets go of Mr. Doyle, who painfully gets on his knees — the perfect position to beg for his life if need be.

"It's complicated," he says. "I might be able to locate it, give me a few days."

Boris grabs onto his suit again, ripping off the sleeves, using them to tie Mr. Doyle's hands behind his back.

Mr. Heinrich approaches. He takes off his second glove, uncovering a wooden hand with metal wires running across the palm and connected to each finger.

"Do you know what this is?" he asks, making every articulation of the prosthesis move like tentacles.

Mr. Doyle shakes his head, nervous.

"This is an automaton," says Mr. Heinrich, "one of the first robotic hands. A pure marvel of technology, nearly four hundred years old. Unfortunately, it was built with a flaw," he explains, clutching the frame of a chair. "See, instead of just grabbing onto things, this hand would compress them, crush them, break them," he says, as the piece of wood in his grasp starts cracking and splintering.

Mr. Doyle looks terrified. Mr. Heinrich lets go of the chair.

"A shame really. The first owner of this automaton killed his wife and child because of it. A tragic accident really. Needless to say, he was not thrilled with it. I, however, happen to find the flaw... very useful," he continues, approaching Mr. Doyle, whose shattering teeth have now detached from their gums.

"I wanted it to be fully mine, to be a part of me. So I had this machine connected to my nervous system, which can cause it to act... a bit erratically. But don't worry, you have nothing to fear, as long as you don't get on my nerves of course," he warns, moving that fidgety claw close to Mr. Doyle's face.

"That girl," lets out Mr. Doyle, "she was here yesterday, she has the globe, she refused to sell it to me," he explains.

"What girl?" asks Mr. Heinrich.

"I don't know who she is," he says.

Mr. Heinrich seems about to grab onto Mr. Doyle's neck.

"I swear I don't know," says Mr. Doyle, "but my son, my son knows."

"So where is he?" yaps Boris, frowning so much he managed to merge his eyebrows with an exceptionally low hairline.

"I have no idea," assures Mr. Doyle, "but he gave me some information about that girl, I can help you find her..."

Mr. Absconce is alone in his classroom, getting ready for his next batch of students. The subject will be "The Superpowers' Race to the Moon," as he wrote on the chalkboard. Now he is trying to draw that moon, biting his tongue. He can't quite draw a perfect circle. And that makes him awfully mad! To make matters worse, he has just heard someone open the door behind him. He sure didn't need to be disturbed.

"What now? Please, I'm busy," he shouts, annoyed, erasing his drawing one more time.

"Professor Absconce?" a deep voice asks.

"Just Mister Absconce would do but thank you anyway," he says, turning around, discovering Mr. Heinrich and the same loyal Boris standing by the door. He is a bit taken aback. Not only has he never seen these two men before but they are also not the kind of people who usually step into his classroom. Mr. Absconce's visitors are more three-piece suit or tweed waistcoat kind of fellows than leather coats and combat boots —although he had that angry parent who showed up in yoga pants a few years back, threatening him with a curling iron after he gave her son an F for spelling Churchill Tchurtchill.

Hopefully this is not that kind of scenario, he prays.

"Gentlemen, how may I help you?" he says.

"Professor, I'm terribly sorry to disturb you," replies Mr. Heinrich. "I'm trying to get in contact with one of your students."

"And who would that be?" inquires Mr. Absconce.

"A young lady, about five and a half foot tall, brown hair, light brown eyes."

"That sounds like a police report!" comments Mr. Absconce.

"Well, we'll get to that later perhaps," says Mr. Heinrich in a cryptic tone.

"Is she in trouble?"

"Possibly."

"What's her name?"

"Hailee," says Mr. Heinrich.

"Surely an unusual young lady that Miss Finch."

"Hailee Finch," whispers Mr. Heinrich.

"Is this a police matter?" asks the professor.

"Not exactly. Not yet. I just need to locate Miss Finch. And I would be thankful if you were to help me in my quest," says Mr. Heinrich.

"Well, I can't just share my students' information with anyone, I don't know what this is regarding but if you contact the administration, I'm sure they will help you," he says, returning behind his desk, a bit shaken.

Mr. Heinrich approaches the desk and opens his coat slightly, just enough to reveal a clerical collar. Mr. Absconce looks immediately at ease. He breathes a —deep— sigh of relief.

"Hailee Finch brought you a globe recently," inquires Mr. Heinrich.

"Yes indeed."

"We have reasons to believe that globe belongs to the diocese. It was stolen just a few weeks ago."

"I asked her whether that was a family possession, but she wouldn't say," notes Mr. Absconce.

"I'm truly sorry," says Mr. Heinrich.

"I really thought that globe belonged to her, with her family moving in that manor and all," lets out Mr. Absconce

"A manor?" asks Mr. Heinrich.

"Her grand-mother's house, in Cuffley. She just moved there with her family. I was so naïve. I feel like she took advantage of her brother's disappearance."

"What do you mean?"

"Yes, her brother, he vanished, into thin air really, just a few days before she brought the globe to me."

Mr. Heinrich seems troubled by that story.

"We should call the police," suggests Mr. Absconce.

"No," says Mr. Heinrich immediately. "We are trying to keep the police out of this. That's why I preferred to come and see you directly."

"Now I wonder whether that other kid is an accomplice of Miss Finch," Mr. Absconce mentions.

"What other kid?" asks Mr. Heinrich.

"A young man, Oliver Doyle his name was, I believe.

"Doyle?" exclaims Mr. Heinrich.

"Yes, he said he had some textbooks to give back to Miss Finch. He needed her address. Very strange request really, I'm not even sure he's a student here. He came in just a few minutes before you."

Without saying another word, Mr. Heinrich and his bodyguard leave Mr. Absconce's classroom. Down the hall, Oliver Doyle is still there, talking to a group of students. He is the only person without a uniform in the hallway. Mr. Heinrich spots him immediately.

"Doyle!" he shouts in his direction.

Oliver looks at him and puts two and two together in an instant. He starts running the opposite way. Mr. Heinrich's bodyguard charges toward him but bumps into clusters of students getting out of class. Oliver disappears down the stairs.

"You can run boy…" whispers Mr. Heinrich.

Δ

Hailee is in her parents' garage, going through drawers, shelves and boxes. It's dark out and fairly dark in this garage as well, green of faint fluorescent light. The lonely bulb hanging from the ceiling certainly won't help Hailee find what she is looking for. She strides out into the hallway to shout something:

"Dad! Dad I can't find those candles, they're not here!"

No answer.

"And of course he can't hear me," she mutters. "How convenient!"

Hailee comes back in and starts looking again. Her task is not easy. It's like trying to find a hair on Mr. Absconce's head. The garage is so big. It was designed for a large fleet of cars, six to eight easily —which means about fifteen the size of the family Fiat. Right now it's the only one parked in here, along with the mess from their last place. Oddly enough, every piece of furniture from their old living room is laid out pretty much the way it was in the London flat.

For Hailee, it's like stepping into a time capsule. She sits on the spongy foam couch, as uncomfortable as it is cozy, because full of memories. She rubs that stain embedded in the middle cushion. That's from three Wimbledon tournaments ago. It was on her birthday. Archibald dropped his piece of cake on her lap — officially by accident— while she was opening her gifts. She was so mad that night. Now she smiles thinking about it. Hazy with tears, her gaze has paused on the dining table. That's where that tiny Christmas tree was sitting a year ago. At dinnertime, Archibald was adding his own ornaments to it, the beans and pasta he refused to eat, making everyone laugh, except Hailee of course. Now, grasping the value of the normality that was lost, she would give up everything —even her phone— to go back to that moment.

Some noise behind the car interrupts her daydreaming, bringing her back to reality. She jumps.

"Great house! Full of rats!" she mumbles.

She doesn't see any. Instead though, she finally spots the candles, on the very edge of a shelf. As she extends her arm to grab the box, she notices a weird shadow, in the corner behind that shelf. Following the curves of that shadow, she slowly makes out the contours of a chin, a nose and some hair... Someone is standing there. Hailee has stopped breathing.

Did that shadow just move?

Hailee gasps at the sight of —Oliver Doyle, who comes at her all of a sudden. He claps his hand over her mouth. Hailee is terrified. She is gagged but her eyes are screaming.

"I'm here to help you okay, to warn you actually," he says. "Please don't scream, I'm going to remove my hand from your mouth, can I trust you?"

She nods. He lets her go.

"What are you doing here? Are you crazy?" she says.

"I know it looks like it but I had to come over before they do."

"What are you talking about? Who's '*they*'? It's your dad isn't it? He sent you to get the globe from me," she says.

"No, yes..."

"Yes?" repeats Hailee, getting ready to scream again.

"I mean no, it's not my dad. But yes they want the globe."

"Who are you talking about then?"

"That guy, he came to my dad's shop. He's looking for that globe you have. For some reason, he wants it really badly. I think it's the same guy who was at your school this morning."

"What? My school? He was at my school? Wait, how would you know?"

Oliver hesitates to tell her, for obvious reasons.

"Because I was there too," he finally says.

"You were at my school? That's it! I'm calling my Dad," warns Hailee.

"I had to. You told me about your History teacher. That's how I figured out the name of your school. I mean, there's not that many teachers called Absconce in London!" he explains.

"But why would you go there?" she asks.

"Because I knew that guy would do the same. It took me what, five phone calls to locate your teacher. Then ten minutes for some students to tell me you moved here."

"This is crazy," mutters Hailee, her eyes fluttering.

"That guy has a lot of money, I'm sure he has a lot of power too. There's something wrong with him, I can tell," says Oliver.

"What do you mean?"

"I don't know. I think he's a priest but it doesn't make sense."

"A priest?"

"I saw his collar, you know, that white collar priests wear," says Oliver, pointing at his throat.

"Why would a priest be interested in that globe?" asks Hailee.

"I'm not sure but maybe I should look at it more closely?"

"What?"

"The globe, if I get a closer look at it, maybe I can find out why that priest wants it so bad."

"Oh I see now, this is what it's all about isn't it?" says Hailee. "You made up this whole story just so you could convince me to sell my globe to your dad! I might not know much about Leonardo Da Vinci. But I'm not *that* dumb you know."

"What? No. I swear! I'm just here to help."

Hailee walks towards the hallway again and presses a switch on the wall, opening one the four garage doors.

"If you don't leave right now, I'm going to scream, and my dad will be down here in seconds" (though she knows he probably won't hear anything). "Then I'll call the police," she assures.

"No, don't call the police, that guy has not done anything yet," notes Oliver.

"Yet?" asks Hailee. "Oh so what is he going to do next?"

"I don't know but I have a bad feeling about it."

"I'm going to give you five seconds before I scream," she warns him.

"Let me just have a quick look," he suggests.

"Four," Hailee replies, starting the countdown.

"I'm begging you, it won't take long."

"Three."

"Just a few minutes, I promise."

"Two."

"I'm doing this for you. Don't you get it?"

"One…"

"Fine! Good luck to you then," says Oliver before he drifts away, disappearing into the night.

Another troubled night for Hailee. More tossing. More turning. More grunting. And barely any sleep. She just couldn't stop thinking about everything Oliver told her.

Between Archibald, the globe, that weird priest and Mr. Doyle, this is becoming too much to handle for her. She misses the time when her life was simple, made of texting, shopping and interneting —oh and yes, going to school sometimes. It actually just occurred to her: she has an early class today.

She leaps from her bed, puts on her uniform quickly, grabs her small backpack and leaves without having breakfast, just giving a quick kiss to her mother.

With Bartholomeo now gone, Kate has been trying to take care of this gigantic house on her own. It takes her two hours just to clean up the living room and library floors.

She has just started scrubbing the kitchen stove when she sees someone wandering around in the backyard. Because of the fogged up windows, she can't really tell who that is. With his long coat, he looks like one of those inspectors who came over after Archibald's disappearance.

Kate opens the back door.

"Can I help you?" she shouts.

The man approaches slowly, his head down to avoid the rain, pressing on his hat to prevent it from flying away. He only lifts his head back up when he reaches the house —it's Mr. Heinrich.

"I'm truly sorry, I didn't want to scare you. I knocked at the front door but nobody answered," he says, forcing his face into a smile, which seems particularly painful.

"I know, I'm sorry, we need to install a doorbell. I can usually hear those big knockers though," says Kate, clearly on the defensive.

"I'm really sorry, I didn't mean to scare you," he says, shaking his coat, opening it up slightly, on purpose, to reveal his white collar.

On Halloween night last year, Archibald managed to collect treats from the same neighbors' house three times, simply by switching disguises. (They had the best candy in the neighborhood). Mr. Heinrich would probably pull off the same feat with only one disguise. His trick worked with Mr. Absconce. It does once more with Kate.

"You don't have to be sorry," she says, suddenly with her nicest voice. "Please come in, you wouldn't want to stay outside in this weather."

"Just a drizzle, really, but thank you," says Mr. Heinrich as he comes in, drenched.

"So how can I help you?" asks Kate, now completely at ease.

"Oh quite the opposite Mrs. Finch, hopefully *I* can help you," he says.

Kate is intrigued.

"I'm with the local church," he explains. "We heard from the Police about your son. It is in our tradition to try to help as much as we can, to bring comfort to families."

"How kind of you, thank you so much, but to be honest, my husband and I have not been involved with any Church so…"

"There's no need to feel bad, Mrs. Finch," he says, cutting her off. "We help people regardless of faith or religion, we are all neighbors before all."

"Sounds good, I agree," says Kate.

"See," continues Mr. Heinrich, "we have a large network of followers, each with a good pair of eyes the Lord gave them, and good ears as well, which can be of great help in your son's case."

"Well, I really appreciate it. Would it help if I gave you a picture of Archibald perhaps?"

"It certainly would," says Mr. Heinrich.

"Why don't we go to the living room, we'll be more comfortable, I'll make a fire, and a tea perhaps?"

"That would be lovely."

Kate leads Mr. Heinrich to the living room. On the way, he comments on the beautiful library.

"What an impressive collection!" he says.

"We are actually thinking about donating some of these books, maybe your Church would be interested?" she says.

"Maybe, maybe…" says Mr. Heinrich, suddenly back to his old weird self. Something else has caught his attention it seems: a picture, sitting in a frame on one of the shelves, between two rows of books.

"That's Archibald's Grandmother, my husband's mother," she says.

Mr. Heinrich moves closer to it. He looks stunned.

"What's her name?" he asks, without parting from the picture and now looking even more strange.

"Celestine, Celestine Finch," she says.

"Is that so?" he comments, producing that scary cough and growling sound again.

"I'm sorry?" asks Kate, a bit troubled.

"Is your mother in law around by chance?" he asks, going back to a nicer voice and demeanor.

"I'm afraid not, this is the picture we used at her funeral. Celestine passed away last month," says Kate.

Mr. Heinrich finally detaches from the picture, takes a large breath and closes his eyes for a few seconds, a slight smirk on his face.

"Her death was very sudden," says Kate. "She left us with this big house, and to be honest, we don't know what to do with all of this."

"Well, this house is beautiful Mrs. Finch, you'll make good use of it I'm sure," says Mr. Heinrich.

"Would you like a tour?" suggests Kate.

"I didn't want to ask," he says with another smirk.

"There's something I'd like to show you upstairs," says Kate.

Hailee is seated at her desk, in Mr. Absconce's classroom. On the chalkboard, the same title as yesterday, The Superpowers' Race to the Moon. Right underneath, that same drawing of the moon, still unfinished.

Hailee is thinking about the crazy story Oliver told her. She seems worried and lost at the same time. A third paper ball from William Tanner just landed on her lap. She turns to him with such a furious look on her face that he literally swallows back that whitish tongue he had unleashed out of his dirty mouth.

It's 10.05 at the wall clock and Mr. Absconce is not here yet. Five minutes late; a very unusual occurrence for a man who puts punctuality as the top of a long list of manners and principles to respect —three-foot tall and pinned by the entrance. Everyone is waiting for him. Instead, it's the headmaster who shows up, looking even more somber than usual. A fairly bad omen. She goes down the aisle and steps up on the podium. She clears her throat. She seems distraught. The students have never seen her like this.

"I'm sorry," she says in a chocked voice, "there has been a terrible tragedy. Mr. Absconce's car swerved off the road inexplicably this morning. As a result of that accident..." adds the headmaster, taking a large breath, "Mr. Absconce is as we speak fighting for his life."

Her announcement draws loud gasps from the room. William Tanner digs deep to find an appropriate reaction.

"Cooooool," he lets out, cracking a smile.

"Willam Tanner!" shouts the headmaster.

For Hailee, aghast at the news, it echoes as a scary reminder of Oliver's warnings. She can't imagine the events of the past 48 hours to be unrelated to one another.

"Given these rather tragic circumstances, class is dismissed," says the headmaster. "You are invited to go back home for the day and not return tomorrow. And since your Christmas vacation starts the day after that, we will see you in two weeks."

"Sooo cool!" tops William Tanner.

By the time the headmaster is done, Hailee has already left the room.

Hailee gets off the bus at the Culpeper Lane stop, facing that gigantic manor she still has to get used to. She starts walking down the interminable driveway. The rain is getting heavy but she doesn't care. Her light makeup is already smeared on her cheeks. She has obviously cried a lot on her way back home.

As she gets closer to the house, she notices a car coming towards her —a long black Mercedes. She has never seen it before.

It's not Grandpa Harvey's car —she would have seen the heavy clouds of smoke coming out of the diesel tailpipe.

Maybe her mother just hired a new maid to replace Bartholomeo? —no, that seems way too nice to be a maid's car.

Maybe the police inspectors came back with some good news about Archibald? —no, at this point, Hailee knows it will take more than the Police to get her brother back.

Soon the car drives past her. She can clearly see the driver and his creepy bulldog face but she only gets a furtive glimpse of the person on the back seat, just enough to see a white priest collar under his chin. Or at least she thinks so. Did she see that collar for sure? Or did her mind make her believe it because she has been obsessing over it so much? Hard to tell with the rain and that dark tint on the car window.

Suddenly, the worst feeling invades her. She stops dead, drops her backpack, and starts running towards the house, a million scenarios twirling in her head about what might have happened to her parents —well, mainly one actually, closely related to Mr. Absconce's fate.

"Mom! Dad!" she screams out of her lungs as soon as she pushes open the entrance door.

The five agonizing seconds that follow seem like an eternity. And then suddenly, coming from the kitchen:

"Hailee? What's going on?" asks Mom.

She comes over to the foyer. She seems fine. But Hailee asks anyway:

"Everything okay?"

"Are *you* okay?" asks Kate, seeing Hailee out of breath, completely soaked, her make-up a mess.

"Where's Dad?" asks Hailee.

"He is at one of Grandma's orphanages. There was a problem. Why aren't you at school by the way?"

"What problem? What happened?"

"We're not sure. Nothing too bad."

"Who was that in the car?" asks Hailee.

"Oh, you saw Mr. Heinrich leave? Very nice man."

"Mr. Heinrich?"

"Yes, but I guess I should say Father Heinrich, he's a priest."

Hailee's heart stops beating.

"Oh my God!" whispers Hailee, in shock, and scared.

"What's wrong? You're so weird today. You want a hot chocolate?"

"What did he want?" asks Hailee.

"Who?"

"The priest."

"He is with the local church. He just wanted to know whether he could be of any assistance. He heard about Archibald from the Police and volunteered to help. Such a pleasant man! He loved the house. I gave him a tour."

"What? Are you crazy?"

"Hailee! I was just being polite!" says Kate.

"Did he go into my room?"

"Yes, as a matter of fact he did. I just wanted him to see where Archie was when he disappeared."

"Oh my God the globe!" mutters Hailee.

137

"What's happening?" shouts Kate as Hailee sprints up the stairs as fast as she can.

She reaches her bedroom door. It's closed. She takes a large breath and gets in swiftly, her eyes riveted on her nightstand. The globe is gone. It was there when she left this morning. And now it's gone.

Kate comes in, beyond worried.

"Hailee you have to tell me what's going on. You're scaring me now."

"The globe is gone," mumbles Hailee.

"The globe? Archie's globe? I just put it in the living room."

Hailee takes off again, this time dashing back downstairs. She heads straight to the living room…

The globe is there, on a table, right by the Christmas tree. Hailee squats down on the floor to enjoy this moment of relief.

"I'm losing my mind," she whispers.

Kate follows in a few seconds later.

"Okay please talk to me," she says.

"It's nothing really," assures Hailee.

"I'm sorry I shouldn't have moved it without asking you," says Kate. "I had no idea this globe meant so much to you. I just thought it would be better here, so that everyone can enjoy it. Mr. Heinrich liked it very much as well, that's what gave me the idea actually."

Hailee stands back up swiftly, her fears awoken anew.

"What did he say about it?"

"I'm sorry?" says Kate.

"What did he say about the globe?"

"Nothing much, he just told me he had one exactly like this when he was young. That's why he'd like to have it."

"Did he offer to buy it?"

"Yes he did actually," says Kate. "But I told him this had become Archie's favorite thing, so there was no way we would part with it. He looked disappointed. But he didn't make a big deal about it."

After staring at the globe for a few seconds, Hailee goes by the fireplace to grab an empty gift box. She places the globe inside, and adds sheets after sheets of wrapping paper around it.

"I hope you're not planning on giving it away!" says Kate.

"No don't worry Mom. But I have somewhere I need to go," says Hailee, heading to the door.

"Can you tell me what's going on at least?"

No answer from Hailee.

"Please Dear make sure you don't get back too late," adds Kate, looking at Hailee as she gets smaller and smaller on the driveway.

Though ice on the railway added twenty minutes to her ride, it was still not quite enough time to convince Hailee her next move was the wisest one. But it sure feels like the only one.

She is back at the heart of London, breathing clouds in the freezing air. It is snowing now. People are milling around with bags full of Christmas presents. Hailee is holding on to her box as if it were everything she has in the world. Her eyes seem full of doubts, focused on the store across the street: The Realm of Antiques.

After several minutes, she finally convinces herself to go in. She pushes the door quietly and closes it behind her. She can't see anyone around. But the piles of antiques could easily conceal someone.

"Oliver," she asks, her voice shy.

Getting no answer, she walks deeper into the store. Each corner she passes is a source of fear and anguish. What if Mr. Doyle is standing right behind that mountain of books? Or behind that tall pedestal clock?

Hailee has found a trick. She uses the mirrors of all sizes, scattered around, to navigate the room and tell her more about those hidden corners she dreads.

One more turn and she will have reached the end of the store. Hailee braces for the worst —seeing Mr. Doyle's face pop up out of nowhere for instance —when a voice catches her by surprise.

"Can I help you?" it says, coming from behind her.

Hailee jumps in surprise and wheels around right away, to discover Oliver, who also jumps as a result.

"You scared the hell out of me! You're good at that!" she says, startled.

"Sorry but, what are you doing here?" he asks, a bit cold.

"You were right. I should have listened to you," says Hailee, apologetic.

"What do you mean?"

"That priest, he came to my house and talked to my mother. He asked about the globe. And my History teacher, Mr. Absconce, he is..."

"What about him?" asks Oliver.

Hailee has a hard time just saying it.

"He's at the hospital. Between life and death," she says.

"What?" exclaims Oliver, in shock.

"They're saying it was an accident, a car accident, but this can't just be a coincidence."

"This is crazy," says Oliver.

"Is your dad here?" asks Hailee, obviously fearful.

"No."

"Is he at the pub?" she asks, looking across the street through the window.

"No, actually, I have not seen him in two days. I'm starting to worry, especially after what happened to your teacher," says Oliver. "He might be back soon though, come with me," he says, leading her just a few steps away, to one of the bigger mirrors attached to the wall.

Oliver applies a slight pressure on the ornate frame. A spring-like noise later, the mirror swings opens like a door, leading to a hidden, secret room. It's pitch black in there. Oliver turns the lights on, unveiling a small chamber, so clean, so well put together, and so organized, it doesn't seem to belong here.

"It's like a museum in here!" says Hailee. "A war museum."

Covered with tufted red velvet, the walls are lined with all sorts of ancient weapons —swords, muskets, halberds, pistols, spears, bows, crossbows, axes and full body armors.

"We'll be okay here," he says, closing the door. "This room is only for special clients."

"Freaks you mean?" she says, exploring this cave-man's cave further.

"Huge freaks!" he says. "When it comes to killing, Men's imagination knows no limits. People love this stuff."

"What's that?" asks Hailee, gesturing towards a wooden target on the wall, pierced by multiple arrows near the center.

"Let's just say I get bored sometimes," explains Oliver.

"Can't you just play darts like everyone else?"

"Sorry I don't really want to be like everyone else."

"I know, you're different. That's why I'm here," says Hailee, "I feel like I can trust you."

"Oh *now* you trust me?" questions Oliver, noticing the rounded bulk of the globe sticking out of Hailee's box.

"I want you to have it," she says.

"Why?" he asks.

"Just for now. For some reason, I feel it will be safer with you" she says, handing him the box.

"Are you sure?" he asks, reaching out to take it.

She nods.

"There's something else I need to tell you," says Hailee. "Something I have not told anyone."

"Okay," says Oliver, curious.

"My brother, Archibald, he disappeared a few days ago."

"Really? How?" he asks.

"I'm not sure. The only thing I know is that this globe has something to do with it."

"I'm sorry what? You think that priest took your brother or something?"

"No, that's not what I'm saying."

"I don't understand then," says Oliver.

"The night Archibald disappeared, I was with him, at home. He was playing with this globe. I kept telling him to turn it off."

"To turn what off?"

"The light. The globe was glowing. Then suddenly, it became even brighter, like lightning. There was that loud thunder sound too. I got so scared, you have no idea. The next thing I know, I opened my eyes and Archibald was gone."

"What do you mean he was gone?"

"Gone. It's like he had... evaporated," says Hailee, about to cry again.

"This is insane," says Oliver.

"I know. But you have to believe me," she says. "I have to go but please don't tell anyone about any of this."

"I won't, I promise."

"This is my number," she says, handing him a piece of paper. "You seem to know so much about everything, I was thinking, maybe you can find something about this globe. And help me get my brother back."

"I'll definitely look into it," says Oliver.

"Thank you. And by the way, sorry I didn't believe you the other day," says Hailee, heading out.

DAUGHTERS
OF NIGHTFALL

Archibald is back in his cabana/prison, only this time, the door is unlocked. He could leave. But to go where? He doesn't even know where he is! So, like any other 11-year-old boy after dinner, Archibald is studying. Cross-legged on his bed, the *Bestiary of Marodors* spread open on his lap, he is getting ready not for an exam, but for a looming battle. That's what it means to do your homework in Gristlemoth.

At his feet, partially hidden under a blanket, the target pillow has found a resting place, and some temporary relief. He is shivering though, his eyes bouncing from side to side, and up, watching out for the next incoming arrow.

"Don't worry Paws, you're safe here", says Archibald, giving his makeshift pet a gentle stroke.

He takes the book outside, where a couple of girls are running through high grass, waving nets, trying to catch fireflies. Sitting on the cabana steps, he can't take his eyes off the beast he is to face tomorrow —the Krakatorum Gargantus. The lack of details in the drawing would almost make it more frightening.

Dad was right, thinks Archibald, *the unknown is always scarier than what you can see.*

The stats alone on that monster don't bode well for the fight ahead. With an average height of 20 feet and a weight (estimated) of 12 to 15 tons, the Krakatorum is a heavyweight in the world of Marodors. Under the influence of the night fires burning around the village, the terrifying beast would almost seem alive, undulating between shadows and sudden flashes of light. Besides the lack of nickname, two facts on the monster's chart worry Archibald more than others, the date of capture and the list of weaknesses —both left blank...

It was not so long ago that Archibald learned in school about rites of passage in certain tribes, from Asia to Africa. In his eyes, fighting that monster represents just that, a leap into manhood that would be second to none; more unpredictable than the Massai initiation, leading wannabe tribal warriors to stalk and kill a lion armed only with a spear; more daring than the *Naghol* from Vanuatu, in which daredevil boys have to throw themselves from huge bamboo towers, tied to tree vines wrapped around the ankle, aiming for a well calculated brush with the ground —and death.

Archibald is looking at his flashlight, turning it on and off, over and over, until the shaft encircles some of the graves next to his cabana. He has never dared getting too close to them. But on a night that feels like his last, he finally does, his eyes lingering on one particular aspect of each grave —the dates, of birth, and death.

"There must be a mistake," he mumbles.

If he believes the markings, one girl, Forestyne Emma Payne, was born in 1501 —and died in 1733! Another one, Abellana Wren Brickenden, lived from 1487 until 1608. And what about Alvina Millicent Ashdown, who passed in 1869, at age 351...

"This doesn't make any sense," says Archibald.

Two people holding torches are heading his way. Even from afar, he can tell one of those silhouettes is Wymer —a fairly easy assumption, since that big guy is the only person in the village over six feet tall. He is coming over with Faerydae.

"What have you been up to?" she asks.

"Nothing really, just getting ready to die," he answers, somber, glancing at the graves.

"I made a little something for you," shouts Wymer, holding that little something in his hand. "Stand up, let's see if it fits," he says.

"What is it?" asks Archibald.

"Well, any knight deserving of that title needs a proper armor!" says Wymer.

"A knight? Me?" asks Archibald, his face now lighting up.

"But of course!" confirms Wymer. "We had a castle already, now we have a knight!"

The armor is very rudimentary, made entirely of rough slices of bark. Wymer places one piece on Archibald's chest, and another one on his back, connecting them together with ropes over his shoulders and two more tied up at the waist.

"It's a bit tight on the chest, I'll have to adjust the bark a little, you're stronger than I thought," says Wymer jokingly, winking at Faerydae.

"You must be kidding!" shouts Archibald. "My armor is made of bark! What's supposed to protect me from that Gigantus is made of bark?"

"Oh but not just any bark," corrects Wymer, "a mighty strong bark, from Dalbergia Melanoxylon."

"That'd better be some magic bark!" hopes Archibald out loud.

"It's blackwood, from Umbraea, the same wood I used to build the tank," notes Wymer.

"Okay but… wait, what? You said tank? You have a tank?" asks Archibald, eyes and mouth wide open.

Wymer just nods and smiles really big, his eyebrows arched high on his forehead.

Wymer is showing the way but he can barely walk, with Archibald stepping in front of him every five seconds, assailing him with questions. His gesticulation makes Faerydae chuckle.

"How big is the cannon?" asks Archibald.

"Big!" assures Wymer.

"Wow!" says Archibald. "How big is the tank?"

"Big!"

"Wow! How fast does it go?"

"As fast as you want it to go!"

"Wow!"

"Can it shoot from any direction?"

"From *any* direction that's for sure."

"Wow!"

Wymer comes to a stop suddenly.

"I'm sorry, I'm in your way?" asks Archibald.

"No, we have arrived!" simply says Wymer, motioning to a house on the side of the road. Unlike the other homes up and down the street, this one has a huge garage door almost covering up the entire façade.

Archibald is puzzled. In his mind, if a tank there was, it had to be hidden in the castle, at the heart of Cleofa, sheltered behind the ramparts, maybe in a secret passage. *Not in a barn!* he erupts internally.

"Welcome to my house!" says Wymer. "Well, this is actually my workshop, *that* is my house," he says, pointing at a tiny hut about ten times smaller than the workshop it's attached to. As a result of that rather unique floor plan, the building as a whole is profiled like a snail. The head of the mollusk —AKA the living hut— is so little that both Archibald and Faerydae wonder how Wymer can even fit in there. It seems hardly bigger than his body!

"I only go in there to sleep. And I never sleep!" he says.

Wymer cringes as he cranks up the garage door. He goes in first, using his torch to light up four more, anchored to the walls around. Little by little, Archibald discovers the silhouette of Wymer's work of art. Not quite what he had in mind, which in many ways makes this combat vehicle even more impressive — unique for sure.

Wymer didn't lie. The tank shell is entirely made out of wood. Circular at the base, with a cone-shaped body ending with a pointy observation turret at the top, it can be best described as the product of a marriage between a turtle and a teapot.

"I have to say, when we got the plans for it, I didn't really know what I was building at first, I had never seen anything like this before," says Wymer, showing a couple of sketches pinned to the wall —which look strangely similar to the Da Vinci sketches Oliver showed Hailee in his dad's store.

"It reminds me of your hat!" Archibald tells Faerydae.

In fact, the wood panels are also covered with the exact same cloak of camouflage material.

"It does, doesn't it?" says Wymer. "I never thought about that!"

Archibald has already shifted his attention to the detail that matters most to him: the cannons, sticking out from small openings all around the tank.

"These are so cool!" he says, trying to count how many there are —eight total.

"Just like I told you, there's no blind side, you can fire from any angle, 360 degrees," explains Wymer.

Archibald notices something by the turret.

"What are those lines up there?" he asks. "Looks like that wave rune from your flag? Nice touch!"

"No that's no rune," corrects Wymer, "those are scratch marks, from a Marodor's claws. That's from last year."

"The Tormentare Arnicolare, that was a toughie!" recalls Faerydae.

"It sure was," notes Wymer. "But hey, at least the tank came back in one piece!"

Archibald sits on the ground, overcome by doubt again.

"I don't think it's going to work," he says. "I mean, no offense Wymer, this tank is awesome but, that beast seems so big. It's just crack-brained!" he says. And looking at Faerydae: "You know, crazy!"

"You gotta believe in this baby. It can withstand a great deal of firepower," assures Wymer, petting his tank. Adding: "We've only lost twelve on the battlefield."

"Only twelve! Oh that's encouraging!" says Archibald, sarcastic of course.

"Don't forget, we also have your special weapon," Faerydae reminds him.

"And that's what's *really* crazy! This is not a special weapon," explodes Archibald, pulling the flashlight out of his pocket. "Don't you understand? This is just a flashlight!" he adds, turning it on and off.

"Don't you point that thing at me again!" says Faerydae, hiding behind the tank.

Even Big Wymer seems afraid. Right now he would gladly hide into a deep hole if he could. And he does, going down a ladder into a deep pit dug underneath the tank —a regular pit hole like you'd find in any other repair shop!

"I just remembered I have to fix one of the pulleys," he argues.

"This is only a flashlight, it's never going to work," repeats Archibald.

"Well it certainly worked the last time you used it," says Faerydae.

"That was just luck," replies Archibald.

"Luck? Archibald, nobody has ever defeated a Marodor that fast before!" she notes.

"Really?" he asks.

"Trust me, you've got something special there, special powers," says Faerydae.

"Special powers?" repeats Archibald, inspecting his flashlight closely again.

Would he actually be starting to believe that flummadiddle?

R

The Sun has barely come out on Gristlemoth. Wymer's tank is rolling through the village, under the applause of many girls lining the streets. Archibald is enjoying the glory. The top turret is flipped open. He is standing up there, hitting his chest armor with his fist while holding his flashlight high in the air. Yesterday a sword, it is now an Olympic torch!

"Here I come!" he shouts, the battle cry he rehearsed in his Grandma's library.

Each time he points his flashlight down, many in the crowd, scared and panicked, duck as if trying to dodge a bullet.

Down below, in a cabin lit solely by fireflies twirling around in jars, Faerydae is driving, looking at the road through a slit cut into the slanted face of the tank. Seated on a tree-stump stool, she has her hands solidly wrapped around the control stick, and her right foot drumming on the brake pedal. Both are connected to a complex system of pulleys and cranks, themselves linked by ropes to four wagon wheels —also made of wood of course.

Right behind Faerydae, Maven and Rhiannon are using golems to activate and feed that ingenious engine.

Conveying the not so discreet grinding sound of a steamboat engine, the wobbly chariot is actually throbbing down the road at a remarkable speed, threatening to topple Archibald from the rickety ladder he is standing on.

Soon, they cross the limits of Gristlemoth, entering the darkness, and Marodor territory. They follow a sinuous path carved into the woods, without a glitch, only a few bumps in the road. Still posted at the turret, Archibald has abandoned his earlier chest thumping. Holding the hatch slightly open above his head, he is trying to hide 99.9% of his body inside the tank, worried of what might pop out from the creepy woods around.

"What's that dust everywhere?" he asks, referring to the thin powder coat he noticed the day he arrived.

"Ashes, not dust," says Maven.

"Ashes? From what? Is there a volcano around here?"

"Not nearby. But your bet is as good as ours," says Rhiannon. "Most likely just Marodors' breath, we're not too sure."

"You're joking right?" he says.

"Nope," they respond in one voice.

"Wymer says the nutrients in ashes are great for fertilizing plants," adds Rhiannon. "If that's true, this land should expect spring to one day prevail over any other season," she says with a smile.

"Well, in the meantime, it's stuck in winter," says Faerydae.

After a six-hour "drive", the tank has a harder time advancing. Behind them are the flat plains and gentle slopes of Gristlemoth. The terrain around here is much more difficult. For the last mile, Faerydae has had to maneuver around rocks and huge tree stumps —a challenge that pales in comparison with what's lying ahead. Slapping the murky surroundings with his flashlight, Archibald is first to spot the problem: the dirt trail will soon shrink to nothing.

"Trouble at twelve o'clock. There's no more road!" he says.

"No, there is, just not quite a road though," says Faerydae.

Archibald's eyes go from squinting to wide open, as he discovers a crumbling cut in the middle of a sheer cliff face.

"That's the Neander Pass," says Rhiannon —more of a mule route in fact, barely wide enough for a car, let alone a tank.

"We can't go through that!" whines Archibald.

"We have no choice," says Faerydae, slowing down to a crawl.

"Have you done this before?" he asks.

"Not with a tank," she says.

It's a tight squeeze. Faerydae is biting her lip, trying to stay within the limits of the narrow path carved right off the cliff's edge. Archibald looks down with a fearful gaze, peaking into the blackness of a seemingly bottomless ravine.

What if that Gargantus showed up now? Archibald thinks to himself, right when a loud walloping noise rattles the cockpit.

"Landslide," whispers Maven, as more rocks come tumbling down from the peaks above.

For everyone onboard, the entire stretch of the pass is a heart-stopping experience —300 mountain-hugging yards of high stress and sweat.

"We made it!" celebrates Rhiannon when they finally reach the end.

"Naida spotted the Krakatorum a mile north of here, only a few minutes away. We could see him at anytime now," says Maven.

"As soon as the Marodor shows up, you hit him with your magic light okay," Faerydae tells Archibald.

"Okay," he says, glancing forward. "But maybe you should get the cannons ready, just in case..." he adds.

Suddenly, the glow from Archibald's flashlight gets dimmer.

"Oh no. No no no, please no," whispers Archibald.

Despite his incantations, the glow gets even dimmer, and dimmer, and dimmer —until it completely dies.

"You wouldn't have any batteries by chance?" he asks the girls, getting a concert of "What?" and "Huh?" in return.

"Two C batteries," he says after unscrewing the bottom of his flashlight.

"C what sorry?" asks Rhiannon.

Archibald is getting dizzy. His body is boiling up, inside and out. He is sweating profusely. He wants to vomit but he's afraid his guts would come out all at once in one chunk —big as a pea. And that paralyzing tingling is back in his legs.

"We have to go back to the village!" he says.

"Have you gotten mad?" says Maven.

"We have to turn around!" he now shouts.

Archibald has turned into a pressure cooker —with no safety valve though. Seeing that the girls have no intention to change course, he pulls himself up, slides down the tank and falls onto the ground.

"What is he doing?" screams Faerydae.

Maven removes two of the golems that were feeding the pulleys energy. A quick loud snap later, the engine has stalled. The tank comes to a grinding halt. The girls leap out through a side hatch. Archibald is sitting on the ground, his flashlight next to him. He looks knocked out.

"Are you okay?" inquires Faerydae.

"No I'm not okay," he whispers to himself. Then repeats it louder: "I'm not okay!"

"What's wrong?" asks Faerydae.

"What's wrong? My flashlight's dead. That's what's wrong!"

"It can't die! It's a magic weapon!" says Faerydae.

"This is bonkers!" he says. "How could I be stupid enough to believe you with that whole magic thing? This was never a magic weapon, it's just a flashlight, you didn't want to listen, and now it ran out of batteries, that's it!"

"You're saying the magic died?" asks Maven.

"I can't believe this. Why don't you guys use your own magic, huh? What kind of witches are you anyway? Don't you have a magic wand like all witches?"

Faerydae looks furious.

"Maven, hand me that please," she says, referring to a crooked twig lying at her feet.

Maven picks it up.

"This?" she questions, wondering what Faerydae could possibly do with it. Sure she knows her friend has more than one trick up her sleeve, like the one (still unexplained) she used a few years back against that vulture Marodor (the Barachia Milamporis, page 105 of the *Bestiary*), to defeat him with his own claws. But "this twig here?" as Maven asks again, she really has no clue what Faerydae has in mind. Archibald wonders the exact same thing —except he is worried about it.

Faerydae grabs the twig, bends it to straighten it up a bit, and brushes her fingers on the tip, before pointing it at Archibald in a threatening manner.

"I told you to not lie to me anymore. Or I would turn you into the little weasel that you are deep inside," she says.

Archibald is crawling on the ground, trying to escape. But Faerydae won't let him. She gets closer, now aiming the twig directly at his face.

"Here is what a magic wand can do," she thunders.

Archibald cringes and closes his eye nearest to the twisted twig.

Faerydae seems about to strike! Instead, she breaks the piece of wood in half and throws it on his lap.

"Nothing, that's what a magic wand can do," she says. "And no, we don't have any flying brooms either!"

Rhiannon lets out the most mischievous, spooky, almost devilish cackle.

156

"Some of us do have a wicked laugh though," admits Maven.

Archibald picks himself back up, still shaking.

"Now get your weapon to work again," says Faerydae.

"It's not a weapon, don't you get it? And the letters on my sweater, that's just from my mom's sorority at Harvard."

"Oh so you like to wear girls' clothes? Maybe your name *is* Ivy?" jokes Rhiannon.

"Don't listen to him, that's just his flummadiddle again!" laments Faerydae.

"You're so disguisy," Maven tells him, coming closer, looking mad as well.

"So *what* now?" he asks.

"Beffudling, always mealy-mouthed," says Rhiannon, moving nearer as well.

"Huh?" lets out Archibald.

"Bamboozling, confusing, full of tricks that's what you are," thunders Faerydae.

"No, I'm not making this up," says Archibald, now surrounded on three sides by menacing figures. "I have no clue where I am or what I'm supposed to do. I just arrived here a few days ago. I had never seen a Marodor before that. I have no magic, the flashlight just followed me here, when I got sucked up into that globe…"

All three girls seemingly freeze at the same time. It takes a few seconds for Faerydae to digest what she has just heard.

"What did you say?" she asks.

"About my flashlight?"

"No, you said something about being sucked up into a globe."

"Yes I did, in my bedroom."

"Who are you?" asks Faerydae, using that threatening tone again.

"We're not going back to that, please!" he says.

157

"There is no globe. They were destroyed a long time ago," says Faerydae.

"Wait, you know about the globe too?" he asks. "Is that the way all of you came here?"

Faerydae is stunned. Maybe he's not a hugger-mugger after all.

"Tell us about that globe you speak of," she says.

"I found it at my parents' home. I mean, my Grandma's house. We had just moved there."

"What did it look like?" inquires Faerydae.

Archibald doesn't know where to start.

"It was round, like a globe, brown, old looking and… with a weird smell."

"What else?" asks Faerydae, visibly impatient.

"There were monsters all over it. I drew several of them. Some looked like the beasts in your book. What else? Oh yes, there was a crack in the globe. But it was not really a crack, more like a button you could press up and down. And I got that key that unlocked the globe. Then I could spin it, and boom, a big flash of light and I was here."

Faerydae is staring at Archibald. He doesn't know how she's going to react.

"You are speaking the truth!" she says, with astonishment in her voice.

The next second, Maven and Rhiannon start jumping up and down and screaming at the top of their lungs.

"What's happening? We are stuck in this nightmare, what's there to celebrate?" asks Archibald.

"You don't understand. We thought all globes had been destroyed," says Faerydae.

It took some time but the girls have now calmed down. Everybody is back in the tank, sitting in a circle. Silence has taken over, so deep and heavy it gave a buzzing life to the fireflies' usually silent symphony, increasing the drama of the moment — the moment of truth for all.

"So, when did you get here?" asks Maven.

"Just a few days ago. The day I met you," says Archibald.

"What was the year?" she asks.

"What?"

"When you left, what year was it?" asks Rhiannon.

"2018," he says. "What about you? When did you get here?"

The girls hold each other's hands for a few seconds.

"We stopped counting a while back," answers Faerydae. "But based on what you just said, about five hundred years ago."

"Yeah right!" chuckles Archibald. He quickly stops though, realizing this is no joke, just by reading their startled faces.

"But... you don't... look 500 years old," he says.

"In Lemurea, you don't get old. Only your mind grows. You learn, you expand your way of thinking. But your physical body doesn't change," she explains.

"What's Lemurea?" he asks.

"It's here, in the Earth's underbelly if you prefer," she says.

"No I don't prefer. I don't prefer at all actually! What kind of country is that?" asks Archibald, with fear and concern in his voice as this new reality sinks in.

"A country far far away," says Faerydae for short.

"How far? Like Ireland?" asks Archibald, seriously.

"Are you sure you're ready for the answer?" asks Faerydae.

"Yes," he says, while shaking his head at the same time.

"It all started at the end of the fifteenth century. Thousands of women across Europe were hunted down, just because they were different, just because they didn't think like everyone else. And when they were caught, they were tortured and put to death in the worst imaginable way, some drowned, many burnt alive."

Faerydae's story reminds Archibald of that shocking scene carved on his Grandma's fireplace. And the same question comes to his mind once again.

"Those women, what did they do?"

"What do you mean?" asks Faerydae.

"To be treated like that," he says. "They must have done something really bad right?"

"If you believe the flummadiddle in that book, they were real monsters. They killed babies, some say they devoured them even. Let's see, what else? Oh yeah, they could trigger hailstorms, rain, and turn into animals! And of course they also cast spells on people, causing them to lose some body parts and things like that."

"Is that true?" asks Archibald, terrified.

"Not really, greatly exaggerated!" says Faerydae. "Their only crime was to be too caring, and way too smart."

"You can never be too smart!" objects Archibald.

"Oh yes you can, trust me, especially women. They offered an alternative to medicine, to religion, to teaching in general. They had become a danger, they were the enemy, they were... witches."

"That's why they were called witches?" he says.

"Yes. I know it sounds crazy, but it didn't take much to be called a witch back then. In reality, they were just nature lovers, believing in the power of plants and herbs. They were healers, they were life worshippers, they were... our mothers."

"Your mothers?" exclaims Archibald, not quite following.

Maven and Rhiannon just nod to confirm.

"Imagine what those women had to go through, every single day," says Faerydae. "Imagine what it means to live in constant fear and terror, being forced to flee your village or town to survive, moving from one place to another, hiding. Based on what was happening to them, it was easy to assume that their daughters would meet the same fate. *We,* would grow up to suffer the same persecution. Our mothers knew they had to do something to protect us. We were birthed as the daughters of nightfall."

"Is that why they sent you here?" asks Archibald. "To save you?"

"That was the idea, yes," says Rhiannon.

"But it's a bit more complicated," adds Faerydae. "Something else was happening in the world. Always more wars, more massacres, more blood being spilled. What our mothers were trying to heal, or protect, Men were busy destroying. At one point, the Earth couldn't take it anymore. Even our mothers couldn't do much. All that blood seeping through the ground gave birth to demons… the Marodors."

"Wait, the Marodors are demons?" asks Archibald.

"That's why they can't be killed. In a way, they *are* death," says Faerydae.

Archibald's world is thrown off balance suddenly:

"I don't understand. Those demons live inside the Earth? We are inside the Earth?" he asks, panicked.

"Not exactly no," says Faerydae. "Lemurea is more like a parallel dimension, some sort of underworld. At first, the Marodors were confined here, with no direct access to the Earth. Nobody could see them. That was until the winter of 1482, when some sailors from Ireland got caught in a storm…

Through the power of lightning, that storm created a temporary passage that brought them to the underworld. They were the first ones to witness the demons. The same storm carried them back to Ireland, where they told their story. They thought they had landed on an island nobody had discovered yet. So people started drawing that island on maps.

"And they drew the Marodors too!" notes Archibald.

"They thought they were just sea-monsters," smiles Faerydae. "But our mothers knew better. They knew about Lemurea. They knew those monsters were demons. More boats followed. More storms. More stories. More mysterious islands started to pop up on maps everywhere. And more Marodors. A handful of them even managed to escape Lemurea through those storms. One sank boats off the coast of Ragusa. Another terrorized a village in Carinthia. And the wars didn't stop. With more blood seeping into the ground, there were more and more Marodors. Their power was growing by the day. Our mothers knew it was only a question of time before they could access the Earth... and take their revenge against Men."

"So why not let them if those men were also trying to kill your mothers?" remarks Archibald.

"I know right, you would think! Sometimes I wonder why they didn't," says Faerydae.

"Instead, they turned you into guardian-angels," he notes. "Guardian-angels fighting demons."

"I never thought about it that way," says Faerydae. "But that's the thing, our mothers also believed in the best in Men. They believed the human race was worth saving. And more importantly, they believed people could change."

"So what happened?" asks Archibald.

"They had two goals in mind. First, put us out of reach of the witch-hunters, but at the same time, they knew someone had to fight those demons, not on Earth, but here, in the underworld. So they passed on their knowledge and powers to us. Then they sent us here."

"That's what the globe was for?" asks Archibald.

"The idea was to recreate the conditions of those storms that allowed sailors to travel to Lemurea. To do that, witches from all over Europe combined their powers. But it was not enough. They had a dear friend in Italy, a great inventor. He found a way to build a machine powerful enough to make us travel here. He had to hide that machine, so he put it in a globe. He actually used the globe itself to make the machine inside easy to use, with just a spin."

"He's also the one who came up with the idea for this tank," says Rhiannon.

"Really?" asks Archibald.

"That man was brilliant," says Maven.

"He built a total of five globes," points out Faerydae. "They were taken to all corners of Europe, to make it easier for us to travel, and save as many young witches as possible."

"What happened to those globes?"

"Two of them were found by witch-hunters, and smashed to pieces. Two were lost in wars. We used the last one, which was destroyed as well. At least that's what we thought... until today."

"What does it change anyway?" asks Archibald. "I'm here and the globe didn't come with me."

"It never does. The globe always stays where it is used, that's just the way it works. The storm it generates will take anything, and anyone, within a twelve-foot radius. You just can't take the globe with you when you travel. There's a trick though: someone else *can* use it to bring you back."

"How?" he asks.

"I'm not sure but I think that's why the globe stays behind."

"Maybe you can come back with me then!" says Archibald, with a half smile, thinking maybe this nightmare could end soon.

"I'd rather not get my hopes up," says Faerydae.

"You know, where I come from, people don't burn witches anymore," says Archibald.

"Maybe they don't, but I'm sure they still find a way to keep them silent," notes Faerydae.

"And what about wars? There are no more wars either?"

"Not too many," says Archibald.

"Really?" says Maven.

Archibald nods.

"So why are there more and more demons down here then?" questions Faerydae.

Archibald doesn't quite know what to say to that.

Another question he doesn't have any answer to: why would his Grandma have that globe in her house if she hated witches so much, as proven by that horrible fireplace in her living room?

ß

Archibald spent the next fifteen minutes trying to convince Faerydae he was ready for battle. He argued passionately that not only he had the necessary experience, but also the required skills to take on the Krakatorum Gargantus. It sounded very much like a job interview.

He bragged about catching a "ginormous" lizard with his bare hands once, so big his arms wouldn't stretch wide enough to describe the size of that creature —in fact a sixteen-inch gecko that had escaped its container at the pet store and that he held by the tail for two seconds, before screaming for help. But why bother the girls with such insignificant details —clutter to the story really.

He also mentioned his extensive training in aikido, once a week for five months, two years ago. Key to that martial art: "You use your opponent's strength against him, the bigger the opponent, the easier it will be to defeat him," explained the white belt champion. How that technique would translate into fighting a beast like the Krakatorum, he did not elaborate.

"Just trust the ancient Japanese," he simply said, "and Mr. Edwards," his aikido teacher from the Mall, who doubles as security guard at that same Mall on the weekends.

At the bottom of his resume, if needed to close the deal, Archibald threw in two side accomplishments, admittedly more minor but still with the potential to tip the balance in his favor.

One: Diving from the highest board at camp last summer —it was five feet high but who's keeping tabs.

Two: Holding his breath under water for a full minute —more a surviving necessity than a shot at a medal really, since Tanner was pressing on his head the whole time, trying to drown him.

Surprisingly, Archibald left out one truly remarkable skill, that no one would question or take away from him: always being the first one to run from danger —real or perceived, like that time he escaped his gym class thinking he was chased by a bee.

When it became clear he had exhausted that highly remarkable collection of exploits, Archibald left it for the girls to judge.

"What do you say?" he asked.

Probably because she didn't understand half of it, Rhiannon almost bought his spiel. Maven, not so much. In fact, she cracked up so hard her sudden laughter made Archibald jump, which in turn helped brush aside any doubt Faerydae could have —and she had very few.

In the end, Wymer's tank is back on the march. But it made a U-turn, headed back where it came from. Archibald is not at the turret anymore. He is sitting in the cockpit alongside Rhiannon and Maven, with Faerydae still at the commands.

"Why do we have to go back to Gristlemoth?" he complains.

"I told you already," says Faerydae, "since that magic weapon of yours happens to not be so magic after all, we have to put you in safety. We're going back to Gristlemoth, then we'll go fight that Marodor without you."

"I feel so useless," says Archibald grumpily.

"Look, you have to face reality," says Maven, "you don't know anything about golems, in the middle of a fight, you'd be a total nuisance for us. Not only would you be of no help whatsoever, but you could get hurt."

"You should consider yourself lucky," says Rhiannon. "Back in Gristlemoth, you can have fun with the girls."

"And do what? Laundry?" he jokes.

"And what's wrong with doing laundry?" ask the girls all at once.

"Look, no offense" he says, "I'm not sure if you guys are trying to make me feel better, but just so you know, it's not working for some reason."

"We're just telling you the truth," says Maven, bluntly.

"I think I've had enough truth for today thanks," he says. "Enough to last me my whole life actually, which now might last a thousand years, who knows?"

"Maybe not!" comments Faerydae, who has switched back to grave and serious.

"What's happening?" asks Rhiannon, getting up right away.

"Marodor, right ahead," shouts Faerydae. "That's the Krakatorum."

"He's attacking Gristlemoth!" echoes Rhiannon.

This is the worst-case scenario Faerydae warned about. In a wheeling movement worthy of Napoleon's most brilliant tactic — or just because he likes to venture off the beaten trail—, the Krakatorum Gargantus must have crawled in a semicircle from the

Neander Pass, through the woods. That's how he avoided their tank.

Peering through the slits in the planks, Rhiannon and Archibald discover the giant beast. Tall as a palm tree, the Krakatorum is as scary as the drawing could suggest —and then some. He is pushing against the wall of golems using his spider legs, some with sharp pikes, and some, with human hands. Sticking out from that dark mound of fur and leaves are not three, but four worm-like necks, confirming Naida's description. Lined with a mohawk of branches, each of those necks ends with the most ghoulish face, lost in patches of swampy hair.

What makes the Krakatorum so awesomely creepy is the look on those faces, utterly blank, lifeless, until the mouth gapes open, so wide it eats up everything around, eyes, nose and chin. One of them just did, spitting fire between fences of crisscrossing teeth. The flames go over the rampart of golems, but luckily bounce off the wall of light.

"Holy, giant, Bejabbles," lets out Archibald.

"We've got a dragon on our hands!" says Faerydae.

Even though the necks are also covered with lizard scales, for Archibald, something doesn't add up.

"That thing is no dragon," he says, sounding disappointed almost.

"And what do you think it is then?" asks Rhiannon.

"I have no idea," he says, "but not a dragon!"

"Because you know so much about dragons!" says Rhiannon.

"That thing can't even fly!" he argues.

"We don't have time for this!" yells Faerydae. "He's trying to break through the wall. If he does, more Marodors will come in, we all know what that means," she adds, looking at the girls with her most severe face yet.

All four of his heads are seemingly acting independently from one another, some focused on the village, the others on the incoming tank. It's like fighting an enemy equipped with a second pair of eyes behind his head —three extra pairs in this case!

"Let's fire at him!" says Archibald.

"Where are the cannonballs?" he asks, lifting blankets but finding only crates of golems underneath.

"Cannonballs wouldn't do anything, Marodors have thick skin!" says Rhiannon.

"Then what do we do?" he asks.

"We fire these golems at him," she says.

"But *you* don't do anything. You just stay put," says Rhiannon.

"No!" shouts Faerydae, "We'll need all the help we can get, let him shoot too."

"Are you sure?" Rhiannon asks her.

"Yes, I'm sure," confirms Faerydae.

Then, sharing a deep stare with Archibald: "You can help us right?"

He nods, thankful, smiling with his eyes.

"You know how to aim?" asks Maven.

"Do I know how to aim? I went through all the missions in my sniper game in one week-end!"

"I have no idea what you just said, but okay," says Maven.

"A video game!" exclaims Archibald. "That's what I'm best at, I can't believe I forgot to mention it earlier."

"Look," explains Maven, "the goal is not just to hit the Marodor, that would be too easy. Remember the chalkboard, the golems work together. So we have to fire three of them pretty much at the same time."

"How do I know which golems to fire?" he asks, lost just looking at all the different runes in front of him.

"Don't worry about that. I'll pick them for you. Just make sure you aim right, okay?"

"Okay," says Archibald, taking position behind two cannons.

"Hurry!" shouts Faerydae. "We are almost within range."

Maven is holding her head between her hands, scanning the golems, trying to figure out which ones will work best.

"Perfidrae, Eolare, Draconia," she finally says, handing one golem to Rhiannon, one to Archibald, and keeping one for herself.

Rhiannon and Maven place their stone into a slot located at the back of the cannons. Archibald just mimics them.

"How do you fire?" he asks, seeing no trigger.

"Each cannon is mounted on powder golems, the same that heat up Karl and Karla, only much more powerful," says Maven.

"When you're ready, just push your golem into the slot and say 'Propellia Momentum', the cannon will fire," explains Faerydae.

"Propel what? Couldn't you guys just say fire!" he whines.

The Krakatorum is finally within striking distance, about two hundred feet off. Rhiannon taps on the golem to load it fully, and pronounces the triggering words... Her cannon goes off in an ear-splitting roar. It's a hit! The golem doesn't quite penetrate the Marodor's body but it gets stuck right under his skin —his scales to be exact, layered like the flower buds of an artichoke.

"Your turn Archibald, quick!" says Maven.

One sharp poke and his golem is in. He points his cannon at the beast.

"Propellia Momentum!" he shouts.

Another loud bang resonates through the cockpit... And it's a hit too! The golem disappears among the multitude of eyes studding the spider's face.

"So much better than my video game!" says the sharp shooter.

They have to switch positions though since the tank is now facing the wrong way.

"To the other side," says Rhiannon.

That's the point of having cannons all around the tank. Maven fires the last golem of the spell, Draconia, hitting the Krakatorum in the belly. All three golems glow at once. Seconds later, the beast starts coughing. And choking.

One after another, the Marodor's heads are rendered all but useless, collapsing and dangling on the side of his body like dirty old socks —two out of four.

"Hurray!" shouts Rhiannon, high-fiving Archibald.

"What was that? Internal boiling?" he asks.

"Close. More like a crushing of the lungs!" says Maven.

"What about that looping tail? Why don't we use that spell to finish him?" suggests Archibald.

"He doesn't have a tail!" notes Rhiannon.

"So? Maybe we use his necks to tie up his legs?" he says.

"Too complicated, too many limbs to worry about," gauges Maven. And she obviously has the last say.

"Well we need something, and quick!" says Faerydae. "Two of his heads are still working! That's enough to destroy Gristlemoth."

In fact, the Krakatorum has managed to partially push aside one of the huge golems of the wall. The breach allows him to spew some of his lava breath deep inside the village, spreading panic. He is now trying to squeeze in. On the other side, Naida and others are pushing back, armed mostly with bows. But as feared, their arrows are too weak to pierce the beast's carapace.

"The wall won't last much longer," says Faerydae.

She slaloms between trees to avoid the balls of fire the Krakatorum is spitting. One of them comes near to burning the tank turret. Another one is aimed at Gristlemoth, setting ablaze a guard tower where several girls had taken position, trying to set up an extra cannon. As the tower collapses on the outer boulders, one of the girls is snatched by the spider half of the Krakatorum.

"That's Willow!" screams Faerydae, recognizing the girl who alerted her a few days ago in the Marodor's pen.

Maven is trying to pick a new set of golems. But panic has taken over. She hesitates.

"Please hurry!" says Faerydae.

Prisoner of the monster's arms and claws, Willow, already injured by the fall, has no wiggle room to put up a fight. Only when the spider brings her close does she try to kick that ugly face. But the danger comes from above. One of the Marodor's necks plunges on the young girl and anchors itself to her chest. In frightened awe, Archibald witnesses that hug of death Faerydae talked about. The embrace is horribly peaceful, with Willow seemingly suffocating, as if every ounce of life was being drained out of her. A spark slowly spreads to turn her pupils bright red, the flame soon engulfing her eyes almost entirely.

"Maven! What's taking so long?" yells Faerydae.

The rune expert seems at a loss.

"Maybe this," she says: "Achillae, Moonesterum, Fraxinus."

"What's that?" asks Rhiannon.

Maven just nods, meaning, "trust me". She fires her golem first, again hitting the Krakatorum, in the chest. It's Rhiannon's turn. She missed. The golem gets lost in the trees.

"Sorry," she sighs. "I was afraid to hit Willow."

"Hurry or soon she won't be Willow anymore," says Maven, handing her another golem.

This time, Rhiannon adjusts her aim and hits the Marodor in one of his front legs. Her perfect shot causes the beast to let go of Willow, by throwing her aside, against the wall of golems.

"What have I done?" gasps Rhiannon.

Unable to say another word, or make another move, she is all but paralyzed. Maven tries to shake her out of her torpor. But nothing will. It all depends on Archibald now. With all that firing, smoke has engulfed the tank cockpit. Archibald can't see much. He squints, trying to tune out all the noise and craziness around him. Finally, he gives one more yell:

"Propellia Momentum!"

It's also a hit —a close call though. The golem lodges itself in one of the Marodor's limp sock faces.

"Does it count?" asks Archibald.

"It will do," says Maven. And sure enough, the three golems light up. Their combined energy seems to act as a giant hammer. The Krakatorum is hit with such force to his head(s) that he loses his balance. He is staggering, growling —and about to collapse. And that's just the first effect of the spell. Next comes the impact from Fraxinus: several of the spider legs get entangled, and more importantly, the two dragon necks still alive roll around one another, to end up tied into a knot.

"We got him!" shouts Maven, confident they have the beast at their mercy.

Suddenly though, one of the golems detaches from the Marodor's body, making the other two fade and quickly go dead. Nearly unconscious, two of the beast's faces reopen their glaring eyes. The fire-breathing demon regains his full strength in an instant, using one of his necks to hit the tank ferociously.

The shock is tremendous.

Da Vinci's war machine is sent flying through the air. Countless flips later, it comes crashing against a tree.

Wymer witnesses the drama from another guard tower inside Gristlemoth. His growing eyes soon match the diameter of the binoculars, some funky periscope rising two feet above his head — a complex system of concave mirrors and optical glasses linked together through strings and putty.

The Krakatorum approaches the tank, now upside-down like a spinning top. Rhiannon is the only one still inside, pinned underneath the planks, one of her legs crushed by a cannon. She's trying to grab her bow and arrow, but her favorite weapon is out of reach.

Lying nearby, the other crewmembers have been ejected on impact like ragdolls, along with the rest of the cannons and all the ammunition. They are barely moving. Archibald's vision is blurry but he sees the Krakatorum getting closer. Faerydae is lying right in the monster's path.

"Careful, he's coming!" Archibald warns her.

Faerydae stands back up painfully. She's not in good shape either. Noticing the golems scattered on the ground, she picks up two of them and punches the dirt, sticking the stones deep inside. After murmuring a few words, she runs out of the way. When the Krakatorum charges toward her, the ground opens underneath him, right where Faerydae placed her golems. The Marodor falls down into the hole and breaks several of his spider legs at the bottom, thirty feet below.

She's amazing! Archibald says to himself.

Faerydae huffs. But the Krakatorum claws his way back up, and rears his head out of the hole, —the one still up and brewing. He switches his focus on Maven, still unconscious on the ground, creeping toward her with wide-open jaws.

Sensing the imminent danger, Archibald looks to Faerydae for another spell or miracle parry, but she is now too far to intervene.

Archibald has to improvise. He makes a "T" with his hands — one of the signs Faerydae taught him. She got it. He is ready for a diversion —his specialty since he tried getting those keys from Bartholomeo.

Faerydae shakes her head, worried, but Archibald has already made up his mind. Surprisingly, his legs are not tingling.

He runs behind the Krakatorum and hurls both golems and insults at the Marodor, now only a few feet away.

"Hey chicken dragon! Hey you giant turd!" he screams out of his lungs, taunting the beast.

Taking the bait, the towering monster turns his neck around and spews his embers at Archibald, who disappears in the blast.

"Noooooo!" screams Faerydae.

Archibald's desperate move has given Maven precious time to grab some golems from the ground. She crawls to a large oak tree nearby and hugs it, holding the golems in her hands. Her eyes are closed. She whispers something, as if she was talking to the tree.

When the Krakatorum turns back to her, the tree bends towards the Marodor and swats his last remaining head with a branch. Two more blows, and the beast is twisting in agony, ready to give up. The tree unleashes more branches to grab the Marodor and squeeze him against its main trunk, each head and neck now firmly held prisoners in a tight armlock.

Ambers are still floating in the air when Naida arrives with a handful of young fighters, reinforcing the end-of-the-world atmosphere of the scene. Carefully extracted from the tank wreck, Rhiannon is relieved to see Willow coughing her way back to life —not a speck of red left in her eyes.

"That was close," says Naida, squatted down, her hand on Willow's chest.

On the other end of the battlefield, it's bad news. Faerydae is desperately looking for Archibald. Among burnt out trees and shrubs, the only thing she finds is a piece of breastplate armor — carbonized. Tears start mounting in her eyes, when she hears a faint cough coming from a bush nearby.

"You're alive!" shouts Faerydae, discovering Archibald entangled with creeper branches, his hair partially burnt in the back and his face darkened by the Krakatorum's fire. Deflected for the most part by Wymer's armor, the blast has poked dozens of small holes through his skin. They are now glowing like lava craters, dotting his face and his hands.

"This was just a bad, bad dream," Archibald mumbles, looking at his fingers sparkle in the dark. His body is so numb he doesn't feel any pain.

"How do you like that blackwood bark now?" she asks, taking him in her arms.

By nightfall, Gristlemoth has switched to celebration mode. The town fared relatively well, and is back to —kind of— safe. Yes, a handful of homes have gone up in flames. Maven has a black eye. Faerydae has bruises on the side of her pretty face. Archibald's head looks like it was toasted on medium, and he had to trade his Mom's sweater, in tatters, for a medieval style tunic. They all know it could have been much worse though. Even Rhiannon's shattered leg seems like a small price to pay to stop the Krakatorum. Smoke has not completely cleared yet but everyone has assembled in Cleofa to enjoy the feast Wymer prepared, the tables piled high with food.

"Mmh! This Marodor is cooked just right!" he says, stirring Karl's insides from the top of a ladder.

The whole kitchen/dining hall falls silent suddenly. All eyes are on Wymer, who couldn't feel more uncomfortable, unless his beard was half-shaven, his flummadiddle had not risen and his fly was left open —all at once.

"Not amusing," Karl tells him.

"I'm kidding, you know it's mostly veggies!" corrects the Chef, allowing the room to go back to loud and festive.

Maven is at a table with Archibald. Corn chowder is the soup of the day. She is sort of the hero of the day. Sparing her audience no detail, she explains which golems she picked to defeat the Krakatorum Gargantus —and why.

"See, when you combine Moonesterum with the Achillae rune, the Marodor is going to be destabilized," she explains, using breadcrumbs and beans to reenact the battle. "But if you add the twisting of the Fraxinus rune, that's it, the beast doesn't stand a chance, doesn't stand at all actually," she chuckles, pushing a larger crumb that finishes to collapse her already shaky six-bean high tower.

"What about the tree though? How did you do that?" he asks.

"I just asked him for help," says Maven. "You've never talked to trees before?"

"Not like that no," he says.

"I'll teach you if you want," she says.

"I want to know!" says Lenora, joining them.

Archibald doesn't say no. But he's had another question on his mind: "The Krakatorum, is it really a dragon?"

"You still have doubts? Look at your face!" jokes Lenora, referring to his forehead and cheeks, tan to a reddish pecan brown.

"It's just that… it doesn't look like a dragon."

"So tell us, what's a dragon supposed to look like?" she asks.

"You know, big nostrils, scissor-sharp teeth, flaming eyes, a snake's tongue, huge batwings and a spine of horns, everybody knows that!" he says.

"Have you seen one before?" asks Lenora.

"No," he admits.

"So trust me, *this* is the real thing!" she says, pointing at the beans now scattered on the table.

"You're right though," adds Maven, "some Marodors have all that, the bat wings, the snake's tongue, the scary looking teeth, the flaming eyes, and yes, even a spine of horns sometimes. But that's not what makes them dragons."

"What does then?" he asks.

"The fire they spit!" says Maven.

"So, all those monsters in the Bestiary, the wolf owl, the beetle skunk or the rat raven, they're all dragons?"

"Many of them are, yes," she confirms.

For Archibald, it's years of certainties, fed by books, movies and tales from all continents, that suddenly crumble.

Two tables away, a girl just started playing a weird instrument that vaguely resembles a guitar. Another joins her with a flute. And another with a harp. A bunch of people quickly surround them, singing and swaying as one.

"Sounds like Grandpa's music," says Archibald. Not quite the kind of beat that will inspire him to show off those moves he's managed to keep private.

"Wait, is that Rhiannon?" he wonders aloud, surprised to see her among the growing crowd of dancers.

"Yes," confirms Lenora. "Willow is still at the hospital but Rhiannon is already back on her feet" —limping a little on those feet, but incredibly, her wounds and pain seem to have all but vanished.

"How's that possible? I thought she broke her leg in the tank?" says Archibald.

"She sure did," says Maven. "So many broken bones, it took hours and four golems to fix them all."

"You can do that?" he exclaims, amazed.

"Of course!" she says, almost offended that he would doubt her powers. "Do you want to know how?"

"Maybe later," says Archibald, scanning the room, obviously looking for someone.

Now Maven's feelings are truly hurt.

"Have you seen Faerydae?" he asks.

"I think I saw her step outside a few minutes ago," says Lenora.

Archibald finds her on a terrace in the very back of the dining hall. She is looking at the sky, the most somber look plaguing her face, observing the Marodors flying near the Gristlemoth perimeter. With the music playing in the background, the contrast is startling.

"Are you okay?" he asks.

"What will happen next time?" she says.

"What do you mean?" asks Archibald.

"What if we had come back an hour later? Even just half an hour. What would we have found?" she asks.

Archibald understands. At the same time, his doubts and questions are still of the most basic kind.

"Demons? Dragons? What are those things really?" he asks. "I know you said they were born from the blood spilled on Earth but… it just doesn't make sense."

"Well, the story goes that the first breeds of Marodors were just insects, feeding off that blood directly from the ground. That's why many of them still have body parts from termites, beetles, spiders, you name it."

"And you guys thought that eating bug burgers would be a good idea!" jokes Archibald. "No wonder why Marodors are so angry, you're eating their cousins, their kids maybe!"

Faerydae chuckles.

"What about the other parts by the way?" asks Archibald more on a more serious note. "The animal and people parts…"

"We're not sure, probably a mix of humans killed in battles and animals slaughtered on Earth. If you believe that, demons just haunt this underworld, waiting for their return, for their revenge."

"Look at their faces, they look so human," says Archibald. "Have you thought about treating them differently," he suggests.

"What do you mean, differently?"

"I mean, what's the point of capturing them? To keep them in cages forever?"

"That's what we do, that's what we're here for, to keep them under control, so they can't access the Earth," says Faerydae. "And don't get me wrong, they might look human, but they're mostly animals."

"I don't think they're just animals. Actually, I don't think animals are just animals. Anyway, humans or animals, are we really that different?" Archibald wonders aloud.

"Maybe not on Earth, but in this world we are," she says.

"I'm not sure," mutters Archibald.

"Do you think someone will get you back up there?" she asks.

"I really don't know," says Archibald. "By the way, when we met, you called me an accident. What did you mean by that?"

"I don't know if you've noticed but, there are not many boys around. Only girls were sent down here. They were the only ones in danger. Boys, not so much. So when we find one, we know for sure he was a mislimp, an accident."

"Is Wymer a... mislimp too?"

"One hundred percent," she confirms.

"How did he get here?"

"He was drunk! He fell asleep under the table where we had put the globe. We didn't see him. He got absorbed with everyone else in the room."

"So no then," says Archibald.

"What do you mean, no?" she asks.

"It's just a better answer to your question. No, I don't think anyone will get me back up there. Because you were right, I was definitely an accident too. And see that's the problem. I'm just like Wymer. It's not like anyone else knows how I came down here, so I doubt anyone will ever bring me back."

"Can you do me a favor then?" asks Faerydae.

"I don't know. What is it?"

"Don't say any of this to the girls. They all think they'll be coming with you when you leave..."

HUNTERS AND PREYS

Pancake flipping on Shrove Tuesday is a big thing for the Finch family. That, and watching the Queen's speech on Christmas day. But five days before is another ritual, this one dreaded by all: visiting Grandpa Harvey —or as Hailee puts it, prayer day. It has nothing to do with saying grace before dinner —even though a few uttered words might not be unwise for those hoping to survive the food. Hailee's consideration is somewhat more down to Earth. Each time, she calls upon the skies for help, wishing for a hail-storm, a tornado, a swarm of winter locusts, or just more snow, anything that would derail this annual event. With Archibald gone, she found some solace in the certainty that the gathering would be cancelled. But Grandpa Harvey insisted...

"He'll be back before Christmas," he assures, cutting his tradi-tionally overcooked meatloaf.

"We surely hope so Dad," sighs Kate.

"Trust me, this kind of thing gets resolved quickly, on TV at least..." he says.

"*What* kind of thing?" asks Hailee.

"It's okay, we don't need to know," says Kate, a bit nervous.

She knows her father has lost some of his marbles in the last few years. He is notorious for saying the most unpredictable — some would say inappropriate— things. Just last week, Kate had to call the local bakery to apologize on his behalf, after he told the sales person she had, quote, "the most beautiful buns"...

At 87, he is still jelly though. Tonight, he is wearing a snowman sweater with a blinking carrot nose. He matched that with a small green elf hat on his shiny white hair, the same he strapped around

Stuart's head with a rubber band, making his cheeks all puffed up as if he had a tooth infection. Kate can consider herself lucky. She got a cute reindeer's hat.

"Put your branches on like your Mom!" he tells Hailee.

"Not branches Dad, they're antlers," Kate corrects nicely.

"Oh that's what those are huh!" he says, nodding.

"I'm good thank you," says Hailee with a fake smile, while staring at her phone on her lap.

"Hailee, I told you a thousand times, it's very impolite to be on your phone during dinner."

"I'm not Mom," defends Hailee. "I'm just expecting something important."

She has not heard from Oliver in two days. She is starting to wonder whether she gave him the right number —or if something terrible happened to him too.

"Have they asked you for a ransom yet?" Grandpa Harvey asks out of the blue, making Stuart finally swallow that piece of meatloaf he had been chewing on for the last five minutes.

"Dad no!" gasps Kate, dropping her fork. "Archibald was not kidnapped! Please don't say that. We don't know anything."

Hailee rolls her eyes. The truth, nothing coming out of Grandpa Harvey's mouth can hurt her anymore —except for that spluttering of course. Besides, if she needed a good excuse to be a no show next year, he has just offered it to her on a platter —and that's a much more enjoyable course than his meatloaf.

"I'm sorry," says Grandpa Harvey. "You're right, it's too soon."

Kate can breath, for about half a second…

"If they don't ask for money by next week, you should start to worry though," adds Grandpa Harvey, bringing consternation back on Kate and Stuart's faces.

Hailee checks her phone again. Still no message from Oliver.

"What about those orphanages Celestine left behind?" asks Grandpa Harvey.

"It's all good, they're well taken care of," answers Kate.

"Except for one of them where half the kids disappeared," mentions Stuart.

"What do you mean disappeared?" asks Grandpa Harvey.

"Yes, what do you mean disappeared?" asks Hailee, maybe seeing a link with what happened to Archibald.

"They didn't disappear sorry, escaped would be more accurate," corrects Stuart. "They packed all their things and left. Nobody knows where they went. It happened around the time of Celestine's death. Maybe they got upset. They were all so close to her."

"We don't have much to do with the orphanages. She had good people taking care of them, nothing will change really," says Kate, worried her loose cannon of a father will start talking about Archibald's adoption in front of Hailee.

"Before I forget, I have a gift for you young lady," Grandpa Harvey tells Hailee.

All giggly, he heads to the kitchen, the second of his three-room charming house, where he kept his surprise present.

"Great!" says Stuart, eager to switch to a different topic —and leave.

"Great," cringes Kate, much less optimistic, still remembering what he bought her daughter last year. Hailee has not forgotten either.

"Another gift card for a tattoo, Grandpa?" she asks.

"What's wrong with that? Kids love tattoos these days!" he says.

"Not thirteen-year-old girls," says Kate.

"Well, *this* will be useful," he says, excited, placing the roughly wrapped gift next to her on the table.

"Maybe I should wait until Christmas?" suggests Hailee.

"No no no, I want to see the look on your face," he says, grinning widely.

Hailee unwraps her gift slowly. Her parents brace for the worst.

"Surprise!" shouts Grandpa Harvey as Hailee discovers a brand new... pocket knife and mace spray kit.

"For self-defense," he points out.

"That's not bad!" comments Stuart.

"Not *too* bad," whisper Kate and Hailee at the same time.

"Like that you won't get kidnapped like your brother!" says Grandpa Harvey. "Anyone wants more meatloaf?" he asks.

But Kate has gone very pale. And everyone has definitely had enough —meatloaf and all.

"Why did you guys accept his invite in the first place," Hailee yells at her parents from the back seat of the car.

"Give him a break. He has a good heart," says Stuart.

"Just not a very sound brain," adds Kate. "I feel bad having him alone in that tiny house."

"How could you even think that going there would be a good idea, especially without Archibald?" says Hailee.

"Look, we all miss Arch very much," says Stuart. "But we have to keep our spirits up, that means living as much of a normal life as possible. Tonight was exactly about that, focusing on something else just for one evening?"

"Oh that was the point? That definitely worked Dad!" reacts Hailee with a sarcastic tone.

Thankfully Grandpa Harvey doesn't live too far —for everyone's sake in the car. They are back home in fifteen minutes. They were away for less than two hours total but it felt like eight. They are drained. Kate and Hailee head to the front door while

Stuart looks for something behind one of the two winged lions guarding the entrance. From an empty flowerpot, digging through a few dead leaves, he pulls out that famous ring of keys Bartholomeo carried around everywhere.

"We really have to change the locks," he says. "I mean, look at the size of this thing! We can't even take our house keys with us, it's ridiculous! Can you imagine me going to the office with this?" he says, posing with that huge cumbersome set of skeleton keys.

"Or maybe you could do the opposite," Kate says, "and get matching keys for the car?"

"My chariot you mean?" he says.

Kate and Stuart share a laugh and even manage to crack a faint smile on Hailee's face.

"I don't even know what some of these open," he says, "especially these four small ones, I've tried everything."

As soon as he enters, Stuart knows there's a problem. Something seems stuck between the door and the wood floor. It sounds like gravel. Stuart turns the lights on, realizing a marble goddess statue has fallen off its pedestal and is now strewn in pieces all over the foyer.

"Careful where you step?" he warns.

"What happened?" asks Kate.

"The statue fell down," he says.

It's more than the statue though. Kate pushes the door wide open, revealing the full extent of the damage. Jackets and rain boots seem to have flown out of the coat closet and landed on the stairs nearby. The rugs are folded in half. Each drawer lining the side of the staircase is open, its content scattered around, mixed with the debris from two other sculptures broken on the floor.

"Maybe an animal snuck in?" says Stuart.

"And went through the drawers?" snaps Hailee.

"Maybe it was that thunder again, the same thing that happened the night Archie disappeared?" says Kate. "Maybe he was right. Maybe this house is haunted," she whispers.

"Guys, I'm no Sherlock Holmes but this was no thunder," says Hailee, pointing at dirt shoe prints on the steps and on the rugs.

"Burglars!" says Stuart, making Kate jump. "Maybe they are still here, we have to call the police."

Stuart pushes everyone outside. The only one not to panic is Hailee, as if she knew who was behind this and what they were looking for.

Perhaps because of what happened to Archibald less than two weeks ago, no less than three police cars are dispatched to the Finch residence. Wearing fluorescent yellow jackets, their guns drawn, it takes 8 officers nearly an hour to clear all 56 rooms of the house. Two things for sure: based on the footprints, there were at least two burglars —big guys, with large shoe sizes. And they came in from the back, by breaking a window in the kitchen.

Since the Police didn't find anyone, Kate and Stuart can now go through the house to assess the damage. It's even worse than what they feared. The library has been completely ransacked. Only a few books are left standing upright on the shelves. The rest are on the floor. Same thing in the kitchen and the pantry, where everything has been taken out of the cupboards. In the living room, Celestine's old china has not been spared. The cabinet it was in has been knocked down. Even the Christmas tree is lying on its side. Surprisingly though, nothing seems to be missing.

"You're sure they didn't take anything?" asks one of the Police officers. Twice.

"We still have a few things to check but no, I don't think they did," says Stuart.

"Some paintings perhaps?" inquires the officer, pointing at the two empty spots on the wall in the staircase.

"No," says Stuart. "Those were missing already when we moved in."

"To be honest, Mister Finch, there are lots of break-ins and burglaries at this time of the year, especially in neighborhoods like this one," says the officer. "However, something here is rather unusual."

"What do you mean?" asks Kate who just joined the conversation.

"Well, you have many valuable possessions in this house, why would they break all those things instead of stealing them?"

"I have no idea," says Kate.

"Could this be some kind of revenge? Family or work related perhaps?" continues the officer, taking notes.

"No," answers Stuart right away. "I mean, we've had issues with people at work but nobody we know would do something like this."

"There's just one other hypothesis then I guess," says the officer, closing his notepad.

"What are you thinking?" asks Kate.

"Based on the evidence I see here tonight, I believe that whoever those people were, they were looking for something very specific."

"For what?" asks Stuart.

"Well, *that* was the question I had for you, Mister Finch."

Stuart shakes his head in dismay.

"Any visitors in the last few weeks that might have seemed suspicious to you?" asks the officer.

"I don't think so, why?" answers Stuart.

"You see, Mister Finch, skilled burglars usually like to scout the premises before committing their misdeeds. So they come to your house first under the pretext of, let's say, offering their services, to renovate your house for example. It's a ploy of course to identify what they're interested in stealing."

"No, no one like that," confirms Stuart.

"There was that priest who came over yesterday," says Kate, "but I can't imagine…"

"A priest?" asks the officer.

"Yes, from the local church. He wanted to know if he could help with our son's disappearance."

"I'm aware yes I'm sorry Madam," says the officer. "Did that priest give you his name?"

"Heinrich, yes Mister Heinrich I believe it was," says Kate.

"A robber masquerading as a priest, that would be new, but you never know," says the policeman.

"He was a very nice man," assures Kate.

Upstairs, Hailee discovers her room, which has been vandalized as well. It's the second time in a short amount of time that her bedroom suffers heavily due to some dramatic event. Even though she has no doubt Mr. Heinrich is behind this, Hailee can't make any sense of it.

"I have to tell the Police," she mutters.

She wants to run downstairs, tell the officers everything she knows. But *what if that mysterious priest is also keeping Archibald captive?* she wonders. She has never experienced such a dilemma before. In her mind, it's a question of life or death —for Archibald of course.

191

She has to make a decision, fast, as she hears the officers getting ready to leave. She heads towards the stairs, when her phone suddenly rings. An "unknown number" is blinking on the screen. She swallows her saliva, afraid of whom it may be. Mr. Heinrich himself perhaps? She gathers all the courage she has left in one deep breath. And answers.

"Hailee?" says the familiar voice.

She relaxes her whole body in a sigh a relief, recognizing the voice right away.

"Oliver! I'm so glad, I've been waiting to hear from you."

"I'm sorry, I wanted to call you earlier," he says.

"No worries, listen, something happened."

"What now?"

"My house. Burglars. I think they were looking for the globe."

"What? Are you sure? Maybe they just wanted to steal stuff, there are tons of break-ins right now."

"No, listen, they didn't take anything. I have no doubt. It's that priest. That's why I gave you the globe. I knew he was going to come for it."

"Hailee, this is crazy!"

"I know, trust me, I have no idea what to do. I don't know what it is about that globe, but there has to be something special about it to explain all of this."

"I'm not sure," says Oliver, "but I think I found something."

"You did?" asks Hailee, excited.

"It's just weird, I have to show you. When can you meet me?"

"The Police are here right now so it's probably not the best time. What about tomorrow?"

"We should meet in a public place, with lots of people around," suggests Oliver.

"Good idea. Where?"

"St. James Park, by the blue bridge, you know where that is?"

"I'll find it. What time?"

"Noon?"

"Okay, says Hailee, see you there."

"See you there."

"And Oliver..."

"Yes?"

"Be careful, I don't know what else that priest is capable of."

"Don't worry," says Oliver before hanging up.

Of course Hailee barely sleeps again, especially with her room now in shambles. She actually doesn't even bother putting her mattress back on the bedframe. She gesticulates all night. And wakes on the floor, late and full of sore muscles. She is on time for her meeting with Oliver though. In fact, she is starting to worry. It is now half past twelve and Oliver is still a no-show.

It was easy for her to find the blue bridge. Not only is it the only bridge in St. James Park, but it's also, well, blue. The view on Buckingham Palace from here is just enchanting. For a second, Hailee imagines that green slime on the lake to be floating lilies, as painted by Monet in the "Nymphéas." She dreams of different circumstances, in which this could be a normal date. But nothing seems normal anymore, as Oliver arriving pale and out of breath quickly reminds her.

"What happened?" she asks.

"Maybe I'm paranoid, but I think I was followed," he says.

"All the way here?" worries Hailee.

"No, I'm pretty sure I lost them," he says. "I stopped by at my dad's shop earlier, it's a mess, someone went through it also."

"The globe!" reacts Hailee.

"Don't worry, they didn't find that secret room. I left the globe in there," he says. "Still no trace of my dad though."

"I'm so sorry, your mom must be so worried," says Hailee.

Oliver chuckles.

"What did I say?" asks Hailee.

"I've not seen my mother in a long time. To be honest, I barely remember her. She left us when I was two," he says, looking down.

"Where do you live then? You're on your own?"

"Look, my mother is long gone, my dad is a drunk, I have not been in school in three years, I have pretty much always been on my own," says Oliver, giving Hailee a forced smile. "Now, you want to hear what I found?"

"Yes, please."

"Don't get too excited. This might be nothing."

"Tell me."

"Okay this is it," he says, opening a binder with plastic sleeves containing a bunch of brownish old documents.

"Newspapers?" questions Hailee.

"Kind of, not really" he says. "This is one of the first tabloids ever printed. There are only a few copies left. I had seen these years ago at the shop but I only thought of them yesterday."

"A tabloid?" asks Hailee, "I don't understand, what does it have to do with that globe or my brother?"

"Look at the date," says Oliver, "it's from 1519. People wanted to know the same thing they're interested in today, what rich folks were doing with their money, and who dated who. Back then of course, there were no actors, no reality TV. The celebrities were the kings, queens and princes. That's why the name of the tabloid was 'crowns', see. Not sure if you can read this, it's in old English and an old-fashioned font."

"Wait, I thought you found something about the globe?" says Hailee, looking disappointed, mad almost.

"I did," says Oliver, taking one of the papers delicately out of its sleeve. "Look, this is the interesting part. Like in any tabloid today, there's always some crazy story somewhere, something completely made up or hard to believe, right?"

"Right," says Hailee, "like the guy who married his vacuum or the woman who got abducted by aliens."

"Or that kid who got absorbed into a globe," suggests Oliver.

"Please don't make fun of that," says Hailee.

"I'm not," he says, opening the old tabloid on the last page.

"In January 1519," explains Oliver, "the crazy story of the month *was* about a globe. Look at the title."

"Sorry I can't really read that, what does it say?"

He reads it for her:

"Tavern owner claims globe stole customers and best shanker, his best bartender basically," translates Oliver.

"Is this a joke?"

"You tell me," says Oliver. "The story says that the tavern owner saw, with his own eyes, I quote, eleven young girls being sucked up into a terrestrial globe, along with his shanker sleeping under the table. The story doesn't say why that guy, who goes by the name of Wymer, was sleeping under the table."

"Does it say what happened to the globe?" asks Hailee, now starting to understand the point of this demonstration.

Oliver starts reading again:

"According to the tavern owner, a mysterious woman arrived a few minutes after the incident and took the globe with her."

"This sounds completely made up!" says Hailee.

"Is that why you didn't want to share your story with anyone? You were afraid they'd think you made it up?"

"You're right," admits Hailee. "But I mean, the guy owned a tavern, a bar right? Don't you think he was just completely drunk and hallucinating!"

"Maybe," says Oliver, "except there's one detail in here that tells me he didn't lie."

"What is it?"

"It's right here," says Oliver, pointing at the middle of the article. "The tavern owner said that right before the young girls and his helper disappeared, he saw, and I'm quoting again, a tremendous flash of light, as bright as the Sun, followed by a loud bang that sounded like thunder. It reminds you of something?"

Hailee is speechless. The drawing in the article features that bright light coming out of a globe, and radiating towards a group of girls standing in a circle around it.

"Don't get me wrong," adds Oliver, "if you had not told me about your brother, I would have never taken this story seriously."

"What about now?" she asks.

"If I believe you, then I don't have a choice, I have to believe this story," says Oliver. "And I do want to believe you," he adds.

"You think it's the same globe?"

"Possibly," says Oliver, "this story is from 1519, that's four years later than the date carved on your globe."

"This is unbelievable," says Hailee.

"Wait," says Oliver suddenly, grabbing Hailee's arm.

"What's wrong?" she asks.

"I thought I saw that guy," he says, trying to see through the clutter of tourists cramming the blue bridge. "Heinrich!" he shouts in the same breath.

Hailee turns around, seeing Mr. Heinrich's face clearly for the first time. He is standing at the opposite end of the bridge, his hands in his coat, looking at her with a smirk on his face.

"That's him?" whispers Hailee.

Mr. Heinrich's bodyguards are already running towards them, pushing people aside bluntly.

"Let's go!" says Oliver, pulling Hailee by the cuff of her jacket.

They also have to make their way through dozens of people strolling the narrow paths of the park. One of their two huge pursuers has collided with the bridge railing and fallen into the water but the other one, Scary Boris, is still chasing them.

"Stop that kid!" he keeps shouting. "He took my wallet!"

Hailee has taken the lead. Constantly looking back to check on that second henchman, Oliver doesn't see the baby stroller standing in his way. He trips over it and falls to the ground. Boris yanks him by the collar.

"You're not going nowhere!" he says with a croaky voice, dragging Oliver towards Mr. Heinrich.

"Let go of me!" screams Oliver.

"Quit jiggling or I'll break your neck," warns Boris.

"Oliver!" shouts Hailee, turning around to help him.

She grabs Oliver's arm and tries pulling him the other way but she is no match against that 300-pound gorilla. It hits her suddenly. She remembers that can of mace her Grandpa gave her. Her gut feeling told her to put it in her pocket before she left this morning. She pulls it out and sprays Boris's face profusely. He lets go of Oliver in a painful scream.

Hailee and Oliver run away and soon break out from the clout of people.

"Thank you, that was amazing!" says Oliver.

"Thanks Grandpa Harvey," she mutters.

HOW TO TAME A MARODOR

For the first time, Archibald wakes up in Gristlemoth knowing this is not a dream —though yesterday felt like a nightmare—, knowing where he is —more or less— and not wanting to leave — not really. His loud yawn slowly mixes with the whiny howling from Paws, the loyal and comfortable pet pillow he slept on all night.

Archibald has not quite recovered from his encounter with the Krakatorum Gargantus. His neck is stiff and those burn marks on his face and hands have turned into black freckles, big and small. Not to mention that smell of carbonized hair he carries around with him. At the same time, he doesn't want any of those "war wounds" to go away. They are much more meaningful than any medal he could have gotten —and definitely something to brag about when he goes back to Cuffley.

Going through Gristlemoth, he seems to be walking a little taller today. He truly feels like the knight of the village. No one is going to slap him behind the head here. He might be called a liripoop from time to time, but it's not that bad, and it still sounds better than "dweeb". Everywhere he goes, girls wave and smile at him. One of them just pinned a flower onto his chest. Wait, *this might be a dream after all.*

He passes Wymer's house. The garage is open. His tank is there —or what's left of it to be more precise. A few blocks down, near the village entrance, a well-organized team effort is at work, some taking away the debris from homes destroyed by the Marodor, while others are already bringing new planks to fix them up. No trace of Wymer around though. Archibald finds him by the Marodors' pen...

Gristlemoth's main and only handyman is building a new cage for the Krakatorum. The existing cages were just not big enough for that Gargantus, levitating nearby, for now. The new one is dramatically larger, and reinforced in each corner with nails as big as heron beaks. Archibald would say as big as those carrots Naida pulled out of the ground. But that's just because he's obsessed with carrots.

Proud of his contribution in capturing the colossal Marodor, he can't help but also feel terrible for him. The beast's long necks are now hanging down like deflated balloons, with all four of his partially human faces seemingly fighting for the saddest face award. Soon the Krakatorum's wailing will get lost among those rising from other cages. One, in particular, catches Archibald's ear. It would almost sound like "Help" —a long, painful, drown out call for help. As far as he knows though, Marodors don't talk.

Is this like looking at clouds? he wonders, when one can pretty much make any shape or form out of those constantly morphing cotton balls. No, here it echoes again.

"Heeelp," says the distant cry.

Archibald sets out to pinpoint it.

After a few detours, backtracking and zigzagging through the woods, he finally finds the source of that peculiar plaint. It's coming from Parnel's cage. Or so he thinks, as she is now silent.

"Did you call for help?" he asks her.

Lying on the ground, she is contorting her body to try to stand up, obviously in pain.

"It's your arms, isn't it?"

Archibald gets closer to the cage. Parnel is just staring at him.

"Do you need help?" he whispers, getting even closer.

The next moment, Parnel throws herself at the cage, scaring Archibald so much he gets knocked off his feet. Parnel crawls back to the shadows, moaning louder now as she probably hurt her arms further.

"I get it, you're mad," he tells her. "But I know you need help. And I'm going to give it to you, whether you want it or not!"

Archibald hurries off to Cleofa, to the Golem workshop. Maven is there, still bragging about defeating the Krakatorum single-handedly. He takes her aside.

"I have a question for you," he says.

"Sure," she shrugs.

"You told me you fixed Rhiannon's leg right?"

"I did," confirms Maven.

"How did you do it?"

"You didn't seem to care about it yesterday?" she says.

"I know, I'm sorry. I really want to know though."

"Okay let me show you then," she says, taking him to a shelf where she keeps her personal golem collection.

"How many do you need?" asks Archibald.

"It's not about how many, it's about choosing the right ones!" corrects Maven.

"Sorry, so which ones then?" he asks.

"Okay it's also about how many," now says Maven, making Archibald's head spin. "When it comes to golems," she says, "you need a minimum of two. Three is definitely the magic number, but personally, I always like to add one extra."

"I'm sorry but, are we talking about eggs or golems?" asks Archibald, semi-serious.

"What? Golems of course!" says Maven, annoyed. "See for Rhiannon's leg, I used Prama ($\approx$) as a base, then I added

Mallemendia (∞), which facilitates the renewal of things, especially when combined with this one here, Durare, (ß).”

"The angry B!" notes Archibald.

"Is that the way you call it? You're right, it kind of looks mean.
But this golem is mostly known for its hardening power. This
would have worked fine, but I wanted her arm to heal fast, so I
added one more, Vitarespare (⼂), to accelerate the whole process.”

"You talk about it like it's a recipe!" says Archibald, amazed.

"Because it is," says Maven. "You need all the right ingredients,
from A to Z, starting with the right herbs by the way.”

Archibald cracks up.

"I'm serious," says Maven, with a straight face.

"How does it work?" asks Archibald.

"I just told you!"

"No, the spell I mean, how do you *activate* those powers?"

"That's the easy part!" says Maven. "Once you have all your
golems lined up, you just speak their names, one after another,
then you pronounce the key word.”

"The magic word you mean?" he asks.

"If you want to call it that, yes.”

"I knew there was a magic word!" he exclaims. "So, what is it?"

"Malenvoli," says Maven. "The only time you don't need it is in
the tank. The cannons activate the golems directly.”

"So that's it? Just the names of the golems, plus the magic
word?"

"Yes," confirms Maven. "And the golems will just do exactly
what they've been told.”

Archibald now comes really close to Maven.

"Can I borrow these?" he whispers.

"For what?" she asks.

"I can't tell you but it's for someone who needs help.”

Maven hesitates.

"Just have your friend come over and I'll take care of her."

"No she won't, she can't walk, she is in really bad shape," says Archibald.

"Who is it? I didn't know anyone else got hurt," she says.

"I can't really say, I'm sorry," he explains.

Maven hesitates again.

"Okay," she finally says. "But at one condition…"

"Anything you want."

It's her turn to whisper.

"You have to take me with you!" she says, all excited.

"I can't, my friend is very shy."

"No, not to your friend," says Maven, "when you go back, you know, up there," she says, pointing heavenward.

Archibald is embarrassed, since he has no clue how, when or even if he'll go back home.

"Okay," he finally says, without *really* lying.

Maven exults and gives him a hug.

"One more thing though," says Archibald, "you'll need to write down the names of the golems for me. They're too complicated!"

"Only from great efforts comes great power," says the golem master. Hard to understand for a boy whose motto has always been: "why do today what you can put off until tomorrow!"

"You know what would be easy?" he says. "Give each golem a number, and replace that Malenvoli by something more punchy, like *boom* or something, for more impact. So when you read your spell, you can just say one, twelve, twenty three, and boom, instead of all that mumbo jumbo."

"That's a good idea, I'll think about it," says Maven.

"Really?" he asks, proud of his find.

"Of course not!" she cracks up.

"That's not funny," he says.

"What do you think?" she asks. "That we just made those names up? The runes get their names from plants. Don't you remember when I talked to that tree?"

He nods.

"When we spell out each formula, we do nothing more than calling upon those plants to wake up the golems," she explains.

Archibald doesn't seem convinced:

"Still way too complicated if you ask my opinion…"

"Good," she says, "cause no one's asking!"

Archibald is experiencing something entirely new. He has never been excited this much for anyone other than himself. Just a few days ago, this kind of feeling would have been so foreign, and so counter-nature.

When he gets back to Parnel, she seems to be sleeping. He tries not to make any noise and places the four golems around her cage. Time to read that formula Maven gave him. He pulls out the piece of paper from his pocket, but can barely understand a word of it. As if this exercise was not complicated enough! Now he has to try and decrypt Maven's writing, made of intricate cursive letters, as curvy and beautiful as they are gobbledygook to Archibald.

"Who writes like this?" he fumes, still giving it a try: "Malle… media, Vi… tares… pera, Prama, Mephisto… pera?" he says aloud, stumbling over every syllable. And then in a more solemn tone, the magic word: "Malenvoli!"

Archibald waits a good half-minute for the golems to light up. But nothing happens. He taps on one of them but still nothing. Not even a spark. Maybe he made a mistake (three in fact).

His eyes back on Maven's notes, Archibald tries again, this time more carefully:

"Mallemendia, Vitarespare, Prama, Mephistopare... Malenvoli!"

The golems light up almost instantly.

"Yes!" exults Archibald.

Parnel wakes up in a jolt. Her body starts jerking, as if hit by internal spasms.

"What did I do?" mumbles Archibald, worried.

Suddenly, the convulsions stop. Parnel collapses to the ground.

"I killed her," gasps Archibald.

Maybe he misspelled the spell and triggered a completely different outcome. But Parnel's eyes soon reopen. A few more seconds and she springs back up, now standing firmly on her arms.

"I did it! We did it!" shouts Archibald, trying to get a closer look at Parnel's arms. But again, she rushes toward him and bangs against the cage, hissing some more.

Archibald is back on the ground.

"Are you a pincher bug or a cat?" he asks her. "I guess it will take a little more than fixing your arms..."

♫

The morning after, Archibald pays a visit to Wymer. They are both sitting on the ground in his garage. Gristlemoth's number one —and only— handyman has a daunting task standing in front of him. Not quite standing actually, since his tank has been reduced to a heap of splinters.

"How could I put this back together? It's like an impossible puzzle," complains Wymer. "I'm a repair guy, not a magician!"

"Why don't you ask Faerydae for some magic then? Isn't there something she can do with golems?" suggests Archibald.

205

"No, unfortunately, this is pure engineering. Golems might be able to fix a leaky roof, but this tank is like the gout in my foot, too many moving parts," explains Wymer. "It'd be easier to build a new one!" he notes.

"A new foot?" asks Archibald.

"I wish!" says Wymer, laughing.

"You know, if one day you do build a new tank, maybe you can tweak the design a bit," recommends Archibald.

"Oh yeah? Tweak it how?" asks Wymer, skeptical.

Archibald starts drawing something in the ground with his finger.

"It's just an idea," says Archibald, "but see instead of having cannons all around the tank, you could have just one bigger cannon, which means bigger golems, and more power."

"Nice try but that would never work, you could only fire in one direction," comments Wymer, shaking his head.

"Not if you put that cannon on a rotating tower," says Archibald. "Then you could still fire from any angle, but with only one cannon to worry about and reload."

Archibald has essentially drawn a modern tank, similar to the ones you could find on battlefields nowadays. Wymer is looking at the rough sketch, scratching his head, now impressed.

"Not bad kid!" he exclaims. "See that's what happens when you eat your vegetables!"

"Yuk!" objects Archibald.

"Are you hungry by the way?"

"Not for veggies. I miss ice cream," he says, salivating.

"None of that here sorry Son."

"I can't believe you guys don't use sugar, that's the best stuff," laments Archibald.

"Nope, though we could get it from beets," notes Wymer.

"What do you mean?"

"Beets. You know beets?"

"Of course I know beets, I hate beets, they taste like radish, celery and eggplant mixed together, disgusting!" says Archibald, wrinkling his nose.

"Sounds like a nice stew to me! But yes, there *is* sugar in beets. You just have to extract it," says Wymer. "After all, we use black treacle in Flummadiddle, that's sugar, kind of."

"There's sugar in Flummadiddle? That thing does not taste like sugar!" says Archibald.

Wymer gives up. Even his broken tank is not as much of a headache.

"Go ask Naida, she'll tell you all about it."

Sugar from beets? For Archibald, that just doesn't sound right. But he still wants to get to the bottom of it.

∴

Five minutes later, he shows up in Naida's garden. There she is, that criminal, planting more carrots.

"Don't you think we have enough of those?" he asks her.

"Carrots are so good for you!" she says.

"What about beets?" he says.

"They're great too, and even better when cooked together with carrots!"

Archibald's gagging reflex takes over. He struggles to remain focused.

"Is it true you can get sugar from beets?" he asks.

"Black treacle. You know, molasses? We put that in…"

"Flummadiddle, I know. But I'm talking about real sugar, you know, the good stuff," says Archibald.

"You don't need that, it's bad for you," she says.

"It's *not* bad. And it's not for me. I mean, I'm not going to lie, I will probably eat some too. But it's for someone else."

"Who's that?"

Archibald is not sure he wants to tell her.

"Parnel," he finally says.

Naida shakes her head and chuckles.

"What? Are you all here?"

"What's that supposed to mean?"

"That maybe you left some brains behind when traveling through the globe!"

"Why?"

"Marodors don't eat," she says.

"Well, they have a mouth, don't they?"

"To spit fire, not to eat! Don't you think we thought about that? Trust me, we've tried everything, bell peppers, carrots, Brussels sprouts, celery…"

It takes a lot of self-control for Archibald not to throw up. And Naida is not even done yet:

"…cauliflower, asparagus, eggplants, I'm telling you, we tried e-very-thing," she says, "and guess what, they didn't want any of it!"

"Shocker! Of course they didn't! I wouldn't want it either!" says Archibald. "And you're wrong, Marodors do eat."

"Oh yeah, so what do they eat then?"

"Candy bars! When that Marodor was chasing me, I dropped a Kit-Kat on the ground. And he hate the whole thing, I'm telling you."

"I doubt it, but go ahead, feed'em your candy," she says.

"That's the problem, I ran out."

"I'm sorry, we don't grow those around here."

"But you know how to make sugar!" he says.

"I guess," she admits.

"Can you show me?" he asks.

Naida thinks about it for a minute.

"Okay I'll show you but only this one time," she says. "And at one condition…"

Somehow, Archibald fears he already knows the nature of her request.

"What would that be?" he asks anyway.

"If you go back up there, you have to take me with you," she whispers.

"Who told you about that?" he asks, even though, again, he's pretty sure to have the answer already.

"Maven," she says. "She told me about your globe."

Archibald sighs. He really doesn't want to lie —too much.

"Okay, I'll take you with me, but I'm not even sure I *can* go back."

Naida smiles really big and gives him a long hug, then runs to another aisle to get some beets. She has so much energy suddenly that she pulls five large ones out of the ground in no time.

"They grow in the dirt?" says Archibald, stunned, with that familiar look of disgust back on his face.

"Of course, they are roots!" says Naida.

"No wonder! Now I know why they're so gross! They're like carrots," he says.

"Once we cook them, they won't be that bad," assures Naida.

She leads Archibald to Wymer's kitchen, which has four huge baskets of carrots ready to be peeled, chopped and roasted for tonight's supper.

"What is wrong with you people, you're all going to turn orange!" he warns.

"Take a seat, this might take a while," says Naida. "Ready Karla?" she asks the small cauldron sitting on the table.

"I just need a few minutes to warm up," says Karla in a yawn, obviously waking up from another nap.

Archibald would have never imagined it was so complicated to make sugar. Naida spends hours preparing the beets, cooking them, extracting their liquid through a cloth and spreading the precious nectar on a baking tray. When she's finally done, Archibald has fallen asleep.

"Voila!" says Naida, awaking his senses with a striped bar she placed on a knotty birch twig.

She obviously had fun, shaping this improvised lollipop in the likeness of Marodors, with multiple horns and big eyes made of raw beet. To Archibald, who has not had sugar in so long —a record five days—, this honey-colored candy looks like pure gold. All it takes is one bite to trigger a meltdown with a cascading effect, starting with his eyelids, followed by his mouth, his shoulders, his belly, and all the way down to his knees that buckle under pleasure.

"How could you live without this?" he tells Naida.

"Is it that good?" she asks.

"It is," says Karla, her handles still shivering.

"You have to try it. Did you make enough for another one?"

"I think so," she says, moving aside, unveiling a tray with enough caramelized beet sugar to make a hundred more lollipops.

"I must be dreaming," says Archibald in wonder, on the verge of tears.

He places a few pieces of Naida's creation in a towel before heading out. By the time he reaches Parnel's cage, the towel is 80% empty, 20% crumbs.

"Oopsh!" he says, his mouth full.

He throws three surviving chunks inside the enclosure, near the dark corner where Parnel likes to hide. Her reaction is swift, and very frog-like for an earwig Marodor: the initial sniffling quickly gives way to a frog-like leap towards the syrupy candy, which disappears in one frog-like gulp, followed by a no less frog-like burp.

But what matters most to Archibald is that purr she soon lets out —the very same purr that first Marodor produced when eating the Yorkie from his desk.

"Better than turnips, isn't it?" says Archibald.

Unsurprisingly, Parnel retreats back into her favorite corner in no time. But the purring doesn't subside.

"You're part cat, aren't you?" says Archibald. "You were hissing at me. And now you're purring. That's progress…"

Archibald starts spending most of his time in the Marodors' pen.

"Have you seen Archibald?" keeps asking Faerydae around the village. She's not too worried though. As far as she's concerned, he is busy drawing Marodors, the Krakatorum in particular, making the Grand Bestiary slightly less incomplete. Besides, he still shows up every evening for dinner —never that hungry anymore though, for some reason…

On most days though, Archibald just devotes long hours entertaining feeding and Parnel. He loves to lie down by her cage, reading her that book he found at Cleofa: *The Facetious Nights of Straparola*, a collection of many fairy-tales, some very strange, some fun, some scary.

"Which story do you prefer?" he asks Parnel. "The one about the Pig-King or the one about the living doll?"

Archibald is not sure Parnel can understand a word that he is saying but he doesn't mind. What matters is that she seems to feel better. She is more calm. She has not tried to attack him in two days now. Archibald also noticed something curious: her eyes are not as glaring as they used to be. The red has dimmed down to a pale pinkish color. Maybe it also has to do with all the beet sugar lollipops he has been sharing with her. She can't get enough of them. Archibald had to ask Naida to cook two more batches since the first one.

Today, Archibald has brought a guitar he borrowed —not stole— from Rhiannon's friend. It's not really a guitar. It ends in a strange bend resembling a crane's neck. They call it a lute. But to Archibald, it doesn't make much difference. A lute or a guitar, it's all the same to him, since he doesn't know how to play either one of them anyway. He just likes to brush his hand against the cords and see Parnel react to a particular note. Each time, the expression on her face changes slightly, her neck moving up, left or right depending on the melody.

"Are you dancing?" asks Archibald, not expecting any answer, just enjoying the moment.

The sun is out but can't quite reach Parnel, due to the bundles of wood stacked on her cage. *If only I could move those a little*, thinks Archibald.

He leaves for a few minutes and comes back with a ladder under his arm. Wymer agreed to give it to him, wondering what he could need that for. Archibald refused to say, well aware that the foliage was placed on all cages for a specific purpose: as a secondary shield, besides the natural umbrella of trees above, to keep the Marodors as restrained as possible, in the dark.

He places the ladder against the cage.

"You won't jump on me, right?" he asks Parnel.

213

Even though she's been more peaceful lately, he knows she is still highly unpredictable. Faerydae's words are echoing in his head: "They might look human, but they're mostly animals…"

Archibald has made up his mind. He shall —not— heed Faerydae's warning. He starts going up the ladder. Parnel does react but she seems more scared than anything. Reaching the top of the cage, Archibald pushes some branches aside, allowing in some light, but not nearly enough. He decides to step on the cage itself.

He is now hopping from one wood beam to another, trying to avoid the gaps in between, his arms up, like a tightrope walker.

He stops suddenly.

The worst fear has just settled on him. He is standing right above Parnel. At any time, she could jump up and catch one of his legs. Or both at once!

What am I doing? What am I thinking? Why would I take such a risk?

He is sweating even more than the day William Tanner held him upside down by his underwear in the gym locker-room —and that was a big sweat.

It's the peace on Parnel's face that eventually makes Archibald calm down. He removes more branches from the roof of her cage, creating a well of sunlight that reaches the edges of her body.

After initially folding up into a ball and covering her head, Parnel extends her neck to fully enjoy the rays of sunshine. Archibald is in awe. He gets ready to come back down, when his foot slips off the edge of the cage. He loses his balance and falls backwards, letting out a shriek. His whole life goes through his mind in one instant. An impressive eleven years of souvenirs condensed in one quick slideshow: images of his mother, his Dad, Hailee (very very quickly), that cute cat he saw at the pond —and ice cream.

The cage must be twelve feet in height. Archibald is on his way to break his neck for sure. Maybe worse. He cringes, bracing for impact. For some reason though, this fall is taking much longer than he expected.

Maybe I already reached the ground and died instantly? he wonders.

Archibald opens his eyes, to realize he is lying in Parnel's arms —those arms he healed for her. She passed them through the cage and caught him right before he hit the ground. They are now staring at each other.

"Faerydae!" Archibald tries to scream, letting out nothing but a squeaky chirp. His tongue has dried up like a giant prune tasting of rubber. Sweat is pouring off him from head to toe. Parnel seems to be probing him, the same way a predator would before devouring his prey. Based on what he knows, Marodors don't eat humans. But Archibald has been eating so much candy since he was born that half his body must be made of sugar by now —so who knows!

"You're not going to hurt me, are you?" he asks.

But what if she does? What if this is the final embrace, that hug of death that Faerydae told him about? Parnel cuts short this brainstorming that nearly cost Archibald a heart attack. She releases him, slowly and carefully.

"Thank you," Archibald tells Parnel, who nods and blinks gently in return, her eyes now fully back to normal —green, deep, sweet, beautiful.

In the village, no one could suspect what had just happened. All girls are doing what they normally do in Gristlemoth —the usual gardening, planting, schooling, fishing, carving, polishing...

Rhiannon is talking to Wymer about ways to improve his new tank. The master builder is just nodding, stroking his beard. Suddenly though, his eyes get bigger, and bigger, and bigger!

"Are you okay Wymer?" asks Rhiannon.

"Ma-ma, Ma-ma…" he mumbles.

"What? Are you calling your mother?" she asks.

"Ma-mmm… Marodor!" he finally lets out.

"What are you talking about?" she says.

Wymer points at something coming from the East, on the edge of the village —it's Parnel, standing in between two cabanas. Rhiannon screams so loud she communicates her fear to everyone around in a second.

"Marodor on the loose!" she shouts, sowing panic throughout Gristlemoth.

Archibald is nowhere to be seen. What happened to him is a mystery. Did he get overly optimistic thinking Parnel could be tamed? And more importantly, what did she do to him?

When Faerydae shows up, she can't believe her eyes.

"To your golems," she shouts, as most people seem to be looking for shelter.

"I'll get some cannons just in case," says Wymer before running away, perhaps headed back to his pit-hole.

Parnel seems headed straight for Faerydae. Surprisingly though, she doesn't show any sign of anger, like other Marodors would if they escaped from their cage. Faerydae was not born yesterday though —definitely not. She knows looks can be deceiving. As the saying goes, don't judge a book by its cover, especially in Gristle-moth where all book covers are essentially identical —brownish or greyish, worn, rubbed, with no title and for sure no pictures.

A few hearts have paused. Maven has just handed Faerydae two powerful golems, that will stop Parnel in her tracks if need be. Far from flinching, Faerydae starts walking towards her former best friend, ready to confront her.

Parnel stops suddenly. She slowly turns her neck around, seemingly looking at something behind her.

"Has another Marodor escaped?" murmurs Faerydae.

"Let's hope not," says Maven, knowing such a scenario would probably mean the end of Gristlemoth.

Instead of a Marodor, something else steps out of Parnel's shadow —Archibald, drawing a the loudest gasp among the girls surrounding Faerydae.

"What the heck!" says Wymer as he hurries back with a cannon.

To make it perfectly clear to everyone that Parnel is not a danger anymore, Archibald places his hand on her arm.

Faerydae drops her golems, and approaches them.

"Hello Faerydae," says Parnel, with the most tender of voices. "I missed you."

MALLEUS MALEFICARUM

Hailee and Oliver have not stopped running since they escaped Crazy Boris in St. James Park. In fact, they look poised to never stop, not until they've reached a sea or an ocean at least. But Oliver has just given up it seems, grabbing onto a lamppost to use it as a crutch, stooped and out of breath.

"You think we're far enough?" asks Hailee, panting as well.

"I'm not sure but this is it, this is my place," he says, motioning to the building behind her, an apartment complex twisted like a politician, leaning left at the bottom, and veering right at the top.

"Great!" says Hailee, just relieved to have found a hideout.

They look both ways, repeatedly, before stepping inside, still worried Heinrich's henchmen might be around the corner. The building is old, completely run down, with a strong smell of mildew hanging in the air. It stings Hailee's nostrils as soon as she enters. Caught off guard, she covers her nose with the sleeve of her jacket.

"Sorry, I know, it stinks in here! It's mold, among other things," says Oliver. "This place is so ancient. Holes everywhere, it's like a giant colander."

"No worries, what floor are you on?" asks Hailee.

"The last one. Sorry, no elevator!"

"It's okay, we ran for over three miles, I think we can do this," smiles Hailee.

"It's not that, you gotta watch your steps!" he says.

Oliver was not referring so much to the six floors they have to climb. What concerns him most are all those broken planks leading to his place. Combined with water infiltrations and the freezing cold, the stairwell has turned into a skating ring. Oliver was right to worry. Hailee slips over and falls on her butt —twice.

"I'm sorry, this is not quite like your house!" he says as they reach the top floor.

"Maybe, but at least it's safe, right?" she says. "I mean, do you think Heinrich could find us here?"

"I doubt it," says Oliver as he unlocks the door. "We moved here just a few months ago, we couldn't pay our rent in the last building. Slightly better than being on the street, I think that's next though," he predicts.

His first priority when they get in is to empty out the five large buckets that have been collecting water from leaks in the ceiling, black with mold. He doesn't look too surprised. This is something he is obviously used to.

"You can always sleep at the store," says Hailee.

"Nah, my dad can't afford the rent there anymore either," he comments. "And now that Heinrich sent his guys to wreck the whole place, I really doubt things are gonna get better."

There are only six pieces of furniture in the room: a carved dining table and two matching chairs, a sofa, a small one-person bed against the opposite wall next to a corner kitchenette, and a desk by the window —all beautiful antiques that stand out like a gold tooth in a pirate's mouth (full of cavities).

"I'm sorry," says Hailee, pausing. "I feel like this is all my fault."

"Why would it be your fault? You didn't force my dad to drink. Oh wait, did *you* tell my mother to abandon me?"

"You know what I mean," she says.

"Trust me, you have no reason to feel bad about anything. This disaster started way before you came into my life," he says. "Do you want a tea or something?" he asks, emptying the last bucket in the tiniest of sinks.

"If you use that water to make it, I can't wait!" she says.

He cracks up.

"I'm okay though thanks," says Hailee, crossing the living area in nine short strides.

"Wow you've got an amazing view," she says, looking out the window.

They are obviously in the suburb. From here it seems that they can see nearly all the way to the Center of London.

"That's the only good thing about this place," says Oliver, now grabbing towels to wipe the floors, since the buckets overflowed. "That, and the charm of living under a tin roof of course. Freezing in winter, boiling in summer. The first five days of April are pretty enjoyable though!" he jokes.

Something catches Hailee's attention —a business card, sitting in an open folder on the desk.

"Did you see this?" she says.

"What is it?" he asks, still sponging up water.

"A business card."

"Yeah, that's my dad's desk, I usually leave it alone, he hates it when I touch his stuff."

"I think you should have a look at this," she says, showing him the card as he comes closer.

It reads "Jacob Heinrich" and has two phone numbers, one in London, one in New York.

"That's that priest's card!" says Oliver.

"Is that an hourglass?" says Hailee, rubbing her index on the blazon embossed on each side of Heinrich's name:

⧖   Jacob Heinrich   ⧖

"I think it's heraldic. Pretty normal stuff. People who are into History and relics love this kind of symbol, like crosses, lions and all that stuff. I'm actually surprised this guy is not using the swastika!"

"The Nazi symbol you mean?" asks Hailee.

"Exactly," he confirms, "that would fit him better!"

She nods. She couldn't agree more.

"Anything else in there," asks Oliver.

Hailee pulls out another piece of paper from the folder.

"Just a receipt," she says, handing it to him.

"It's from a delivery company. My dad uses them only for expensive stuff," explains Oliver. "This is for that book he sold Heinrich years ago," he adds.

"Which book?" she asks.

"It's written right here. It's just an abbreviation."

Across the receipt are two abstruse words.

"Mal Mal" reads Hailee. "What is that?"

"It stands for 'Malleus Maleficarum', I remember because Heinrich paid a fortune for it. My dad took care of a lot of debt with that money."

"Just the title sounds creepy," says Hailee. "What is it about?"

"It's in Latin. It means 'the Hammer of the Witches'. I don't know much about it but I think it's about witch-hunting, you know, Middle Ages stuff."

"Fun guy that Heinrich!"

"Right? Let's find out who he is, we have his full name now, you wanna search him on your phone?"

"Sure," she says, spelling out each syllable of his name as she types: "Ja-cob Hein-rich"

"Anything?" asks Oliver.

"Not really," she says, scrolling down.

"What about 'Father Jacob Heinrich' or 'Jacob Heinrich priest'? Maybe you should try that."

"Good idea," she says.

Hailee shakes her head though.

"Nope, nothing," she says. "Oh wait, this is weird."

"What?"

"You won't believe this."

"Tell me."

"How did you say that book was called?"

"Malleus Maleficarum," repeats Oliver.

"That's it, there's a link to it right here."

"Really? Under Heinrich's name?"

"No, that's what's weird. It's under Jacob Sprenger. But guess what, he's a priest, one of two priests who wrote that book," says Hailee. "You want to know who the other priest is?"

"Who?"

"According to this, his name is Heinrich Kramer."

"Let me get this right," says Oliver, "the guy who's after us, his name is a combination of those two guys, Jacob Sprenger and Heinrich Kramer? That can't be just a coincidence."

"I definitely think Heinrich is a freak, look at this picture, it's a painting actually," says Hailee, showing Oliver an image of the two priests/authors side by side. "Not only he took their name but look at this, it seems he's also trying really hard to look like one of them."

"That's crazy! Says Oliver, "Kramer looks exactly like Heinrich! Or Heinrich looks like Kramer actually!"

And indeed he does. Same creepy haircut, same chiseled features, same gaunt, elongated face —and the same dark emptiness in his eyes.

"They could literally be twin brothers," sums up Hailee.

"Does it say anything about a globe in there?" asks Oliver.

"I don't think so," says Hailee, still looking. "You were right though, that book *is* about witches. It was like a weird step-by-step manual, telling people how to find them and get rid of them. It sounds like they're talking about rats, but no, this is actually about people.

"The good old times," jokes Oliver.

"This gets even weirder, it's like those dolls in my Grandma's library…"

"What are you talking about?"

"When they caught those witches, they shaved their heads."

"Yeah I've heard that before."

"But do you know why?"

"Uh uh why?"

"Listen to this," she says, "shaving a witch was meant to locate a scar or a mark that would provide the undeniable proof of her pact with the devil."

"You'd better not bump your head back then!"

"You're not too far-off. It seems even a birth mark would qualify," says Hailee. "You want another fun fact?"

"I'm not sure," says Oliver.

"You know Sprenger, the second writer?"

"Yeah, what about him?"

"It says here he was murdered."

"What? Who did it?"

"It doesn't say, but it seems Kramer and Sprenger didn't get along. They were fighting about who actually wrote the book."

"Are you saying Kramer had him killed?"

"I don't know."

"If that's true, then Heinrich has definitely found his mentor in that guy Kramer! A priest, slash crazy person, slash killer, the perfect role model!" says Oliver.

"It's interesting but, it doesn't tell us much about Heinrich himself," sighs Hailee.

"Or maybe it tells us everything, and we don't really know how to read it," he says. Adding: "Sometimes things are right in front of your nose and for some reason you're just blind to them."

"Are you sure you've not been in school in years?" asks Hailee, half serious, half kidding. "I mean, you're smarter than most students in my class. And I'm not just talking about William Tanner. It's pretty sad. You should come with me some time and you'd understand."

"Nothing better than the school of life!" says Oliver. "I'm just street smart I guess. Too bad they don't have a degree for that," he jokes, now looking at that book receipt again.

"Maybe we should try something else," he suggests. "What about this address we have here for Heinrich?"

"What are you thinking?"

"I'm not sure. It's been four years since that book was delivered but you never know, maybe he still lives there."

"What's the address?" asks Hailee, ready for her next search.

"44 Wilton Place, in Belgravia. Our priest is loaded. That's an expensive neighborhood," he comments.

Hailee starts searching.

"Okay, directions to, no, find on map, no, for sale nearby, no, let me see…" she mumbles.

It started raining again, as the trickling in the buckets indicates, getting thicker, and louder. Oliver moves each of them slightly to better catch the drips.

"Wait!" exclaims Hailee.

"You found something?"

"People are exchanging that address on forums," she says.

"What kind of forums?" asks Oliver.

"They don't say much, they are just talking about an event that's supposed to happen at that address."

"When?"

"December... 21ˢᵗ, 6 pm."

"Hailee that's today! That's tonight!" shouts Oliver. "It's in a couple hours, we can make it."

"What do you mean we can make it?"

"I mean we have to go Hailee, what else do we have?"

"I'm not going to that crazy guy's house."

"Do you want to find your brother or not?"

"Of course," she says.

"Something tells me this is your best shot."

"And something tells me this is crazy," she says, showing him something on her phone.

"What's that?"

"Just look," she says. "The people talking about this event, they're saying Master Kramer himself is going to give a grand speech tonight."

"Okay so they call him Master, big deal. Are you really surprised? I mean, look at the guy. He's probably a cult leader or something."

"You don't understand. They're going to that event to see *Kramer.*"

"So? That's his house right!" says Oliver.

"No, you're missing the point," she says, frustrated. "That house is supposed to belong to *Heinrich*. Kramer is that guy he looks like from 500 years ago!"

Oliver looks suddenly as puzzled as she does.

The night has just finished settling upon London, blanketing every rooftop, every wall, every street.

"This is crazy," says Hailee as they walk out of the subway.

"But exciting, right?" says Oliver.

He obviously managed to convince her to go to that event.

"Actually, *you* are crazy!" she corrects. *And exciting*, she admits, keeping that part for herself though.

Once on Wilton Place, they don't have to wonder long as to which one of those large five-story houses is Heinrich's. The traffic is at a complete stop due to a long line of taxicabs dropping off guests at the entrance of a large courtyard. Hailee and Oliver slowly mix with other people, men mostly, arriving on foot. Looking around, Oliver knows that something doesn't add up.

"No tuxedos, not even suits, this is weird," he mutters.

"Why? It's just like people going to church," says Hailee.

"Except this is not a church, this is Belgravia, an island for rich folks, and these are not rich folks, it doesn't make sense" he says.

Given the neighborhood, he expected Heinrich's guests to be more fancy. These are just regular people, most of them wearing shabby clothes —if not raggedy. Oliver's dad could be among them. In fact, he is!

"Dad?" says Oliver, walking up to his father, in line, waiting to get in like the others.

"Oliver! What are you doing here?" says Mr. Doyle, shocked.

"I thought you were dead," says Oliver.

His dad looks terrible, with a shaggy beard, tousled hair and mud stains on his pants, as if he had been drinking and sleeping outside —which wouldn't be something new.

"You've gotta go Son."

"Dad, these people destroyed your shop!"

"What are you talking about?"

"The shop Dad, it's been ransacked."

James Doyle keeps blinking his eyes, speechless, obviously unaware of any break-in.

"I've not been there in a few days. I was... busy," he says.

"It's Heinrich, Dad. His guys did it, I know it."

"You don't know nothing! It could have been anyone."

"That guy is crazy. He's been following me."

"Mister Heinrich is a noble man. He'll help us."

"Dad no, you've got to trust me."

"Don't go make things worse than you did already," says Mr. Doyle, grabbing his son by the collar. "You gotta go home, now. I'll deal with you later," he says, pushing him away.

Oliver goes back to Hailee.

"What is he doing here?" she asks.

"I'm not sure," says Oliver.

"Not him," sighs Hailee, spotting one of Heinrich's bodyguards posted by the gate, the one she coated with mace —Crazy Boris.

"We can't go that way," she says.

"You really thought we'd go through the front door?" he says.

"I don't even want to know what that means," she says.

"Follow me," he says, leading her to the house next door.

It's nearly identical to Heinrich's, except with no guard blocking the entrance. Better yet, the courtyard gate is unlocked. Oliver pushes it open.

"Where are you going?" asks Hailee.

"Trust me," he just says, grabbing her hand.

They go in heads down like a pair of ostriches, and head straight to the tall wall separating the two properties. Within a second, Oliver disappears into a tree. Hailee tracks his climb through the cracking of branches and the shaking of leaves.

"Oliver?" she whisper-shouts.

"Right here," he says, as he pops up at the top and crests the wall.

"I can't do that!" she says.

"Of course you can."

She hesitates for a moment but eventually follows him, taking the same improvised path. Oliver extends his hand, pulling her up for the last stretch of this escalade.

They slide down on the other side, hiding behind a hedge of trees. The darkness also helps them reach the side of Heinrich's house without being seen.

"What now?" asks Hailee.

"These homes usually have some kind of basement access," mutters Oliver while looking around.

"Here," he says, kneeling down to clear ivy from a small window close to the ground. One sharp hit from his elbow and the window snaps open.

"You've done this before, haven't you?" she suspects.

Oliver heaves a sigh.

"How do you think my dad got some of his antiques?"

Hailee gasps, covering her mouth to abort a louder reaction.

"You're a robber!" she says.

"I'm not proud of it," says Oliver. "That's just the way I was brought up."

Hailee has a doubt suddenly.

"The break-in at my house, that wasn't you, was it?"

"Don't be ridiculous, we both know who that was, that's why we're here," says Oliver. "So, are you coming or not?"

She shakes her head, speechless.

"Okay I'm going in, it's up to you," he says, going through the small opening, legs first, soon disappearing.

Hailee looks around and ponders one last time.

"Wait for me!" she says all of a sudden, following Oliver down that creepy hole.

Hailee enters the gloom of the basement, where light filters in solely from those narrow windows squinting all around at ceiling level. She lands on a cardboard box, one of many piled up throughout the room.

"Congrats, you're officially a criminal!" jokes Oliver.

"It's not funny," she groans, "and what's that smell?" she asks, groaning a bit more.

"The sewage?" he guesses. "Anyway, we gotta find the stairs."

"Over there," she says, pointing to the other side of the room.

Slowly, they wade their way through the mountains of boxes.

"I'd really like to know what's in these," says Oliver.

"I'm sure you would, but we don't have time," says Hailee. Yet she is the one who stops suddenly. Something has caught her eye — something shining beneath the staircase.

"Wait, what is that?" she asks, squinting.

"I thought we didn't have time?" he smirks.

Hailee suddenly leaps backwards in horror.

"Are those… eyes?" she asks, nodding at one of many glass jars crammed on four layers of shelves.

Oliver comes closer to give his expert opinion.

"They sure are!" he exclaims, "pigs' eyes," he adds, reading from a half-gone yellowish label.

"That's gross!" says Hailee.

"Well I guess we've found the source of that delicious smell," he says, knocking on the cork top.

"Does it say owls' feet on that one?" asks Hailee, pointing at another jar.

"It sure does," says Oliver, "but if you find that gross, check these out... rabbit brains and... cockroach juice, not your usual preserves, that's for sure!" he jokes, sorting through a sordid inventory including but not limited to: beetle horns, owl legs, raven beaks, bat wings, rat tails, lizard scales, moth powder, snake skin, tick blood, spider legs and toad saliva...

"This is so bizarre. Is Heinrich a priest or a sorcerer?" Hailee wonders aloud, keeping her distance with this wall of horrors.

"What could he possibly do with these? Do you think he eats them?" asks Oliver.

"I think I'm going to be sick," she says, looking a bit like Archibald when he explored the pantry.

"You never know with rich folks! Always looking for the next thing," sighs Oliver.

"Whatever this is for, it's a pretty odd thing to have in your basement," says Hailee.

"Yes and no," he argues, "I've met people at the store who collect the weirdest things, you'd be shocked."

"I don't even want to know," she blurts out, walking away.

"Let's just go," says Oliver, going up the stairs.

At the top, each shadow passing by the door makes Hailee suspend her breath. Oliver opens it slightly. Through the narrow slit, he can see the main entrance. A couple of guests are still streaming in but it seems as though most people have arrived.

He also spots another flight of stairs, small as well, probably used by the maids, waiters and other plethoric staff taking care of this enormous house.

"As soon as I get out, you follow me, okay," he tells Hailee.

Hailee nods, obviously paralyzed with fear.

The hallway is finally clear. Oliver runs out. Then Hailee. They go up the stairs on their tippy toes. About half way up, they freeze.

Someone is coming down.

They have nowhere to go.

Hailee cringes...

It's a waiter, carrying a pile of empty trays.

"Hey kids!" he just says, passing by without paying much attention.

Hailee and Oliver look at each other, sighing in concert, their eyes wide. They keep climbing and soon reach the second floor. It's crowded. People are lining up at several counters, trading their jackets and scarfs for some kind of thick, chocolate brown coats.

"This is a weird coat check," whispers Oliver. *Why would they want to wear something like that inside?* he wonders.

It's only a question of time before someone sees those two kids who kind of look out of place —since they are the only kids around.

"We can't stay here," Oliver tells Hailee.

The service stairs seem to continue up at least one more floor. They rush forward as fast as they can. The next level is much more peaceful. In fact, it seems completely deserted.

Oliver and Hailee advance carefully, guided by a strange and sinister humming sound. It seems to be coming from those doors lining the hallway on their left. Oliver opens one of them, again, carefully. It leads to a balcony, empty as well, with a view on a grand ballroom packed with people.

The garbs guests picked up before entering are monk robes with wide hoods hanging on their shoulders. Everyone is wearing the same costume, making all of them blend into one another, creating an anonymous, uniform, and docile crowd. Standing in tight ranks, dozens at a time but proceeding as one, they each raise a tall candle up in the air, the only source of light in the room.

No shouting, no talking —no thinking— is emanating from this sea of brown, only that constant buzzing, disturbing and chilling.

Facing a large stage with a carved arch and multiple layers of curtains, everyone seems to be gearing up for a show, a one-man-show obviously.

"This guy has his own theater," murmurs Oliver.

"Look, it's that hourglass logo again," says Hailee, pointing at an emblem detaching from a white circle on long banners hanging from the ceiling —the same emblem they found on Heinrich's card.

"Not quite an hourglass," he says. "Look closely, it's actually two letters, facing each other."

Hailee indeed distinguishes a gap in the logo, splitting it vertically in two identical halves, twin halves.

"Two Ms," she says.

"As in Malleus Maleficarum," adds Oliver.

"The guy really loves that book!" comments Hailee.

The stage lights up suddenly.

The main curtain is pulled up.

Heinrich makes his grand entrance.

The humming stops instantly. A searchlight is tracking Heinrich's every step. He, too, is wearing a monk robe, but his head is partially uncovered.

"My children," he begins, "I have come back again, I have come to save you!" he says, his voice echoing through speakers in the giant ballroom.

"This has been an extremely long and difficult journey. For the last five centuries, I have worked tirelessly to protect you," he continues, each of his words paired with grand gesture, in a perfectly choreographed —and probably rehearsed— speech.

"I have been your shield. And your sword. I have been your prophet. And your servant. In 1487, in the Darkest of ages, I started this fight against the most wicked, vile and maleficent enemy —witches!" he whispers in the microphone pinned to his habit. "Most of them were caught. But many escaped. Once again, they are standing in our way, plotting in the shadows, in a world unknown to most of you. That secret underworld has allowed them to disrupt the natural course of History. It has allowed them to delay the inevitable, the Apocalypse and the necessary cleansing of this Earth."

"This guy is nuts," says Oliver.

"Shh," says Hailee, fearing someone might hear him.

Heinrich has grabbed a silver goblet on a pedestal next to him. He takes a large sip of the viscous mixture bubbling inside, slime sharing the surface with unidentified chunks.

Nothing happens, until he drops the goblet to the floor.

He cringes suddenly, his face crisscrossed by painful twitches and convulsions. His entire body is soon afflicted, seemingly growing under his robe, nearly doubling in size within seconds — both in height and width. When he reopens his eyes, they are glowing red...

"I can see them..." he whispers, his voice trembling.

The audience is conquered and bewitched. Hailee and Oliver are speechless.

"I am watching them," continues Heinrich. "Soon I will lead you to their hideout. The witches can't get away," he says, shaking, slowly getting back to his still pretty creepy self.

"The time has come to complete our mission," says Heinrich, placing his hand on a mysterious object covered with a black cloth on the table.

"Today, I bring you the key to their secret world," he murmurs.

All eyes are now on Heinrich's hand, or more exactly, on whatever is sitting underneath it. Lost in the crowd, Mr. Doyle is smiling really big, seemingly hypnotized by Heinrich's words.

"I give you… the Orbatrum," shouts the man on stage, pulling the cloth off, unveiling —a globe, apparently identical to Archibald's, from the lions' feet to the crank on top.

In theater, Heinrich's dramatic move would be called a Deus-ex-Machina, something that appears out of nowhere to change the outcome of a story. And sure enough, Heinrich gets the effect he counted on, triggering a gasp that reverberates among the audience.

The loudest reaction comes from above though, from the balcony.

"No!" shouts Hailee, recognizing her brother's globe.

Oliver pulls her away from the balustrade. But Heinrich's bodyguards are already headed upstairs.

"We gotta go!" he yells, grabbing Hailee's hand.

They retrace their steps back down, while Heinrich's men are coming up through the grand staircase.

Seeing the main entrance unobstructed, the two intruders run outside without looking back. They soon reach the street and mix with the Christmas crowd.

"Did you see his face? And his body? Was that some special effect?" asks Oliver.

"I don't know," utters Hailee, still in shock —but for another reason.

"He has my brother's globe," she says, while slaloming around pedestrians and traffic.

"How could he get it?" shouts Oliver.

"Don't you understand? It's your dad, he gave it to him!" says Hailee, angry.

"That's impossible. My dad didn't know where I put it."

"He must have found it, in that room!" she says.

"He didn't even know the store had been wrecked."

"I'm telling you, he just lied to you."

"There's no way, I stopped by this morning and I swear, the globe was still there," says Oliver. "We're not far. I have to go check."

"What's the point? He has the globe now," says Hailee, as they reach the "Realm of Antiques."

Oliver doesn't want to say anything until he sees it —or not— with his own eyes. He unlocks the door. The store is a mess, reminding Hailee of her own house following the break-in. They have to carve a path through broken lamps and upside down furniture, their eyes riveted on that large mirror commanding the entrance to the back room.

One tap on the mirror frame and they are in. No globe in sight though.

"What are we doing? Oliver, he has the globe, see, there's nothing here," repeats Hailee.

Oliver remains silent and walks to the circular ottoman in the middle of the room.

He kneels down, detaches one of the top cushions and pushes it aside.

"I knew it!" says Oliver as he looks inside.

"What?" asks Hailee.

Oliver slowly pulls something out and turns around to show her —it's Archibald's globe.

"That's impossible! How can it be?" lets out Hailee, surprised and relieved. "What was that other globe then?"

"I have no clue. But the real question is: why would Heinrich want this globe so bad if he has one already? It doesn't make sense," says Oliver.

Now backstage, Heinrich has taken his monk robe off. In pants and tee shirt, a towel on his shoulders, he seems exhausted, like an actor after a demanding performance. In fact, he is sitting in front of a Hollywood-style mirror, with a 20-bulb frame —the same kind of mirror you'd find in the dressing room of a professional theater.

"This was a great speech, Master," says one of his minions, the one who drives him around everywhere. A few punches on the nose have given him a bulldog profile and a twangy duck voice.

"Thank you Edward."

While petting a snow-white cat on his lap, Heinrich is inspecting the globe he unveiled earlier to his followers. It looks exactly like Archibald's, to the last detail it seems, including the imaginary islands, the missing American continents. And all the monsters.

"May I ask you a question Master?"

"You may Edward."

"I was wondering, what would those people think if they knew this globe was broken?"

"Those people don't think Edward, they follow," says Heinrich.

"I understand but…"

"Soon, we'll have a new globe, all questions will be answered, all doubts will vanish, and the prophecy will be realized," assures Heinrich.

"Yes Master," says Edward, about to leave the room.

"Edward," says Heinrich, calling him back.

"Yes Master."

Heinrich reaches into his jacket folded on the counter in front of him, and pulls out a picture of Archibald —probably the picture Kate gave him when they met.

"Find this boy, I think he has the globe," he says. "And Edward…"

"Yes Master."

"Don't forget about the Grandma," he says in a cryptic tone.

ᚾᚾᚾ

MARE

DAMNVM

GALLI TERRA

KAKKEN

srinkiden

melwinne

urlagone serpentis

MARE

MYRMECIA

PERDITVM

tungo

MAXIBVL

rarund

MANDIBVLA TORR

Bunung

LOBVL

sarauna

ARACHNAGAR

Heolstor

VMBRA

THE JOURNEY TO BELIFENDOR

A deep turmoil has gripped Gristlemoth. Except for Archibald, nobody quite knows how to deal with Parnel's rebirth. The whole village has assembled at Cleofa to see her. She is standing in the schoolyard, in front of the chalkboard still full of drawings, warnings and instructions. Until this morning, this is where they studied Marodors, how to identify their weaknesses, how to fight them, how to fear them. Everything they knew, everything they thought true, now seems uncertain.

"Everyone please be quiet!" demands Faerydae, facing an over-whelming barrage of questions from many, waving their hands and shouting over one another.

"Is this really Parnel?" asks one of them.

"How do we know it's not trumpery?" asks another.

"A ruse," Faerydae translates for Archibald.

He gives her the most confident "I know" nod, even though he surely didn't remember.

"Maybe she's like a Trojan horse, a way for the others to get in," says Naida, adding her voice to the swell of concerns.

"Why don't we let her answer for herself!" suggests Maven.

Parnel waits until everyone has gone silent to speak.

"I understand your doubts," she says, serene and peaceful. "I'm not asking you to trust me. I'm not even sure I can trust myself."

Her remark sets off more commotion.

"Put her back in her cage," screams someone.

"Lock her up," echoes another.

Even Rhiannon has doubts.

"This is too risky," she says.

Parnel starts speaking again.

"My friends, my sisters, I don't know if I'm fully back to myself, but I know what brought me back among you," she says, turning to Archibald. "What brought me back is kindness, attention and care. That's what our mothers taught us. That's what I'm asking you to trust, what's in your heart."

In the crowd, it's shakers versus nodders. Many, like Naida, don't seem convinced. They are shaking their heads. Still, Parnel seems to have won over a few people, ready to give her a chance. They are the ones nodding. Some of them are even tearing up.

"We have to heal more Marodors," shouts Archibald.

"What do you mean?" asks Naida.

"We know how to do it," preaches Archibald. "We know how to treat them, we know what to feed them. We can heal them all."

"The rest of them are different, they're not like Parnel, they've always been Marodors, they've got nothing to get back to," notes one girl.

"She's right Archibald," says Faerydae, "what worked with Parnel might not work with all Marodors."

"We don't know that, we just have to try!" says Archibald. "You told me yourself, we don't even know what Marodors are to begin with. Maybe they are the products of wars and bloodshed. Maybe they are demons. But maybe they're just people, trapped in this world, like all of you, just in a different way. And what about the other girls, your sisters, all those who became Marodors while fighting them? Don't they deserve a chance to be cured? We have to help them! Some of them might even be here, in those cages."

"What do you know about this world?" Asks Naida.

"You're right, Not much. But what do we have to lose? Why don't we uncover their cages at least," pleads Archibald.

"Crack-brain!" yells Rhiannon, who has joined the shakers.

"Think about it, why are Marodors so attracted to the lights of this place? Look at them!" says Archibald, pointing at the beasts flying around Gristlemoth. "Maybe it's the sun!" he says. "Maybe they know the sun can heal them!"

"What are you suggesting?" asks Naida. "That we just let them in and see what happens. You're right, maybe they'll just get a tan and be on their way…"

"That's not what I'm saying, I'm talking about healing the Marodors we have here first."

"You can't tell us what to do," responds Naida. "*We* have to decide what's good for us."

"I'm sorry Naida but as you know, only one person can make such a choice," corrects Faerydae.

Naida backs down in agreement.

"Who's that?" asks Archibald.

"The Queen!" she answers.

"The what?" he asks.

"Her name is Helena. We call her our Queen," says Faerydae. "She is the mother of us all, she is the one who sent us here, and taught us everything. If we're going to change the way we treat Marodors, she'll have to approve it first. Maybe *you* can convince her."

"Okay let's go talk to that Queen then, where is she?" asks Archibald.

"That's… complicated," says Faerydae.

Archibald and Faerydae have walked up to the library. From a long leather tube, she pulls out a rolled up map, and spreads it flat on a study by the window. It was drawn on parchment paper. At the top, it reads:

THE WORLD OF LEMUREA

"It looks very much like… Europe", says Archibald, discovering a continent with extremely rough and approximate coastlines, yet also familiar contours.

"I know. Only with time did we realize that. A very long time. It took nearly three hundred years of exploring to make this map," notes Faerydae. "In many ways, Lemurea is all but a mirror image of our old world, only, its darkest side."

And dark this world certainly is, with mountains shaped like fangs, erupting volcanoes throughout, and creatures roaming the lands and seas, from Mare Monstrum in the south to Mare Damnum in the north.

"The main purpose of the map is to locate our colonies, see, each of them is symbolized by a different rune," says Faerydae, showing him signs he has become more or less accustomed to, scattered throughout the map.

"How many are there?" asks Archibald, his eyes travelling from one bizarre name to another, from Agrestal to Marrowclaw, Beorbor, Spinkiden, Yolkenrof and others…

"Twelve," she says.

"How come those are different?" he inquires, pointing at Tungolwald, south of a region called Myrmecia, and Arkæling, in the far eastern reaches of Lemurea, right by a vast Terra Obscuria.

"Those are marked with a flower of life turned black," says Faerydae. "It means the colony has fallen to Marodors."

"Scary," lets out Archibald. "Where are we exactly?" he asks.

"Right here, this is Gristlemoth," she says, her index pinned right in the Center of Lemurea, in the land of Kakkerlakan. It matches the area Archibald selected by pressing that pin down into the globe with his pen —but he doesn't make that connection.

"How did I land here?" he laments. "I'm so far from home."

"This is where we want to go," explains Faerydae, moving her finger to the East, all the way to a city surrounded by mountains, between Gurguria and Worgonia.

"Belifendor?" reads Archibald.

"That's where the Queen lives," confirms Faerydae.

It also happens to be where the first crack in the globe was located. Archibald doesn't remember that either. He just noticed something else though: a small detail standing between them and the Queen.

"Does it say Transylvania right here?"

"Yes, the land beyond the forest, we've got to cross those mountains," she confirms.

"Vampires," murmurs Archibald.

"What was that?"

"You've never heard of vampires?"

"No, what are they?" she asks.

"Maybe it's just a legend but, I've heard they're creatures that suck the life out of you!"

"Oh those! We call them Marodors around here!" she says. "And they're not a legend, they're real."

Archibald lets out a nervous laugh, not too sure how to feel about that. Faerydae goes back to the map.

"See the problem is, there's no other colony between us and Belifendor. The closest would be Marrowclaw, but still way off-course" she explains. "That means no stopping anywhere. That means more supplies to carry, more golems on our backs, more caution, and in the end, more time. That's why the trip is so difficult."

"How long will it take?" he asks.

"The last time I went there was about thirty years ago. Back then, it took me about two weeks," says Faerydae.

A look of bewilderment has gripped Archibald's face.

"What's wrong?" she asks.

"I'm not sure what the craziest part is," he says, "that you were alive thirty years ago, or that it takes two weeks to travel to another country!"

"You don't understand," she says. "Not only it's far, but the area in between is infested with Marodors, land Marodors mostly."

"Like the Krakatorum?" he asks.

"Maybe not as big, but yes, that kind."

"It could take less time if we don't encounter too many of them. But even in the best case scenario, it's still a five to six days journey," notes Faerydae. "No matter what, we can't leave right away, we have to wait until Wymer is done fixing the tank."

"Fixing the tank? You mean building a new one?" says Archibald. "It's going to take months, we can't wait that long."

"I have been here for nearly five hundred years, trust me, I think I can wait a few weeks," says Faerydae.

"But Parnel can't! Naida wants her back in her cage, until we get a decision from your Queen," Archibald reminds her.

"There's no other way," assures Faerydae. "Besides, nobody wants to go. I might be able to convince Maven, but not Rhiannon."

"I thought her leg had been fixed."

"It's not her leg. She just doesn't believe in all this. I don't think she'll come."

"I will," says a voice coming from the hallway.

Archibald and Faerydae turn around, surprised to see —Lenora.

"Really?" says Archibald.

"Don't get me wrong," she says, "I think this whole idea is crazy but hey, it fits me right?"

"I'm sorry Lenora but you can't come," says Faerydae.

"Why?" asks the volunteer.

"You know why. And no offense but we need people with experience," says Faerydae.

"No offense but the casting is rather limited," replies Lenora.

"Thanks, but no thanks," repeats Faerydae.

"I'm so sick of this!" shouts Lenora. "This is why I have no experience. My mother always tried to protect me. And now you're doing the same thing! It's not fair."

Faerydae takes a few seconds to think.

"You know we're not flying there right?" she finally says.

"Unfortunately," grins Lenora.

"Okay then!" says Faerydae, making Lenora grin even bigger.

"Flying would definitely help!" says Archibald.

"It's one thing to levitate Marodors a few inches off the ground, it's quite another to make you fly," explains Faerydae. "No golem is powerful enough for that."

"Why don't we give it a shot?" he insists.

"And you don't think we have?" says Faerydae.

"Maybe not enough," he says.

"Not enough huh?" smirks Faerydae, uncovering her left shoulder. "See this was on my twenty third, and last, attempt," she says, showing a scar as long and wide as the zipper on a pair of trousers.

"Ouch!" says Archibald. "And no flying broom right?"

Faerydae shakes her head.

"Just checking," he says, turning back to the map.

"Maybe there's a shortcut somewhere," he mumbles.

"We know all the shortcuts, it's six days, minimum," she says.

"What if we take this river?" he asks, following the course of the *Urlagone*, running all the way to the *Loch Tenebris*, a nearly enclosed sea right by Belifendor.

"And how do you propose we do that?"

"We have boats, don't we? That way, we can bring cannons with us. And no need to deal with those land Marodors," he says, pretty proud of his idea.

"It wouldn't work," says Faerydae. "Those boats are too small, good enough for the Rhodon but that's about it."

"The Rhodon?" he asks.

"The river going through Gristlemoth," she says. "By the way, yes, we would avoid the land Marodors, but then we'd have to deal with river Marodors."

"There are river Marodors?" he says, surprised.

"Yes I told you, some of them swim," explains Faerydae. "And that's another problem, we know how to handle Marodors on land, but we've never fought them on water," she says.

"I should be the one freaking out, I don't even know how to swim!" says Archibald.

"This is *really* crazy," smiles Lenora, even more excited now.

"So we're going!" exclaims Archibald.

Faerydae rolls her eyes, not too sure what she's getting into.

It's a new day in Gristlemoth —a decisive day. Wymer has abandoned his tank "repair" for a moment, to focus on prepping the boats by the river. The raad fish have been transferred into large buckets nearby. The old canoes are ready to regain their original purpose, after Wymer is done fitting them with an invention of his own.

"What are you doing?" asks Maven.

"Since you won't get any cover from the trees, I'm adding a special camouflage to the boats," he explains, stretching a blanket above the second skiff, fixing it to wooden poles at each end.

"How does it work?" asks Lenora, inspecting the canoe already on the river.

"Well, it's simple really. Instead of branches and leaves, we put water on there!"

"How can you put water on cloth?" asks Maven.

"Archibald painted some waves on it, he's quite an artist actually," says Wymer, showing her the rippling patterns, green, white and blue. "He calls it troopaloy, or something like that, pardon my French!"

"It's a trompe l'oeil!" corrects Faerydae as she walks over, "it means trickery of the eye."

"That's exactly what I said, troopaloy," repeats Wymer.

Indeed, from above, thanks to Archibald's magic, the boats now completely blend in with the water. Wymer can add his final touch: cannons, installed at both ends of each canoe.

Maven and Lenora start loading in bags of food and piles of ammunition —meaning golems.

"Looks like we're ready to go," says Faerydae, helping them. "Where's Archibald?" she asks.

No one seems to know.

Archibald is with Parnel. As planned, Naida —and many others still wary of that hybrid Marodor— had her put back into her cage. Parnel didn't resist. She looks terribly sad though.

"I'm sorry," Archibald tells her through the bars, "they didn't want to see you roam around the village, they're worried."

"I understand, this is still unknown for most of us, including me. People always fear the unknown," says Parnel.

"Still, it's not right," says Archibald.

"I want you to know something," she says, "I am so thankful for everything you've done for me already."

"Hopefully I'll have more luck with your Queen," he says. "I just have to tell her how special you are and I'm sure it will work!"

"I'm not that special," says Parnel.

"I don't know how you were before this," says Archibald, "but I find you pretty awesome now."

"Thanks," says Parnel.

"And don't worry," he adds, "I made sure they'd give you all the sugar you want."

"You know, I've started eating regular food again," she says.

"You mean, carrots and stuff?"

She nods, looking ashamed almost.

"See you're more courageous than I am!" he says. "Be careful though, I might start to believe there's something wrong with you after all!"

Parnel smiles at last. Archibald walks away, trying to hide from her the tears he is fighting back. He squats down by Paws, who now follows him everywhere.

"You take care of her okay, I trust you," he tells the rectangular "dog", who stops wagging his tail, crashes to the ground, and pouts.

Thirty something girls have gathered by the Rhodon River to bid the four adventurers farewell. If Archibald and his comrades wanted to know how much support they have in Gristlemoth, this would be a good way to gauge it: 30 something out of 287 —just about a 10% approval rating. Hopefully Archibald won't be running for mayor anytime soon.

"Where's everyone?" he asks.

"I guess they're not crazy about this whole plan," says Faerydae.

Fortunately, Wymer has a last minute surprise to cheer them up.

"New armors for all!" he shouts, unloading his bag of treats.

"For us too?" asks Lenora.

"Of course for you too!" he says, handing her a bark body armor carved with Gristlemoth's wave logo.

"Thanks but I don't need it, I only believe in the power of golems and runes," says Maven, a tad condescending.

"Suit yourself, or not!" jokes Wymer. "Seriously though, travelling so far without a tank, you might want to reconsider."

Gathering her armor, Faerydae notices weird objects mixed with the bark body plates, some kind of deep wooden bowls with a handle and straps.

"I don't think we're going to eat much stew on this trip Wymer. What are these bowls for?" she asks.

"They're not bowls you silly, they're helmets!" says the handyman. "I figured after what happened with the Krakatorum, you need to protect those small skulls of yours!"

"Cool!" says Archibald, the only one getting excited about that new piece of armor, pulling his hair back to fit it best on his head. Wymer helps him.

"Young knight, you're wearing it the wrong way," says Wymer, flipping the helmet around. "See this part here is a nose guard, no need to tell you what it's for, the name speaks for itself right!"

That's the part Faerydae confused with a bowl handle. Archibald has a hard time seeing with that narrow piece of wood hanging down the very middle of his face, from his forehead all the way to his mouth. It makes him want to go crossed-eyed.

"You'll be okay!" says Wymer, adjusting the helmet so he can see better. "I also carved a rune on each helmet, see right here, each one is different," he says, pointing right at his forehead.

"Which rune do I get?" asks Maven, now showing interest.

"No magic there Maven, sorry to disappoint, just a good luck charm, that's all!" says Wymer.

But she doesn't mind, happy to have found a helmet with one of her favorite runes, the Perfidrae arrow, ᚾ̂ —even though she loves them all of course.

"What rune did *you* get?" she asks Archibald.

"I'm not sure," he says, taking his helmet off. "Hey I've seen this one before!" he says. He just can't quite remember where.

Was it in the fridge back home? Maybe on that pack of frozen salmon polluting my ice cream? he wonders. It is indeed shaped somewhat like a fish: ᙂ.

For a helmet Archibald picked randomly, it's not a bad coincidence, considering the journey about to begin. But that rune evokes something different to Maven, taken aback the second she sees it.

"That's weird," she says.

"What is it?" asks Archibald.

"It's just that, I've not seen this in so long," she says. "Wymer, where did you find this rune?"

"I don't know, I did it from memory I guess. What did I do now? Am I in trouble again? Are you gonna turn me into an hairy monster? I'm afraid I've already become one on my own," he says, laughing.

"What's wrong with this rune?" Archibald asks Maven. "Is it bad luck or something?"

"No," she says, "it's one of the first runes we worked on when we got down here."

"What does it do?" he insists.

Maven seems hesitant to tell him.

"It doesn't matter anymore," she says, before walking away.

"That girl is so weird," Archibald tells Wymer.

"She's a girl!" simply says Wymer.

Archibald is sharing a boat with Maven. Lenora is with Faerydae. This is no random pairing. They argued about it for nearly an hour before deciding on who was best at picking the golems and who would operate each cannon.

Rhiannon comes running last minute, conflicted at the idea of her companions leaving without her. But the boats have departed already. Within a minute, they reach Gristlemoth's wall. It sure doesn't take long to cross this village. For a few seconds, one of the huge boulders restraining the weak flow of the river is moved out of the way, just enough for the two boats to be set free.

The Rhodon snakes through the forest for miles. It's a calm ride. Archibald is twisting his paddle to try and catch some fish whose eyes are glowing green on the sand bottom of the river. The darkness makes the phosphorescent spectacle even more fascinating.

Lenora is using her paddle to splash everyone. They all laugh. This would almost feel like a camping trip. They are starting to think the cannons are taking up too much room on the boats. Wymer's camouflage is working as planned. The Marodors flying above seem to be completely oblivious to the presence of the boats.

Lenora is acting a bit strange though. She keeps turning around each time Faerydae looks back at her.

"What's with you Lenora?" asks Faerydae.

"Nothing, why?" she answers.

"You're hiding something from me," says Faerydae.

"No I'm not," says Lenora.

"Really? You think I'm buzzard-blind?"

"What's buzzard-blind?" Archibald asks Maven.

"Buzzard-blind, you know, squirrel minded," she says.

Archibald doesn't get it.

"It's like Chuckle-pate but more like lourdish, duncified almost but definitely more boobyish if you know what I mean."

"I don't!" says Archibald, shaking his head.

"You know, witless, frost-brained, mossy, potato-headed?"

"Stupid," sums up Faerydae, "I'm not stupid," she says. "So Lenora, what are you hiding?"

Lenora pulls out several candy bars from one of the leather pouches attached to her belt.

"The sugar is for Parnel and Parnel only!" fumes Faerydae. "It's not good for you!"

"But I like it," says Lenora.

"I do too," admits Maven, pulling a lollipop out of her bag.

"Do I need to tell you what I think?" asks Archibald, sticking one in his mouth.

"Archibald, you are the worst influence on everyone, I swear," sighs Faerydae.

"Thank you!" he says proudly. "By the way, you keep saying sugar is not good for us, but how do you know, if you've not even tried it?"

"It's just bad," she repeats.

"Says who?" asks Archibald.

"Says me. And says the Queen," simply answers Faerydae.

"With all due respect, the Queen is wrong on this one," quips Archibald.

Soon, the quiet, peaceful Rhodon merges with the Urlagone, five times as wide and with a much stronger current. No need for paddles any more. From here, they will only be useful to guide the boats. Archibald realizes the Rhodon was more a stream than a river. He looks down, worried suddenly. He can't see the bottom anymore.

"How deep is this?" he asks. "About three feet you think?"

"Are you serious?" says Maven. "More like twenty."

Archibald is not feeling that comfortable on this boat suddenly.

"Do you know how to swim?" he asks.

"Of course!" says Maven. "You do too right?"

"Of course!" nods Archibald, gripping both sides of the skiff in fear. He might have something else to worry about, something worse than not seeing the bottom of the river. The glowing fish eyes have indeed disappeared, replaced by ferociously red glares, emanating from the forest.

"Marodors!" says Lenora, who first spots them.

"Don't worry, they can't catch us," says Archibald, emboldened to address the Marodors directly: "What's happening guys? You're afraid of the water?" he shouts, taunting them.

"Careful," warns Maven, "some of them might be able to fly!"

"Or swim," says Lenora.

"Or both," tops Faerydae.

Archibald returns to his default mode —scared and quiet—, and puts his helmet back on.

"If we keep up this pace, we could be in Belifendor in less than two days," says Faerydae, as the boats zoom down the Urlagone, out of reach to Marodors on land and invisible to those above.

The night seems darker suddenly. And colder. Archibald is shivering. Lenora is drawing clouds from her breath, blowing them upwards, adding a layer to the thick blanket of fog hovering above the river. Faerydae and Maven, steering the boats, can barely see where they're going.

"Am I dreaming?" Archibald wonders aloud.

He could swear he has just seen a church on the left bank of the river, a tall building with a cross at the top.

"That's Uvarok," says Faerydae.

"There's a church over there," he says.

"There *was* a church there," she says. "In fact, a whole city once."

Spectral in the mist, the church blends in with other ruins around. Nothing much is left standing, some buildings partially burnt down, others completely flattened, covered with moss.

"Marodors…" utters Archibald.

"Don't be mistaken," says Faerydae, "the devastation you see here was not caused by Marodors, it's the result of Men."

"I don't understand?" says Archibald.

"Our mothers used to visit this place long before they sent us here. They told us of a world frozen in time, something resembling the Earth, only, the worst parts," explains Faerydae. "The Queen warned us though: Lemurea is also a glimpse into the Earth's future, of what it could become, if Marodors take over."

"How?" asks Archibald.

"How what?" asks Faerydae.

"Your mothers, how did they come here? Before the globes I mean."

"Secret potions, deep meditation, allowing them to have a foot in both worlds," explains Faerydae.

"Why would anyone want to come here? Do you think London looks like this?" he asks.

"I know it does, I saw it with my own eyes," says Faerydae.
Archibald gapes at the ruins. As if the fog was not
bad enough, the current is getting even stronger,
causing the boats to turn upon themselves,
seemingly caught in a powerful whirlpool.
"I can't control the boat!" shouts Faerydae.
She realizes her paddle is not even touching
the water anymore. The boat she shares
with Lenora is being lifted off the river.
"I think we hit a tree," says Lenora. And indeed,
leaning to the starboard side, she finds a giant root,
woven in strips not unlike those of her braided hair.
"That's no tree," whispers Faerydae.
A large bulging eye has just opened on those gnarled
vines —inches away from Lenora's face. Almost
instantly, her eyes grow to mirror the one staring at her.
"Marodor!" screams Maven, pointing at multiple tentacles
holding onto the canoe from underneath. At the end of
those arms is a dark hole, ancestor of the garbage disposal,
with a blend of small suckers and teeth like splinters.
"Holy Bejabbles!" exclaims Lenora.
"Just what I was thinking!" mutters
Archibald, glad —and stunned— to finally
hear someone else use that unique expression.
"Is that an octopus?" says Maven.
She can't really see a face
anywhere, just plenty of eyes,

human eyes. Scattered on each tentacle, they open one after another...

"Use your cannons!" shouts Faerydae.

"Prama, Inflecto, Brachiamorphis," says Maven, sharing her picks with Lenora.

"She wants to turn him into ice!" translates Faerydae. But Lenora's cannon has just fallen overboard and drowned. Maven herself is unable to follow through. Sucked up by the current, she can't turn the boat to adjust her fire.

Whatever breed he is, this Marodor got some smart genes. He is using half of his tentacles to grab onto the boats, and spinning the other half under water at high speed, turning them into huge propellers. Not only that balancing act allows him to move around quickly, but it also feeds that tornado-like swirl to confuse his preys and disable their boats. The situation is dire.

Suddenly, a loud bang echoes through the mist. That shot came from Archibald. He literally fed the golem to the Marodor, lodging it in his mouth.

"That's one out of three!" he shouts.

Faerydae is now struggling to just stand on her feet. She manages to fire the second golem but it flies right past the beast. She turns to her paddle, hitting the Marodor right where it hurts —in the eyeballs!

"Aim for the eyes!" she screams, which is not the hardest task in the world since that beast must have two hundred of them!

Archibald is pretty good at this game, wielding his paddle as if it were a sword.

"Bulls' eye!" he shouts each time he pokes one.

Maven is not bad either but she can't avoid that wide swing from the Marodor.

She is thrown off the boat. Her cannon follows. Archibald pulls her back in, rescuing her seconds before a tentacle could grab her. Shivering from the icy water but looking angrier than ever, Maven is back hitting the Marodor with all her strength. She might be little, but she is fierce!

Lenora has picked up another Inflecto golem. Since her cannon is gone, she has a different idea in mind. Climbing onto the edge of the boat, she seems to be bracing herself for a dive.

"Lenora no!" yells Faerydae, doubtful of her companion's intentions.

Undaunted, Lenora jumps off and lands on one of the beast's tentacles. She struggles to grab onto that woodsy worm undulating underneath her. When she finally gets a good grip, she sticks her golem into one of the Marodor's eye sockets, right before letting go. She lands back onto the boat —with Faerydae's body acting as a protective buffer, absorbing the shock from that harsh dismount.

"You really want to get killed!" yells Faerydae, glad nonetheless to have her back.

Even by Lemurea's standards, Lenora's move was unorthodox. And daring for sure. But it paid off. Combined with Prama, the Inflecto golem is already having an effect, freezing some of the water on the beast's tentacles, which get paralyzed one by one.

Already crumbling under an avalanche of paddle hits, the beast recedes back into the water with a few dozen black eyes —half shut or blinking like stroboscopes.

Archibald and his friends can catch their breath, emerging mostly unscathed in a scene of confusion and chaos. Most of their food and provisions are floating around. Many golems are missing. Faerydae and Lenora's boat is severely damaged, suffering several leaks at the bottom. Wymer's camouflage is also gone, now leaving them vulnerable to flying beasts.

They are definitely not out of danger. About two hundred feet away, the Marodor has just resurfaced, only two eyes at first, bug eyes, detaching from the gloom. Perched at the end of long antennas, they are acting as periscopes. They recess back into the submarine body as it finally emerges, massive and deceiving. It's a toad, mainly. But unlike other Marodors covered with leaves, this one looks as though it was literally leaf-wrapped, like a stuffed appetizer. With moss, roots and mushrooms as toppings, the beast could easily be confused with an island, if not for the two sets of jagged tusks bulging out from both sides of a haunting face, part owl, part human.

Archibald and his friends realize the octopus represented only a portion of that monster —the tip of a dark iceberg.

The flip side they are now facing is even more terrifying —a threat of titanic proportions, with potentially fatal consequences on their journey.

"What the hell is that?" asks Lenora. "A different Marodor?"

"No, I think it's the same," says Maven.

"I've never seen anything like this," says Faerydae.

In fact, this monster is nowhere to be seen in the 182 pages of the "Grand (purposely incomplete) Bestiary of Marodors" —hence the "incomplete" part, and the many pages left blank at the end.

It will surely deserve a place of choice in that book, thinks Faerydae — only if they manage to escape him of course.

If bad news for sure, this Marodor is not entirely news to Archibald, who has the same sense of déjà-vu he had with that bear in a porcupine coat —only this time, it's not from the globe, it's from school. The beast's partially human face and his sparse moustache remind Archibald of Mrs. Richards, his Math teacher.

Hopefully this monster is not as mean, he prays.

"Let's not panic," says Faerydae, in a somewhat panicky tone.

"I thought he was frozen," says Archibald.

"Only partially. We need the last golem to trigger the full spell," says Maven.

"Hit him hard," she tells Archibald, handing him the key stone of the formula, Brachyamorphis, the one carrying probably the most whimsical rune of all, a swirl: ☉. A simple but deadly rune, which will complete the formula and turn the whole Marodor into ice. Archibald loads it quickly into his gun.

"Propellia Momentum!" Bang! His aim is perfectly in line with the target. But the golem falls short, into the water, ten feet away from the beast.

"We've got to get closer," says Lenora.

"I don't think we'll have to," says Faerydae.

The beast is on the move again, now using the non-frozen tentacles of his secondary body to propel himself.

Maven was right. The Marodor has been slowed down —but not stopped.

He is speeding up towards the boats, letting out a gurgling roar that ripples across the water. He is so massive that he is parting the river in his wake.

Lenora hands Faerydae another magic stone.

"This is our last Brachyamorphis, make it count," she says.

Faerydae wastes no time.

"Propellia Momentum!" The cannon fires. The golem and the Marodor are on a collision course. Faerydae's aim was dead on, right in the monster's face. But the golem bounces off one of his tusks...

Back on the boats, everyone knows what this means.

It's too late for Maven to come up with another spell.

Archibald exchanges a brief panic-stricken glance with Faerydae, right before the Marodor hits her boat.

She gets the brunt of the impact. Her helmet gets knocked off her head. She is projected all the way to the back, against Lenora. The front cannon flies over their heads. The monster lifts their canoe again, like a toy, with his tusks this time —and much higher. Both girls are just holding on to their seats, screaming.

"Jump!" Archibald shouts at them, seeing no other way.

It's probably the least bad solution at this point. Faerydae and Lenora look down, considering that option. They must be at least twenty feet in the air. They are hesitating. The Marodor makes the decision for them. Against all odds, he lets go of the boat.

Released from the monster's grip, the skiff levitates in the air for a second, before plummeting like a rock.

The drop is spectacular and frightful. Rhiannon covers her mouth. The small canoe crashes onto the water and breaks in a million pieces —literally a million! Both Faerydae and Lenora seem unconscious. They're about to drown.

Archibald and Maven scramble to get close to them. They manage to draw Faerydae out of the water. They are now paddling towards Lenora but the Marodor reaches her first. His tentacles are back in force, wrapping around her tiny body. Lying side by side, Maven and Archibald are using their paddles to attack the beast. Suddenly back to life, Faerydae joins them, using Rhiannon's helmet to punch a few eyes. But she is no match either.

The Marodor now has a strong hold on Lenora, who's still not moving, and he won't let go of her. He seems ready to settle for one prey. Using some of his tentacles as propellers again, he detaches from the boat and swims towards shore.

"Let's go, we have to follow him!" shouts Archibald. But neither Faerydae nor Maven seems eager to go after that beast.

Archibald can't contain himself.

"What's wrong with you?" he shouts. "We have to save her!"

"There are too many Marodors around," says Maven.

"We can't abandon her," he begs, paddling on his own.

Faerydae sits at the bottom of the canoe, shaking her head.

"Maven is right," she says, "we might catch up with him, but with one cannon left and just a handful of golems, we don't stand a chance."

"Faerydae please!" he shouts, tears coming to his eyes.

"I'm sorry Archibald, it's too late," she says.

The Marodor has reached the bank and started crawling in the mud. Soon he disappears through the ruins of Uvarok, dragging Lenora behind him.

THE ORBATRUM

Hailee's room has become the subject of an inquiry once more. Her parents are filling in for Scotland Yard's sleuths —for now. They both have the same look they had on their face the night Archibald disappeared.

"Maybe she missed her train last night," says Stuart.

"And went where?" snaps Kate. "She would have called."

Going through Hailee's nightstand drawers, Stuart finds the picture of a young man.

"Could this be something?" he asks Kate.

"Stuart please, that's that kid from that band!" she sighs.

"I dunno. How would I know?" he says.

"Maybe that's the problem, we are so out of touch our kids just can't connect," comments Kate.

"So they just leave, that's it?" asks Stuart. "I don't watch TV so it's my fault now," he says, visibly upset.

"I'm sorry, I'm just tired," she says.

"It's okay, we're both exhausted," says Stuart, switching to Hailee's desk, while Kate frantically explores the pile of curled up blankets on the mattress, still sitting on the floor.

"Maybe she stayed at a friend's house," he thinks aloud.

"I called Emily's parents, and Ella's parents. Nothing," she says. "Besides, Hailee doesn't do that, she would have left a note or something."

"Did you check in the kitchen?" he asks.

"Yes," says Kate.

"Did you see anything on the fridge?"

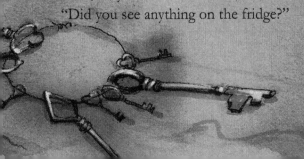

"I'm not sure."

"Let's check again," says Stuart.

They head downstairs, when they hear the tires of a car crushing the gravel in the driveway. Hopeful, Kate rushes to the front door and swings it open quickly. She is stunned. The two inspectors in charge of Archibald's disappearance are coming up the stairs. *What a strange coincidence,* she says to herself —unless it's not...

"What happened?" she asks right away, now imagining the worst about her daughter.

"I beg your pardon?" says one of the inspectors as they both reach the landing.

"Our daughter is missing," she says. "Do you know what happened to her?"

The two inspectors look at each other, dumbfounded. They obviously had no idea.

"Please come in," says Stuart.

The two police officers step in the foyer. The house is almost back to normal. The only trace of the break-in —in this room— is the marble statue still lying in pieces by the front door.

"Any news about Archibald?" asks Stuart, taking his wife's hand in his.

"I'm afraid not Sir," responds one officer.

"Is this regarding the break-in?" asks Stuart.

"No, we are not in charge of that, although the cases might be related," says the inspector.

"I'm sorry, what is this regarding then?" asks Stuart, looking even more worried now.

"I'm afraid we have more bad news," says the policeman.

Kate has placed her hand on her heart. She seems on the verge of a panic attack.

The officers exchange one more look. They seem much more careful with their words than the first time they came over.

"It's about your mother," says one of them.

"My mother?" says Stuart, with split feelings, relieved and astonished.

What could be worse for my mother? he thinks, *she's been dead for nearly two months now!*

"It's about her grave," says the inspector.

"What happened?"

The inspector clears his throat.

"Someone desecrated your mother's grave," he explains.

"What?" asks Stuart, in shock.

"It happened last night, most likely," says the other officer.

"This is crazy," says Kate.

"It gets worse," adds the inspector. "They broke into your mother's grave and… dug up the coffin."

"What?" exclaims Stuart.

"They stole her body," adds the officer.

"And replaced it with sandbags," completes his colleague.

Kate gasps. Stuart is speechless.

"Have you found her?" asks Kate.

"No Madam, I'm afraid the body is still missing."

"Who would do such a thing?" shouts Stuart.

"We don't know Sir," says one inspector.

"Although we have a theory," says the other.

"What is it?" asks Stuart. "Tell me."

"We think the people who broke into your house are the same who broke into your mother's grave."

"How do you know?" he asks.

"We think perhaps what they couldn't find here, they were looking for it in her coffin."

"That's crazy!" says Stuart.

"Yes it is Sir. We agree on that point. But it's also possible," says one inspector.

"Do you know of any jewelry, or any possessions, that would have been added into your mother's coffin?"

"Not to my knowledge no," says Stuart. "My mother was very... particular, she left precise instructions before her death. Bartholomeo, her butler and longtime friend, he took care of all the arrangements."

"If I may," asks the officer, "you said something about your daughter missing as well when we arrived?"

"We've not seen her since yesterday morning," notes Kate. "She didn't come back home last night."

"How old is she?" asks one of them.

"Fourteen," says Kate. "She'll be turning fourteen in a couple of months," she corrects.

The inspectors exchange another one of those perplexed looks.

"How was her relationship with your mother, Mister Finch?" one of them asks.

"Not too bad, we rarely saw my mother. She was very... secretive. We didn't even know she owned this house. Why are you asking this?"

"Any grudge your daughter could have had against your mother?" asks the other officer."

"Are you serious?" says Stuart. "You think Hailee..."

"You never know with teenagers nowadays!" says the officer with a serious face.

"As you know," explains his colleague, "we have to explore every option."

Stuart sits on the stairs, shaking his head. *This is such an absurd theory*, he thinks. He prefers not to comment, afraid he might not be able to parse his words carefully enough. Kate is not as diplomatic:

"So, let me get this straight," she says, "if I understand you correctly, we abused our son and now our daughter is a criminal?"

Hailee wakes up on the ottoman in which Oliver hid the globe. She is lying right above that secret compartment. They obviously spent the night in that hidden back room at his dad's shop. Not a chance that they would have swung by Grandma Celestine's grave.

Oliver has been up for a while. He is sitting on the other side of the large bench.

"Everything okay?" asks Hailee.

"I borrowed your phone," he says. "I hope it's okay?"

"Yes sure," she says. "What are you looking for?"

"Do you remember what Heinrich called the globe?" he asks.

"His globe or this one?" she asks, pointing at the one sitting next to Oliver.

"Both I guess! They look the same to me," he says.

"He called it Orbator or Orbatrum, or something like that?"

"That's it, the Orbatrum. I searched it online."

"Why are you asking if you already knew?" she asks.

"Just making sure I heard that right," he says.

"Did you find anything?"

"Nothing came up," says Oliver, "until I found this website about weird inventions."

"What kind of inventions?"

"All kinds," he says, seemingly hesitant to say more.

"Tell me," insists Hailee.

"Mind-reading machines, alien detectors, that kind of thing..."

"Are you serious?"

"I know right! Between this and the tabloid story, we're definitely dealing with a *special* kind of people."

"Loonies you mean!" sums up Hailee.

"Look," he says, "I agree, it all sounds crazy, but you heard Heinrich. It's not like he made any sense either. If you believe him, he is the one who started the whole witch-hunt thing with that book, five hundred years ago! And did you see his eyes after he drank from that cup? He looked possessed!"

"So what are you saying?" asks Hailee.

"What I'm saying is that pretty much everything surrounding this globe sounds crazy. So we might as well look into this website, even if, yes, I agree, it seems a bit nuts."

"Okay so what does it say about that... Orbatrum?"

"That's the thing," says Oliver, "it just lists it with other inventions but doesn't say anything about it."

"So we're stuck," she says.

"Maybe not," says Oliver. "I called the guy behind the website, he is right here in London."

"Great! Our own crazy professor!" jokes Hailee.

"Funny you said that!" says Oliver. "The guy is actually not a quack, he has a PHD in Astrophysics from Oxford and a degree in Biology from Cambridge."

"Really?" she says.

"I'm not joking, look, this is the guy, Professor Malcolm Brimble," he says, showing Hailee a picture on the phone.

And indeed, Professor Malcolm Brimble looks like the serious kind, a mix of Sigmund Freud and Albert Einstein, bald on top, curly on the sides, bushy above the eyes and tufted on the chin. Not to mention that pipe that couldn't be better angled in the corner of his furry mouth.

"We are meeting him at two o'clock," says Oliver.

"What? Why don't we just ask him questions on the phone?"

"That's the problem. He wants money."

"How much?" asks Hailee.

"Fifty pounds," says Oliver. "I have only fourteen."

Hailee checks her pockets, pulling out a few bills.

"And I only have twenty six," she says, "we are ten short."

"It should be fine," says Oliver. "It's not like the guy is starving, he's a professor!"

It's five to two. Hailee and Oliver arrive at the address Malcolm Brimble gave him, in Twickenham. At 52 Heath Road, they find —a carpet store.

"I knew it was a scam!" says Hailee.

"Maybe he lives up there?" suggests Oliver, looking at a couple of red bricks apartments above the store.

"Did he give you an apartment number?" she asks.

"No he didn't," says Oliver, checking the names listed on four doorbells next to a staircase stuck between the carpet store and a tanning salon.

"Here!" says Oliver, showing her the printed name on the bell: "Profesor Brimble."

"Professor with one s? This is a joke right?" she says.

"Maybe he ran out of room for the second one," says Oliver, not quite convincing Hailee —not quite convincing himself in fact!

He rings the bell.

"Yes," answers an old, moist voice with a Scottish accent so strong no one could ever get rid of it —not even the best Scottish actor in the world.

"It's Oliver, we talked on the ph…"

He gets cut off by a loud buzzer, which unlocks the gate.

"See!" Oliver says proudly. But Hailee has a doubt suddenly.

"Don't you think it's weird?"

"What?"

"That a renowned professor with two PHDs, from Oxford and Cambridge, would have nothing better to do on Christmas Eve than meet with us? That doesn't seem weird at all to you?"

"Not at all, quite the opposite actually," says Oliver. "Think about it, the guy is a scientist. He is so into his research that he doesn't care about Christmas!"

"Do you have an answer for everything?" asks Hailee.

"Not always, I remember one day when I didn't actually, it was a Monday a couple years ago I think, I was so mad," says Oliver.

"You're something else," says Hailee, grinning.

They go up to the first floor and come face to face with two doors. The left one reads: "Mr. Zolthar, Psychic." The right one: "Profesor Brimble," written by hand this time, with the same spelling error.

"Not enough room huh!" quips Hailee.

Oliver shrugs again. And knocks. A moment later, the tiny dot of light in the door peephole is eclipsed. Someone is looking at them.

"Fifty pounds, under the door," says the same voice with a slightly different accent.

"The guy sounds like he's from Istanbul now," worries Hailee. "Or some place even more exotic, I can't tell."

"Relax," says Oliver, not too concerned. He gathers their 40 pounds. Each bill is yanked from the other side as soon as Oliver slides the money under the door.

"We said fifty?" complains the voice, kind of back to the Scottish accent —and now with an angry undertone.

"Sorry Professor that's all we have, we hope it will be okay with you," says Oliver.

No reaction. In fact, Hailee and Oliver don't hear anything for a whole five minutes. Oliver knocks several times but still gets no answer. What can they do? Call the Police? They are actually about to leave, when the door finally opens.

"Please come in," says a young man of Indian origin, in his mid-20s, with tall fluffy hair, barefoot, in bottom pajamas cut roughly at the knees, and a tee shirt that reads: "1N73LL1G3NC3 15 7H3 4B1L17Y 70 4D4P7 70 CH4NG3, a quote by 573PH3N H4WK1NG.

"Hi," says Hailee.

"Please," says the young man, motioning for them to sit on the sofa, covered with blankets and bed pillows —and crumbs.

Oliver sits down right away, Hailee more reluctantly, pushing aside a sock and a cookie. This looks like a student's flat, the walls and bookshelves papered with post-it notes —definitely not what they expected. What they had in mind was closer to an old interior, with Professor Brimble seated behind a rich mahogany desk, with rows and rows of books behind him.

"So, how can I help you?" says the young man, slumping his lanky body in a rocking chair.

"Where's Professor Brimble?" asks Hailee.

The young man doesn't answer. And keeps rocking.

"Is he getting ready in the back?" asks Oliver, pointing to a door behind him.

"Oh no that's the bathroom," says the young man. "And... I am Professor Malcolm Brimble," he says, switching from his strong Indian accent to a weird Scottish one, arching his eyebrow into a Freudian curve.

"What? I knew it was a scam!" fumes Hailee, standing up.

"You gotta give us our money back," says Oliver, up as well.

"Relax," says the young man. "What did you expect? An old professor, seated behind a rich mahogany desk, with rows and rows of books behind him?"

"Yes!" Hailee and Oliver answer at once.

"See that's the problem!" shouts the young man. "Nobody would take me seriously if I posted my own picture, not to mention my real name, Philip Vivekananda."

"That's not true!" says Hailee, "we don't judge people based on their name or the way they look."

"Really?" insists Philip.

Hailee doesn't answer, while Oliver nods, both admitting grudgingly that he has a point.

"Who's Professor Brimble then?" asks Oliver.

"I made him up! I borrowed the picture from the guy next door."

"The psychic?" questions Hailee.

"He's not really a psychic. He's an actor. It was either that picture or another one of him as a dentist."

"You're such a liar!" shouts Oliver.

"Yes," says Philip, proudly almost.

"And a fraud!" adds Hailee.

"No, *that* is not true," objects the young man, visibly offended. "I know my stuff. And I know a lot about the Da Vinci globe."

Hailee and Oliver freeze suddenly. And sit back on the sofa.

"How do you know Da Vinci made it?" asks Hailee.

"I told you, I know my stuff."

"The Orbatrum?" asks Oliver.

"Yes, I might have not gone to Oxford or Cambridge, *yet,* but I have studied time travel in great lengths," says Philip.

"Time travel?" asks Oliver.

"That's what the Orbatrum was for!" says Philip. "I think."

"What do you mean you think?" says Hailee.

Philip jumps off his chair to go through post-its glued to the window frame.

"Here, Orbatrum!" he says, peeling off one of them. "It is a combination of two Latin words," he explains, squinting at his scribbles: "Orbis, which means world, and Atrum, which means dark and obscure. To me, there is no doubt, the globe was a gateway, between two worlds. Now did it mean traveling to a different time? Or a different dimension? Or both? That, I am not one hundred percent sure."

"How's that possible?" asks Oliver.

"How can you travel through a globe?" adds Hailee.

"Da Vinci was a genius," says Philip. "He studied electricity before it was called electricity. He studied clouds and thunder. Some people think he succeeded in harnessing the power of lightning, creating an enormous vortex, some sort of wormhole, that could warp the limits of time and eliminate the boundaries of space."

Hailee's head is spinning.

"That's what the globe does?" she mutters.

"That's what it was capable of, yes, if you believe all those legends I read," says Philip. "I *do* believe them by the way!" he concludes.

"Obviously," comments Oliver.

"They called it the Ark," says Philip, with poetry in his voice.

"What?" asks Hailee.

"The Orbatrum, some people referred to it as the Ark," he explains.

"Why?" asks Oliver.

"I don't really know," admits Philip. "Maybe it was like a wink, a reference to Noah's Ark. But instead of animals, it was meant to save people, from some kind of catastrophe. It could have been anything. They had the bloody Plague back then, so who knows!"

Hailee and Oliver exchange a deep gaze, trying to make sense of everything.

"Why a globe by the way?" asks Oliver.

"What do you mean?" says Philip.

"Why would he put that time machine in a globe?"

"*That's* interesting!" shouts Philip, who stands up again to grab another post-it, on his bookshelf this time. "What is a vortex?" he asks, almost professorial.

Both Oliver and Hailee shake their heads.

"A vortex," says Philip, now reading from his note, "is a region in a fluid where the flow rotates around an axis line."

Oliver and Hailee seem pretty lost.

"Don't you get it?" says Philip. "Remember, Da Vinci created a vortex to allow time travel, or multi-dimensional travel. So… what better than a terrestrial globe to have the flow of that vortex rotate around an axis line?

They don't have an answer —shockingly.

"Nothing!" shouts Philip. "Nothing is better than a globe to achieve that. It is pure genius!"

"How does it work exactly?" asks Oliver.

"It's a globe Man! You spin it! And then you travel!" says Philip as if it were self-evident.

Hailee has an important question on her mind, probably the most crucial for her:

"How do you come back?" she asks.

"You guys are pretty smart!" says Philip. "Well, that is a tricky question. Most stories I have read speak of people who never came back. They were just stuck wherever or whenever it was they traveled, with the globe staying behind."

Hailee tilts her head down. *I'll never see Arch again*, she thinks.

"But…" adds Philip, "*I* personally believe anyone traveling through that globe *could* potentially come back."

"How?" asks Hailee, her eyes regaining some hope.

"Think about it, how did you come in here?" he asks.

"We walked in?" says Oliver, hesitating for fear of sounding stupid.

"Okay but how did you come in?" repeats Philip.

"Through the door?" tries Oliver.

"Exactly!" shouts Philip. "And which door will you use when you leave?" he now asks, looking at his watch and whispering: "soon I hope, this is worth much more than 40 pounds."

"The same door?" says Hailee.

"The same exact door!" confirms Philip. "You'll open it from the opposite side, yes, but still, it will be the same door!"

Neither Oliver nor Hailee quite gets the analogy.

"Oh people!" laments Philip, rolling his eyes in a loud sigh, getting up again, this time going to the bathroom.

"Man, can't you wait until we're gone?" asks Oliver.

"Would you mind closing the door at least?" adds Hailee, grossed out, as she's just realized her hand was sitting on that sock she pushed away earlier.

"Relax," says Philip, coming back out right away with a tube of toothpaste that he throws on Oliver's lap.

"Open this!" he tells him.

"What?"

"Just open it," he repeats.

Oliver twists the cap of the tube to undo it.

"Happy?" he says.

"Now close it," says Philip.

"Sorry Man, we don't have time for games," says Oliver.

"This is not a game, trust me," says Philip. "Go ahead, close it," he repeats slowly.

Oliver screws the cap back on.

"So?" asks Hailee.

"This, I believe, is exactly how the Orbatrum worked!" says Philip.

"Like a tube of toothpaste?" she questions, doubtful.

"Exactly!" he repeats.

Oliver and Hailee are staring at him, waiting for more.

"Look at the cap," he says. "You screw it counterclockwise to open the tube. And clockwise to shut it."

"I don't understand," says Hailee.

"I don't either," says Oliver.

"They would have had to spin the globe the other way!" says Philip.

"What?" says Hailee. *Could it be that simple?* she wonders.

"You heard me," says Philip. "Look, I'm not sure of this but, I believe that if they wanted to come back, those traveling through that globe would have needed someone to spin it in the opposite direction, opposite to the one they picked when they left that is."

Hailee is trying to manage mixed feelings of excitement and fear.

"What if it doesn't spin, if it's broken or something?" asks Oliver.

"What do you mean?" asks Philip.

"Is it possible that the globe stopped spinning at one point?" rephrases Oliver.

"Of course, it had too! Think about it, the globe couldn't just be spinning at all times," says Philip. "How could people transport it otherwise? No, there had to be some kind of locking mechanism. Da Vinci was way too smart to not have thought about that."

"So maybe it's not broken?" mutters Oliver.

"What do you mean? What's broken?" asks Philip.

"Nothing," says Oliver.

"You guys are not just smart, you're weird," notes Philip. "You're talking about that globe as if…"

It hits him all of a sudden:

"Oh my God! You found one. You found Da Vinci's globe!" he exults, his eyes wide and wild.

"Nah, we didn't," says Oliver, trying to deny it as well as he can. Hailee also shakes her head in the most overacted manner.

"It all makes sense," says Philip. "Why would you guys be asking so many questions about the Orbatrum otherwise? And why would you be willing to pay 40 pounds for answers, to me, Philip Vivekananda?"

Hailee gets ready to leave, heading toward the front door. Oliver follows her.

"I have to see it, please, just a few minutes, let me just have a look," he begs.

"This was so worth it, thank you so much!" says Hailee, as she opens the door.

"Will I get a tip then?" Asks Philip.

"We didn't lie to you, we only had 40 pounds," says Oliver.

"Actually, here's a tip, and this will help you gain both credibility *and* money," says Hailee, "there are two 's' at professor."

Oliver nods, pointing at the tag on his front door. Philip frowns.

Hailee and Oliver hurtle down the stairs. They can't wait to go back to the store and find that locking mechanism on the globe…

LA GIOCONDA

The journey to Belifendor has turned into a nightmare. Faerydae and Maven have been taking shifts, one steering the skiff, the other keeping the one surviving cannon ready —both battling exhaustion. They had to do without Archibald. Sickened by guilt, he has remained seated in the back, head against knees. No one onboard has talked since that deceitful Marodor took Lenora.

In the last 36 hours, the landscape has gone through wild changes. The thickest woods have morphed into the barest of valleys. In between, stood a wall of high peaks only the current of the Urlagone could have pierced through. At one point, the mighty river shrank to nothing, squeezed within the guts of the mountain. The bottleneck effect turned the canoe into a runaway ride. That's the only time Archibald lifted his head up, unable to resist the thrill of that rollercoaster —and a bit scared as well.

The Urlagone has now returned to its regular width and strength, more manageable under Faerydae's paddle.

"Everyone okay?" she asks her still traumatized crew.

"Yes," says Maven, while Archibald remains still and subdued.

"It's not your fault, there was nothing you could do," says Faerydae, trying to lift his spirit one more time.

"You know it's a lie," he says, breaking his silence.

"Maven knew the risks, we all did," says Faerydae.

"I'm the one who created the risks!" he argues.

"Now you listen to me," yells Faerydae, "see Maven here, her great-great-grandmother was a witch. She was enslaved by the Mongols, taken from China, and brought all the way to Europe,

just so they could use her powers in battle. Same thing with her great-grandmother, but with the Persians this time. They were after the same magic. Then it was her grandmother's turn. She refused to share her knowledge. So the Russian Cossacks made a big fire. And threw her in there. If you wonder about her mother, don't, she was also burnt alive. You want to know what her crime was? She used an herbs potion to save her sister's life."

As Maven nods mutely, Faerydae pauses to catch her breath for a second, before concluding her point:

"Trust me Archibald, you have nothing to do with this. The risks have always been there."

"I made things worse," he mumbles.

"You care about Lenora?" she asks.

"Of course I do but…"

"Then finish what we set out to accomplish," she snaps. "That's what Lenora would have wanted. She'd never give up."

Maven takes it from here.

"You know," she says, "Lenora lost her brother a few years back. One of the only boys we ever brought to Lemurea. She was devastated. But she remained strong."

"What happened to him?" asks Archibald.

"A disease," explains Faerydae. "Even the Queen couldn't save him. That's when Lenora left Belifendor for Gristlemoth."

Archibald shakes his head.

"We cannot get her back," says Faerydae, "but we can turn our anger into strength, and use it to convince the Queen."

"She's right," says Maven.

"You'd better make up your mind quickly," says Faerydae.

"Why?" he asks.

"Because Belifendor is right there," she says, motioning to a dim dot on the horizon.

His eyes riveted on that tiny beacon of light and hope, Archibald wipes the tears he has been fighting off. A few seconds later, he grabs a paddle to help Faerydae. She turns around. No need to say anything. No need for sign language. The quick smile and nod they exchange are worth a thousand words.

ᚾ↑

Belifendor is obviously more than a village. It's a city. Still a few miles away, the hole in the sky already looks as big as the one above Gristlemoth from up close. Another sky within the sky.

"Look at the size of that thing!" says Archibald, not blasé yet.

"It was the very first colony in Lemurea," says Faerydae. "We grew from here, but we grew here first."

"For over two centuries, Belifendor was all we knew," adds Maven. "Every year, we pushed the city limits farther and farther, until we expanded to other lands of Lemurea.

"What about Gristlemoth? When was it created?" he asks.

"It was our second colony. It's about three hundred years old," says Faerydae, her hair blowing in the breeze, making her even more beautiful in Archibald's eyes —if that's possible!

The wind has picked up strength though, quickly losing its charm. "Swishhh" on the right. "Whooshhh" on the left. Coming in ravening gusts, it billows through the camouflage cloth, turning it into a sail. Out of control, the boat suddenly takes off and soars in the air. In only a few seconds, it's gliding 30 feet above the river.

"So we *can* fly!" says Archibald.

"We've gotta go back down," shouts Faerydae.

Indeed, if they go any higher, they will soon walk into the lion's den —or more exactly, fly into the Marodors' orbit.

"Let's jump in the water," suggests Rhiannon.

"No we can't," says Faerydae, "we're already too high" —and not even quite above the river anymore.

The skiff is acting erratically, threatening to tip over any second. While Maven and Faerydae are grabbing onto each other and whatever else they can, Archibald stands up and climbs one of the poles supporting the cloth.

"What are you doing?" shouts Faerydae.

Archibald uses his paddle to cut a hole in the sail. The boat stops ascending immediately, then starts losing altitude when he tears the sail further. That second breach was a bit too bold though. From a gentle glide, the skiff goes into a free fall. They all let out a piercing scream before crashing on a swampy beach.

Maven and Faerydae quickly extract themselves from the entangled cloth. They are unharmed but fear greatly for Archibald. They scramble towards him, only a few feet away. He is sitting in deep mud, dazed, his vision blurred.

"Are you okay?" asks Faerydae, waving her hand before his eyes.

"This dream is never gonna end, is it?" he mumbles.

"That was genius!" says Maven, tapping him on the shoulder.

Faerydae just smiles at him and sighs, relieved.

"I guess we'll continue on foot," she says, inspecting the wrecked boat.

At least they landed on the right bank of the river, on Belifendor's side. They take cover under the long sad branches of a weeping willow. The tree happens to have the same haircut as Archibald's, a shabby chic haystack do. As far as the eye can see, the land is covered with the same kind of tall puffy wigs, probably grown for bald giants —naturally the main and only explanation Archibald could come up with.

Faerydae leads the way, running from one furry mound to another, seeking cover from Marodors. Many of them are flitting around Belifendor like mosquitoes drawn to a bug bulb on a hot summer night. And this bulb is bright! The city glows of the same magical lights as Gristlemoth's, but with an orange cast instead of green, radiating upwards, and out through swirling loops.

Following an hour trek from the river, Archibald and his companions finally reach the outer wall of Belifendor. They are dripping in sweat. Faerydae is about to blow into her horn when someone beats her to it —a girl, perched on a watchtower, about fifty feet above ground, just behind the boulders marking out the limits of the city.

"They saw us," says Maven.

To everyone's surprise though, a few minutes go by and nothing happens. In fact, the girl who spotted them is nowhere to be seen anymore. She seems to have disappeared down a ladder.

"I don't know what's going on," Faerydae wonders aloud.

"Why don't we call someone?" suggests Archibald.

"The horn was bad enough, shouting would only attract more Marodors," warns Faerydae.

As a reminder of the clear and present danger, one of them comes flying low to the ground, and brushes the top of the trees when shooting back up. Part lion —most of his body, the paws and tail—, part eagle —the wings and the beak—, part human — his face and front legs—, this monster is a flying copy of the sphinx, that statue lying by the pyramid of Giza, in Egypt.

"What is that?" asks Archibald, crouching down in fear, gazing through the branches.

"*That* is page nine of the Bestiary," says Maven, "the Sphinoxis Rapatoris, one of the fastest Marodors you'll ever see."

The terrifying beast comes swooping down twice before one of Belifendor's boulders finally moves out of the way, only slightly, creating a small breach in the fence.

"One more thing before we go in," Faerydae tells Archibald.

"Don't tell me my name is Ivy again!" he pleads.

"No, but keep your helmet on," she says. "Nobody knows you here, let's avoid problems until we meet with the Queen."

"Fine by me," he says.

About a hundred feet separate them from the safety of Belifendor. It is the last stretch of this perilous journey. But not the easiest by any means: a football field length, of bare dirt, with no tree, rock or deep crevice to use for protection. Each nibbled yard will be a challenge.

"You've got to run and never look back," Faerydae tells Maven and Archibald. "You understand?"

They both nod. Faerydae starts the eerie countdown: "All right, three, two, one…"

They all rush through the open terrain at once, Maven first. As planned, none of them looks back, or up. But Faerydae forgets to look down. They have almost made it across when she trips over a root. And collapses. The Sphinoxis Rapatoris is coming back, flying towards her at full throttle, his wings swept back alongside his body for optimal velocity. Unaware of anything, Maven presses ahead. Archibald did hear something —a loud thump. He glances back and sees Faerydae on the ground, holding her leg in pain. He turns around right away and helps her up quickly. She leans on his shoulder as they head toward the opening. The Rapatoris waits until the very last moment to unfold his wings and legs. Faerydae cringes as she hears the snap of his jaws coming together, falling just short of reaching her. The beast comes within a short lock of hair from grabbing onto her. Instead, he crashes into the boulders as Archibald and Faerydae plunge through the narrow passage.

They join Maven, who has just realized what happened. Faerydae collapses again, this time of total exhaustion. A buzzing crowd has gathered around them to get the story. This is no greeting committee but a wide display of wary faces.

"What took you so long to open the gate?" yells Faerydae.

"You Gristlemoths are so much better than us, poor Belifendors," says a voice rising from the group of girls. "We figured you'd find a way in," the voice adds scornfully, triggering laughter among the locals.

"Breena! I should have known," says Faerydae, rolling her eyes.

As she slowly gets back up, Breena emerges from the crowd.

"Aye up Old Friend!" she says.

They look around the same age, but there's something on Breena's face that gives her a somber appearance. It takes Archibald a few seconds and some squinting to figure it out. It's not her skin, even though it's pale as a corpse. It's her eyes, displaying almost no color, only darkness, like two dead moons.

"You have not changed a bit, have you?" says Faerydae with the most sarcastic tone.

"None of us do, remember," sneers Breena.

"You know what I mean," says Faerydae with the same tone.

Breena just smiles, obviously not that eager to change her ways.

"What's the reason for your visit?" she asks.

"I didn't know we needed a reason!" says Faerydae. "Isn't this home forever to all of us?"

"You know what I mean," says Breena, mimicking her.

"We are here to see the Queen," says Maven.

"Why?" asks Breena.

"*That*, is something only the Queen will hear," says Faerydae.

"She's busy you know. She might not have time," says Breena.

Faerydae doesn't even bother with a comment. She just shrugs and shoulders her way through the crowd, Archibald at her heels. Maven stays behind to talk to some old friends.

"What's wrong with that girl's eyes?" whispers Archibald.

"That's just a trick she uses. Some belladonna berry juice."

Archibald looks baffled. He has never heard of belladonna berry juice. He's had lots and lots of strawberry juice, cranberry juice and blueberry juice. He even mixed them all together once. He got an upset stomach within two minutes —but certainly nothing that would turn his eyes black.

"It must taste awful to do that to her!" he winces.

"You don't drink it," says Faerydae. "You put a few drops in your eyes. It enlarges your pupils. Very powerful. And poisonous."

"Why would she do that then?" he asks.

"To look scary. If you ask me, I don't think she needs that!" jokes Faerydae.

"Who is she? She sounds weird."

"Breena and I grew up here together, she always tried to compete with me for everything, the Queen's attention especially. That's why she was so happy when I left," explains Faerydae. Adding: "She never plays fair, she's a witch!"

"Aren't you all?" Archibald wonders aloud, chuckling.

"No, Breena is a real witch," says Faerydae, "She's a guiler."

"What's that?" asks Archibald, lost once more.

"You don't know what a guiler is? A bobber, a fob, a deceptor!"

"A cheat you mean?" says Archibald.

"Yes, something like that," she says, "a cheat and a snake!"

They stop suddenly as they hear someone shouting Faerydae's name. It's not Breena, nor is it Maven. It's another girl, running up to them, with a huge grin on her face.

"Finally, someone happy to see you!" jokes Archibald.

"Rhoswen!" exults Faerydae, arms open wide.

They give each other the warmest hug and connect their foreheads together, covering each other's ears with their hands.

"It's been so long," mumbles Rhoswen, in tears.

"I know, too long," says Faerydae, crying as well. And turning to Archibald: "Archibald, this is Rhoswen."

"My name is Ivy remember."

"It's okay," says Faerydae, "she's my sister."

"Real sisters or BFFs kind of sisters?" he asks.

It's Faerydae's turn to look lost.

"You know, BFFs, best friends forever…" adds Archibald.

"No, real sisters," says Faerydae, holding Rhoswen's hand.

"Well, one more boy in Belifendor!" says Rhoswen.

"What do you mean?" asks Faerydae.

"Believe it or not, we've got eighteen here now," says Rhoswen.

"What? You're pulling my leg," says Faerydae.

"No I'm serious, they all arrived at the same time, about two months ago, along with a hundred new sisters," she explains. "BFFs," she adds, for Archibald.

Faerydae looks around more carefully, and indeed she spots two boys just within a twelve-cabana-and-fourteen-tree radius.

"Mislimps?" asks Faerydae.

"Nobody knows, Helena just introduced them as our new brothers," says her sister.

"Is she here, the Queen?" asks Archibald.

"I believe so, I'm just not sure she's available though," says Rhoswen.

"Where could she be anyway? Shopping?" he jokes.

Both sisters look at him with dismay. Not only was his tone totally disrespectful but also… what does "shopping" even mean?

"We have something important to tell her. I really hope she's here," says Faerydae.

"Let's go check!" says Rhoswen, bowing, and unfolding her arm, showing Archibald the way forward.

Belifendor has obviously had time to experiment with architecture. Besides the same little huts that dot Gristlemoth, the city includes a number of more elaborate dwellings, up to four stories tall. Though crafted of wood and mud as well, they definitely reflect bold creativity and imagination. Some are shaped like pyramids, carrying tiered gardens on one or two sides. Some are just tall circular towers, with an outside staircase swirling all the way to the crenellated flat rooftop. Straight walls and square windows would almost make other buildings look oddly normal and boring —if they were not twisted like fusilli pasta, with each floor out of line by 90 degrees with the one underneath.

LA GIOCONDA

Add the winding streets, the guard towers, narrow alleyways and a few cabanas built in tall trees, and you will have built the ultimate playground. And that's not even mentioning the entanglement of rope bridges linking homes to one another.

Archibald marvels at a couple of girls running right above him. "It must have been fun growing up here!" he says.

"It was," confirms Faerydae.

"Especially when you never really grow up!" adds Rhoswen, grinning wide.

The road winds its way to Belifendor's castle. Perched on a hill, it looks very similar to the one in Gristlemoth, only with many more flags, featuring the colony's

GOLEM SHOP

N D O R

rune of choice —Moonesterum, the pyramid rune, in black, on a yellow background. Another notable difference: the high ground confers it a much more impressive stature, as it towers over the whole city.

"Helena spends most of her time inside Cleofa so hopefully she's here today," says Rhoswen.

"Wait, I thought Cleofa was Gristlemoth's castle?" questions Archibald.

"They're all named Cleofa," explains Rhoswen. "Every colony has one. It means shelter. That's what this was for many years for us, before we built Belifendor."

The castle now serves mostly as a school, just like the one in Gristlemoth. The same effervescence and excitement fills the main courtyard. Looking around for familiar faces, Faerydae bumps into a cluster of boys. She turns red in a flash and giggles in concert with her sister.

"What's wrong with you? They're just boys," says Archibald, obviously missing his Gristlemoth status as the only knight around.

Faerydae and Rhoswen exchange one more high-pitched laugh and a few whispers while running inside the castle. Archibald follows, visibly annoyed, trying to digest his first scoop of jealousy and the bitter taste attached to it.

On the third and last floor, down a long hallway, they reach a rather simple door —not quite the entrance to a Queen's palatial quarters.

"She's here," says Rhoswen.

"How do you know?" asks Archibald.

"The scarf," she says, pointing to a green piece of fabric wrapped around the knocker.

"If it was brown, it would mean the Queen is away or doesn't want to be disturbed."

"We're lucky, that brown scarf can be there for months, even years sometimes," says Faerydae.

"Okay I'm going to let you handle this," says Rhoswen, hugging her sister heartily before walking away.

"We'll see you later," says Faerydae, turning back to the door, about to knock.

"Wait!" says Archibald.

"What's wrong?" asks Faerydae. "I thought we talked about this. Just tell her what you've done in Gristlemoth, that's it."

"It's not that," he says.

"What then?"

"How should I call the Queen?" he asks. "Your Highness? Your Majesty?"

"Don't worry, she's not that kind of queen," grins Faerydae. "Just call her Helena. But remember, you mustn't make a noise before I tell you to…"

∴

Archibald heard what Faerydae said. Even so, he has never met a queen before. He feels overwhelmed —almost tingly. Maybe he needs more time to get ready.

It's too late. Faerydae has just knocked. He draws a deep breath and looks as though he is planning on holding it in for the whole meeting, his lips pursed.

A faint voice answers.

"Come in," it simply says.

Faerydae pushes the door open and steps in first. Archibald adjusts his helmet and hides behind her, tilting his head to catch a glimpse of the Queen.

She has her back to them, looking out a large window, her body silhouetted against the bright lights of Belifendor's outer wall.

Faerydae was right, Helena is definitely not like other queens he saw on TV, or in books. No royal dress. No silk taffeta or tulle embroidery. No satin bows. No fluff. Just a simple ivory lace dress. No tiara or crown either. Just a few daisies woven in a beautiful headdress.

Though comfortable, the Queen's interior is also very humble. In lieu of a throne, a tufted bench is sitting in the middle of the room, among layers of rugs, one of them even covering an entire wall —like the tapestries at Grandma's house.

"What is this regarding?" asks the haloed figure.

"We came from Gristlemoth to see you," says Faerydae.

Helena turns around immediately.

"Faerydae!" she says with much surprise and inversely little warmth in her voice. "I have not seen you in ages, what brings you here?"

"I have some important news," says Faerydae.

"Good or bad?" asks the Queen, concerned.

"Both, I think," she says, hesitant and confused. "But that's for you to say my Queen."

As Faerydae readies for her big announcement, the Queen walks closer to her visitors and detaches from the window glare.

Archibald squints to get a better look at her. The voice was already strangely familiar but now he slowly recognizes her face — a face he thought never to see again.

"Grandma?" he blurts out, loud enough for both Faerydae and the Queen to hear, bringing astonishment on their faces.

"What are you doing? Have you gone mad?" says Faerydae.

Taken aback, the Queen has brought her hand to her mouth. But she can't quite hide her shock.

"Remove your helmet," she orders with a trembling voice.

Archibald complies, revealing his face.

In a loud gasp, the Queen faints in an instant, folding onto herself, like a puppet losing its strings.

"Helena!" shouts Faerydae, rushing to help her.

"Grandma!" says Archibald, unable to move, still in shock.

Sitting on the floor next to her, Faerydae helps the Queen regain consciousness, tapping her gently on the cheek.

"Helena? Are you all right?" she asks. And then turning to Archibald: "I don't know what's going on but you'd better tell me. And fast!"

"I dunno," he says, shaking his head.

The Grandma he thought dead for months is right there, before his eyes, possibly now half dead, yet half alive nonetheless!

"How is this possible?" he mumbles.

He has no idea. Doubts and questions are again gripping his mind. Did Celestine die and get reincarnated in this world? Does it mean he is dead too?

He finally moves closer as she slowly and painfully gets back up.

"What are you doing here Archibald?" she asks in a weak voice.

"You know him?" exclaims Faerydae.

"I should be asking you that, you're supposed to be dead!" he tells the Queen.

"How did you get here?" she insists.

"The globe," he says, "I used the globe."

"How? How could you possibly know?" she asks.

"I didn't. I just found it in your library. I took the key from Bartholomeo. I unlocked the globe and I got sucked into it."

"What have you done?" sighs Helena.

"Can anyone tell me what's going on? Who's Bartholomeo?" asks Faerydae. And to Archibald: "I knew you were trouble!"

"He's not trouble, this is all my fault," says the Queen.

She grabs Archibald by the shoulders.

"Does anyone know? Does Bartholomeo know?" she asks him.

"I don't think so," he says. "I gave him the key back, so he probably didn't even notice I took it."

"Something else must have happened, he was supposed to bring me back a month ago," she says.

"Wait, what do you mean *bring you back*? You knew about the globe?" asks Faerydae. "But... you told us they had all been destroyed?"

Helena lets out another deep sigh.

"I lied," she confesses. "But it was for your own good, to protect you and your sisters."

Faerydae is speechless. There is so much disappointment in those watery eyes. The Queen was the only person she always trusted, blindly, the one person she would have followed anywhere, no matter what.

"Who are you?" asks Archibald.

"Yes, who are you?" repeats Faerydae.

"I thought you were just... Grandma Celestine," says Archibald. "I thought you were dead! And now you're a queen? The Queen of all witches?"

"Faerydae, would you mind leaving us for a moment?" asks Helena.

"I was going to leave anyway," says Faerydae, in the coldest tone she has ever used to address her queen. She would almost tell her to go "shopping", whatever that means, something spiteful enough hopefully.

She slams the heavy door on her way out.

Celestine/Queen Helena sits down on her bench, crumbling under the weight of all her lies and secrets.

"Ask," she simply says.

"I'm not sure where to start," says Archibald.

"I'm not sure either," she replies. "Well, my name is not Celestine, it's Helena," she says. "And all of this was my idea, the colonies, bringing the girls down here…"

"That's impossible, you hate witches!" says Archibald.

"What? Why would you think that?"

"That fireplace, in the living room," he says.

Helena slips a brief and furtive smile in her sigh.

"I found it at an antiques store in London. I thought to myself, how could someone want something so despicable in their house?"

"That's what *I* thought," says Archibald.

"I bought it to make sure it would be destroyed," she says. "But then I decided to keep it, to remind myself, every day, of how dark the human spirit can be. Certain scars are there so the pain can stay alive."

"So… you're a witch too?" asks Archibald.

"One of the worst, if you believe the legends," she says. "That's why the girls call me the Queen. I have never quite liked that title though."

"And… you're also five hundred years old?"

"A bit older actually. But who's counting?" she says with her signature smirk.

The Queen walks across the room.

"I have a question for you. Do you know that painting?" she asks, motioning towards a portrait on the wall behind him, near the entrance.

He doesn't need to get a closer look. He has definitely seen that woman before, seated with her arms crossed, her hair parted in the middle and a slight smirk on her face. It's probably one of the most recognizable works of art in the world —one that even Hailee could identify in a glance.

"I saw this before," he says. "It's the Mona something."

"You're right, they call it the Mona Lisa," says Helena. "But that's not the way the painter called it."

"Who painted it?" he asks, having no clue —surprisingly.

"A great man, a truly inspiring figure, from Italy. The same person who built the globe."

"And the tank?" exclaims Archibald.

"Yes, he was very fond of animals. He imagined that tank to replace horses and elephants on the battlefield. But most of all, he designed it for us, to face the Marodors."

"I like that guy! Who was he?" asks Archibald.

"Leonardo da Vinci," says Helena.

Archibald nods. That name definitely rings a bell as well.

"He called this painting Happy Helena, or the Smiling one, *La Gioconda* in Italian."

Archibald is stunned, his eyes travelling from the Queen to the painting, now noticing the obvious resemblance.

"This is you?" he exclaims.

"It is," she proudly says. "A few copies were made later on, one of them became rather famous, it's at the Louvre now, in Paris…"

"Holy Bejabbles! He must have really liked you!" Archibald lets out.

"He sure did," utters Helena, turning her gaze to the door opened to the room next door.

"Everything okay?" asks Archibald, noticing the blank look on her face.

"Yes," she whispers, still lost in her thoughts.

"Can I ask you something?" says Archibald.

LA GIOCONDA

"I guess," she answers, turning back to him.

"How did you fake your death? And why?"

As if she expected another question, Helena flutters her eyes, escaping a temporary torpor.

"The how part was fairly easy, a few herbs and plants did the trick," she says. "In fact, the potion worked almost too well. It put me in a deep comatose state for two full days, instead of one as planned. I nearly didn't wake up. Bartholomeo was so worried. I think I added too much willow bark and cloves to the mandrake. Unless it was the hemp, I'm not sure."

"But why? I don't understand," says Archibald.

Helena sighs heavily once more.

"My time had come," she says. "After all those years, I became quite certain of one thing: Men will never change. They'll continue to ravage the planet, through wars, pollution, and greed, triggering one disaster after another. I have come to the conclusion that the human species is not worth saving, not on Earth at least."

"What do you mean, not worth saving?" asks Archibald, scared almost.

"You know, shortly after I was born, they discovered a new continent. They called it the New World. It would later be known as... America. There was so much hope. But as it turned out, it didn't take long for that New World to look awfully like the Old one, shaped by violence and bloodshed. Only History will tell but I am convinced that Men have put the Earth on a path of self-destruction."

"So you just... left?" says Archibald.

"I waited for five hundred years Archibald. I didn't just make up my mind overnight. I left because I believed in something different, something better. Down here, we were given a second chance. A chance to start a new life, based on simple values. No need for weapons, no need for technology we would end up using to destroy our own world, to destroy ourselves."

"But how can you build that world with only witches?" asks Archibald.

"You're right. I cannot. That's why I started bringing in new souls, pure souls, who had suffered enough and deserved a second chance as well," says the Queen. "The last time I travelled, I took many children with me. They came from one of my orphanages, they'll be happy here," she explains, looking out the window, trying to spot some of them.

"You brought orphans here?" exclaims Archibald. "But they don't know anything about Marodors!"

"They will learn," she says. "When the girls came down here, they left their dolls behind. I told them they wouldn't be kids anymore."

Archibald surely doesn't mind that those creepy dolls stayed up in the library.

"Besides," says Helena, "the danger my orphans will face here is nothing compared to what they endured on Earth."

"I'm not sure about that," says Archibald, remembering his first minutes in Lemurea, chased by a nightmarish beast —let alone the surreal fights against the Krakatorum Gargantus and that river Marodor!

"At least down here, they won't have to suffer from war," she says.

"But, there is a war already!" snaps Archibald. "Do you ever go out? Every colony is under siege!"

"Trust me, everything was going to be just fine," says Helena. "With hundreds more orphans coming here, we were going to expand all the colonies. And create new ones."

"That was the plan?" asks Archibald.

"It was," confirms the Queen, "until you used the globe. Now I'm afraid the elevator is broken…"

"Maybe it's better this way," he says.

"Why would you say that?"

"I don't know, sometimes I feel like an orphan too, like I don't belong anywhere. At least here I have friends, and people kind of like me."

"I'm sorry," says Helena.

"Are you even my Grandma or was that just part of the lie?"

She comes close and puts both her hands on Archibald's shoulders, staring deep into his eyes.

"I spent so much time with you when you were a baby," she assures.

"I don't remember any of it," he says. "And if you cared about me, why did you convince Mom and Dad to give me that stupid name? They told me you know."

Helena smiles.

"I told you so many stories, narrated so many tales and legends, I taught you so many things, big and small. Have you never wondered why it is you know so much?"

"Holy Bejabbles!"

"Yes, that too," she says.

"It was you? But how? Did you use magic on me?" he asks.

Helena closes her eyes. And turns away.

"It's complicated. I'm not sure you're ready for that just yet," she says, going back to the window.

"I'm tired of people telling me I'm not ready," snaps Archibald. "I'm not a kid anymore, I'm the one who cured that Marodor."

"You did what?" asks Helena, frowning.

"Back in Gristlemoth. I cured a Marodor. That's what we came here to tell you," he says cheerfully.

"What are you talking about? This is non-sense, Marodors cannot be cured," says Helena, dismissive and almost angry.

"I know, I've been told. But trust me, it *can* be done. I did it."

"How?" she blurts out.

"I just took care of her," he says.

"Her?"

"She was Faerydae's friend," he explains. "She turned into a Marodor. I healed her wounds, spent time with her, talked to her. The sun did the rest."

"The sun?" asks Helena.

"Yes, the sun, and sugar!" he adds.

"That's impossible," utters Helena.

"See, another proof sugar is not *that* bad for you," he says with much enthusiasm that the Queen is far from sharing.

"This cannot happen. I won't let it," she assures.

"But… why?" questions Archibald.

"For all your wisdom, you have no idea what it is we are facing here. This discussion is over."

"What? How can you say that?" he snaps. "We've come all the way here to talk to you. We risked our lives! One of our friends was taken by Marodors! You can't just say this discussion is over!"

"Who? Who was taken?"

"Her name is Lenora," he says.

The Queen is visibly shaken again. She tilts her head down and remains silent while Archibald continues his plea.

"Her dream was to fly, to fight Marodors. But if we cure them, there will be no more fighting."

"Where? Where was she taken?" asks Helena, having difficulty breathing.

"On the river, about half way into our trip. That Marodor was really freaky. Some kind of toad and octopus mixed together."

"Isolda…" lets out Helena.

"Who's Isolda?" asks Archibald.

The Queen just sighs.

"Why did you have to come here? This is all your fault," she says with an accusing stare. "I think it's time for you to leave."

Archibald is in shock. But not really.

"Just when I started thinking you're not so bad," he says bluntly, while heading for the exit.

HEADS
OR TAILS ?

Oliver and Hailee look possessed. The spell was of the most enchanting nature though. They have been incapable of wiping those grins off their faces since they talked to Philip Vivekananda —AKA "Profesor" Brimble.

They get off a bus a few streets away from the Realm of Antiques. They race to the door and once more make their way through the messy shop. Half way through, between a stuffed ferret and a monkey toy both about to come alive, Oliver stops abruptly, signaling Hailee not to make another sound.

"What's wrong?" she murmurs.

Oliver points at the secret passage leading to the back room. The trick mirror is slightly open, enough for him to see the light inside. Maybe Oliver forgot to latch that door. However, the odds of him also leaving the lights on are nil.

"There's someone in there," he whispers.

Hailee's first reflex is to take a step back and freeze.

Then her instinct kicks in, telling her to head back out. And run.

"Let's go!" she says, mouthing her words.

Oliver shakes his head, asking her to stay put. He will go check himself.

Since he can't hear anyone talking, there might be only one person in there —unless Heinrich's bodyguards are just waiting for him to step inside, and ambush him.

Oliver takes a quick peak through the crack. He doesn't look too surprised or scared, but rather embarrassed. He motions for Hailee to come over.

It's her turn to take a look.

"I can't believe this," she utters, apparently relieved.

Indeed, no monster bodyguard in there —only Oliver's father, probably drunk, apparently sound asleep, positively slouched on the ottoman at the center of the room.

Only one little problem: one of his arms is lying on the part of the circular sofa that opens up. To get to the globe, Hailee and Oliver will have to move his body.

"I need your help," says Oliver, low still.

"Can't you do it yourself?" she murmurs.

"Sorry, team work," he says.

They cross the room on their tippy toes and squat right by the ottoman. Oliver gives directions through basic mime motions. Hailee is to lift Mr. Doyle's arm high enough for him to remove the cushion cover off the secret compartment.

Begins a seemingly painful grimace contest in which Oliver cringes while Hailee bites her lip during the whole procedure. But it works. Oliver pulls out the globe gently and exchanges a smile with Hailee. She gladly lets go of his father's arm and they are soon on their way.

Such was the plan at least, relying upon a rather fuzzy assumption: that Mr. Doyle was drunk enough to not wake up. Whether he was even asleep, or faking it to know what those kids were up to, is a whole other question —irrelevant now that he turns out to be fully awake.

"Not so fast!" he shouts as he grabs onto Hailee's leg.

She screams.

"Dad no!" shouts Oliver.

Mr. Doyle stands up quickly to get a better hold of Hailee. She doesn't even try to fight him. She is scared to death.

"Give me the globe Son," he orders.

Oliver shakes his head, of course to say no, but also in disbelief. He hates that feeling —of having been played.

"I can't believe I was sleeping on it this whole time!" says Mr. Doyle.

"Dad let her go," pleads Oliver.

"I can't do that Son. That globe is a lifesaver for me."

"You don't understand, we need it," says Oliver.

"Well, I need it more!" responds his dad.

"Maybe we can give it to you later, when we're done with it," suggests Oliver.

Mr. Doyle lets out an intimidating laugh.

"You're funny but I don't have time for this. Give it to me!" he yells. "I will hurt her, you know that," he adds.

"I know you will," says Oliver, reading the insanity on his dad's face —and the anguish on Hailee's.

He places the globe on the floor at his feet, but instead of backing off, he grabs one of the crossbows from the wall. It's loaded.

"Here's our hero!" cracks up Mr. Doyle. "What are you gonna do with that, huh, Robin Hood?"

Oliver clears his throat and takes aim at his father, right between the eyes.

"Careful now, you wouldn't wanna hurt your friend here, would you?" warns Mr. Doyle, hiding behind his shivering prey.

"Ready Hailee?" asks Oliver.

But neither she nor his dad have a clue as to what he has in mind.

Oliver winks at her, and in the blink of that eye, changes his aim, to the left, by about three feet. Now in his sight: a rope, holding straight against the wall a full body suit of armor.

Oliver looses the arrow.

The rope is shattered instantly. All that target practice pays off at last.

Suddenly unbalanced, the medieval armor wobbles for an instant, before keeling over. Caught by surprise, Mr. Doyle lets go of Hailee to shield himself. But he gets trapped under the heavy armor. Oliver and Hailee dash to the street with the globe —back on the run.

It is the night before Christmas. The sidewalks are crowded, the cobblestones freshly coated with frost. And yet, it is highly possible our young fugitives just set a new world record for the 2000-meter steeplechase. In 5 minutes and 31 seconds, they leaped over two benches, five piles of snow of various heights, and nine street bollards. A true feat, especially with the multiple bends they took left and right —all that to get out of reach of the Realm of Antiques madman.

They found refuge among the shadows of an old pub, the *Three-legged Trout*. And picked a corner table. Not for privacy, but mostly in a bid to avoid the waiter's gaze, since they don't have any money left to even share a hot cocoa (which is not on the menu anyway).

Oliver unveils the Orbatrum, smothered in his jacket to protect it from the snow. They've been waiting for this moment for hours.

"Do we even know what to look for?" asks Hailee.

"That guy Philip, he talked about some kind of locking mechanism," says Oliver.

"Like a keyhole?" she asks.

"It's funny, the first time I looked at it, I thought this thing, up here, was some kind of key," he says, putting his hand on the crank. "I turned it as far as I could but it ended up getting stuck. I hope I didn't break anything."

"What about this, right here?" asks Hailee, trying to stick her finger in that dent on the globe.

"I doubt it," says Oliver, "that just looks like a crack."

Hailee still tries to stick a straw into it.

"What are you doing?" asks Oliver, worried.

"I don't know," admits Hailee, sighing. "Maybe it *is* broken, maybe Philip made this whole thing up."

"It's possible. But for some reason, I don't think he did," says Oliver, running his hands on the globe's surface and on the meridian at the same time.

"Wait," he says suddenly, "I think I found something."

He flips the globe over, uncovering the keyhole underneath.

"That's it!" exclaims Hailee.

"Look at that pin going into the globe," says Oliver.

"Is that why the globe doesn't spin?" she asks.

"Probably," he says, "but without the key it's useless."

"Why don't we just break that pin then?" suggests Hailee.

"I can't imagine it could be so easy. We don't know what it's connected to, it would probably disable the globe for good," notes Oliver. "We can't risk that."

"What do we do then?" she asks.

"We don't really have a choice, we have to find the key."

"We've gone so far, I can't believe this," sighs Hailee.

"I'm afraid we've reached a dead-end," says Oliver. "That key could literally be anywhere, at your house, at my dad's shop or maybe it fell off when we were running with the globe."

"Wait," mumbles Hailee, as though if she had suddenly tuned the whole world out.

"What is it?" asks Oliver.

"Could those be?" she mumbles again.

"Please tell me. I'm dying here!" he begs.

"My dad," she says, "he mentioned some keys a few days ago, he couldn't figure out what they were for."

"Keys? There are several? It doesn't make sense, we only need one," he notes.

"I don't know, your guess is as good as mine," says Hailee. "That's the only lead we've got though, unless you have a better idea. I just don't want to go back to your dad's shop."

"Where are those keys?" asks Oliver.

"At my house," says Hailee, excited again. "My parents always leave them there, that's what my dad was complaining about, they're too big and awkward to carry around."

"This is made for a small key though," he notes.

"Yes, and I think some of them *are* small," she says.

"That's a long shot but who knows!" says Oliver.

By the time the train brings Oliver and Hailee to Cuffley, it got dark out. The snow packed on the driveway is brightening up the night, showing the path to the house. But the house itself is shrouded in darkness.

"Seems like no one's home!" says Hailee, surprised.

"Where could they be? It's Christmas Eve," says Oliver.

My brother is gone and I didn't come back home last night, I'm not sure they're up for a big celebration," notes Hailee. "They're probably just freaking out, I feel bad actually."

"How are we going to get in though?" asks Oliver.

"I told you, that's the good thing about those keys, my parents never take them with them," explains Hailee, digging through that pot behind one of the lion sculptures.

"Got'em!" she shouts, dangling the keys.

She uses the largest one to open the front door, and starts going through the four little ones as soon as they get in.

"Which one is it?" asks Oliver.

"Who knows? Let's try them all."

While Oliver holds the globe, Hailee inserts the first key into the hole. But stops suddenly.

"Wait," she says, "we can't do this here."

"What do you mean? Where then?" asks Oliver. "It's not like we have an instruction manual."

"I don't know, maybe we should put the globe where it was when my brother… vanished."

Hailee leads Oliver upstairs, to her bedroom.

"So where was he?" asks Oliver.

"Right over there," she says, showing him the area where Archibald's desk used to be. She grabs a chair and moves it right on that spot. Oliver places the globe on top.

"Keys please," he asks, like a surgeon requesting a scalpel.

Each key going in has Hailee taking a deeper breath. Three times.

"This is not going to work," she whispers.

"Last chance," says Oliver as he tries the fourth one.

Hailee closes her eyes, to reopen them seconds later at the sound of an awaking rattlesnake —a mechanical rattling that is.

The pin is out. Oliver is as amazed as she is. They both step away from the Orbatrum, scared of it all of a sudden.

"What now?" he asks.

"As you said, there's no instruction manual," quips Hailee.

"I have to admit, I'm a little freaked out," says Oliver.

"I won't blame you," she says.

Hailee approaches the globe again. Oliver takes position on the other side.

"Remember Philip's theory. If we follow it, to reverse your brother's travel, we just have to spin the globe in the opposite direction," he says.

"I get it but, the opposite direction compared to what?" says Hailee.

"That's the problem, we don't know which way he chose to begin with."

"So what? We're supposed to guess?" asks Hailee.

"Kind of. As long as it's an educated guess."

"Educated guess? That sounds like 'crash landing', or 'only choice', or one of those bizarre combinations of words, it doesn't make sense," she says.

"You're almost exactly right!" jokes Oliver.

Hailee smiles.

"Okay it's funny, but I'm not following," she says.

"I don't know if you've noticed but when you look around, everything in life is based on patterns," says Oliver.

"In English?" asks Hailee.

"Habits, things people do automatically, without putting much thought into it, you know, like shaking hands or putting their socks on. We just have to ask ourselves: what would most people do? *I* think most people would spin it like this," he says, slicing the air with his right hand, counterclockwise, the same way a tennis player would to give a wicked effect to a ball. "That means we have to do it the other way."

"Are you sure about this?" asks Hailee.

"Of course not! I told you, it's just an educated guess!"

"We can't base our decision on that!"

"What else then? I'm sorry but we'll never be sure Hailee. We just have to try," he says, switching hands and getting ready to spin the globe.

"Wait!" yells Hailee.

"What's wrong?" he asks.

"Not Archibald," she murmurs.

"What was that?" asks Oliver.

"You're right, most people would probably spin it that way," she says, mimicking his slicing motion. "Most people, but not my brother."

"Why is that?" he asks.

"Because Archibald is a lefty," she explains.

"So let me get this right," says Oliver, "if he used his left hand, which he probably did, he would have rotated the globe clockwise, which means we have to spin it the other way."

A rather scary thought just went through Hailee's mind.

"Oh my God," she lets out.

"What's wrong?" asks Oliver.

"I just realized something, if we're wrong, wherever Arch went, we're going," she says, triggering a long silence.

"Only one way to know," says Oliver, reaching for the globe again.

"No," says Hailee, "you've done way too much already. He's my brother. *I* have to do it."

"Are you sure?"

"Yes I'm sure," she says. "Besides, if anything goes wrong, at least you can get *me* back."

"What if I get sucked up with you?" he fears.

"I was in the room when it happened," recalls Hailee. "The globe absorbed everything around. But not me. I was obviously far enough, right there by the bed. I think as long as you stay away from me, you'll be fine."

Oliver grabs her hand and kisses it lightly.

"For luck," he says.

Hailee comes close, twines her arms around his neck, and gives him the same gentle kiss —on the lips.

Oliver slowly steps back, all the way to her bed.

Hailee turns back to the Orbatrum, giving it her most intense gaze yet. She extends her arm above it. Her pointing finger starts swirling, alternating between clockwise and counterclockwise, as if mixing an invisible batch of whipped cream.

"Eeny, meeny, miny, moe, Arch please tell me what to do," whispers Hailee.

Her next move will be, without doubt, earth shattering.

THE DAY THE FISH RUNE DIED

Was the trip to Belifendor just utterly pointless? Archibald is starting to wonder. And who would blame him, looking back at what it took to get here? Imagine confronting a two-sided Marodor with a severe personality disorder —not sun in Scorpio and ascendant in Taurus kind of disorder, but a giant Toad with an Octopus rising up her bottom. For most people, that reason alone would have made a change of heart legitimate —and a U-turn a no-brainer. But Archibald didn't stop there. He braved the waters of the Urlagone, survived a 200-foot drop from the sky in a boat turned airborne, and won a sprint against flying sphinxes.

Worst of all though, he lost a friend along the way.

Convincing the Queen to cure Marodors sounded like a noble endeavor. The end goal seemed great enough to justify the worst hardship, and the most painful sacrifice. Now, exiting his meeting with Helena, Archibald is left with more doubts than certainties.

Faerydae is waiting for him, sitting on the floor, her back against the wall. And she doesn't seem too happy.

"You two had a lot to talk about, didn't you?" she says with a dose of sarcasm, two spoons of resentment and a hint of anger.

"Too much for one day, that's for sure!" responds Archibald.

"I bet it helps you both speak the same language though!"

"What's that?"

"I don't know, whatever tongue liars speak."

"I'm not a liar," he objects.

"Maybe. But *she* surely is," says Faerydae, standing up as to make her point more forcefully. "The Queen of lies!" she adds, turning to the door.

"Shh," whispers Archibald, a silencing finger on his lips, worried Helena will hear.

"Don't shush me! What is she going to do? Turn me into a saddle-goose, I'm already a big one, just for believing her."

"Maybe she didn't lie," says Archibald, "maybe she just wanted to protect you like she said."

"Did she brainwash you too?" shouts Faerydae. "Don't you understand that she's been lying to us for five hundred years! She was going back and forth this whole time, and abandoned us here whenever she felt like it."

Archibald walks away, motioning for Faerydae to come along.

"I don't want to be insulting but… couldn't you figure that out before though?" he says.

"What do you mean?"

"I mean, she put that scarf on her door and you guys would leave her alone for months right?"

"Yes, we respected her wishes."

"I get that, but didn't you ever wonder what she was doing in there, how she could even survive?"

"Of course not. She's a witch, she's the Queen, we figured she found a way… somehow."

"And what about the fact that she got older and you guys didn't? You never found that… odd?"

"That's a good point but again, she's the Queen! I thought that kind of logic didn't apply to her."

"I see," says Archibald, "I guess being a Queen is pretty convenient huh! It kind of explains things that would make literally no sense otherwise."

"Are you saying I'm unguileful?" asks Faerydae.

"No, I would never say that," says Archibald.

"Thanks!"

"I would never say that," he clarifies, "just because I have no clue what that word means!"

"You know, plain-hearted, naïve!"

"Oh that's what it means! Then yes I would say that!"

Faerydae pouts, the way Archibald used to just fifteen days ago, before this adventure changed him radically, before he became a man —about a quarter of one but the ersatz of a man nonetheless.

"What now?" he asks.

"Now I need to sleep. I've barely closed my eyes since we left Gristlemoth," she says. "We should head to my sister's place."

"Are you going to tell her?"

"About Helena you mean?"

Archibald nods.

"I'm not sure," says Faerydae.

Since Belifendor doesn't seem to believe in street names or house numbers, Rhoswen's address would be rather fun to spell out. Someone asking for directions might describe it as "the house brushing the clouds, perched on the tall sequoia by the golem shop, between branches 33 and 36" (out of 47). There are indeed two other cabanas built up and down that giant tree, on branches 9 and 21, respectively.

"Yes, my sister lives at the very top," confirms Faerydae.

"Where's the elevator?" asks Archibald, quite seriously, expecting some kind of gadget dropping down and sweeping them up their feet.

"E-le-va-tor?" spells outs Faerydae. "Let me guess, you're talking about a giant slingshot! No wait, a catapult maybe? Something that would throw us all the way up there in one big swing!"

"Not… quite. That just sounds crazy. Fun, but crazy. You were close though," he says.

"That's a good idea, I'll keep it in mind. In the meantime, this way," she says with a smile, showing him, well, the —hard— way.

First, they have to access the pyramid house next door, which happens to be a library, then walk out to one of its tiered gardens. Only from there can they cross over to Hailee's sequoia, through a suspended bridge. Then comes the trickier part: climb a ladder to cabana number two, cross a second bridge going from the north branches to the south branches, and finally go up another —much taller— ladder straight to the top.

"Don't look down," says Faerydae, which Archibald didn't — until now. Of course he's going to look down! Doesn't he always do what he's not supposed to? And that's not going to change anytime soon. Needless to say he regrets it right away, hugging the ladder like he would his pillow on a thundery night.

They are so high that the wind is blowing ten times as hard up here, making it that much difficult for Archibald to scrabble up the last few steps.

If Faerydae was tired before this obstacle course, she is now completely worn out. She almost feels relieved that her sister is not home. As soon as they arrive, she crashes on her bed and falls asleep almost instantly.

"You cured a Marodor!" is the phrase —more of a shout really—, that shakes Faerydae out of her dreams 5 hours later.

Rhoswen is back, lounging on the floor among piles of blankets with Archibald. Obviously those two have been talking.

"I can't believe it, I never thought it would be possible!" she says.

Faerydae sits up on the bed, wiping the moist blur out of her eyes.

"Did you tell her everything?" she asks Archibald.

"Pretty much," he says.

"Why would you do that?"

"She asked!"

"Sooo?"

"So you told me not to lie anymore!"

Faerydae shrugs her shoulders and shakes her head in dismay.

"I know about the globe," says Rhoswen. "It's so exciting!"

"What about the Queen?" asks Faerydae, a bit worried.

"What *about* the Queen?" asks her sister, now even more curious.

Archibald and Faerydae look at each other, wondering how to answer that.

"You've got to tell her what you did with that Marodor," says Rhoswen.

Archibald and Faerydae look at each other once more.

"Wait, that's why you came to Belifendor, isn't it!" realizes Rhoswen. "You came to tell the Queen about it."

Faerydae nods.

"Are we going to try it here?" asks Rhoswen, staring eagerly at her sister.

"Don't ask *me*!" she says. "I'm not that close to the Queen, like some people, right Archibald?"

He just rolls his eyes.

"What did she say?" insists Rhoswen.

"She didn't have an answer yet," he explains, "she said she'd think about it but she didn't seem too convinced."

"That's impossible, how could she think that?" says Rhoswen.

"She was pretty upset about Lenora getting caught."

"You told her?" erupts Faerydae.

"Yes, why?" he asks.

"I don't think we'll get anything out of her now," sighs Faerydae.

"We have to find a solution," says her sister. "We can't continue to capture Marodors and put them in cages, we'll be running out of space soon."

"How many do you have here?" asks Archibald.

"I don't know exactly. Maybe three hundred."

"What? That's crazy!" he exclaims.

Rhoswen goes to the window.

"Let me show you," she says.

Archibald looks out and takes in the dizzying view. It is simply breathtaking. Remove the Marodors flying in the background and you'll have a place of unspeakable wonders, the most idyllic postcard panorama of rooftops, treetops and hilltops —not to forget golemtops and their runes that read like a giant alphabet, carved on those imposing boulders surrounding the City.

Rhoswen points towards the area beyond the castle, a blanket of green with only a few holes.

That forest spans from one side of Belifendor to the other.

"All that is the Marodors' area?" asks Archibald, stunned.

"All of it," says Rhoswen, visibly sorry to confirm.

"Belifendor is turning into a prison," laments Faerydae.

"I'm afraid you're right," says her sister.

"The rivalry between colonies has only made it worse."

"Which rivalry?" asks Archibald.

"This hunt for Marodors has pit us against one another for centuries. It's Belifendors versus Gristlemoths, or Marrowclaws versus Nifequods. Pick your team. We all try to outdo each other by capturing more beasts," explains Faerydae.

"This can't work for much longer," says Rhoswen.

"What's going on over there?" Archibald wonders aloud, focusing on a large square they crossed earlier, at the foot of the castle. Preparations are being made for something, a wooden structure erected right in the middle of that square.

"It's really strange, I didn't hear about this," says Rhoswen.

"Let's go check!" suggests Faerydae, heading to the door.

"Couldn't you live on the first floor?" whines Archibald, cringing at the idea of using those perilous ladders again.

Getting closer to that mysterious wooden structure doesn't quite make it less mysterious. Braced to scaffolding made out of bamboo, what resembles a totem pole is being anchored to the ground through two additional legs at the base. The weird looking tripod gets even more suspicious when Faerydae spots Breena nearby. Her old friend seems to be supervising the construction.

"What's going on Breena?" she inquires.

"Oh you're still here?" says Breena. "I thought you left already."

"What's all this for?" asks Faerydae.

"Queen's orders," she simply says.

"What orders?" asks Archibald.

"That I cannot say," replies Breena with that default look on her face —malicious.

Before Faerydae can ask another question, Helena shows up, flanked by four young men —obviously some of the orphans she brought here with her a few months ago.

"Can you tell us what's going on?" Archibald asks her.

"Do you know the meaning of that rune?" she asks, pointing at the helmet Archibald is holding.

"The fish rune?" he wonders aloud.

"Yes, that *fish rune*," she says, smiling.

"I'm not sure, I asked Maven but she didn't remember."

"Oh no, Maven remembered, trust me," says the Queen. "She just couldn't talk about it."

"Why?" he asks.

"She worked on that rune, along with me and a few others. That was many many years ago. We called it... Hesperialis."

"I've never heard of it," says Faerydae.

It even seems to come as a surprise to Breena, who frowns.

"What was it for?" asks Archibald.

"A better question would be: *who* was it for? And *where* was it for?" says Helena.

"I don't understand," he says.

"It was not made for use in Lemurea," she says, looking up. "It was designed to be used on Earth, on people."

"You can't use runes on people!" exclaims Faerydae. "It's too dangerous!"

"That's why Hesperialis took so long to craft," says the Queen. "The goal was not to hurt people, but to change them, to make them better humans. The idea was to use it on a few, and make those few the vanguard for a wider change, the disciples of a new ideal, our ideal, which would spread, to eventually vanquish greed and violence. And who knows, stop the wars maybe."

"I don't understand," says Faerydae. "How could Maven believe in this? She didn't even know you had a globe, did she?"

"No, I never told her. She just trusted me to find a way back," explains Helena.

"So you deceived her too?" accuses Faerydae.

"It's a way of looking at it. I just wanted to keep her dedicated and focused," replies the Queen.

"You've played us all," sighs Faerydae.

"As I told you before, it was for…"

"Our own good? Is that the best you can come up with?"

"Silence!" shouts Helena. "There is no point arguing this any further. Hesperialis was a dream, and a dream only. That's why I had that 'fish rune' drawn on my casket, remember," she tells Archibald. "I wanted it buried forever. That idea was naïve. It would have never worked."

"How do you know?" asks Archibald.

"Because I know people Archibald," she says. "Mankind has repeated the same mistakes, over and over, for centuries now, never learning from them. I have come to believe that people don't *want* to change their ways. Therefore, they don't deserve that rune, they don't deserve to be saved. Anyway, this debate is now closed. It's time for plan B."

"What's plan B?" asks Faerydae, fearing the worst.

"The *fish rune* was not the only one I worked on," says Helena. "There always was another option, involving a rather different scenario."

"What was that?" asks Archibald.

"Kill all Marodors," says Helena, cold.

"What?" exclaims Archibald.

"How?" asks Faerydae.

"I thought they *couldn't* be killed!" says Rhoswen.

"I made another rune," reveals the Queen, "a unique rune, so powerful it doesn't need to be combined with any other. I never thought I would use it, even though deep inside, I was afraid I'd have to. By coming here Archibald, by closing the door on us, you left me with no choice."

"But there's another solution," insists Archibald, "I told you, Marodors can be cured."

"It's too late," says Helena. "I had my doubts. But now that they took my daughter, it's over. The Marodors have to go."

Archibald is startled. It takes him a while to understand.

"Lenora? Lenora was her daughter?" he asks Faerydae.

"I thought you knew," she responds.

The Queen points her finger at Faerydae.

"I trusted you to protect her," she says.

"I'm sorry for that, I failed you," says Faerydae.

"If we don't do anything, you'll be next Archibald," warns the Queen. "Complete eradication is now the sole option moving forward. And it starts tonight, right here," she says, gesturing towards the strange looking totem.

"You can't do that!" he exclaims.

While Rhoswen is speechless, next to her, Breena can barely contain her joy.

"It is I who will decide. I won't let you disrupt my plans again," says the Queen.

"What if it doesn't work?" worries Faerydae. "What if trying to kill them ends up creating more Marodors? It could even make them stronger, maybe strong enough to access the Earth!"

"That's a risk I'm willing to take," says the Queen calmly.

"Why rush into this? Let's talk about it," implores Faerydae.

Helena turns to the four young orphans behind her, and to one of them in particular, his hair so short he looks bald.

"Theo, please make sure they don't cause any problems," she asks him, while walking away.

"Please don't do this," pleads Archibald as Theo, nearly a head taller than him, comes standing in his way.

"Don't make me hurt you," warns the tough guy.

The others have grabbed onto Faerydae. Rhoswen wants to intervene but her sister motions for her to stay put.

"Do you wish to follow them?" Breena asks her.

Rhoswen shakes her head.

"I'm loyal to the Queen," she assures, quite convincingly.

"Good girl," says Breena. "Do me a favor though, make sure you stay home tonight."

"What's going to happen to them?" asks Rhoswen.

"A little time in jail has never killed anyone," says Breena.

Rhoswen looks with concern as her sister and Archibald are escorted away.

"Those Belifendors," mocks Breena, "a bunch of idealists."

It's the second time in two weeks that Archibald is thrown in jail. One more and his reputation as a teacher's pet and a wimp might be history, making way for a new boy in town —a *bad* boy.

He's already starting to act like one. He yelled at the guards when they threw him and Faerydae in this cell. He even pushed one of them. Yes it was a girl, but still, at least he resisted. Better yet, Archibald kicked the door a few times, hurting his foot in the process, realizing that door is there to stay —probably made of that same unyielding blackwood Wymer built his tank with.

For the last three hours, Archibald has been inspecting every square inch of the cell. Looking for weak points or flaws, he finally turned his attention on the two metal bars anchored into the tiny window. Archibald is now digging into the dried mud around them, using one of the dead batteries he kept in his pocket. At this pace though —a quarter of a teaspoon of powdery mud removed in fifteen minutes—, it would take him days of non-stop grating to clear a path out.

"I've seen this in a movie," he mumbles.

"I'm not sure what you're talking about or what it is you're trying to accomplish, but you should stop," says Faerydae, seated on the opposite side of the room.

"We have to do something! We can't let her kill that Marodor!" he says.

"There's nothing we can do," she says. "Trust me, I've been in here before."

"You have?" he says, surprised.

"Four times," she says, running her finger into a series of tally marks etched into the wall.

Based on that count, Faerydae spent at least 25 days locked up in this cell.

"What happened to your 'door unlocked' concept? You know, the whole 'it's not a prison, just a time to reflect'?"

"It's different here," she sighs.

"So, what did you do to end up here so often?"

Faerydae looks embarrassed. She definitely regrets mentioning that detail about her past.

"Let's just say that Helena doesn't like to be challenged."

"Wait, you were thrown in jail because you disagreed with her?" asks Archibald, stunned.

"The Queen's a meanie huh!" he comments.

"It was pointless. After the third argument, I gave up. That's when I left to create Gristlemoth."

"So what did you do the fourth time then?" he asks.

"What do you mean?"

"You said you were sent here four times, so three because of those fights with the Queen, and once for... what?"

"Oh, that was nothing really."

"For what?" insists Archibald.

"Nothing," says Faerydae, looking even more embarrassed.

"You... stole something, didn't you?" says Archibald with a gotcha kind of grin.

Faerydae shakes her head but struggles to offer a strong denial.

"You did!" shouts Archibald, realizing he might be right.

"Fine. Yes. But only once," she says. "And it was not really stealing. I just couldn't find my own herbs and I really needed to finish that potion I was working on."

"Let me guess, you *borrowed* those herbs?" he says, cracking up.

"Not funny," says Faerydae, smiling, admitting it kind of is.

Archibald's laughter is interrupted by the sound of horns reverberating all the way to the prison cell.

"What was that?" he asks. "Someone at the gate?"

"No," says Faerydae. "Three horns at once, that's the signal for some kind of ceremony. I think the killing is about to begin."

Archibald stops digging, the anger accelerating the flow of blood to his brain, fueling the search for a way out. He looks up and gets an idea.

"If you step on my shoulders, maybe you can squeeze between those beams," he suggests, showing the narrow openings in the ceiling.

"What do you think I am, a cat? Not even a squirrel could fit through that!" she says.

"Maybe the beams can move a little, that's our only chance," he insists.

"Okay fine, I'll try," she says.

Archibald puts his back against the wall and braces for Faerydae to step onto his cupped hands. She takes a few steps back to get a good run-up, when the door suddenly shakes —a jolt as violent as it is brief.

"Was that a knock?" he asks.

"From what? A twenty-foot giant?" she says. His idea exactly.

Another tremor hits but this time, it's not only the door but the entire room that also vibrates with it. Archibald and Faerydae hold on to each other, nearly losing their balance. The door is about to come off its hinges but the doorframe itself suddenly detaches from the walls around and collapses flat onto the ground.

Emerging from a cloud of dust, Maven steps in, coughing and spitting, holding two golems she used to knock down the door.

"I was just trying to open it," she says, looking sorry.

"Maven!" rejoices Archibald.

"How did you know we were here?" asks Faerydae.

"Everybody knows! But your sister told me what happened. She couldn't come, Breena had her followed," she says.

"Give me some golems, I might need them," says Faerydae.

Maven hands her one.

"Do you have more?" asks Faerydae.

"No but I know where to get some," says Maven.

"We don't have time, we've got to hurry," says Archibald, leading the way as they run out from the crumbling prison.

When they reach the execution area, the night has already come down on Belifendor. The darkness about to prevail would have far longer-lasting effects though. Large fires have been lit all around the square. Packing the streets, picking through windows or standing on rooftops, countless onlookers are gearing up for an event most don't know anything about.

A cortege shows up on the horizon. The image is surreal. A Marodor is levitating above ground, gliding through the crowd. Kept at bay by four guards armed with golems, he looks dead already, his body and expression seemingly frozen. Chosen to star in this grand premier, the unlucky beast is paraded through the City like a war trophy. The final stop is near the totem built in a hurry this afternoon —more of a gibbet, it turns out. The creature is tied roughly to the pole with heavy chains, on a short leash.

"That Marodor is so small," notes Archibald.

"It's a young one," says Faerydae. "Helena is not sure her new rune will work, that's why she didn't pick a full grown."

We are still talking about a rather healthy baby, probably nearing 8 or 900 pounds. Compared to his 5 to 15-ton relatives though, this Marodor is definitely a lightweight —and a casting error. Not quite the most convincing specimen for a Queen trying to convince her people an entire species must be wiped out. He has probably not even made it in the "purposely incomplete bestiary of Marodors" —Or perhaps just as a footnote.

The usual circus aggregate of countless animals, this Marodor doesn't resemble any in particular. From behind, just based on the brown fur and long hind feet, one might think of a hare. That's if one can look past the scaled armadillo tail of course. Pan 180 degrees to the front, and a wild boar is what comes to mind — only, a boar with two mouths framing his snout, horns sticking out of his neck, and a torso resting on human arms! Against all odds, this Marodor would almost look cute, with his pink belly gut and that mossy fuzz growing on his forehead. You could definitely be tempted to pet him —though it might mean getting your hand gnawed off by one of those mouths...

Now released from the spell of the transportation golems, the young Marodor has regained some of his wild spirit. He is roaring and growling again. A chill spreads through the crowd but quickly fades away. The Queen has just shown up, on the second floor balcony of a house facing the square. Same simple dress as earlier, but a face carrying the gravity of this momentous turning point.

"This is a historic day, the beginning of a new chapter in our fantastic journey," she says with a calm voice. "When we got here, the hope was always to go back to a better world. A world that would not only accept us, but that would be guided by new values: tolerance, love and compassion. Unfortunately, after all these years, we have to come to terms with our reality. The dream we had will remain a dream only. There is no way back. Our future is here. The path we're about to take will help us secure that future."

Archibald, Faerydae and Maven worm their way through the silent crowd, getting closer to the soon to be slayed Marodor.

"Time has come to eliminate the remnants from the Old world," says Helena, continuing her sales pitch, now raising her voice. "Marodors do not belong here. We have been struggling with those demons for centuries, even though we had nothing to do with their birth. Today, we say enough. Today, we part ways with the beasts. Only with a new rune can we lighten our burden, a rune powerful enough to kill Marodors!"

The Queen's last two words sow shock and stupor through her followers' ranks, igniting conflicted feelings of hope and fear. But all eyes quickly turn back onto Helena.

"I give you… Venomurtis," she says.

In her hand, a golem, held high for everyone to see.

Scattered throughout the square, Breena and the Queen's loyal orphans show the crowd other golems carrying the same rune, a strange E shaped like a lightning strike, presumably the one about to pelt down on Marodors: ⋛

"Now what?" Archibald asks Faerydae.

"I don't know," she says, looking around frantically in search of an answer and strategy.

Helena raises her voice again, by a couple notches, as she nears the height of her speech.

335

"We cannot do anything for the old world," she says, "but we can save this one, our new world, a more perfect world."

All of a sudden, Archibald runs to stand between the Queen and the Marodor.

"She's lying to you!" he shouts to the crowd, pointing dramatically at the Queen. Then addressing her directly: "If this world is so perfect, why do people want to leave then?"

"Who? Who wants to leave?" she thunders, casting a fiery gaze on the audience.

Her tone makes an impression. Scattered booing erupts — aimed at the rebels. But just in Archibald's vicinity, there are also some Belifendors, a few, visibly shaken, having doubts, and tempted to raise their hand. At the same time though, who would dare challenge the Queen? In the end, no one does.

Faerydae manages to join Archibald but Maven is caught by one of the boys under Breena's command.

"What if they do want to leave? Are you going to throw everyone in jail?" asks Faerydae.

"There's no leaving anymore, this is the only way," says Helena.

"Who are you to decide who will be saved?" asks Archibald.

"Everyone will be saved," she assures.

"Here maybe. But what about Mom and Dad? What about Hailee?" he says.

"I can do nothing for them," says Helena, her voice broken.

"Look around," says Faerydae. "Doesn't it remind you of something? The hellish fires, the crowds, incited to violence, extremism, feeding people's fears. This is what you saved us from. This is why we escaped."

"You can't understand. You have not seen what I have seen, you don't know what these beasts are made of," says Helena. "I won't let anyone stand in my way."

"This is not the Queen I used to love, and respect," says Faerydae, tears welling in her eyes.

"Proceed," Helena tells Breena.

Faerydae and Archibald move back, their arms wide open, as if to shield the Marodor. They are only a few feet away from the beast, getting dangerously close.

Breena moves towards them, holding two Venomurtis golems.

"They're in the way," she tells the Queen.

"Proceed," repeats Helena.

Breena gets even closer.

"You don't have to do this," says Faerydae, armed with one regular golem, making it as useless as an unloaded gun.

Breena freezes.

"I can't do this. What if I harm them," she now tells Helena.

"These golems can't hurt people," assures Helena.

"Are you sure?" asks Breena.

"You don't trust your Queen? Perhaps I should have Theo take care of this instead?"

Seeing Theo step forward with no doubt on his face, Breena tightens her mouth and clenches her teeth. She turns back to Archibald and Faerydae, takes a large breath and extends her arms.

"Please don't," whispers Faerydae.

Breena seems ready to activate the golems. She has not pronounced her fateful words yet, when a halo of light appears on the ground, right under Archibald's feet...

The bright ring with wavy contours slowly grows to soon include Faerydae, flabbergasted, seemingly unable to make the slightest movement.

"What's happening?" utters Breena, wondering whether the golems might have started acting on their own. After all, no one quite knows how the new rune works since it has never been used.

"What is this?" echoes Faerydae, staring down at her feet now covered with a blurry veil.

"It can't be," lets out Helena, the only one who seems to have an idea of what's going on.

"I can't see my legs anymore," says Archibald.

Part of his body seems indeed to have vanished, as though he was slowly sinking into a pond of fog. Same thing for Faerydae, who can't even utter another word.

After stabilizing and hovering at ground level for a few seconds, the halo erupts into a ball of light that tears through the sky. No golem could ever release such power. Everyone on the square is in total panic mode. Those who have not fled yet are desperately looking for cover. Hundreds of screams are suddenly silenced, intertwined with a loud suction sound that vanishes into the sky, along with the beam of light.

The commotion is over. It gave way to an eerie silence. Archibald is squatting in a fetus position. Faerydae is still standing, and squinting, her head tucked into her shoulders. Once free of the high-pitched whistling going through her temples, she reopens her eyes, to discover someone she has never seen before: Hailee, her butt on the floor, palms down, stunned.

"Aye up," mutters Faerydae, dumbfounded.

But Hailee actually seems even more shocked than her. In fact, both she and Oliver, slouched against the bed, have a mix of fear and astonishment on their faces —mouth and eyes wide open. They are not quite looking at Faerydae. Rather, they are staring at something right behind her. Faerydae swivels her head slightly and quickly understands the reason behind their paralyzing anguish.

THE DAY THE FISH RUNE DIED

Groggy as well, understandably jet-lagged, Belifendor's
not-so-unlucky-Marodor-after-all is leaning against the
bedroom wall, still chained by the leg to a huge chunk
of the gibbet that travelled with him. Archibald gets
back to his senses but doesn't have much time to enjoy
his family reunion. The second he breaks a smile,
Faerydae plunges to tackle him aside. She just saved
her friend from the charging Marodor, who darts
past them and goes smashing through the
window. The beast crash-lands in the garden
and disappears through the night, dragging
bits of gibbet behind him. Archibald, Faerydae, Hailee and Oliver are left staring at
one another, wondering what has just
happened. At their feet, lying still in the
middle of a fresh set of black streaks,
the magic globe swallows back the
last remnants of the formidable
energy just released. A feeble
glow travels the surface,
zigzag of slow-moving
lighting strikes that
come dying into
their Maker's
initials…
LDV.

(To be continued…)

𐤗𐤀𐤅𐤅𐤊⊙𐤍

It was 1539,
when Swedish writer Olaus Magnus
created an incredible map,
haunted by the weirdest beasts...

At a time when Science was in its infancy, the unknown
represented an endless source of fears, rumors and legends.
People's imagination was running as wild as the beasts
populating the surrounding darkness.

While werewolves, griffins, manticores,
bonnacons, leucrotas and basilisks
were believed to roam the thickest of forests,
under Olaus Magnus' pencil,
the oceans gave birth to a new breed of nightmarish monsters,
from sea-serpents to owl-sharks and pig-whales.

Incidentally, the Carta Marina also happens to be the main source
of inspiration for the adventures of Archibald Finch.
As an homage to Olaus Magnus, several of his creatures
were included in the Map of Lemurea, page 240.

∴

11538192R00214

Made in the USA
San Bernardino, CA
05 December 2018